A Death in Auvers

Copyright © 2019 Steven Schaefer.
All rights reserved.

ISBN 978-1-880977-50-7
Library of Congress Control Number: 2019955517

This is a work of fiction. Names, places, characters, and incidents are the product of the author's imagination and are used fictitiously. Any resemblance to actual events or persons, living or dead, is coincidental.

Distributed worldwide by Ingram Content Group
Available via independent booksellers and Amazon

First edition by XOXOX Press
402 Chase, Box 51
Gambier OH 43022

A Death in Auvers

a novel by
Steven Schaefer

XOXOX
PRESS
Gambier, OH
2020

I owe a great deal of thanks to so many people for their help and encouragement during the writing of this book: Jerry Kelly for his guidance and mentoring; Kaitlin Tebeau for her skillful edits; my book club friends for their suggestions, including Cheryl Matthias, Osher Pais, Linda and Jeff Riach, Robin Ulanow, Mark Kane; and especially my wife, Ellen. Her unfaltering faith in me (plus a few edits here and there) helped me to never lose sight of my goal.

To my girls: Ellen, Andrea, and McKenna

Auvers-sur-Oise, France
27 July 1890

Vincent was thrown backward off his stool by the force of the blast. The pain was immediate and excruciating as the bullet entered his lower abdomen, perforating a portion of his liver and colon. The lead slug tore through muscle and tissue then stopped, remaining lodged in his body. His hands jerked to the gushing wound. Blood, deep and red, seeped through his fingers like sap from a maple. It smelled metallic, sickly. He laid his head on the ground, eyes rolling back.

A voice screamed in the distance but Vincent could not identify it. "Mon Dieu!" Vincent groaned, white dots floating beneath his eyelids. "Why?" he gasped, "why?"

He felt the dry grass caressing his head. So soft, he thought. A thud brought his attention back to the pain jarring his body. Footsteps running toward him. Or were they running away? He wasn't sure. Theo appeared before him, hazy in his vision. There was so much he wanted to tell his brother, but all he could muster was, "Theo. Theo. I did not mean to let you down."

The pain intensified as he felt hands on him, pushing his body one way and then the other. He half-opened his eyes. His vision wavered and he vomited. He looked into a familiar face, struggling.

"Theo?" he whispered, spittle spraying from his dry lips. "Is that you?"

The face stared back at him, mouth twisted cruelly. The scornful smile reminded Vincent of the whores in Arles as they took his money.

"Leave me," he wheezed. Then suddenly, he felt his body being pulled across the grass onto rough dirt and gravel. He tried to raise his head, but his body would not obey him, and the pain was immense. Darkness was dropping into him. Demons returning? He wondered if this was the entryway to paradise or the gateway to hell. He heard a voice hissing, "You should die alone, just as you have lived."

Then, total darkness.

Chapter 1
Ville d'Avray, France – Present Day

The stone house sat back from the road that meandered through Ville d'Avray on the outskirts of Paris. By American standards, the house was ancient, dating back to the early nineteenth century, but by European standards, it wasn't even middle-aged.

Mark and Maggie McFadden fell in love with it at first sight. As smitten as they were with the old house, they were even more enamored with the prospect of owning a home outside Paris and dividing their time between their home in San Francisco and a new life in France. Mark's career in cancer research, and the breakthrough technology he had developed and licensed, provided all the money they'd need for this new adventure. Nearing forty and with no children, they now had the means to add a new dimension to their life together, and were ecstatic about their Grand Adventure.

Of course, the house needed extensive renovation. But, Mark and Maggie were undaunted at the prospect of replacing the small portico that once graced the front door, adding a garage, knocking out walls, plastering, painting, and refinishing the pine floors, not to mention all the plumbing and electrical work that needed to be done. They agreed that the place had "good bones," and could see through all the required renovation—a vision that made them both smile inside.

The first floor boasted an ample but outmoded kitchen, a large dining room, a small den and functional sitting room, along with two tiny but serviceable bedrooms. At some point over the years, a previous owner had thoughtfully added two full baths and a powder room to the first floor. A second floor had been added long after the house had been built. The addition proved to be a real plus—adding two good-sized bedrooms, each with its own separate bath, along with a reading room and a laundry room.

The windowless basement was musty and damp. A stacked stone foundation surrounded the packed dirt floor, with six massive piers supporting the upper levels. The only access to the basement was through a small doorway in the kitchen.

Judging from the numerous fireplaces and various improvements throughout the years, Mark and Maggie supposed that the previous owners had possessed a fair amount of money. They had taken the time to install critical modern conveniences, such as a gas stove and central heat. But there was no doubt that Mark and Maggie would have to invest a considerable sum to bring the home into the twenty-first century. The first item on their agenda was installing internet access and WiFi—this was accomplished immediately after they moved in.

Then there were the grounds themselves: expansive but unkempt. The east side of the house had a small stone wall surrounding an abandoned garden overrun with nettles, thistle, purslane, and bindweed. To the west was a small copse of dwarf shrub trees. A path of pea gravel led from the driveway to the front door, which was overpowered by a pair of unpruned Wych elms that cast ephemeral shadows over the grounds. A larger stone wall buffered the house from the street. Two sets of wrought iron gates admitted guests—the larger one, automobiles, and the smaller, pedestrians. If not for the ornate gates, no one would suspect that a beautiful estate lay beyond.

Ville d'Avray

The morning sun shining brightly through the kitchen windows revealed a century of dust motes hanging in the stale air. Steam rose from a freshly brewed cup of coffee. Mark sat woolgathering while Maggie carefully examined the built-in corner cabinet.

"I think I'll like it here. I know it's only been a few days, but I feel at ease," Mark mused.

"I think this is original to the house," said Maggie.

"What? I'm sorry. I was distracted. What did you say?"

"I said, I think this corner hutch is original to the house."

"It very well could be," he said. "Look at the rest of this place. I think the only thing the last owners did was move the dust around."

"Well, they did add the second floor and put in bathrooms, even if it was seventy or eighty years ago."

"Thank heavens for indoor plumbing, right? But it would have been nice if they had at least kept up with modern technological and structural improvements. The electrical is a nightmare and the plumbing is ancient."

"Come on, Mark, this will be fun and you know it!" his wife cajoled. "You've never shied away from a challenge before." Maggie sat down at the table across from Mark. She put her hands on his as he held the mug. "I still can't believe we own a house near Paris! This is a dream come true. I hope you're feeling as excited as I am about this house."

"Of course! I'm thrilled that we could get this place."

Mark smiled as they locked eyes. It was her penetrating green eyes and long lashes that first captured his attention when they met at Stanford University. He had been a doctoral student in bio-medical engineering and Maggie had been a senior studying anthropology. They quickly became an "item." Their backgrounds and personalities were similar; both had a lust for knowledge, both were headstrong, and both came from families that valued diligence and hard work. Their courtship ended when Mark was awarded his Ph.D. They married and he began work at a start-up company in Sunnyvale focusing on targeted cures for cancer. When one of Mark's research programs went into clinical trials, a large pharmaceutical company acquired the start-up. Mark continued to work with the acquiring company until the trials were successfully completed.

Maggie was an only child and grew up in an academic household where both of her parents taught at a local California community college. Her father died when she was ten. Her mother was a native Parisian and taught Maggie to love everything French. One of her great ambitions was to live in or near Paris and experience not just authentic French culture but to live as a Parisian.

"Maman would be so pleased to see us having a home near her birthplace," she said. "Paris is her favorite city. I never understood why she never came back. Not even to visit relatives."

"Now that you are a true Parisian, maybe she'll come for a visit."

"I hope so. You know, you'll have to learn French…"

"I know," he assured her.

"By that I mean becoming fluent, not just taking the speed course for tourists." She swatted him playfully.

"Ok, ok. I get it. I'll learn French." He chuckled.

"Come on, lazy bones. Finish your coffee and help me

take this hutch out so I can refinish it."

"Can't we just restore it where it is?" moaned Mark.

"No, we can't! Anyway, I may want to move it elsewhere."

"Ok. Let me get some tools. Maybe a chain saw or a hatchet," Mark grinned.

"Just get what you need and quit your griping, mister! Come on! We've got work to do!"

The two of them stood in front of the hutch, hammer and small pry bar at the ready. Mark gently inserted the pry bar between the hutch and the wall, loosening it just a bit. Slowly, the cabinet came away from the wall and they were able to move it from the corner.

"There! That wasn't so bad, was it?" Maggie asked him with a hopeful smile.

"No, I guess not," Mark admitted grudgingly. "I think I'll go look at the basement while you ponder the beauty of your treasure. I'm a bit concerned about the structural integrity of the house. I don't want this place to collapse right after we bought it!"

The basement stairs groaned under Mark's footsteps and led him into the dark cavity which stank of musk and mildew. The basement covered the entire footprint of the house. The stone columns supporting the first floor were unusually high, allowing him to stretch his arms above his six-foot frame and still not reach the beams crisscrossing under the main floor.

"At least we have electric lights down here," he thought. "Curious… this floor is so well tamped. I wonder what this place has seen. I can't imagine spending any time in this smelly hole. More than likely it was a storage area."

He roamed the basement, shining a flashlight in corners

and nooks, then at the rough beams overhead. Dust fell through the overhead floorboards, creating a light fog. He stifled a cough. There were scorched areas on the beams where lanterns had been hung. "Amazing," he thought, "that in all these years this place hasn't burned down."

As he peered at the old beams Maggie trotted down the steps into the basement. "You won't believe what I found in that old hutch!"

"Gold nuggets? Gold bars? No wait! I know! A map to the fabled treasures of the Templars?"

"Look, a newspaper article about a Russian train wreck. It's dated November 18, 1888!"

"That's certainly intriguing." Mark looked at the paper. "Can you read it?"

"So could you if you knew French, Doctor McFadden."

"In due time, *ma chérie*. So, what does it say?"

"It mentions the Russian Tsar being injured in a train derailment. Let's see. It goes on to say that a French radical group called 'The Commune' is responsible for the assassination attempt. It quotes the French President as having denied any French involvement."

"Fascinating! Anything else in the hutch?" he asked.

"No, just this. Stuck under a shelf in an envelope. You couldn't really see it unless you were almost inside the hutch."

"I wonder why it wasn't thrown away. What significance did it have that someone saved it?"

"I don't know. But it did seem like it was hidden," Maggie looked at him and pursed her lips.

"I wonder if there are any other surprises tucked away in this house," Mark said. "Let's keep going."

Work lights, shovels, measuring tapes, and carpentry tools were scattered around the basement. Mark had purchased the bare necessities, anticipating that someone else would be doing most of the restoration work.

"Hand me that tape measure?" he asked. He took the tool from Maggie and began measuring the distance between the support columns and the walls. "Oh, I forgot to tell you, Anton called yesterday. We should receive our invitation to the French Cancer Research Fundraiser in a couple of days. He thinks it was sent to our U.S. address. When he realized we hadn't RSVP'd, he figured we were already here in France."

"The gala slipped my mind. It's at the Musée d'Orsay?" she asked, suppressing a smile.

"Yep. How can you go wrong with French wine, French cuisine, and magnificent art?"

"You simply can't. But there's always a catch—how much do they want as a donation?"

"To tell you the truth, I don't know. I'm sure they'll use our connections in the biomedical industry, though." He continued inspecting the stone pillars.

"You mean, they'll use your connections. I don't have any patents for cancer research," Maggie said dryly.

"Hey, Mags. Look at this," Mark said. He was staring at a massive two-foot by two-foot support column toward the back of the house. Maggie peered over his shoulder.

"So, what are we looking at?" she chirped.

He was squinting, poking at the column gently with a small chisel. "This part of the column looks like it was patched. And not very well."

"Well, it probably was at some point. This house is pretty

old. I'm sure someone did some work on it over the years."

"Yeah, but this really looks out of place." He scraped at a deeply pitted piece of stone. "Here, look. This mortar is made with horsehair. It's crumbling and the stones are loose. They don't fit. It doesn't look like the patch was meant to correct a structural defect." He tugged at one of the stones.

"Be careful," Maggie cautioned, as a part of the column yielded and several flat stones fell to the floor. Dust flew everywhere. Maggie turned away, shooing at the dust as though it were a swarm of gnats. "Ugh! My hair will be all gray now!"

"Auburn or gray, you're still beautiful either way. Hey, look here." Mark shone his flashlight into the hole from which the stones had fallen.

"What is that?" asked Maggie, sidling up to him and peering into the niche.

"It looks like a box. Help me clear these loose stones. See if we can get it out without causing a major catastrophe."

"Why would someone put a box in a column?" Maggie asked as she pulled at a couple of stones.

"Probably to hide it. Maybe stolen treasure?" he quipped.

"Maybe your gold and the map to the Templar treasure!" she giggled.

"The box seems fairly substantial in size." Mark picked up a larger scraper and dug a little further. The mortar crumbled and more fragments fell out. Mark gently pulled the box from its cache. He blew dust off and turned it around in his hands. "It's heavy," he said to her, shaking it gently. "Let's take it upstairs so we can get a better look at it. It's tough to see anything down here." They scrambled up the stairs to the kitchen where there was ample light and set the box on the kitchen table. It was about the size of a breadbox. Mark brushed away some dirt and looked closely at the edges. "I don't see any locks or hinges. I think it may be nailed shut."

"Be careful opening it," Maggie cautioned.

Mark slid a knife under the lid, moving along the edges, using the knife as a lever. The nails had rusted and gave way easily with each tug of the knife. He raised the lid slowly.

"What the hell?" he exclaimed.

"Geez, Mark! It's a gun!"

Mark carefully picked up the gun—an old revolver, dust covered and slightly rusted. He turned it over in his hands, examining every detail, removing the cylinder and looking through the barrel. The cylinder held six cartridges. Using his fingernails, he removed them one by one. "One of these bullets is just a casing. Looks like the gun was fired once."

"What's this underneath?" asked Maggie. She peered into the box and carefully removed a folded sheet of paper and a leather-bound notebook blotched with dried paint.

"This looks like a letter. It's addressed to someone named Marguerite," she said, turning over the paper. "The handwriting isn't too good. The ink is faded, too, but I think I can make out some of the words." The paper was brittle and yellow with age, so Maggie handed it gingerly, afraid she might tear it. As she read the short note, she translated the French into English for Mark.

27 Juillet 1890
Marguerite,
I secured the journal you so sorely desired. I hope it was worth the life of that poor wretch.
Please do remember me to your precious benefactors.
Yours,
FE

They looked at each other, stunned. Maggie laid the letter on the table and turned her attention to the notebook. She blew the dust from the cover, and gently stroked the paint marks. She slowly opened the leather cover. To her amazement, the notebook was filled with drawings and notes.

"Some of this is in French and German, or maybe Dutch?" she said, carefully turning the pages. Then she stopped. "This looks like our house! And our basement!" She looked at Mark. "This note in the margin says something about a 'Commune.'"

"The same 'Commune' mentioned in the newspaper you found?" Mark wondered.

"I have no idea. But, wow!" She took a deep breath and beamed a huge smile at him. "We have a mystery to solve!"

Chapter 2
A Train to Paris – March 1886

The train swayed back and forth on the noisy tracks, jerking the travel-weary passengers in their seats. Outside, the bleak countryside slid by in the cold night air. Inside the train, the temperature was not far above freezing. The old coal stoves in each car were insufficient to ward off the chill of an unusually cold March night. The wooden benches set on either side of the aisle had become even more uncomfortable for Vincent and his fellow travelers as the journey wore on. The only good thing about the trip, he thought, was the relative quiet of the night. Nearby, two men lay sleeping across the hard seats, snoring out of cycle with one another. A baby wailed its displeasure, then fell silent. The heavy smell of rotted manure recently spread on the passing fields permeated the car, mixing with cigarette smoke.

Vincent sat by a window fogged by his warm breath. His coat was pulled closely around him, shielding him from the cold draft that filled the car. His bag of clothes and his painting supplies rested in the rack above the seat. His hat tilted slightly forward on his head, his sharp angular face vaguely reflected in the window as he stared out at the frost-rimmed countryside. He twisted uncomfortably in his seat as his stomach growled, not so much from hunger as from nerves.

"Paris will be different this time," he mused. "Theo will be happy to see me. I know he will. He cannot remain angry at his older brother. At least I hope, not for very long."

The train was scheduled to arrive in Paris in early morning, with numerous stops along the way, including Namur,

Bastogne, Reims and Meraux. As the train pulled out of Bastogne sharply at 6 a.m., a lone woman entering the front of the car. She was attractive, attired in a simple gray wool skirt, plain white blouse, small beret, and a long overcoat. An overnight bag was her only piece of luggage.

When she opened the door to the car, a gust of cold air rushed in with the noise of the train pulling away from the station. A few people stirred but most passengers took no notice of her.

She hesitated at the front of the car scouting for an open seat. Vincent watched her movements down the aisle. When she reached the row where he was seated, she perched gracefully on the bench opposite him, placing her bag on the floor.

A striking woman, Vincent thought, catching his breath. Deep blue eyes and light brown hair. She was slightly taller than Vincent, with full breasts and round hips that made her waist seem especially tiny.

She smiled at Vincent. "Do you mind if I sit here?"

Vincent stared at her in a manner that tended to unsettle strangers. After several seconds, he said, "Please, sit." His voice was moderate but his manner of speech was abrupt. She did not react to it, sitting with a quiet smile.

He wanted to hear her speak again, but before he could think of something to say, the woman commented in perfect French, "I think it is as cold in the train as it is outside. Are you going all the way to Paris?" Her voice was earthy and smooth, almost melodious, with a tonal quality that greatly appealed to Vincent.

"I am going all the way to Paris," he replied, his own French guttural and accented with his native Dutch. When

Vincent was lucid and not in one of his depressed states, he spoke pleasantly, but with a certain formality. On this morning, across from the beautiful stranger, he began to feel unusually light.

Offering her hand, the woman introduced herself. "I am Marguerite."

Vincent stared at her long fingers in the brown leather of her gloves. He raised his head from the window and grabbed her hand, shaking it vigorously. "I am Vincent van Gogh from Antwerp."

Marguerite pointed to Vincent's easel and the paint-daubed bag above him. "Are you an artist, Vincent?"

A jolt of excitement rifled through him. "I am! Although I have painted for only a few years. I took an interest in art while I worked at Goupil, an art dealer and supplier. I am on my way to Paris to see my brother. He manages one of Goupil's art galleries. Perhaps you have heard of Theo, Theodorus van Gogh?"

"No, I have not had the privilege." She hesitated.

"No mind. I will introduce you in Paris."

Marguerite let out a gentle laugh. "My, Vincent! Are we going to see each other in Paris?"

Vincent looked down sheepishly at his well-worn boots. If Marguerite could see his face, she would have thought he resembled an abused puppy—albeit, a puppy with a large nose and ears that did not fit his face.

"I did not mean to imply that we would not see each other in Paris, Vincent. You just startled me with your conviction that we would meet again. Perhaps if we talked for a while and you told me about yourself, we could get to know one another. Then see where that leads us."

Vincent reddened. He started to speak but thought better of it. Finally, he smiled. "I'll tell you about myself and my work. Someday, all of Europe will know my paintings."

Marguerite chuckled, "Vincent, humility is lost on you. Please, tell me about yourself. I would love to know more."

"I am the eldest of six in my family. I am the only artist," he began, sitting upright in his seat.

He went on to tell her about his childhood in the village of Zundert, a short distance from Antwerp; about his father, who was a minister in the Dutch Reformed Church, and of his mother, a strict disciplinarian. Vincent spoke about his time preaching the gospel in the Borinage. He spoke of art and philosophy, of family and passion. He avoided telling Marguerite about how his mother had ostracized him from the family because she thought him destined for failure in the art world. He did not discuss her inability to tolerate his moodiness and unpredictable behavior, nor his spendthrift ways that had caused the family much financial distress. Above all, he did not discuss the constant loneliness from which he suffered. He chose instead to speak of his younger brother Theo, the most accomplished among all his siblings, and his dreams of joining Theo in his art business in Paris.

"My mother and brother have encouraged me to draw and paint. That is one reason I am going to Paris," he lied. She studied him as he uttered these words. His eyes were cast downward and she sensed that there was more to his story than he was telling. She listened without interruption.

When the train pulled into Gare du Nord, Vincent, unaware they had reached their destination, continued talking animatedly.

Marguerite raised her gloved hand, interrupting him gently, "Vincent, it has been a delight meeting you." With that, she rose from the bench, clutched her bag and gently put a hand on Vincent's cool cheek. Vincent gaped upward at her.

Marguerite turned toward the aisle and an elderly man let her pass in front of him. Vincent hurriedly grabbed his bags from the overhead compartment and pushed his way thoughtlessly in front of a woman with two small children. Jostling his way to the door, Vincent discovered his sight was blocked by puffs of steam rising from an adjacent train.

"I must find her! I must know who she is!" He rushed across the cavernous station. It was early morning and all around him people walked with purpose. Marguerite was nowhere to be found. Vincent dashed up and down the main thoroughfare, eager to catch sight of her. After long minutes of futile searching, he felt himself sinking and stood slump-shouldered in the middle of the terminal. With a bag in each hand, he trudged slowly toward the south portico exit.

Marguerite concealed herself behind a pillar in the terminal gallery. A tall thin man clad in faded trousers and a long heavy coat stood alongside her, intently twirling his broad mustache. Together they watched as Vincent walked distractedly through the terminal door into the early morning sunlight. Without moving her head, she remarked to the gentleman, "This Vincent could be just the person we've been looking for."

Chapter 3
Paris, France – March 1886

Vincent looked around the terminal for a messenger service. He jotted a note to his brother announcing his arrival. As he handed the note to the courier, he told him, "Please make sure this is delivered to Theodorus van Gogh this morning. You can find him at the Goupil Gallery on Rue Chaptal." He thought, "I hope Theo is not so angry with me that he will not come to meet me." Vincent knew that his timing was not exactly agreeable with Theo but had forged ahead anyway.

Theo had asked Vincent to delay his trip to Paris until the summer and had made it clear he was not eager to take his brother into his small apartment and put up with his erratic behavior during high season. The brothers had written back and forth several times over the past months, with Vincent pushing his brother to accept him in Paris and making overtures about going into business together.

Theirs was a complicated relationship. Even as a child Vincent had been difficult. His parents, exasperated and bewildered by his moodiness and occasional epileptic seizures, sent him away to boarding school when he was ten years old. Not surprisingly, school did not work out, and after a few years Vincent was sent to work for his Uncle Vincent, his namesake, who was a very successful art supplier and art dealer partnered with a large art firm called Goupil.

Vincent became captivated with art while working for his uncle and applied himself to studying different artists' work and techniques. He was, however, incapable of dealing with the public. His managers kept him busy with back room tasks such as inventory, packing, and delivery. On the rare times when he had to deal directly with a patron, Vincent invariably alienated the customer with his brusque and odd manner.

Theo was also sent to work at Goupil at an early age because the Van Goghs had spent so much money on Vincent's schooling and upkeep that they could not afford the same for Theo. While Vincent was anything but a success at Goupil, Theo became quite accomplished. He gained a keen knowledge of art and, more importantly, developed an engaging personality. People liked Theo and wanted to be near him. Because of Vincent's odd ways and his inability to sustain work for any length of time, Theo eventually became his benefactor and protector, taking over for their parents and financially supporting his older brother. Unfortunately, Theo's role as a surrogate father led to frequent awkwardness between the brothers.

Vincent emerged through the south portico of the Gare du Nord into a blisteringly cold morning. The blue sky and bright sun promised a beautiful day and Vincent paused outside the door to take it all in. People were pushing past him but he took no notice.

Weighted down with his belongings, he needed to find transportation. Walking along the curbside, he soon found an open carriage for hire. He put his bags on the carriage floor and climbed in behind the driver. "The Louvre–and with speed!" he barked.

The driver snapped his whip and the carriage jerked forward. After a sudden start the trip to the Louvre was quite pleasant. Vincent thought wistfully of all the possibilities awaiting him and Theo. He had lived in Paris once before while at Goupil, but it had not been a pleasant experience. Vincent's uncle had initially hired him to work in the Goupil offices in the Hague. However, his behavior and personal crises interfered with his work, and he was transferred to the offices in London. Despite the change in scenery, Vincent continued his self-destructive assignations in the dark bedrooms of dockside brothels. His taste for absinthe only contributed to his wayward lifestyle. As a last effort, Vincent was transferred to the Goupil offices in Paris in hopes that he would perform better closer to family. Unfortunately, the liveliness of the city was to his immense liking. After several months, Vincent was sent home in disgrace. His reckless lifestyle, moodiness, and insubordination were simply too much for his Uncle to tolerate.

He shuddered. This time would be different. Vincent and Theo had each other. Together, he hoped, the van Gogh brothers would create an art haven. Vincent knew that he would have to be on his best behavior, but having Theo as his emotional anchor would make it easier.

Theo arrived at the Goupil offices on Rue Chaptal in late morning. He completed his normal routine of unlocking the studio and stoking the fireplaces in the public rooms, then crossed the street to a café for coffee and baguettes.

Theo had just sat down to review the schedule of events for the day when the bell over the door announced the first visitor. He rose from his small desk at the back of the gallery and walked briskly toward the door. Standing in the doorway was a messenger with a cable. Theo signed for it and opened the envelope, quickly reading the short message. "Merde!" he muttered. "He never listens. He only thinks of himself! I wrote him just last week and told him that now was not a good time. This is so characteristic of Vincent."

Theo stared at the note for a few seconds, steeling himself to meet his brother. He should have expected this, given Vincent's egocentric behavior, his lack of concern for others, and his impulsiveness. He is wholly absorbed in himself, Theo thought. Slowly, he calmed and settled on the actualities of the day. He grumbled, "He is here and I must make the best of it."

At eleven, Theo put on his tan overcoat and matching fedora and stepped into the bright Paris sunlight. The day had warmed since his arrival at the office so Theo decided to make the long trek to the Louvre from the ninth to the first Arrondissement on foot.

Vincent arrived at the Louvre just as it was opening. He set down his bags in the coatroom and hung his coat and hat. He opened the paint-spotted bag and withdrew a notebook and pencil, then stuffed the bag onto a shelf. He intended to make the next few hours waiting for Theo as productive as possible.

His excitement rose as he roamed from salon to salon studying the artworks. When he believed a work to have little value he passed by quickly, but before others he lingered, studying the brush strokes, the colors, and the use of shading. As he made his way through the Grand Salons, Vincent stopped to examine the details of Rembrandt van Rijn's *Landscape with Castle*. Vincent had incorporated Rembrandt's use of shadowy hues in his own work, in particular, a recent painting of peasants. Dark and somber, with only a single source of light, he had sought to depict the human struggle to find hope in impoverished circumstances in the faces of familiar women sitting at a table, peeling potatoes.

Continuing his leisurely walk through the galleries, Vincent took interest in *Ray of Sunlight* by Ruisdael, Brouwer's *Interior of a Smoking Room,* and *Portrait de Famille* by Van Ostade. Oblivious to all else around him, occasionally he would stop and take out his sketch book and draw something that piqued his curiosity. He paid close attention to details and added notes beside each sketch. The Dutch painters were his favorite.

Theo found Vincent in the Salon Carré engrossed in his sketch book across from Rembrandt's *Holy Family.*

"Ever the student of the old masters," Theo said, standing behind Vincent.

Vincent looked around at Theo, leapt to his feet, and hugged his brother. "I knew you would be glad to see me, brother! It was important for me to come to Paris now and not wait!"

"Vincent, I asked you to delay your arrival until I could find a larger apartment. June was all I asked. Could you not wait just three months?"

"No, I was so eager to see you! To start a new life with you as my mentor, my business partner, and my friend! And now that I am here we shall make the most of it!"

"Vincent…" Theo shook his head. "Never mind. Please gather your belongings. I will take you to my apartment, but then I must return to the Gallery."

The brothers turned toward one of the salon exits, then retrieved Vincent's bags and coat. As they walked toward the exit, Vincent turned to Theo. "I met the most wonderful woman on the train. Her name is Marguerite."

Careful not to be noticed, the tall mustachioed man from the train station peered around a massive Corinthian column. With watchful eyes, he followed the brothers through the Paris streets.

Chapter 4
Ville d'Avray – Present Day

"This house has quite a history, I think," Mark said, carefully paging through the notebook with Maggie.

Maggie pulled her chair closer to Mark to examine the open page. "Some of these sketches look vaguely familiar. I just can't place them."

"Mags, can you read any of this?"

"The writing is faded and difficult to decipher but I can make out a lot of it. Here," she pointed to an entry next to a sketch of a field with a stone wall running through it, "this is a description of the field. It says, 'the day is overcast and few shadows appear. The greens must be emerald and the browns must have a tincture of cerulean.'"

Maggie turned several pages. "This portrait is called 'Pierre.' No other notation." Further in they came to several pages of writing devoid of sketches.

"This reads more like a diary. Let's see. Hmmm… 'Theo should have written by now. I may have caused him and Jo much angst before I left. I must take care to appease Jo. She means a lot to Theo. If I lose Theo, then I am truly lost forever.'" Maggie continued to thumb through the notebook.

"Let's see… okay, here he says, 'Émile is a frightened boy. He worries about things that are unimportant.'"

Maggie continued. "This last sketch is of a big house. 'I will spend time completing my study behind the manse. The weather has been hot and the fields are truly colorful and inviting.'" She turned the next few pages. "Over here he writes, 'That damned cowboy taunts me. He is the worst of this wretched place.'"

"'Cowboy'? Did you read that correctly?" Mark asked.

"Yes, I think so." Maggie's brow furrowed.

"What's the date on that letter?" asked Mark.

Maggie slid it across the table to Mark. "27 Juillet 1890."

"And that's the date of the last entry in the journal?"

"Yep. Both written at about the same time. The letter implies that someone died. Do you think this notebook could belong to the person that died?" she asked.

"Well, makes sense, maybe. If that's the case, then this gun might be a murder weapon."

Mark leaned closer to Maggie as she thumbed through the notebook again, and spoke softly. "These sketches are amazing. Look at the detail—so intricate."

"I swear I've seen some of these before," she said. "See, this one of a vase of sunflowers and this one of a bridge? Some of these are so familiar. Van Gogh loved sunflowers. They were the subject of many of his works. I wonder if he's somehow connected with this journal," she mused.

Mark leaned back in his chair, hands clasped behind his head, brow wrinkled in thought. "So, how can we figure out whose journal this is and who put these things in the box and buried it?"

"We can start by discovering who owned the house in 1890," Maggie suggested.

"The local courthouse might have that."

"Yes. But better yet, we can ask the neighbors. I'm having coffee tomorrow morning with Madame Rousseau next door. She might know."

"She's probably old enough. She reminds me of an ancient skeleton. She's positively antediluvian!"

"Mark! You are so naughty," she scolded.

"Well, she is, isn't she?"

"She is elderly but she's not that old!"

"I'm just teasing. Say," he hesitated. "Let's not tell anyone about what we found. I'm not sure what we have here."

"I agree. That newspaper I found in the corner hutch was from roughly the same time. I wonder if somehow the paper and these artifacts from the box are related."

"They could be. Perhaps it would help to jot down some notes—let's keep notes on this."

As he uttered these words, Mark sat down at the computer to search the internet for information on the gun while Maggie delved into the journal with her tablet by her side.

"Mags, it looks like the gun is a standard issue Chamelot-Delvigne 11mm Modele 1874 Revolver d'Officier. It says here on the website that it was 'issued to French military officers from 1874 through the end of World War I. Many French police continued to use the revolver until the end of World War II.'"

"My search is not going as well as yours. But if I had to guess, I would say this journal really did belong to Vincent van Gogh," she speculated.

"That seems a stretch, don't you think? What would one of his journals be doing buried in a pillar in our basement?"

"I know it seems improbable, but many of these sketches are so like his paintings. And the last entry is around the time of his death."

"Who would want to hide van Gogh's work? And why?"

"I don't have an explanation for any of this but I can tell you that I've looked up several names in the journal. Many correspond to people van Gogh would have known, including his brother Theo and his wife Jo, Paul Gauguin, Émile Bernard, and Toulouse-Lautrec. Look, there are references to 'The Commune' here where he drew our house. But who is this Marguerite? I can't find anything on her."

"Well, Mags, I'm bleary eyed... I have to hit the sack. This is going to have to wait until tomorrow when I'm feeling more clear-headed."

The next day brought with it a perfect "April in Paris" morning—a little cool with clear blue skies marred only by a small scattering of wispy clouds. Maggie hugged a steaming cup of coffee between her hands.

"I couldn't sleep last night thinking about that journal," she said.

"I know. I had the same problem."

"So, what are we going to do?"

"First thing, you have to prod Madame Rousseau's memory when you meet her for coffee. But I would keep our find a secret for now."

"I can do that."

"I'm going to see if there is anything else in the basement," Mark said, rising from the table.

"Should we plan to hit the town hall records later today?" asked Maggie.

"Definitely."

Mark spent the next few hours puttering around in the basement. Before long, he heard the door open and Maggie's call. "Mark, I'm back!"

"Down here!"

Dust drifted through the air as Maggie trotted down the old stairs. Mark looked up from his kneeling position to see Maggie's head peek around the bannister. "Find anything?"

"No. Just poking around and examining the structure. How was coffee with Madame Rousseau?"

"She is a delightful woman. I hope I have as much on the ball as she does when I'm her age. She hasn't lost a bit of her sensibilities. Her memory is remarkable."

He looked at her and asked, "Did she have anything to say about who owned the house in 1890?"

"Well, yes and no. She and her family have lived in her house for almost a hundred years. She said this house has changed hands two or three times since she's lived here. She heard there was someone from Paris who used the house as a retreat, perhaps in the 1890's, but she wasn't positive. She remembers hearing rumors of secret meetings and spies in the area after the Franco-Prussian War but could not recall anything specific."

"Guess we'll have to search city records to find out more."

"I think so. When do you want to go?" she asked.

"Let me shower. I won't be long."

"Did you find anything else down here?" asked Maggie, glancing around at her musty surroundings.

"No luck. One surprise may be all we have."

"Something tells me one will be quite enough."

Ville d'Avray's town hall was housed in a modern building near the center of the business district. Mark and Maggie drove their silver BMW i3 around until they found a parking spot.

"I thought parking this little car would be easier than this," complained Mark.

"This is France. There are no public parking garages. Come on! We need to get there before the archives close."

They walked the few blocks to the town hall. The sun was bright, the sky a clear blue. A slight breeze carried a band of warm air that heightened the humidity. Men and women walked purposefully to their destinations, eyes focused straight ahead. There was no idle chitchat among them.

Mark and Maggie approached the frazzled clerk behind the oversized desk in the lobby of the government building. She looked up expectantly at the couple. Her watchful eyes scanned them from head to toe, one eyebrow raised.

"Oui," the clerk said. In French, "You want something?"

Mark detected a twinge of irritation in her throaty voice.

Maggie answered in her perfectly Parisian-accented French. *"Oui, s'il vous plaît.* Yes, please. I am Maggie McFadden. This is my husband, Mark. We recently purchased a home on Rue de Marnes and are interested in learning more about its history. Could you direct us to the proper person?"

"Certainement! Please, come with me. I'll take you to someone who can help." The receptionist led them up a broad staircase to a room on the second floor. "Monsieur Guyier, this couple just bought a house here in Ville d'Avray and wanted to know more about it. I told them you would be the best resource."

Guyier extended his hand to Mark. "A pleasure to make your acquaintance. I am director of records for Ville d'Avray."

"M. Guyier, I am Maggie McFadden and this is my husband, Mark. We wish to know when our house at 30 Rue de Marnes was built and who the previous owners were."

"Ah, I see. Follow me, please."

The couple followed M. Guyier through several rows of

desks to a large table at the back of the room. Three computer terminals sat side by side. Floor to ceiling bookcases lined the wall behind the computers.

"Recent real estate transactions and other data are in the computer system. Older data is recorded in books. It's likely that you would find your information in the record books if the house was built before 1930. Do you have an approximate idea of when your house was built?"

"Our house was definitely built before 1930 but we do not know the exact year."

"Well, then, let me gather the older real estate records. They have yet to be digitized. Is there any other information that I can provide you?"

"We'll want to look at news clippings from 1888 to 1890," Maggie answered. "Do you have them?"

"Unfortunately, another department handles media. I'll be back in a moment." Twenty minutes later he returned with two massive leather-bound volumes. "I believe what you are looking for is in one of these books. Data is sorted by street, then by house number. Please realize that addresses sometimes change with time and the current number may not match our records. I'll leave you to your research."

Mark looked at Maggie with wide eyes. "Well?"

"I guess we're on our own. He said that the addresses may not be the same. That will complicate things. Street names may have changed as well."

"Do you think he has a town map from the 1800's?"

"That would help. I'll go ask." As Maggie trotted off to see M. Guyier, Mark sat down and opened one of the books. "Oh, crap," he muttered, looking at the French text.

"I'll never be of any help."

A few minutes later, Maggie returned with something in her hand. "Well," she announced as she sat down, "this was all he had, or at least all he would give me." She unrolled a copy of a large, hand-drawn map of the town.

"This should help immensely, assuming it's accurate," Mark exclaimed. "Mags, you might want to look at these books and see if you can make heads or tails of them."

"Why, what's the matter?"

Mark looked dolefully at his wife. "They're in French…"

Maggie half-feigned a sigh.

Mark looked at the map and pulled out his phone. He found their location on the old map. "Okay, I think this is our house," he said, pointing to a small rectangle.

"Is there an address?" asked Maggie. She correlated the map with the records and finally found the data she was searching for. "Here. This looks like it. Let me see. Okay. We bought the house from the Bertrands. They inherited it and the owners before their family bought the house from Marguerite Chemin. Looks like Marguerite Chemin inherited the house from Frederic Chemin as the surviving spouse. He must have been wealthy or land was cheap. He owned most of the land behind the house too. Almost twenty hectares. She sold the house and land in 1906."

"Marguerite Chemin could be the Marguerite from the letter we found!" exclaimed Mark. "We need to know more about Frederic and Marguerite Chemin!"

Chapter 5
Paris – 1886

In 1886 Paris was a large city, central to culture, commerce, and government in France. It was the center of French pride and the true heart of France. The city would soon host the 1889 Exposition Universale and celebrate the centennial of the French Revolution. Pockets of the city still held scars of the German siege of 1870. People did not speak of those times. The ceding of Alsace to Germany was a source of anger to the French, especially Parisians.

Since the siege, the French art world seemed intent on replacing all memories of the Prussian occupation with cultural diversions. Paris was feverishly busy, with many exhibitions being held throughout the city. The Louvre was now among the most respected and notable museums in the world.

Vincent moved into Theo's undersized apartment on the outskirts of Paris. With only one bedroom, a sitting room, and a kitchen, Theo found the close quarters stifling. Vincent occupied the sitting room, sleeping on a divan, and setting up his makeshift studio throughout the small apartment. The two brothers quickly fell into a routine. Theo would go off to Goupil in the mornings while Vincent went out to explore museums and galleries or to paint.

Vincent spent his first few days in Paris visiting museums and sprucing himself up so he would not be an embarrassment to Theo. He groomed his unkempt beard and trimmed his unruly hair, relieved that shortly before his arrival, he had his teeth fixed as they had suffered from lack of care. Theo took note of Vincent's attempts to adjust to his new surroundings and improve his personal appearance and made sure to compliment his brother often. Theo did not want to deal with another breakdown.

It was not long before Theo suggested that Vincent enroll in art school.

"Vincent, I think that your time would be well spent studying with Fernand Cormon. You are aware of how sought after he is, aren't you?"

"Yes, of course. He has achieved much commercial success and also a bit of notoriety for his work *The Flight of Cain,* which alienated many devout Christians. Let me think about your suggestion."

Heeding his brother's advice, Vincent applied and was accepted to Cormon's school. Cormon took a novel approach in teaching art, believing that structure, in particular three-dimensional perspective, was the key to skillful rendering.

"Drawing comes first! You must learn to sketch before you can become a painter! Sketching is the purest form of art!" he told his students. But sketching did not come easily to the older and less-skilled Vincent. He worked hard to improve his sketches, constantly drawing and erasing, drawing and erasing, until he was satisfied with the result. Other artists in the school, including Henri de Toulouse-Lautrec, did not find this exercise so challenging.

"Vincent, your figures are lopsided! Look at that one there! Her hips are disjointed and one bosom is shaped like a pear!" Toulouse-Lautrec teased. The constant mocking infuriated Vincent and often, returning home, he would unleash his anger on Theo.

"Out of proportion once again," Cormon noted one day.

"Try again."

"Vincent, are you drawing with your toes? Perhaps if you use the other hand, the sketch might resemble the nude woman it is supposed to be!"

"Now, now, gents. Let's be more considerate of our fellow student. We all go through a learning period. Come Vincent, let me show you some tricks."

Vincent looked up to see who had come to his defense, a situation that rarely occurred. The compassionate remark had come from a young apprentice, Émile Bernard.

Émile was the son of an affluent Parisian merchant and lived a privileged life. Although younger than Vincent, he carried himself with a grace beyond his years. As they came to know one another, Vincent came to appreciate Émile's sympathies for those less fortunate. Because of their shared philosophies, they became friends.

Despite the emotional support that Émile Bernard had provided, Vincent soon tired of the ridicule from the young artists at the school. After three months he decided to leave and broke the news to his brother. "Theo, I am finished with the art school," he announced. "I'm not returning."

"But Vincent, you have a three-year contract with Cormon. You can't simply walk away from your obligation!"

"I cannot endure those miserable miscreants any longer! They won't leave me alone! They mock my work all the time. It's too much to bear, I tell you!"

"What will you do next, my brother?"

"I will seek out street fare for my art. Street scenes, still lifes, the Paris landscape will become my subject. This will work, you'll see! I will fill the apartment with my paintings!" True to his word, Vincent began scouring the avenues for panoramic vistas and willing subjects.

In May of 1886, the last of the eight Impressionist shows was held at a gallery at 1 Rue Lafitte. Theo convinced Vincent to go along with him to view the showings, even though Vincent had stated his distaste for this style of art. Among the artists displaying work at the exhibition were Lucien Pissarro, who was a friend of Theo's; Edgar Degas; Georges Seurat; Mary Cassatt; and Paul Gauguin. Theo and Vincent roamed the salons, Theo assessing the commercial value of various works while Vincent criticized technique and use of color, and bemoaned the lack of portraits, which he thought to be the worth of a true artist.

"I find much of this work disagreeable and meager. Wasted paint on canvas. Compare any one of these to the work of masters like Rembrandt and Brouwer. These are the paintings of children."

"Vincent, must you always see fault in others' work? Please, try a little decorum in the delivery of your opinions!" Theo complained, hoping to quiet him and prevent further embarrassment among the up-and-coming artists that filled the hall.

As they entered a side salon, the brothers noticed a small crowd gathered around a young, diminutive, and bearded gentleman standing in front of several canvases. He was discussing each in turn, pointing to different features with animated gestures. His paintings were much different than others in the show. He used dabs of colors and light to form his images, rather than the long brush strokes and shading that were customary.

Theo and Vincent approached the crowd and listened as he spoke about his dotted brush strokes, his use of blues and greens to soften images, and the contrast in the colors of the sky and water against the surrounding images. He spoke of his desire to transcend a passive, perceptual recording of concepts by using more active, intellectual, and emotional ideas and theories.

Suddenly, Vincent let out a forced laugh. "Color is misused in all of these paintings! The images are less than clear and the subject matter is dull."

Silence fell as the group turned to see who had made these caustic remarks. With all eyes on Vincent, he stared back as if to challenge the onlookers. The speaker said nothing for a moment, then erupted in a roar of laughter. "You are quite frank in your opinion of my work. I must say, outside of art school, there are few people with your audacity. Tell me, why do you think so poorly of my paintings?"

Without hesitation Vincent said, "There is no mixing of color and the images are flat. The blues and greens are used, not to identify images, but to occupy space on the canvas. Where is the physical reality? The sky never looks as you painted and the water—where did you see that? Theo will agree with me." Vincent turned to his brother, who was standing very still and hoping this awkward moment would soon pass.

"I do think this work is very good," Theo demurred. "I happen to like the use of color and the subject matter."

"Theo, do you not see the visual disparity in these works?"

Theo put a hand on Vincent's shoulder and whispered, "Please, Vincent, can we discuss this at home?"

In an uncharacteristic gesture, Vincent stopped and moved away. Theo approached the man and introduced himself. "I am Theo van Gogh, manager of the Goupil Gallery on Rue Chaptal. I apologize for my brother. He is an artist and has strong feelings about... well, everything."

"My name is Georges Seurat. I do not take offense at your brother's outburst. He is welcome to his opinion. As for me, I rather like your opinion better."

Theo and Georges fell into a conversation, discussing the canvases, examining his technique, and debating his color theories. They spoke quietly between themselves. During this conversation, Vincent moved into the next salon and, looking straight ahead, noticed a tall, slender figure admiring a painting by Pissarro. He quickened his pace as he approached her, trying to determine who this vaguely familiar person was.

"Marguerite! I am so happy to see you again! It is I, Vincent van Gogh. The man you met on the train in March."

She spun around, looking both startled and delighted.

"Vincent, what a lovely surprise! Imagine meeting you here among these people! How are you making out in Paris?"

Vincent rapidly recounted his move to Theo's apartment and his enrollment in art school. He sputtered through the painting and sketching he had been doing throughout Paris.

"I see you still have your sketchpad with you," Marguerite noted. "Are you gathering ideas here, Vincent?"

"A few. I find that art fills a void in my life. I breathe in its spiritual force, its intellectual power. For that reason, I simply wouldn't dream of going anywhere without my sketch pad," he replied with unbridled enthusiasm. "Marguerite, you have not yet met my brother, Theo. Let me introduce you. He is in the next salon."

"Vincent, I really must go," she said, clutching her bag and turning away. "I have an appointment that I must keep."

"No! I will get him. Stay here!" Vincent ran into the adjoining salon, finding Theo and Georges still engaged in a discussion of Georges' art.

"Theo, come and meet Marguerite! The woman from the train! She is in the next salon!"

"Vincent," Theo held his hand up to stop him. "I am talking to Georges…"

"I'm sorry to interrupt but you must come now! Continue your conversation in a moment—you must meet Marguerite." Vincent grabbed his brother's arm, yanking him into the next salon.

Vincent looked around, but Marguerite had disappeared. Georges came up alongside Theo and stood watching while Vincent paced up and down the salon, searching for Marguerite. Finally, he returned to Theo's side.

"Sorry, Theo, but I don't know where she went. She was just here a minute ago," Vincent said, bewildered.

"Vincent, allow me to introduce Georges Seurat. He has exhibited with the Impressionists several times. Georges, this is my brother, Vincent."

Distractedly, Vincent shook Georges' hand. Theo led the conversation and Georges spoke to Vincent as one professional to another. Soon Vincent forgot about Marguerite and was absorbed in the art discussion. The three men left the gallery and headed for a café near the Tuileries to continue their conversation.

From her vantage point near the exit, Marguerite saw Vincent, Theo, and Georges turn east and head down the avenue. Standing next to her was the tall, mustachioed man from the train station and a second man.

She addressed the tall one. "Pierre, we must hurry back to the house and meet the others. Émile, keep an eye on Vincent. Stay close to him." Marguerite and Pierre turned toward a waiting carriage, and Émile Bernard hurried off to follow the trio.

Chapter 6
Paris – June 1886

In June, the lease on Theo's apartment was up, and Vincent convinced his brother to search for lodging closer to the burgeoning artist colony of Montmartre, just north of the city center. The arrival of summer in Paris brought with it the sour stench of garbage and sewage accumulating throughout the city. Most people placed their chamber pots outside to help reduce the rancid odor that built up in their apartments. The summer air, heavy with dampness, made parts of the torpid city almost unbearable.

Theo wanted a larger flat on a high floor, far above the unpleasant stench of the street. A bigger apartment would also provide him with much-needed space to isolate him from Vincent's petty outbursts, which he unleashed on Theo almost daily. To make things even worse, Vincent's canvases were collecting rapidly, filling all available space. They were stacked along the walls, under Theo's bed, and in the hallways. Theo felt as if the rooms were closing in on him.

The brothers found an apartment at 54 Rue Lepic in Montmartre. Its higher elevation was a plus during the summer months, providing a slight breeze that alleviated the stifling heat and sour city odor. In addition, there were many open vistas from the spare hilltop village. Theo and Vincent agreed that Montmartre was the perfect place for them.

Vincent painted inexhaustibly, experimenting with natural chalk and lithographic crayon. Despite his initial distaste toward the Impressionists' use of color and street scenes, Vincent began to incorporate more color into his works.

He still wanted to paint portraits, but, lacking the money to hire subjects, he decided to make do with street scenes.

One day Vincent decided to paint a vagrant sitting on a park bench near the Seine. While Vincent was concentrating on perfecting the scene's composition, the elderly drifter kept shifting uncomfortably, always repositioning himself exactly at the moment Vincent achieved the perspective he wanted. Finally, Vincent's frustration boiled over.

"Mon Dieu, must you twist and curl like you're suffering from the DT's? What is your problem anyway? I'm trying to create something of beauty here but you can't even sit still long enough for me to compose the scene! Be still you vile gypsy!"

Vincent's outburst startled the old man. He stared at the strange artist as though hearing the sound of a human voice for the first time in his life.

This lack of response only served to further enrage Vincent. At once he was on top of the unfortunate vagrant, thrashing him with his notebook, whipping his face with his paint rags, and cursing at the top of his lungs. Soon, a small throng of onlookers gathered and jumped in to rescue the man from further harm. Vincent, both annoyed and frightened by the fuss he had created, quickly gathered his paint supplies and fled the crowd.

"What did I just do to that beleaguered soul?" he whispered to himself as he hurried from the turmoil. "Why did I lash out like that? I don't think he's hurt. I... I... I need a moment."

When he thought he was far enough away from the crowd, Vincent parked himself on a bench behind a large oak tree, hoping to further shield himself from view as he caught his breath. Within minutes he had gathered himself and his thoughts had already turned to a more bucolic scene that had captivated him on one of his recent outings.

He walked for several miles before coming upon the familiar spot. Situating himself at the bottom of a sloping hill near a quarry, he proceeded to paint the barns in the background. They appeared almost monochromatic to him, with only a hint of color. But despite the somber tones and his own foul mood, which was beginning to slacken, Vincent managed to incorporate brighter colors than in his previous work.

Potato Eaters was one of his favorites that he had created the year before in Nuenen, before he learned anything about the Impressionist school. He was fond of painting peasants. He loved their honesty, their simple way of life, their coarseness. He had sought realism in the rendering of these figures peeling potatoes by the fire, but he also knew that realism was more than just literal truth and he wanted to learn to paint from his heart. He struggled with the use of local color, a technique that was popular with the traditional schools. This internal struggle led to his study of color, and to his surprise, he discovered that he favored the techniques of his Neo-Impressionist friends. Over time, he began to transition from the shadowy, dark images of Potato Eaters to a lighter and more colorful palette.

In July, heartened by Vincent's jauntier disposition and improved techniques, Theo wrote to his mother:

He is progressing tremendously in his work and this is proved by the fact that he is becoming successful. He has not yet sold paintings for money, but is exchanging his work for other pictures. In that way we obtain a fine collection, which, of course, also has a certain value. There is a picture dealer who has now taken four of his paintings and has promised to arrange for an exhibition of his work next year. He is mainly painting flowers—with the object to put a more lively colour into his next set of pictures. He is also more cheerful than in the past and people here like him. To give you proof: hardly a day passes that he is not asked to go to the studios of well-known painters, or they come to see him. He also has acquaintances who give him a bunch of flowers every week which may serve him as models. If we are able to keep it up, I think his difficult times are over and he will be able to make it by himself.

Increasingly, artists visited the brothers at their apartment in Montmartre. Pissarro, Cézanne and John Peter Russell were frequent visitors. Each delighted in showing Theo their work. Cézanne and Pissarro were enjoying moderate commercial success, but neither were in the league of Claude Monet, who owned his own gallery. Theo thought all of their work held much promise, and he purchased a few paintings and quickly sold them at Goupil. But he did not hang any of Vincent's work in the gallery.

"Theo, why do you not show any of my paintings?" Vincent finally asked, trying to conceal his disappointment.

"Vincent," Theo answered gently, "I think you need more improvement as an artist. I know you have the skills; it takes time to develop them. Don't despair. You will get there one day!"

Vincent knew that his history at Goupil still haunted the gallery halls, and that Theo had to contend with his reputation. He yearned for approval from his brother, whom he depended upon in so many ways. If he could just measure up to Theo's expectations, he might gain some confidence. And if he could garner even a modicum of support from his mother, who likened his painting to a child's finger art, that would feel like winning a Grand Prize.

Vincent continued to search for portrait subjects to further hone his skills. Lacking both the money to pay models and the gift of gentle persuasion, he was often left painting landscapes, flowers, or self-portraits.

He soon met the proprietress of the Café du Tambourin, Signora Agostina Segatori, an aging Italian beauty who was well-known in the art world. Long past her prime as a portrait sitter, now her career was the management of her café.

Vincent convinced Agostina to exhibit his art in exchange for free meals. The Café du Tambourin was filled with art, as much a gallery as a restaurant. People came to browse the art and enjoy a café au lait.

Vincent formed a close relationship with Agostina, then convinced Émile Bernard to exhibit alongside him at the Café. The proprietress was delighted to have new artists filling her walls with their canvases. Vincent, being the more prolific of the pair, had better exposure in terms of the sheer numbers of paintings displayed. But Émile's paintings appealed to the patrons. Unfortunately, Vincent's still lifes did not sell.

Vincent and Émile had become close friends and drinking companions. Theo, no stranger to Parisian nightlife, would occasionally join them. They would often end up at a local bordello, seeking pleasure with women who worked there. One particular night the brothers were at a popular brothel with Émile and John Peter Russell, along with two not so young women clad in tight bustiers and low-cut blouses revealing generous, fleshy bosoms. While Vincent sat staring into his glass of absinthe, the women were seductively rubbing up against John and Émile. Theo had already disappeared upstairs with his favorite whore. The room was filled with laughter and bawdy talk, mostly coming from the male patrons.

Moments later, John and Émile both looked up as Theo re-entered the room with a satisfied grin on his face.

"Another successful conquest!" John raised his glass, "Here's to Theo! Did you leave the dear heart with anything to give to us?"

"She is now a woman!" Theo exclaimed. The men chortled with merriment and one of the women asked John, "Are you ready for your turn or should I send Émile for a go?" Theo turned to Vincent, who was now feeling quite fuzzy from the absinthe. "Vincent, why don't you impale this wench? Show her what a van Gogh can do!"

"No, no. I am not up for screwing tonight," Vincent demurred.

Émile let out a gasp, "Vincent, all real men want sex every night! Theo's right. You go up and give this beauty a real screw." Émile smacked the woman on her ample derriere.

Theo grabbed Vincent's arm and raised him up from the table. Vincent gave a few muffled "no's" but the prostitute came around to Vincent, putting her hands on her breasts and purred, "Sweetie, I really want to see what you've got." With that, she led him through the doorway and up the well-worn stairs.

At the top of the stairs were three doors. Two were closed, a small red plank hanging from a nail, indicating they were in use. The third door was slightly ajar. The woman reached for the glass doorknob, nudging the door open. She turned to Vincent, "My name's Sophie. I've seen you here before but I haven't had you."

The room was spartan. There was a wooden framed bed, a small counter with a washbasin and ewer. A heavy wool blanket covered the single window, giving the room a dark, somber feel that matched Vincent's mood. There was a chair in one corner and a clothes butler in the other. The bed was unkempt and had clearly been used several times that evening. Sophie closed the door behind Vincent, then turned toward the clothes butler and reached behind her to unbutton her dress.

"It's 50 francs, mon cheri. You need to pay first. Do you want to undress me?"

Vincent stood gaping at Sophie. Finally, he replied, "Just take off your clothes and let's get this done."

"Ain't you the charmer." Sophie let her dress fall to the floor. She picked it up and placed it on the butler. Underneath her dress was a plain, drab chemise. She slid her arms out of its thin straps, lifting her soft, plump legs through the top. Her skin was white, almost alabaster, as if she never saw the sun. Her large breasts drooped to mid-torso. She had a roll of fat around her waist that was just enough to get a good grip on. Her pubic area was trimmed. She smelled of stale sex and bad hygiene. She crawled onto the bed, laying on her back spread-eagled, looking at Vincent.

"You want it this way or..." she turned and raised her buttocks in the air, "you want to give it to me like a dog?"

Vincent removed his pants and looked through the

woman as though she weren't even there. "Put your ass in the air and your face on the bed. I don't need to look at you." Vincent hesitated. It was clear that he was neither ready for the task ahead nor interested in any small talk.

"My dear, do you need a hand?"

"No, just get ready for a good screw. This will not take long."

Vincent climbed on the bed behind Sophie, her butt as high in the air as she could make it. The smell coming from Sophie was a distraction that Vincent did not enjoy. He got up behind her and rubbed his penis across her buttocks and, finally erect, entered her. He thrust several times hard into Sophie and with the last thrust, grunted loudly. He let out a sigh, then withdrew. He wiped himself with the sweat-soaked sheets.

"Goodness, that was… well… quick. I appreciate you wasting no time in getting down to business," she said, voice dripping with sarcasm.

Vincent dressed quickly for he did not care to linger and headed for the downstairs parlor. Sophie followed a few minutes later. Vincent sat down in front of his absinthe, which had been refreshed while he was busy upstairs, and lit a cigarette.

"Did he hold up the van Gogh reputation?" asked Theo. Sophie looked at Vincent. "He enjoyed it as if it were his job. He's a real hard character." All the men laughed except Vincent.

Chapter 7
Ville d'Avray – Present Day

"Mags, the car will be here any time. Are you about ready?" Mark was in the makeshift office of what had once been a guest bedroom, adjusting his tie as he surveyed his reflection in the flat screen TV. "Mags!"

"No need to shout. I'm right here."

Mark turned around to face his wife. She was wearing a black gown with a thin strap over her right shoulder. The dress hugged her curves, accentuating her sinewy frame. Dangling earrings, small silver pendant, and black sequined clutch bag were perfect accoutrements to the simple yet elegant gown. "You really are the most beautiful woman I've ever seen," he said softly.

"Oh, stop! You look very handsome in your tux. Here, let me fix your tie. It complements your eyes."

Mark faced her as she straightened his tie. He felt the urge to unzip her figure-hugging gown but thought better of it.

"Tell me again who will be at this soirée?" she smiled.

"Several cancer researchers, the heads of the French and other European medical facilities, a few major donors, and a few politicians, from what I understand."

"And tell me again why we are going?" she teased.

"Well, Anton asked us to go and that's enough for me," Mark explained. "Come on, Mags. You'll have fun. Plus, you'll have the eyes of all the men there. You'll be the belle of the ball," he winked.

"You really are the sweetest," she murmured as she kissed his cheek. Suddenly she heard an engine. "Sounds like our chariot has arrived."

The driver emerged from the private car Mark had hired. Although unaccustomed to such indulgences, they relaxed together in the backseat as though this was their habit. Light classical music floated in the air. They toasted each other with a small glass of champagne. In no time at all, they were in Paris.

"I'm grateful not to have to fight the Paris traffic tonight," Mark said contentedly.

"Yes, this was a wonderful idea to hire a chauffeur. I'm sure we'll both be so worn out at the end of the evening that neither of us will feel like driving. Besides, you would have made me the designated driver – I just know it! Oh, I think we've arrived! Look at that magnificent elephant," Maggie remarked, pointing to a figure across from the museum entrance. "I had forgotten that statue."

"That is something to behold!"

The couple made their way up the main steps to the museum, Maggie careful not to step on her dress. "I've always loved this museum," she whispered.

"Yeah. Pretty grand for an old train station."

The glorious entrance was showered in bright incandescent light. Just inside, a tuxedoed gentleman was checking invitations. Mark presented the gold embossed card to him.

"Monsieur and Madame McFadden. On behalf of the Republic of France, welcome to our cancer research gala. Please proceed through the security screening and follow directions to the visitors' gallery."

Mark and Maggie had no difficulty finding the main gallery. It was buzzing with small talk and the clink of wine glasses. The high-ceilinged room was massive. "There must be two hundred people here," Mark commented as he took in the crowd.

"Well, it is a gala, after all. You can't have a fundraising gala without lots of rich and powerful folks."

"Let's find the bar." Mark led Maggie through the throng to a linen-covered table attended by white-jacketed servers.

"May I help you," a bartender asked, casting a lingering gaze over Maggie's curves.

"I would like a Chardonnay and my husband would like a Bud Lite," she ordered in French. The bartender hesitated.

"Very funny! I caught that Bud Lite request! Excuse me, sir, no Bud Lite," Mark said, waving his finger. "I would prefer a glass of Beaujolais."

Maggie repeated the order in French just to be sure. The bartender cracked a wry grin and went off to fill their request.

"Even the barmen are better dressed than I am," said Mark, feeling uncharacteristically uncomfortable.

"That's not true! You look as handsome as ever!"

"Did you see the way he ogled you?"

"He's French. He will appraise anything with breasts, dear."

The bartender returned shortly with their drink orders.

Maggie reached for her Chardonnay from the serving tray and handed the red wine to Mark. "Shall we find Anton?"

"Sure," Mark answered. He grabbed her hand and they roamed through the throng, admiring the fashionably dressed patrons. "I don't know if we'll ever find him in this crowd."

"Maybe he'll find us."

"I don't know how…"

"I think he just did!" Maggie pointed to a man poking his head above the crowd, waving a slender hand in the air.

"Yes, that's him! Good eye, Mags!" They started toward a cluster of five people, all of whom had turned to face the American couple. A tall but slight man with a full head of wavy jet-black hair came forward and gave Mark a hearty embrace.

"Mark, I am delighted to see you, my friend! And Maggie!" he said, taking her hand and brushing his lips across her knuckles. He stood back and looked her up and down. "Ah, you are as gorgeous as I remember! More so!"

"Anton Lambert, you are a rogue!" Maggie laughed.

"Anton, where is Sarah?" asked Mark.

"Alas, Sarah had to stay home with the boys. Phillipe has a terrible cold. Please, come. Let me introduce you to some wonderful benefactors." He reached for Maggie's hand and led them to a foursome that was watching their encounter.

"My friends, allow me to introduce Mark and Maggie McFadden. Mark and I attended graduate school together at Stanford. Mark and Maggie, this is Guillaume and Sofia LeGrand, and Louis and Andrea Morel. Jacques is National Director of Health Services for France. Andrea is a physician in private practice. Louis is one of the largest donors to the cancer research at my hospital and Sofia is an expert in fundraising for non-profits."

"Are you the Mark McFadden that discovered the receptors and tagging proteins for cancer cells?" Louis inquired in heavily accented English.

"I am," said Mark, "but you must know I was only part of a truly great team."

"But it was your discovery, was it not?" asked Jacques.

"Yes," Mark admitted, shyly.

"Your discovery," said Jacques, "enables direct targeting of certain types of cancer cells with small amounts of chemotherapy. This kills the cancer without going systemic, so the harmful side effects that most chemotherapies produce are essentially nonexistent. Even the most immune compromised patient can tolerate this treatment. This is the most amazing discovery of the decade. You have already saved many, many lives and lessened the suffering of so many cancer patients!"

Mark blushed and murmured his thanks.

"This is the stuff of Nobel Prize winners," added Louis. "How did you get interested in cancer research?" he asked.

"My mother died of breast cancer when I was twelve. I saw what that dreadful disease did to her. My father and I were devastated when we lost her."

"It must have been difficult growing up without your mother," Louis said softly.

"It was. But my father instilled in me a love of science. He saw to it that I received an excellent education."

"Well, I for one am most impressed with your work," Jacques remarked.

"We have been neglecting the other accomplished McFadden, and certainly the lovelier of the two," Anton reminded his colleagues as he turned to Maggie. "Maggie is a highly regarded anthropologist. She is widely published and has either led or assisted archeological digs in Europe, Asia, South America, and Africa."

"But you are so young," said Sophia. "And married as well. How do you find the time for career and family?"

"It certainly is not easy juggling both but we don't have children. At least not yet. Besides, Mark and I have a mutual respect for our individual fields of endeavor. He encourages me to pursue my own interests and is very supportive," Maggie responded in French.

Sophia's eyes grew large. "My dear, your French is impeccable. Where did you learn to speak our language?"

"My mother grew up in Paris. French was our primary language at home."

"Madame LaGrand, Maggie is also fluent in Mandarin, German, and Spanish," Anton added. "How many other languages do you speak, Maggie?"

"I can get by in a few others," Maggie said modestly. "At least enough to order food, tell time, and get directions."

Sophia asked, "How did you acquire such skills?"

"I was fortunate enough to travel to several archaeological sites around the world and one of the requirements was that I learn the language of the country I was visiting. I prepared for the digs by simply immersing myself into the language and culture of the country. I find I learn languages quickly that way. It's very rewarding."

"How did you and Mark meet?" asked Andrea.

"We met at Stanford," Maggie continued in French. "Mark was in the doctoral program in biomedical engineering and I took an introductory biology course that he taught. Then, switching to English, she added, "I guess you could say I became the—how do you say it— *'la chouchoute de professeur?'*"

The group chuckled at this last remark.

"Anton, are you still pursuing a localized treatment for brain cancer?" Mark inquired.

"Yes, but it is slow going. We remain in clinical trials. Being head of oncology at Hôtel-Dieu, I am blessed with generous benefactors and gifted students but, alas, I have many patients and not enough time for research. There are times I long for our days at Stanford and the gentlr pace."

"You are making headway, Anton. These things take time," responded Louis.

"*Oui,* you are correct. But, now, tell me, Mark, how is your summer place in d'Avray?"

"It is coming along nicely. There is a lot to do to renovate the house, but we are making progress."

"My friend, you chose wisely. D'Avray is a lovely village. Quiet, small, yet close to Paris."

"We are thrilled. But I must tell you, Mags is on my case to learn French!"

"And so you must! We have a special love for our beautiful language. You would find inconvenience not to speak our beloved language," Anton said with an earnest grin.

"I know, I know. Maggie has impressed this upon me. But, let me ask you a favor," Mark said, pulling Anton away from the others, out of earshot.

"Anything."

"In our digging around the house we've stumbled upon some curious things."

"Like what?"

"Such as an old wooden box hidden in a stone support column in the basement."

"Really? What was in the box?" Anton whispered.

"It contained a letter, an artist's journal, and a gun."

"*Mon Dieu,* a gun?! Remarkable! How old are these things, do you know?"

"They all appear to be from the late 1800's. I researched the gun online. It looks to be a French Army revolver from around 1870-1880. Etienne is the manufacturer."

"I know nothing of guns. But a letter and journal?"

"The letter mentions someone's untimely death. We think it may be referring to the person who owned the journal. The journal has several sketches and notes written in two or three languages."

"Interesting."

"Yeah. We went to the city hall and found that a man named Chemin owned the house in 1890. We haven't been able to find out anything about him."

"Chemin. That is a fairly common name."

"Unfortunately. Anyway, the sketches in the journal look familiar. Mags and I both think we recognize the work."

"Who is it?" Anton wanted to know.

"I'm hesitant to say. We haven't confirmed anything yet. I was hoping you might know someone in the Paris art community who could help us."

"I do know the assistant director of modern art here at the D'Orsay. His name is Victor Durand. I can call him and see if he can help you," Anton offered.

"That would be excellent. Thank you!"

"*Certainement.* I will call him on Monday."

"In the meantime, I'd appreciate it if you would keep this to yourself. We're not sure exactly what we have here."

"Of course."

A few feet away, an elderly gentleman with rimless glasses had ambushed poor Maggie. As she strained to hear his slurred words, she caught Mark's eye.

"Please excuse me, Anton, but I think I'd better go and rescue my wife," Mark said. "Many thanks, my friend."

"Please do keep me informed of what you find out about your treasures."

Chapter 8
Paris – August 1886

Theo was keeping an active correspondence with several friends from Nuenen. He exchanged frequent letters with Andries Bonger, a longtime friend whom he affectionately called "Andre." Andre had tried to encourage Theo to go into his art business with him. He also tried to act as matchmaker between Theo and his sister Johanna.

Both of Andries' ideas intrigued Theo, but leaving Goupil meant that he would require financial backing, and this would not come easily. The wooing of Jo Bonger, however, was just becoming a priority for Theo. Jo was near his own age and had never married. She lived at home with her parents and was sheltered from outside influences. He liked the idea of marriage and a family, and he was well aware that his health was suffering from his frequent visits to bars and bordellos. So with thoughts of Jo in his mind, Theo went back to Holland to visit his mother in late summer of 1886, allowing him the opportunity to spend some time with Jo as well. Recently widowed, his mother had moved in with his sister Wil in nearby Breda. On this trip he visited Jo as often as time would permit.

While there, Theo approached his Uncle Cent to obtain financial backing to start an art gallery with Bonger. Cent, who still had ties to Goupil, refused to fund Theo whom he thought too valuable to lose. He was also concerned with the type of art in which Theo and Andries intended to trade. He thought it "too modern" and felt the venture was doomed for failure; and so, faced with insufficient means to support a family, Theo left Holland without any mention to Jo of his intentions towards her.

When he returned to Paris, Theo confided in Vincent his plan to marry Jo, an aim that was set firmly in his mind. "I have met my future bride, Vincent. She is lovely, a bit shy, and very sweet."

Vincent was seized with a myriad of emotions. He was all at once aghast, furious, and jealous. His fragile ego could not comprehend why Theo wanted to bring another person into their home. He looked at Theo in utter disbelief. "Where did this come from? Why have you not confided in me before now?"

"Dear brother, I had no intention of leaving you out of my confidence."

"You don't even know her, Theo."

"I know her well enough. I visited her several times while in Nuenen. She is kind, gentle, and beautiful. Our wise father would have approved of her. His counsel was to marry someone decent, someone within our 'station.' She is surely that woman."

"As always, you follow the rules. You are far too bourgeois and much too reserved. Why, you would never think of flouting convention! What about the whores down by the river and the Moulin de la Gallette—are they not respectable enough for you?" Vincent asked sarcastically.

"Vincent, I long for a family of my own. It is what Pa and Ma have always wanted for us… peace and solidarity and a close-knit family. Is that too much to ask?"

"Theo, you are a good brother, but you don't understand life. Women bring only pain. I don't want you to suffer as I have."

"This talk is useless. I am going to the Gallery now. You

are entitled to your opinions, Vincent, but please do not share them with me!" Theo left the apartment in a huff, his anger lingering in the air like a cloud of dust.

Vincent felt miserable but could not put his angst into words. He feared that with three in the household, he would be abandoned and alone once more. It was the same feeling he had when he was sent to boarding school many years before. Finally, he gathered his paint supplies and went to the door. He needed some air.

He headed north, then west, hoping for an opportunity to paint a figure. Failing to convince anyone to sit for a portrait, Vincent hiked further out toward the edge of the city, intending to work en plein air on the beautiful summer afternoon. He wore his blue overalls, those of a zinc worker, spattered with odd little dots of color. He trudged along, lost in thought, forsaking the city behind him and feeling propelled forward by the forces of nature.

He soon reached Asnières on the outskirts of the city, then found the corner of Voyer d'Argenson Park, which was relatively quiet on this calm afternoon. He stopped and looked around. The few strollers passing by had nothing more than sidelong glances for him, for which he was grateful. He was in no mood for conversation. He grumbled as he set his easel on a level spot and arranged his tools—today it was oils. He set his paint box on the ground and placed a small stretched canvas on the easel. He erected his perspective frame in front of the canvas. This prized tool allowed him to compare subjects that were nearer to him with those further away. He believed that it was not possible or even feasible to completely rely on one's sights to gain the proper perspective. Only the best and most experienced artists could do that, and even the old Dutch Masters favored the use of this mechanism.

His anger fading, Vincent focused on his colors—those before him in the scene, and those behind his eyes. He had been talking with Paul Signac the night before about Seurat's intriguing color theories and had been collecting bits of colored paper and yarn to play with color contrasts. Now, he took in the local color–the green of the grass, the near-white of the horizon–inhaling them as if they were mixed with the air. He watched the play of sunlight on the leaves of nearby trees, which were dancing on a soft breeze. Closing one eye, he slowly scanned the landscape, looking for a natural composition in a form given by the world in his eye. His breath caught on a particular view–vibrant tufts of tall grass dotted with wildflowers beside the path, beyond which waved shimmering trees. He could see in this frame a host of greens mixed with a palette of earthen shades from cream to rich brown.

The scene begged him to compose it.

Using his perspective frame, he centered it on the canvas. A grid of horizontal and vertical threads stretched across the canvas. He lined his eye with the frame's rod, which was the same height as the distance from the bottom of the frame to the middle of the grid. He began outlining the park's geometry with light charcoal. He marked the focal center where the light grasses were at their brightest. The scene harmonized with strong horizontals–the pathway snaking from lower left toward this center point and, beyond, the edge of the field and distant hills, then a bit of bright summer sky. But what entranced him was not so much the geometry of this composition, but the richness of color at its vortex. The gentle slant of the background trees and the lean of the path all drew him toward this bright center of grasses.

He saw it now.

The light between the leaves, the vibrating colors, a sense of circling energy. These were essential. He set to work.

First, he drew charcoal lines to depict where trees and grasses grew before adding the oils. He incorporated horizontal lines for a pathway. When he was satisfied that he had captured the geometry of the park, he added some shading and details with a light pencil.

The scene did not call for broad swaths of color, and Vincent preferred to create his own small but varied mix of colors. For this scene, he chose white, Prussian blue, Van Dyke brown, chrome yellow, vermillion, and chrome orange. The canvas had already been prepared with lead white, chalk, and barium sulphate. Its jute-like texture was rough enough to permit the oils to easily adhere to the surface. He painted horizontally across the canvas, careful to follow the perspective he had established. The colors transformed before him, coming alive as if emerging directly from the sky, the trees, and the grasses. He painted quickly but thoughtfully, combining the pointillism technique he had learned from Suerat with the dashed brushstrokes favored by other neo-Impressionists. He worked with the bold colors first, filling in the canvas with greens and blues. Then he added detail with points of red and yellow.

Vincent stepped back from the canvas. He was pleased with his work but had more to do and wanted to finish before the sun went down. He was anxious to show Theo his latest achievement. He finished as much as he could, carefully covered the canvas, then rushed back to the apartment, hoping that Theo was not still angry with him.

When Vincent arrived home, Theo was waiting for him. Ever the patient and loyal brother, he greeted Vincent with open arms. "Please do not be offended, Vincent. You are so very important to me. I want you to be happy. I will not approach Jo Bonger yet with my proposal. But when I do, you will be the first to know."

"I was quite harsh with you, Theo. You know how impulsive I can be and how difficult it is for me to cope with change. I was just taken by surprise. I truly want to live up to your expectations but I fear I have let you down. I hope that you can forgive me. You have done so much for me in ways that I cannot begin to describe."

"Come, let us sit and relax for a while. I have prepared a small meal. But what is it that you have here? Another painting?"

"Yes! I am feeling very confident about this one, Theo. The results are quite pleasing to me. Let me recount my afternoon to you. Perhaps our quarrel provided just the impetus I needed to be productive on this fine day!"

The brothers sat side by side at their dinner table. Vincent described his approach and technique to Theo, speaking of his feelings, the oneness he felt with nature, and the emotions that the colors evoked within him. They talked long into the evening, putting the earlier unpleasant events of the day behind them.

Summer moved into autumn and the brothers continued about their business. Theo was wrapped up in his gallery work while Vincent painted during the day and spent his evenings in the bars, drinking with friends.

One evening in late autumn, Vincent and Émile agreed to meet at one of their favorite cafés on the Rue du Montmartre. As Vincent entered, he spotted Émile sitting, facing the door. Across from Émile with her back to Vincent, was a tall, thin woman wearing a high-collared, gaily flowered dress and a black, brimmed hat. Next to the woman was a large, towering man sitting erect and entirely focused on what she and Émile were discussing. The woman seemed familiar to Vincent, but he could not immediately place her.

Émile spotted Vincent by the door, and he rose and waved for his friend to join them. The café was large, with long tables traversing lengthwise across the room. Serving women were catering to the small crowd.

Vincent walked slowly down the main aisle, never taking his eyes off the pair sitting across from Émile. As he approached, the man came into profile first. He had broad shoulders, an angular nose, deeply shaded eyes, and a thick, downturned mustache. The man appeared not to notice Vincent. Coming around the table on the side where Émile was seated, Vincent finally got a clear view of the woman.

It was Marguerite.

"Marguerite! I did not think I would see you again! This is a pleasant surprise! How do you know my friend, Émile?"

Vincent's voice was high and excited.

"Vincent, it is so nice to see you again." Marguerite stretched out her hand and Vincent took it, brushing his lips across her knuckles. She continued, "It is a small world when people have so much in common."

"Vincent, this is my friend, Pierre." Pierre stood and reached to shake Vincent's hand.

Vincent shook Pierre's hand and perched himself on the bench next to Émile. "Émile, how do you know Marguerite?" he asked.

"We met last year at a meeting of young people concerned about the oppressed poor in Russia."

Marguerite nodded. "The abused are one of my causes, Vincent. It pains me to see people kept under the thumb of a regal few. Birth should not denote one's station in life. But, Vincent, you know this better than anyone."

"Yes, I have not always been appreciated. I served my time as a minister on the docks in Belgium, and now I serve as a chronicler of the poor man's struggles. Only Theo has any appreciation for my true sacrifices. He understands me better than anyone else."

"Vincent, all artists suffer to some degree," said Émile. "It is the nature of our soul. Many of us don't know how to channel our energy, merely speaking of hope and change."

"I am focusing my energy into my work," Vincent rejoined, feeling a bit slighted by Émile's remark. "I want to make this world a better place."

"That is a noble gesture. But you have confided in me that there is a part of you that is unsatisfied, the part that leads you into despair," Émile added.

"My painting and sketches help me overcome my sadness. I always look for subjects to help." Vincent reached into his jacket and withdrew his journal.

"Art is good for the soul, Vincent, but you have more to offer the world. You could join our group and truly benefit others. And, sharing a cause just might help your art find a paying audience."

Marguerite and Pierre sat watching this exchange. A slight smile crossed Marguerite's face as she said, "Vincent, I knew from the first time we spoke that you are a man of strong convictions. A man who wants to be great, not for his own sake but for the sake of others. When I learned that Émile was your friend and I made the connection to you on the train, I could not wait to meet you again. Unfortunately, our encounter at the exhibition was all too brief."

Vincent was staring at Marguerite. He rarely blinked, as if afraid she might disappear if he closed his eyes even for a moment.

"Vincent," she leaned in, "we are part of a group, a commune, brought together in a special brotherhood. We truly care for one another, respect one another's opinions and, more importantly, we reach out to help those who cannot help themselves. Would you consider joining our cause?"

Vincent said bleakly, "But I have no money to give."

Marguerite reached across the table and took Vincent's hand, her blue eyes catching Vincent's unblinking stare. She replied, "We don't expect you to have money, Vincent. We want your talent and time, your desire to correct what is wrong in the world. Do you know the story *'D'où vient le mal'* by Tolstoy? The tale ends with a sentence that has stayed with me: 'It is from our own nature that evil comes; for it is our nature that gives rise to hunger, and to love, and to malice, and to fear.' We are not perfect creatures but we are capable of so much good! Compassion, forgiveness, and love! Would you really like to make a difference in the world, and be respected wherever you go as a man of true noble heart?"

"Of course, yes!" Vincent was eager to hear more.

"We are very selective of those who join, Vincent. If you decide to join us, you will be welcomed, but we would expect your devotion to us, both as a group and—" Marguerite looked straight into Vincent's eyes—"individually."

"I am interested. But what does this group do?"

"Let's say we determine what we can do to help people. I can't go into any more detail until you join us." She looked at him with flashing eyes. "I truly hope you will join us, Vincent. I would like to see you more often. The Commune is a special group of people. You would fit like a glove fits a hand." Marguerite and Pierre rose. Émile and Vincent likewise rose in respect.

"Vincent, there is a meeting coming up shortly. Émile will let you know the time and place. I hope to see you there." As she turned to leave, Marguerite turned back to face Vincent. "But be mindful, Vincent, we are a devoted group. Only come if you are seriously interested in our mission."

Vincent watched as Marguerite led Pierre down the aisle of the café and into the night air. Émile looked at Vincent. "Our drinks have arrived. Let us drink to your health, my friend!" They clinked glasses and took their sips.

Outside the café Marguerite stood at the step of a waiting carriage. Pierre said in a heavy German accent, "These artists are an odd bunch. They are so easily manipulated."

"Don't be so sure, Pierre. What we will ask of them will require them to make life and death decisions. I am worried how they will cope. But we do need them." Marguerite got into the carriage and Pierre walked down the avenue a ways before taking cover behind a building. From there he could watch the entrance to the café.

He waited.

Chapter 9
Ville d'Avray – Present Day

Mark answered his cell on the second ring. "Hello, Anton, how are you today?" he asked cheerily. He and Maggie had driven into town and were enjoying a café lunch.

"Very well, *mon ami*. I'm calling to let you know I talked to Victor Durand at the d'Orsay. I told him I have a good friend who recently purchased a home in d'Avray. I explained that you came across what may be an artist's notebook and asked if he could examine it and evaluate its worth. He said he'd be delighted to assist."

"Perfect," smiled Mark.

"You have an appointment with Victor next Tuesday at one o'clock. Go to the museum and tell the receptionist you have an appointment with Monsieur Durand."

"Anton, I can't tell you how much I appreciate this. Thank you very much."

"Remember, you must let me know what he says. This is a very curious matter."

"Of course, I will. Take care."

"Please give my regards to Maggie. *Á bientôt.*"

Mark shut off the phone and told her about the meeting.

"That's super!" she said. "Maybe Monsieur Durand can confirm that it is van Gogh's journal. What a find that would be!"

"Mags, don't get your hopes up. I mean, really, what are the chances that this journal belonged to van Gogh? It wasn't uncommon for art students to copy the work of other artists, you know, so the fact that the pictures look like van Gogh's work may be meaningless."

"You are always a pessimist!"

"Realist, Maggie!"

"So how are we going to find out anything about the gun and the note?" she asked.

"Well, let's take the gun to the local police department and see if they have any ideas as to how it can be traced."

"Are we even allowed to own guns in France? Who knows what the laws are here?"

"All guns have to be registered. I don't know what they'll say about us finding a gun. They might want to confiscate it or they could help us trace it. Or it could simply be too old for any records to exist."

"Hmm. No other ideas?" Maggie asked.

"Not unless we can find some local gun historian."

"Hmm. So, when do we visit the police station?"

"There's no time like the present."

"You don't have the gun with you, I hope?" Maggie asked with a look of alarm.

"No, of course not. But I have pictures of it on my phone. That should be good enough to start."

"Let's hit the road then!"

Mark left money on the table and they walked out into the bright spring day. Unsure of which way to turn, Mark said, "The police station might be located near the town hall." They headed in that direction and there it was.

They entered revolving glass doors and passed through a metal detector. The station was bustling with people. Some were dressed in suits and others looked like they had worn the same rags for days.

A lone officer sat at a dreary desk in the center of the

atrium. A sign on the desk said "Rancard." There was a short line of people waiting in front of him. He answered their questions brusquely and the line moved quickly. When it was Mark and Maggie's turn, the officer addressed them with a nod and a terse, *"Oui."*

Maggie said in French, "Officer, we just purchased a house outside of town on Rue de Marnes. During our renovations, we discovered a gun. A revolver from the late 1800's, we believe."

"You wish to turn it in?" he asked.

"No. We wanted to talk to someone who might know more about it and, if possible, find out who it belonged to."

"You know all weapons must be registered."

"Yes, we know. But do you think it's possible for us to talk to someone about the gun?"

"We are not the library, Madame."

"I'm sorry, but we thought the police would be the most knowledgeable resource for such things."

The officer sighed and picked up the phone. He explained Maggie's request to the person on the line. *"Oui. Oui."* Looking at Maggie, he asked, "What is your name?"

"Maggie McFadden. This is my husband, Mark."

"Your nationality?" he asked them.

"American."

"Someone will be out to talk to you," he said, resting the phone in its cradle.

"Do you have any idea how long it will be?" she asked politely.

"This is not a priority. Someone will be out as soon as possible. Please, have a seat."

Maggie looked at Mark. "We should sit. He says someone will see us but it is not a priority so who knows how long that will be."

"That doesn't sound encouraging."

"It's as good as we can expect, I think. We're in France. We're on their timetable."

They found a bench along the wall of windows. "Looks like we may be in for a long wait," Mark said, as he eyed the swarm of people milling around.

"By the way, I talked to Maman yesterday while you were out," said Maggie.

"How is she getting along without you? She must miss you terribly."

"She sounded good. She asked about you, of course. I told her about our finds. She is intrigued and wants to know what we uncover."

After a while, an officious man in a dark blue suit appeared at the information desk. He and the desk officer exchanged words, looking in Mark and Maggie's direction.

Maggie nudged Mark's leg. "Looks like our waiting may be over."

The couple watched as he approached. Mark judged him to be about five-foot eight, fiftyish, and in good shape. His hair was mostly pepper with a little salt; most of the gray was around his temples. His gait was brisk and he stared straight ahead at them. They rose from their seats in unison.

"Are you the McFaddens?" he asked in English.

"Oui," Maggie answered, introducing herself and Mark.

"I am Commissioner Phillipe Gastineau of the Ville d'Avray police. Do you both speak French?"

"No, only I do. Mark is learning, though."

Gastineau extended his arm toward the front desk. "Please come with me. We can talk in the back."

He led them to a dimly lit room with a table and four chairs. Mark felt like a suspect just before questioning.

"Tell me, what can I do for you?" Gastineau asked.

Mark explained how they had found the gun buried in the basement of the old house. He didn't mention anything about the letter or journal. "I have some pictures of the gun here on my phone." Mark handed it to the detective.

"Yes. This looks like a French army revolver from the turn of the last century." Zooming into the photo, he pointed to some writing on the side of the gun just below the cartridge cylinder. "See here. 'Saint-Etienne.' That is the manufacturer."

"Is it possible to trace this gun to the original owner?" asked Mark.

"I don't believe so. This gun was issued to many French soldiers in the late 1800's and early 1900's. It was manufactured even through WWII. Detailed serial number records were not always kept for weapons issued to soldiers."

"Do you think it would be worth going to the manufacturer and ask them to search their records?" asked Maggie.

"Saint-Etienne is now part of Nexter. Nexter is a large government-owned weapons maker. I doubt anyone there would take the time to look at their records for you, especially records that are so old. As I've said, such records might not even exist. Why is this gun so important to you?" Gastineau asked.

"It's not every day that you find an old gun buried in your basement."

"No, I suppose not," he admitted.

"We did learn that the house was owned by a Frederic or Marguerite Chemin at the turn of the last century. The gun could have belonged to either of them. Have you by any chance heard of Chemin?" Mark asked.

"Chemin… hmmm… No, it is a common name but I do not know of a Frederic. But you must know the gun may have been buried at any time over the past hundred years."

"True. But we also found a newspaper from 1888 stuck in an old hutch. I just thought there might be a link between the two."

"Perhaps, but somewhat unlikely, I think. Did you find anything else?" he asked Mark.

Mark felt himself flush. He quickly weighed his options, fearing that if he lied to the police, he would surely be caught. Reluctantly, he added, "We found an old journal and lots of dust."

"Did this journal give you any clues about the gun?" asked Gastineau.

"Not really," replied Mark.

"What did you say your address is?"

"30 Rue de Marnes."

"Ah, a very nice area. When did you purchase the house?"

"Just this year. We are just now moving in."

"I hope you will love d'Avray and France as much as I do. But, alas, Monsieur, I don't think I can be of much help to you."

"Thank you for your time, detective," replied Mark, rising from his seat.

"Au revoir," added Maggie.

Gastineau escorted them to the lobby and watched as they exited the building.

"Well, that was a bust," said Mark, not trying to hide his disappointment.

"I guess we'll have to keep looking at the journal and letter for answers," said Maggie. "I still think we have something—I just don't know what."

Chapter 10
Paris – Late Autumn 1886

Theo continued his long-distance courtship with Jo. His increasing interest in her became a source of conflict in the apartment and Vincent became withdrawn and brooding. He spent less and less time at the apartment and more time in cafés and bars drinking, frequently to excess, and listening to fragments of other patrons' conversations. Émile and Vincent were constant companions, at least when they were not busy with their respective paintings.

Late one evening, they were leaving the Café du Parisien on Boulevard de Clichy with a group of friends. The weather was cold and the group quickly dispersed, going their separate ways.

Émile murmured to Vincent: "Vincent, are you in a hurry to get home?"

"No. I have no desire to come home to Theo and face his unbearable criticisms of my drinking habits."

"Remember our conversation with Marguerite? About the Commune?" Émile was whispering now.

"Of course, I remember."

"The meeting is scheduled for next week. Come, let's go and have a cup of coffee and talk."

Émile led Vincent onto the Rue Andre-Antoine. The street was dark and quiet. Émile stopped at the door of a small shop with heavily curtained windows and opened it to reveal a smoke-filled room. At one of the corner tables three men halted their conversation to watch them. The men stared warily until Émile and Vincent found a table on the other side of the room. The men then resumed their hushed conversation.

"What is this place, Émile? I've never noticed it before." Vincent was feeling somewhat uncomfortable with the quiet surroundings and the watchful eyes of the other huddled men.

Émile said, "I come here sometimes when I want to be alone with my thoughts or I have private matters to discuss, like we do tonight."

Vincent instinctively removed his journal from his jacket pocket and took out a pencil. Émile gently put his hand on Vincent's.

"Please, this is not a night for drawing, but for conversation."

Vincent could see the seriousness of Émile's gaze. He slowly put the pencil and journal back in his pocket. A waitress appeared at the table. "What to drink, monsieurs?" she asked.

"Two coffees, black," replied Émile. When she left he lowered his voice again and spoke to Vincent. "Marguerite asked me to invite you to the next Commune meeting."

"Finally," Vincent replied curtly. "I wondered when…"

Émile interrupted. "Wait. I must tell you, Vincent, that the Commune members are serious and single-minded. They believe, as I do, that the world is at a crossroad. The elite few who run governments in Prussia, Russia, Denmark, and even France are evil and entirely self-serving."

"Yes. So?"

"The Commune is committed to change through whatever means necessary. Sometimes the only way to make change is to replace the ruling class—this is often accomplished by force."

"Are you are talking revolution, Émile? Do you mean to overthrow the French government?" Vincent was suddenly alert.

"France is the least of the problem. Prussia and Russia are ruining the chance for Europe to enter a golden age. Look at what Bismarck did to France just fifteen years ago. He lied to give Prussia a reason to invade France. He laid siege to Paris for almost a year! People ate dogs, cats—even rats—to survive! All of this so he could annex Alsace and create a united Germanic republic under his thumb."

"What's done is done. We can't change what happened."

"Would you want it to happen again?" Émile was keenly watching Vincent's reaction.

"No, of course not." Vincent did not quite know what to make of this conversation.

"Vincent, the Commune has very smart people with connections throughout Europe and Russia. The same thing that Bismarck did to France, Tsar Alexander is doing to the Baltic region and in Siberia. He is enslaving people for his own aggrandizement. This is pure malevolence, Vincent."

"I had no idea things were that bad. Although I have lived among the peasants and the dockworkers and have witnessed social injustices, I am not a man of politics. You know that."

"I do. The Commune has the best interest of Europe and its people at heart. If you come to the meeting, all of us there will expect you to be committed to our cause. Are you up to the task?"

The coffees came and the two men sipped in silence.

"Émile, you are one of my only true friends. I accept the invitation. Gladly."

"That is good. The meeting — please do not tell anyone, not even Theo, of the meeting or the Commune."

"I promise. Theo is too busy looking for a wife anyway."

Chapter 11
Paris – Late Autumn 1886

October was nearing its end. The air was bitterly cold, as winter had made an unexpected early arrival. Snow had already fallen and melted, leaving the ground frosty and wet. Vincent and Émile met at La Tambourin at four in the afternoon, and then took a carriage to Montparnesse to catch the five o'clock train to Versailles.

Vincent spoke up. "Tell me, Émile, will Marguerite be at the meeting?"

"Yes, Vincent. She will be leading the meeting as usual."

"How many other people will be there? Where is the meeting to be held?" The questions kept coming.

"There will be about a dozen people, including you and me. Marguerite will probably be the only woman. We will meet at the home of a member of the Commune."

"Is it Marguerite's home?"

"No. I understand that she doesn't live here, only visits."

"I thought she lived near Paris. I am sure that is what she told me." Vincent felt confused.

"I may be mistaken then, Vincent. If she told you that then I am sure she has a home near Paris."

"What will we talk about? Will I be asked to do or say anything? You know I am not good at speaking to strangers," Vincent's voice was mounting with apprehension. "My speaking skills are better if I have prepared something in writing beforehand. My days as a preacher have long passed."

"You should simply listen and observe tonight."

By the time the train arrived in Versailles, darkness had fallen. "Vincent, we are to wait outside the main entrance to the station. A carriage is being sent to pick us up." Émile started towards the door of the terminal.

"How long do we have to wait? It's cold and my coat is thin." Vincent was beginning to wear on Émile's nerves with his constant questions and complaints.

"I don't know," Émile answered. "I was told to wait and a carriage would come for us."

Across from the station's entrance Pierre stood, hidden by his waiting carriage, watching Émile and Vincent exit the large doors. When he was certain that they were alone, he got back into the carriage and instructed the driver to pick up the guests. The carriage moved to the front of the station. The driver called out, "Monsieur Bernard?"

Émile linked his arm with Vincent's and said, "Yes… come, Vincent, this is our carriage." They climbed aboard, facing Pierre as they sat. Émile began, "Ah, Pierre, it is good to see you again! Do you remember Vincent?"

"I do. It is very nice to meet you again, Vincent. Our ride should not take long. If you don't mind, I closed the curtains to keep the cold out." Pierre's manner was pleasant but reserved.

The carriage ride took about forty minutes and the men rarely spoke except to comment about the weather or the bumpiness of the ride. When the carriage stopped, the driver opened the door and all three men descended. Pierre said to the driver. "We should be about an hour and a half."

The house was a simple, two-story stone structure with a gabled roof, set back about forty feet from a muddy lane.

With only a few other houses in sight, it afforded a quiet privacy. A small stone fence encircled the front of the house and a similar fence guarded an unkempt flower garden. A wooden portico with four columns covered the main entry.

Lights flickered in the large windows on either side of the front door. Shadows of people were visible through the opaque curtains. Pierre led the small group down the cobblestone sidewalk to the front door.

Entering the house, Vincent could see several men standing in the rooms to the right and left of the central foyer. The room on the right was a dining room. To the left was a sitting room that boasted an oversized stone fireplace. Marguerite warmed herself in a chair by the fireplace talking to a small group of men. Seeing Vincent and Émile come in, she rose. "Vincent, Émile, thank you for coming! I hope your journey was safe and comfortable."

"Our trip was fine, if a bit exhausting, and Pierre was kind enough to pick us up at the train station," replied Émile. He was relieved to be out of the bitter cold and rubbed his hands by the welcoming fire.

"Vincent, I have been looking forward to seeing you again. You have been well and painting the Paris landscapes, I hope?" Marguerite inquired with her deep, melodious voice that had caught Vincent's attention during their first encounter.

"I am well. My painting is progressing. I am using more colors but my subjects are not what I prefer. I need subjects for portraits. Perhaps you would pose…" Vincent asked hopefully.

Marguerite ignored the request. "Vincent, come, you

and Émile are the last to arrive. I want you to meet the rest of our group." With that, she took Vincent's arm and led him through the foyer. On the left, beyond the foyer, was a weathered oak door that opened to steps leading down to another level. Marguerite descended and directed Vincent, Émile and Pierre to follow. The basement was as large as the main floor of the house, encircled on the perimeter by seven-foot stacked-stone walls held together with horsehair mortar. In addition, there were ample load-bearing stone columns that supported the upper floor. Oil lanterns provided indistinct light throughout the cold, austere room. There were several small wooden chairs on the dirt floor and two large tables placed at either end of the room.

"We hold our meetings here to avoid prying eyes and snooping ears. This room gives us the solitude that we need for open discussions. Émile, please, you and Vincent sit." Marguerite motioned them toward one of the chairs.

The men from upstairs were filling the room. Cigarette and pipe smoke quickly permeated the air. Marguerite strode to the middle seat at the head table. "Please take your seats, gentlemen. We have just a few items to discuss tonight." Marguerite spoke with quiet confidence.

After everyone was seated, stillness filled the room and Marguerite began. "We have very important business to discuss but first, I want to introduce a new member to The Commune, Vincent van Gogh. Vincent shares our passion for the rights of workers and peasants. He has lived among the poor and experienced the injustices of the ruling class first-hand. Vincent is a man of the people and we welcome him."

Clapping filled the room. Vincent smiled sheepishly and lowered his gaze, somewhat embarrassed yet pleased by the attention.

Marguerite continued, "Comrades, as most of you know, we are at a critical juncture in our plans to help free the Russian people from the oppression of the Tsar. Some of our most dedicated comrades in Russia are prepared to act. These men are to be lauded for their selfless acts. If only we had more like them!" Marguerite was staring directly at Vincent. Vincent looked at the sketchbook resting on his lap. He started to draw. Marguerite rose from the page, standing like a goddess before the group of men. He sketched quickly, making long lines, avoiding details that he'd add later from memory.

"Comrades, some of our soldiers are traveling in Prussia and in southern France. Your financial assistance is necessary to continue." A hat was passed around the room, each man adding coins to the collection. Immersed in his sketching, the hat passed by Vincent without his notice.

"Comrades, the small amount you give tonight is not enough to make our plans succeed. I implore you to go and secure more funds." Marguerite was speaking fervently.

Someone interrupted, "How are we to get what we don't have?"

"This is a revolution we are talking about, Comrades. Think of the lives you can save. Every day peasants die at the hands of the Prussian and Tsarist dogs. Are you not willing to sacrifice as our comrades are? Are you only committed when the path is easy?"

"No! No!" came the replies. The audience was roused by Marguerite's impassioned pleas.

"Comrades, you will go down in history as saviors of the working class. But this fight will not be won unless we are successful in bringing the revolution to the surface. We have many men in place ready to act. They are depending on you. Please, do not fail them!"

Marguerite continued. "Comrades, we also need arms to help in the fight against oppression. I know many of you have pistols and rifles. We can get these to the comrades who need them. Please bring them to our next meeting. By then I hope to be able to tell you what precise action we are taking and when you can expect results. Now, comrades, let us go and take our leave. Remember, secrecy is our greatest weapon against tyranny. They will never see us coming!"

Émile looked at Vincent and his sketchbook. "Vincent, it is time to go. Please put that away. We don't want to upset anyone."

"Why would anyone be upset? I am going to make this into a great piece that will survive long after we are gone." Reluctantly, he shoved the book into his jacket.

"Vincent," said Marguerite as she approached, "what do you think of our group?"

"I'm not sure. What are you planning? You know I have no money. What else can I do to help?"

"You may be able to play a very important role in pushing our cause forward. In you I see a man destined for greatness. Not just in your art, but in your humanity. I want to rely on you for a very important assignment."

"What is it you expect of me?" he asked anxiously.

"Nothing now, but soon. Please trust me." Marguerite accompanied them to the door. Émile and Vincent were the last to leave. "I look forward to our next visit. Pierre will see you back to the train station. Thank you for coming."

"When will I see you again?" Vincent's voice had a plaintive edge, like a child asking for candy. Marguerite's lips curled in a half smile, "I am not sure, but soon."

"Will you pose for me? In Paris?"

"I will consider it, Vincent. Now hurry, you don't want to miss the last train." She ushered him out into the waiting carriage.

Pierre paused at the door and watched while Émile and Vincent got into the carriage. In his northern German accent, he said, "You have work to do."

"I know. I still think these two will serve our purpose well."

"Have you heard any word from Moscow?"

"None. They are being quiet now. The time is near for them to act. We should hear soon."

"You know not to over promise."

"Pierre, let me worry about what I promise. All that has to happen is to establish a direct link from Moscow to France. Berlin will handle the rest."

Pierre marched to the carriage and the waiting artists.

Chapter 12
Paris – Present Day

The McFaddens decided to take the train from Sèvres Ville-d'Avray to Paris, followed by a taxi to the Musée d'Orsay for their meeting with Victor Durand. The train arrived at Saint-Lazare promptly at 11:32 a.m.

"Mags, we have plenty of time before our meeting. Want to take a stroll?" Mark suggested.

"Sure. It's a beautiful day and after all, it is Paris."

The couple walked down Rue du Havre, hand in hand, in the direction of the Seine. Mark carried a small black leather briefcase with the journal inside; Maggie toted a woven red, yellow, and green straw bag. Pigeons fluttered past them in search of food discarded by tourists. Street vendors hawked their cheap wares. The couple savored the ordinariness of this day in Paris. They soon came to the sprawling Place de la Concord and the bridge that arched gracefully over the Seine like an overladen bough.

"It's hard to believe that at one time headless bodies from the guillotine were piled up right here," said Mark. He grimaced at the thought.

"Different times, those were," Maggie answered. "I'd like to think we are a bit more civilized these days."

Once across the Seine, they turned down Quai Anatole France. They passed several imposing stone buildings, including the National Museum of the Legion of Honor and Orders of Chivalry, which Maggie pointed out. "The name is as daunting as the building," Mark noted. Shortly, they came upon the stone mall at the entrance to the Musée d'Orsay and entered the expansive atrium. The high rounded ceiling recalled the building's early life as a train terminal. The architecture was a piece of glorious art; even the opaque glass and intricate stonework that form the support columns noteworthy in their beauty. The couple's eyes were automatically drawn to the diffused light high above their heads.

"To think this was a train station. It's all so grand!" Maggie said.

"We don't have much in the States that can compare with this, that's for sure. Come on, let's find someone who can help us," Mark said.

The cordial young woman at the information desk immediately placed a call for them to someone ensconced deep in the bowels of the building. After a few brief words, the receptionist announced that someone would be there shortly to escort them to the assistant director's office.

Before long, a humorless young man appeared before them —tousled brown hair and a rumpled shirt, sleeves rolled up to the elbows. "Monsieur McFadden," he inquired as he approached the couple. "I am Henri, M. Durand's assistant." He shook each of their hands vigorously. "The director is expecting you. Please walk this way."

They passed through security, descended one floor in an elevator, and walked through brightly lit corridors until they reached a door with a placard that translated, "Victor Durand, Assistant Director, Modern Art."

"Please wait here while I get the director," Henri requested.

He disappeared through the adjoining door. Mark looked around the small anterior room. There were windows high on the wall with iron bars on the outside. The room itself was plain and devoid of any warmth; bookshelves lined one wall and a small desk sat opposite the bookcases. A computer terminal sat to one side of the desktop.

They waited in silence. It was only a few minutes before the door opened and Henri reappeared, followed by a short, rotund, bespectacled man. He extended a fleshy hand to Mark and introduced himself as Victor Durand. He reminded Mark of the Pillsbury Doughboy, sans toque.

"It is so good to meet you. Anton speaks very highly of you," he wheezed.

Mark and Maggie found themselves leaning in to understand what the gentleman was saying. "Please come into my office so we can talk."

A colossal desk dominated the office, behind which rested a well-worn leather executive chair. Photographs of the director with various notable people were scattered about the room. One wall boasted certificates of graduation and achievements of various kinds. A gilt framed picture of Pablo Picasso hung in the center of the largest wall looking very out-of-place in the otherwise bleak room.

The director motioned to two straight-backed wooden chairs across from his desk. Mark and Maggie sat down as M. Durand wobbled around to his place at the desk.

"I understand from Anton that you have purchased a house in Ville-d'Avray. Is that right?" he panted.

"Yes, it is a lovely old home not too far from the village center," said Mark. "We plan to renovate it, hoping to return it to its former grandeur."

"Good for you. Few people today have any regard for historical things. It's a shame. Many of the old homes possess such innate beauty and elegance. Have you moved permanently to France then?"

"No, we maintain our principle residence in California. Maggie's mother was born in Paris."

"Excellent! Then you know Paris, Madame McFadden?"

"A little. I grew up in California, just outside of San Francisco, but occasionally vacationed here. My mother tried to instill in me an appreciation for France and its culture. But, please, call me Maggie."

"Parfait! Perfect! And you may call me Victor. After all, we are all friends of Anton. So, how may I help you?"

Mark began. "As I mentioned, we are renovating our house and in the process, we came across some items of interest and wanted your expertise as to what they might be and if they have any value."

"Certainly. I will gladly help you in any way that I can. Did you bring the items with you?"

Mark set his briefcase on his lap and flipped open the two latches. He withdrew the leather-bound notebook and the letter. The letter was sandwiched in a clear plastic cover and the journal was in a sealed plastic bag with a small package of desiccant.

"We were not sure exactly how to protect something this old. This is the best we came up with," explained Mark.

"You are right to seal the book in an airtight bag," Victor said casually.

Durand donned a pair of white cotton gloves and took the items into his meaty hands. He glanced at the letter, then placed it on the desk. He held the notebook gingerly, weighing it in his hands. "Where did you find these?" he asked.

"They were buried in a stone column in the basement."

"Really?" Victor placed the notebook on a tissue he had laid out on his desk and opened the cover. He carefully turned the pages, bending over to get a closer look at them. He then reached into a drawer to retrieve a magnifying glass. He examined the paper alternately through the glass and without it.

"What do you think?" asked Mark.

The director did not immediately reply. He fixed his eyes on the notebook. All Mark and Maggie could see was his bald pate before them, gleaming like polished silver. Finally, he raised his head. "I'm not sure what to make of this. I can see that it is old. From the looks of the ink and the paper, it is from the late 19th century. As for the artist, I cannot say."

Maggie leaned forward and spoke. "We think it looks like van Gogh's work. It's certainly his style."

"Yes. I would agree that the style is very similar to van Gogh's. I hesitated to say that and raise your expectations. To be definitive that this is van Gogh's work, there will have to be several scientific tests and a thorough review by experts."

"Oh, we fully understand. We just wanted your opinion. After all, neither Maggie nor I are art experts."

"You were wise to bring this journal to me. I hate to say it, but there are too many unscrupulous art dealers in Paris. If this is a real van Gogh journal, it is worth millions of Euros."

"What about the letter? Do you recognize anything that could lead us to the author?" asked Mark.

Victor read and reread the letter. "This could indicate that a murder occurred. Did you find the letter with the journal?"

"Yes. They were both in the same wooden box."

"You are aware that van Gogh committed suicide. Just north of Paris in Auvers-sur-Oise."

"Yes, we know. But did he leave a note?"

"He left no note. In fact, van Gogh made it back to the inn where he was staying before he died. He survived for a couple of days; just long enough for his brother to come to his bedside and be with him when he died. The gun was never found. Even his paints and easel were never found. Very odd."

"Do you think this journal could be his?"

"I don't know. We really must undertake a comprehensive investigation. If you will leave these items with me, I will bring the resources of the museum to bear and discover if this is truly a van Gogh journal and what, if anything, this letter means."

"Victor, that is very gracious of you, but I think we would like to keep these artifacts with us," Mark said.

"Mark, Maggie…" The director leaned forward, resting on his elbows. He looked at each of them in turn. "This journal could be one of the great finds of the century. A treasure. A world treasure. It belongs in a safe place where it will not undergo any further degradation and can be studied."

"I appreciate that Victor. And, if you would indulge us, we might bring it back. But for now, we want to keep it. Thank you very kindly," Mark said.

"What can I say to change your mind?"

"Not a thing. But we do appreciate your assistance and your candor."

Mark rose and reached for the journal. Reluctantly, the director released his grip. Mark returned the items to the airtight bag and placed them in his briefcase.

"Before you leave, could I at least make a copy of a couple of pages of the journal? That would help me determine if the handwriting is van Gogh's."

Mark glanced at Maggie and she nodded. Mark replied, "I think that would be all right. If you don't mind, may I accompany you to the copy machine?"

"Very well, please follow me."

The men left Maggie alone in the office. When they returned, the director slowly removed his gloves and asked Mark for his address and phone number. As they bid their farewells, Mark noticed that the director was sweating and that his hands were clammy.

Henri reappeared to lead the couple back to the atrium. Victor stood in the doorway and watched them leave.

Out in the bright afternoon sun, Maggie put on her sunglasses and said, "He was not exactly what I expected."

"No, not exactly the sophisticated Parisian art connoisseur that I envisioned. He was certainly surprised by the journal, wasn't he?"

"He was. Mark, I think we should just go back to d'Avray and put these things in a safe place."

"I agree."

The next train from Saint-Lazarde to d'Avray did not leave for thirty minutes so they ordered a cappuccino in a pâtisserie within the train station.

Taking a seat in the corner of the bakery, Maggie asked, "I'm curious. What pages did he copy out of the journal?"

Mark took the journal and letter from the briefcase and closed it. "He copied the letter and two pages from the journal. I'll show you which ones."

"No," Maggie stopped him. "Don't take the notebook out of the bag. I'm afraid you'll damage it. Do you remember the pages?"

"The picture of the bridge and one of the wheat fields," said Mark.

"I guess those should be good examples to determine if it's VG's work."

"Are we talking in code now?" Mark grinned.

"I admit I am a bit nervous. Victor is right. This could be a significant find."

A voice roared through the loudspeakers in French, then in English: "4:21 train to Ville-d'Avray on Track Four!"

"We'd better hustle." Mark fumbled with the briefcase, then handed the journal and letter to Maggie. "Damn thing's locked. Mags, put these in your bag until we get on the train. We don't want to miss it." Mark said.

The train was filled near to capacity but they managed to find two seats together. They had barely sat down when it began to pull away, swaying back and forth on the tracks as though it were about to teeter over under the weight of all its passengers.

"Do you want these in your briefcase?" Maggie asked.

"No, just hold onto them right now. It's too crowded for me to get into my briefcase."

The train arrived at the Sèvres Ville-d'Avray station, and the platform quickly filled with people exiting the train.

"I didn't realize how packed the station would be. Must be folks coming home from work," mused Mark.

Mark and Maggie jostled their way through the commuters, hand-in-hand, when Mark felt himself start to lose his balance. A sharp pain seared his hand holding the briefcase. Just for an instant, he released his grip and the portfolio was gone.

"Owww! What the...?! Hey! Hey!!" Mark shouted. "Stop that guy! He stole my briefcase!" Mark pointed to a teenage boy running through the crowd.

Mark let go of Maggie and started running, bumping into men and women as he made his way onto the street. Passersby eyed the fleet American suspiciously. When Maggie caught up to Mark, he had stopped and was straining his neck to see over the top of the crowd.

"Honey, are you all right? Your hand! It's bleeding!"

"Shit! I don't see him. I can't believe he stole my briefcase!" Mark looked down at his hand. A clean gash appeared just below his knuckles. Maggie grabbed some tissues from her bag and blotted his wound.

"This is really peculiar," she said. "Of all the people on that train, he picks you to take your briefcase. Was there anything in it?"

"No. I only brought it to keep the notebook and letter from being damaged."

"Thank God we put them in my bag!"

Chapter 13
Paris – Winter 1886-Spring 1887

The winter snowfall on St. Nicholas Day had been light, the air crisp and clear. The Folies Bergère had just introduced their sensational striptease show featuring beautiful women in spectacularly risqué costumes. Theo and Vincent made a point of seeing this novel revue as soon as it opened, but despite the holiday cheer, Vincent was feeling depressed, overwhelmed with all the yuletide hustle and bustle. Theo decided that they should travel to Breda to visit their mother and siblings in the spring when the weather was a bit warmer. Theo privately hoped that the trip would ease the tension between himself and Vincent, whose mood swings were steadily increasing.

Theo had another reason to go home in the spring. He intended to propose to Jo Bonger in April.

Vincent was still resistant to the idea of Theo taking a wife, though he had no personal quarrels with Jo, whom he thought was lovely and intelligent. But when any talk of Jo arose, Vincent felt as if his heart would break in two. He feared he would be cast aside, like discarded ashes, and loneliness would once again befall him.

"Theo, what will I do? Why couldn't you wait for me to find a wife? Where will I stay?" Vincent asked anxiously.

"If she agrees, you can stay here. I expect you to be cordial to her and welcome her into our family," replied Theo in a voice that signaled serious consequences if Vincent behaved badly. "You know what our father always told us: family comes first. All else, second."

Vincent was not at all soothed by this response. He had given up all hope of ever having a wife and children. Given the poor state of his overall health, he was uncertain if he even wanted a family.

In late spring, Theo went alone to Amsterdam, leaving Vincent behind in Paris. Vincent had refused his brother's numerous appeals to join him. Secretly, he felt the need to escape from Theo's paternalistic speeches. Theo, on the other hand, was always afraid of leaving his brother alone for too long, keenly aware of Vincent's self-destructive behavior. Consequently, he arranged for several friends to look in on Vincent.

Early one morning while Theo was still in Holland, Vincent was in the local artists' paint shop chatting with Julien 'Père' Tanguy, the owner. He was doing his best to convince Père to sit for him. Père was accustomed to Vincent's persistent appeals but his wife was not receptive to an interruption of their workday. She gruffly told Vincent, "He is busy today and, anyway, he doesn't need to be the subject of your portraits."

"But this will be a beautiful piece that would do well if you placed it in your window. It will not take long. Sit for me, Père, please." Vincent insisted.

Eventually, over the strident objections of his wife, Père acquiesced and sat while Vincent situated his easel on the sidewalk outside the shop. He did not use his perspective frame, nor did he sketch his subject before painting. He used long, continuous brush strokes to outline Père's head and sloping shoulders. For the background, he used the impasto technique of applying colors straight from the tube, spreading the dark paint with a thick, heavy brush. Père's receding hair and neatly trimmed beard were highlighted with streaks of silver; his jacket, dark cayenne. He quickly but carefully captured the rumpled creases in the shop owner's worn apron.

"Sit quietly, look this way," Vincent said sternly.

"Vincent, I have been here long enough! You will have to finish later." Tanguy was fidgety after having sat for what seemed like an eternity. Although Vincent was a swift craftsman, Tanguy had work to do and was worried that his wife would become infuriated if she was left to look after the business by herself for much longer.

Vincent repeated. "Père, I beg of you, sit down and be still!"

"I will not. I have had enough!" Tanguy glared at Vincent. He didn't know which he feared most—Vincent's rage or his wife's vitriol.

Suddenly, there was a thunderous clamor and a shower of wet paint went everywhere. Vincent threw the brush down on the pallet with such force that paint splattered on the sidewalk, the easel, and himself. Fortunately, none of the oils reached the canvas.

Père rose indignantly, and Vincent protested.

"Where are you going? You cannot leave now!"

"I told you, I've had enough! You are not only insufferable, Vincent, but you are also mad!"

"Merde! To hell with this portrait!" Vincent fussed and began to pace with his head in his hands.

"Stop it. You should leave now." Père strode into his shop, slamming the door behind him. Vincent stood on the sidewalk cursing under his breath. An urgent voice interrupted his muttering.

"Vincent! I have been searching for you all day!" Émile was fast approaching, waving his gangly arm. "Did you see *Le Nouvel* today?"

"No, I have no use for newspapers. Why do you ask?"

"You should start picking up newspapers, Vincent. Today *Le Nouvel* has an article on an attempt to assassinate the Tsar."

"What?" Vincent stopped dead in his tracks. "Do you think this is what Marguerite has been hinting at? Is there mention of the Commune?"

"Shhh. You know that we are not to speak publicly of such things. Come, gather up your things and let's find a quiet place to talk." Émile motioned for Vincent to follow him.

Émile and Vincent found a private corner in a cafe on Rue André Antoine. Émile raised two fingers. The waitress nodded. Émile spread out the newspaper on the beer-stained table. "Here, read this," Émile said, pushing the article toward his companion.

Vincent scanned the article. The headline read *Five Arrested in Assassination Conspiracy.*

"This has to be what Marguerite alluded to at the meetings. You know what this means, Vincent? It means that we are taking action. The Tsar's time is limited." Émile was talking excitedly.

"It says that four of the five arrested are Russians. The blame is placed on Narodnaya Volya. Who is that?" Vincent queried.

"The NV is the organization that assassinated the Tsar's

father. It says that most of the conspirators were university students. We must ask Marguerite what happened."

"When is the next meeting?"

"Soon, I imagine."

Across town in another café on Rue Massenet, Pierre was leaning toward the woman, speaking in hushed tones. "The Chancellor is not happy. There is no clear connection to the French. He wants to know what went wrong."

"We have contingency plans. Does the Chancellor believe that this one attempt is all we have?" she replied. "And I do not appreciate your tone."

"I don't know what the Chancellor thinks. I only know that the next attempt should clearly point to the French. If the Russians decide to form an alliance with the French, it could set the Chancellor's plans for a greater Germany back by years." Pierre's gaze was intense.

"I am aware of this. I will activate the next step in the plan. French nationals will be our scapegoats."

"Do you mean the Commune?"

"Why do you think the group was formed? They are our pawns in this chess game." She continued. "We need to set up the next meeting. Please arrange it. And please tell the Chancellor not to worry. I will see to it that a wedge is driven between the French and the Russians," she assured him.

"All right. But, Marguerite, I warn you, do not fail. I don't want to deliver any more bad news to the Chancellor."

Chapter 14
Paris – Spring 1887

Theo returned to Paris heartbroken. Jo Bonger kindly but firmly turned down his marriage proposal.

"Monsieur van Gogh, we don't even know each other. I did not expect you would propose so soon. I don't really know what to say. We see each other only a few times each year. There is much you have to learn about me, and I about you."

"Say 'yes.' I am not a wealthy man but I do earn a decent living. If you marry me, I promise that you will have a wonderful life. You will be able to mingle among some of the greatest artists of our time. You can continue your musical studies too if you wish. I want you to know how important it is to have you in my life."

"Monsieur van Gogh—Theo," she paused. "I am overwhelmed. I had no idea that you felt this way, but I cannot say yes. It is much too early in our relationship."

"But, Johanna… you mean so much to me."

"Please, Theo. It is time for you to take your leave."

"But may I at least write you?"

"Yes. I believe that would be appropriate."

Theo was humiliated. His mother, with whom he had sought solace, was harsh, advising Theo that no considerate aristocrat would surprise a woman like he did. His sisters tried to console him but Jo's response hurt Theo to his core. The first thing he did when he returned to Paris was tell his brother of the fiasco. "I am a broken man, Vincent. Jo turned me down. I have never felt such disgrace."

"Perhaps it was not meant to be, my brother, at least not now. Even though we have squabbled over this from time to time, my heart goes out to you. Jo is a wonderful woman and I know you love her. The best thing to do is to return to work and focus on our lives here in Paris."

"Jo is the love of my life. She is always in my mind and in my heart," wailed Theo. "I despise the distance between us. It makes things that much more difficult. How can a man woo a woman when he can see her only sporadically? I wish we were closer." The two brothers sat in silence, Vincent staring compassionately at Theo, as Theo sat with his head in his hands, sobbing.

"You know, Theo, you must persist with her. It is possible, perhaps even likely, that Jo will come back to you if you write to her and express how you feel."

"I am doubtful of that."

"You have to be resilient. Women like strong men. If you brood all day, you will accomplish nothing. Tell her what she means to you. If you give up, you will never respect yourself. Persist or you will never attain any peace of mind," Vincent urged.

Theo looked at his brother from behind red, swollen eyes. He was not accustomed to hearing consoling words from Vincent. "You are right. I must carry on. I will convince her to marry me."

If Theo's love life seemed to be falling apart, his professional career was flourishing. A new majority owner took over Goupil and tasked Theo with finding new, up-and-coming artists. He was given the mezzanine as a display area for work that he alone chose to feature. He purchased a few Monet landscapes in an effort to champion the Impressionist style, which he believed to be ripe for investment.

Caught up in Theo's advancement, Vincent made his case for a partnership. He said to Theo, "This is our chance to do something great, my brother! You know I have a keen eye for talent."

"I'm not sure, Vincent... I trust your knowledge but your business sense is lacking."

"Together we will make a great team! You and I will be free to search for new artists. I should like to be a part of your intellectual circle of friends, all working and thinking together, and in no time at all, I am sure we will make headway."

Vincent was right. They were a good team. The van Gogh brothers—in particular, Theo—became the toast of the contemporary art world. New artists came from all over Europe to show off their work. Artists lavished gifts and invitations upon Theo and Vincent in hopes that their works would be displayed in the Goupil foyer where they would surely be seen and admired. The brothers' home on Montmartre was teeming with visitors night and day.

As Vincent advised, Theo continued his relentless pursuit of Jo Bonger. He made plans to return to Amsterdam to propose to her again. He wrote to let Jo know of his travel but her response was the same: please don't come.

Even if professional success was his, Theo was an unhappy man. Jo would not see him and his health was failing. He was weak, losing weight, and had painful sores on his feet, hands and in his mouth. He was often unable to go to the Gallery. Vincent was affected by similar maladies, although less severe than Theo's.

Late one evening after Theo had been home in bed for two days, he came into the sitting room where Vincent was sipping a glass of cognac.

"Brother, you look wretched," said Vincent. "Would you like some cognac or brandy? Perhaps a sip of alcohol will put some color in your pale cheeks."

"No, thank you. I just want to sit up for a while."

The brothers sat in silence for some time, Theo peering absent-mindedly out the window while Vincent sketched in his notebook. Theo broke the silence. "I have been sick for some time."

"I know."

"I want to confide in you but you must not tell anyone."

"You are my brother, Theo, you can tell me anything."

"My sickness is syphilis. I have had it for a long time. The weariness, the sores, the achy joints cause me so much pain."

"Brother, it may comfort you to know that I also have syphilis."

Theo looked up, surprised. "I didn't know. But you are not sick."

"I have the occasional bout with sores and bad joints. I have been to a doctor and am taking the cure."

"We should go to the same doctor. It might save us money and we could look after one another."

Vincent agreed.

"One thing you must promise me: never tell Jo or anyone else. She would not marry me if she knew I had syphilis."

"I won't say a word. This is between us, dear brother."

"Tell me, Vincent, why do you continue to go to bordellos knowing you have syphilis?"

"It is simple. Once you get syphilis, you cannot get it again! You might as well enjoy yourself while you can."

Chapter 15
Ville d'Avray, Amsterdam – Present Day

Maggie listened to the voice on her phone. Mark sat opposite her at the kitchen table.

"*Oui. Oui. Je comprends. Merci. Au revoir,*" she said, disconnecting and placing the phone on the table. "Well, as you can probably guess, the police can't really do anything to recover your briefcase. The man I talked to said we were welcome to come down and file a report, but the chances of ever catching the guy are nearly zilch."

"That's what I figured. I'm sure glad you had the journal and letter in your bag."

"Me, too. I would be devastated if we had lost those."

"I was thinking while you were on the phone that we should go to Amsterdam and visit the Van Gogh Museum. I'll bet by seeing some of his work we could get a better idea if this is his journal."

"That's an excellent idea. I'm not sure we should show it to anyone, though. The more I think about it, I believe the thief may have been after the journal," Maggie said.

"You could be right but I can't imagine how they would even know what we were carrying," Mark replied. "How about I make some train reservations for Amsterdam?"

"I've got nothing on my schedule for the next few days so let's do it. Let me call Maman and let her know our travel plans. Maybe we can convince her to come here after we get back."

"I'd be surprised if she came to visit. She doesn't seem to want to visit France."

"I know. I really don't understand it. She says she loves France. I'm still going to ask her."

Mark made reservations for the following day on the 9:16 a.m. Thalys high speed train. He was searching for a hotel on his phone when it rang. Caller ID told him it was Anton.

"Anton, it's nice of you to call!"

"How are you and Maggie? Still enjoying France, my friend?" Anton asked.

"We are both fine and yes, we are still enjoying your beautiful country."

"Excellent. I wanted to let you know that I talked to Victor Durand after your meeting. He seems to be very excited by your find."

"Yes, he didn't want to get our hopes up but I got the impression he thinks the journal could be van Gogh's."

"Indeed! That is a find. I would truly like to see it."

"Well, I think that could be arranged. Maybe you and the family could come to our place for dinner sometime and we can show you the journal and our home."

"I will have to check with Sarah, but I'm sure she would love to visit."

"Wonderful. We're heading to Amsterdam tomorrow morning to visit the Van Gogh Museum and compare the artwork there to what's in the notebook. We should be back in a few days. Let me know when you are free."

"I will. But Mark, Victor mentioned having experts study the journal. Are you going to have Victor help with determining the provenance of the journal?"

"I'm not sure what we are going to do just yet. If this is authentic, then placing it in anyone's hands is a big decision.

I'm sure there will be several claims to it. Mags and I are going to take it slow."

"Whatever you decide, I suggest you keep it in a safe place. Victor thought it could be quite valuable."

"Oh, trust me, we will."

"I will call you and set a time to visit. In the meantime, be well, my friend."

Mark was hanging up when Maggie appeared at the doorway. "Who was that?" she asked.

"Anton. He wanted to know how our meeting went with Victor Durand. I told him Victor thought the notebook could be van Gogh's."

"How did Anton react to that?"

"He was excited. Said he'd like to see it, so I asked if he and Sarah wanted to come over for dinner when we got back from Amsterdam. I hope you don't mind."

"That's fine. It would be nice to have them over. I'd like to meet their little ones. We can show them our renovation plans."

Mark's phone rang again. This time Caller ID revealed a French number but no name. He raised a finger to Maggie to indicate he'd be a moment and answered the phone.

"Hello, this is Mark McFadden."

"Monsieur McFadden, this is Victor Durand. We met earlier this week."

"Yes, Monsieur Durant. How are you?"

"Um, er, very well! I am calling because I just spoke with Anton Lambert. He told me you are going to visit the Van Gogh Museum in Amsterdam. Is that correct?"

"Yes, that's right." Mark's brow wrinkled.

"It is not my place to tell you what to do, Monsieur…"

"Continue—and please call me 'Mark.'"

"Ah yes, Mark. I want to say, I strongly advise you not to disclose the fact that you have the sketchbook."

"Why is that?"

"Well, the directors at the Van Gogh Museum are very territorial when it comes to anything related to Vincent van Gogh. I am certain they will try to lay claim to the journal. You might not even be able to remove it from the Museum."

"So, you think it is van Gogh's then." Mark looked up at Maggie, eyebrows raised.

"Until I can have experts examine it, I cannot be certain, but in my opinion, it certainly is possible. It is widely known that he kept meticulous notes and sketches."

"Well, rest assured, we are not planning to show it to anyone just yet."

An audible sigh rustled through the phone. "Ah, that is wise. When do you leave for Amsterdam?"

"Tomorrow."

"And when will you return?" Victor asked.

"We should be back very early next week. Why do you ask?"

"I would like to see the journal again to study the figures and writing. It would help confirm my opinion."

"I'm sure we can arrange something. I will call you when we return from Amsterdam."

"Excellent. Until then, safe travels."

"What was that all about?" Maggie asked.

"That was Victor Durand. Anton must have called him right after we hung up and told him we were going to visit the Van Gogh Museum. Durand wanted to warn us not to show the journal to anyone at the Museum because they might try to confiscate it and claim ownership."

"Good grief! Really? Get those hotel reservations made! I want to get going! We've got some packing to do!"

"Yes, ma'am!" Mark said with a grand salute and a click of his heels.

The next morning, they boarded the high-speed train at Gare du Nord. Within minutes they had passed through Paris. A half hour later, they had traded high-rises and smog for verdant French pastures. Fields of wheat, corn, and yellow daisies flew by them as they gazed out the thick Plexiglas windows. They lamented the lack of train travel back in the U.S. and the difficulty of air travel since 9/11. Eventually, Maggie picked up a travel book on Amsterdam to pass her time. Mark was asleep when the train pulled into Amsterdam Central station three hours later.

The couple weaved their way through the myriad of commuters, avoiding construction hazards as they passed through the station and out the double doors to find a taxi. They spied several waiting in line at the far end of the station. The universal sign of the "taxi hail" was immediately understood and a driver quickly picked them up. He maneuvered through the Oude Zijde, then around the central canal ring to the Museum Quarter. The car pulled up to a row of tall, narrow buildings on Jan Luijkenstraat.

"Which one is our hotel?" asked Maggie.

"It's that little hotel at the end of the block."

"Oh, it looks charming," said Maggie.

"I thought it looked appealing," Mark said, handing the fare to the taxi driver. "The reviews I read said that all B&B's

should be like this. I imagine it has a lot more personality than the bigger, chain hotels. And, it's just a block from the Van Gogh museum."

Mark grabbed their luggage and checked in at the receptionist's desk in the tiny but modern lobby. He learned, to his immense relief, that almost everyone in Amsterdam spoke English. After completing the necessary paperwork, she handed him two card keys for a room on the second floor. The single elevator was in use and traveled at the speed of a tortoise, so they decided to ditch it in favor of the steps.

Their room was large, even by American standards, and it had all the modern conveniences: TV, DVD, air conditioning, WiFi, even a computer. Maggie was impressed.

"Would you look at the four-poster bed? This place is spectacular! I love how they've blended the old with the new!" she exclaimed.

"Yes, and a free champagne breakfast comes with the room. Nothing but the best for my lovely wife," Mark said with a smile. "The online reviews say that the owners are very accommodating. They make each guest feel special—as if they were the only ones staying in the hotel. Say, are you hungry?"

"I am, but I would really like to go to the museum first. I'm anxious to see what we can find out. I wish we could have brought the journal with us."

"Yeah, but it's safer in the bank vault. We don't need to take any chances."

"I agree."

The walk to the Van Gogh Museum was short. The museum was massive and comprised of an older section and a newer, oval-shaped wing.

"This is not exactly what I expected," Maggie said.

A glass-fronted ticket booth was recessed into the older, more institutional looking building. After paying for two adult tickets, they walked the short distance to the ultra-modern glass-enclosed art museum. Stairs and escalators descended from the entryway to a large, open atrium. After obtaining self-guided tour earphones, the couple walked up a short flight of stairs to an intimate auditorium. A short film recounted van Gogh's life, his approach to art, and delved into some of his seminal works. At the end of the viewing, they were directed to the exhibits one floor up from the auditorium.

The museum was arranged in chronological order with van Gogh's early work displayed on the ground floor and his last works on the third floor. His letters were exhibited together with some of his journals and studies.

When they reached the third floor, Maggie discovered a lovely rendering of Montmartre. "Look, this one is in the journal!" she exclaimed.

"This one is too," said Mark, gazing at an oil of Moulin Galette. "The possibility of someone simply copying van Gogh's work is becoming increasingly remote. I'm convinced that what we found are really his notes and sketches."

As they walked through the museum, they noted that several entries in the journal were nearly identical to the artwork displayed. Irises, sunflowers, the Yellow House, the Langolin Bridge, the Zouave, Madame Ginoux, even the handwriting appeared to be the same.

"Wow, it's amazing how many drawings in the journal are

actually on display here," said Mark.

After a couple of hours of wandering through the massive collection, they were beginning to feel weary. It was a lot to absorb. They left the museum, exiting through the same doors they had entered. The sun was settling behind the buildings, filling the sky with streaks of red interspersed with deep blue. The air was turning brisk. Maggie pulled her collar up around her neck and wrapped her arm through Mark's.

"He was talented but very disturbed," Mark observed.

"Indeed, he was—on both counts. I find it very intriguing that everyone assumes he committed suicide. But, it does seem logical, given his melancholia."

"There may be other theories, but if the note we found is authentic, we know he didn't kill himself. Since he lived for a few days after being shot, I wonder why he didn't point the finger at whoever pulled the trigger."

"Maybe he didn't know the guy," said Maggie.

"Still, you would think he would have told someone, like his brother or the doctor that treated him, that someone shot him. It's all just so odd that van Gogh would let them believe he tried to take his own life."

"Perhaps he was at a point in his life where he just didn't care. At any rate, I'm convinced this journal is the real thing," she said.

"Yeah, me too."

"So, what do we do now? Turn it over to the museum? Keep it? Sell it?"

"I don't want to sell it. I think we should stop and take a deep breath. One thing I would really like to do is solve the riddle of who wrote the letter, who really killed Vincent, and why his journal and a gun were buried in our basement. Let's lay low for a while."

They spent the next two days roaming the canaled city. They visited the Rijksmuseum, which housed over 8,000 works of art. Because of its vastness, they decided to concentrate on the Old Dutch Masters of the 17th and 18th centuries. Rembrandt's *The Night Watch* was the highlight of their visit.

They admired the unique architecture along the Amsterdam canals: the ornate and simple cornices, the scrolled and crested gables, wall plaques and tilted facades. Het Scheepvaartmuseum, the maritime museum, was of particular interest to Mark. He found the collection of beautifully decorated model yachts fascinating and was equally inspired by the interactive exhibits and displays of maritime objects. Maggie was enthralled by the Royal Palace, the churches, and simple buildings restored to show how common people lived in the 17th and 18th centuries.

After a few days, it was time for Mark and Maggie to leave. They boarded their high-speed train and found their seats. They were weary from the trip yet were in high spirits.

"I think we're going to need a stroke of luck to find out who wrote the letter and what really happened to van Gogh," said Maggie.

"I was thinking the same thing. I've had no break in learning anything further about Frederic or Marguerite Chemin, either."

"Yes. And that detective… what was his name? Gastineau? Yeah, Gastineau. He was not helpful with the gun.

Maybe we should try someone else. What do you think?" asked Maggie.

"Can't hurt. Although, I tend to believe that detective was probably right. How would we go about tracing a military issue revolver to one man? And how would we know if that person actually shot van Gogh?"

"So, we are back to the Chemins as our lead."

They fell silent for a while, staring out at the passing pastures and small villages.

"Now that we are reasonably certain that the journal is van Gogh's," said Mark, leaning toward Maggie, "maybe we should chart out the journal entries against a timeline of van Gogh's life. His movements during the last few years of his life are pretty well documented."

Maggie continued to stare out the window. After a few passing seconds, she said, "Not a bad thought. Plus, knowing what and where he painted alongside the notes in the journal, we might just find something everyone else missed."

The train was at full speed, whizzing through the countryside. Mark looked at Maggie with a wry expression. "You really think that's possible? Two amateur detectives stumbling on the killer?"

Maggie thought for a moment. "No, not really, but creating a timeline is our only option unless you want to turn the journal over to the police or a private detective."

"Not on your life!" Mark growled. "I'm not about to quit! We just have to be patient and methodical. We're bound to turn up something."

The train pulled into Gare du Nord with Paris rush hour well underway. The pair stood in a crowded line for a taxi.

People were scurrying out of the station, dodging cars and scooters as they did so.

"Keep hold of your bag," Mark whispered into Maggie's ear.

"I will. I've learned my lesson," she reassured him.

At last they were in a taxi, headed home at a snail's pace through the maze of traffic. It was stop and go for the next half hour. "I'll never complain about traffic in the U.S. ever again," Mark vowed.

The sun was low in the sky when the taxi pulled through the front gates of the house at 30 Rue de Marnes. The Beemer sat in the driveway exactly where they left it. Mark stood next to the taxi and paid the driver, adding a generous tip to the fare.

As they walked up the stone walkway to the front door, Maggie remarked, "I loved Amsterdam, but I'm glad to be back."

Mark turned the key in the latch and opened the door. The house was dark, engulfed with the shadows of nightfall. He reached for the lamp on the table by the door and felt a crunch under his feet. He moved further inside. More crunching. Maggie was on his heels.

"Uh oh, what was that?" she asked with a trace of alarm in her voice.

"Stay right there. Don't move. Let me find the light," Mark ordered.

"What's wrong?"

"Dunno." Mark finally found the switch. The room was suddenly swathed in light, revealing pandemonium: overturned chairs and bookcases, scattered and broken figurines, a ripped leather sofa, and paintings hanging cockeyed.

"What the…?" cried Maggie. Her heart was in her throat as she surveyed the chaos.

"Oh, shit! We've been robbed…" Mark's voice trailed off and he suddenly felt sick. He turned toward the kitchen with Maggie beside him. Pots, pans, dishes, and pantry stores were scattered about the room. Papers on the floor. Maggie rushed upstairs to see what else had been disturbed.

"Mark! Oh, Mark!" she cried.

Mark came up behind her. The bedrooms had been ransacked as well. The mattresses and box springs had been sliced open. Clothes were strewn about the room. The chest of drawers and armoires were open but nothing was left inside.

Maggie was horrified to a point of confusion. "I can't believe it! This isn't supposed to happen here!"

Mark stood agape, his shoulders slumped low. He looked battered. "Oh, Mags, I'm sorry. We need to call the police and report this."

"I feel so assaulted," she sobbed, bending down to pick up a shard of glass from the antique lamp that had once graced the bedside table.

"I know. Me, too. The glass here isn't the only thing that's been shattered. Come on. Let's call the police," he said, handing his wife the cell phone.

Chapter 16
Paris – Summer 1887

The dingy basement teemed with agitated conversation and rank cigarette smoke. Marguerite strode indomitably down the narrow staircase and headed straight to the table at the front of the room. She leaned over the table and commanded, "Gentlemen, please take your seats quickly. Our meeting will begin."

From the corner of the room someone remarked, "'Le Monde' said five people were hung for trying to assassinate the Tsar. Were we linked to this?"

"Were we?" The noise in the basement mounted. "We must know" and "Give us the details."

"Please, quiet down. I will answer all your questions in due time." Slowly the din subsided.

Marguerite began. "Five men were executed by the Tsar. All were Russian born and most were students. The Tsar claims that there was a conspiracy by the NV to kill him and his family. He also arrested more than twenty others. The Tsar either jailed or killed these men without a proper trial. The families of those arrested are being persecuted by the Russian secret police—the Okhrana. If you need any more proof of how duplicitous the Tsar is, go look behind the borders yourselves."

"Did we have anything to do with it?" The question arose from a casual spectator in the back of the room.

Émile leaned over to Vincent and commented, "Some of the Commune seems worried about being connected to this assassination plot."

Vincent did not respond. He was busy writing and drawing in his journal. Yet despite his silence, Vincent was thinking hard. He was worried about the depression he'd witnessed in business and among the Parisians. The various strikes throughout the city weighed heavily on his mind. He had observed in a letter to his brother before coming to Paris that making a living, especially as an artist, was very difficult and he foresaw that the struggle would only get worse from year to year. "We are still far from the end," he had told his brother. He had hoped that all would be brighter in Paris but it was not.

Marguerite continued. "There is no way to link our group to this assassination attempt but why do you worry so? Are you troubled by your convictions? Do you only want to act if there is no risk? You all joined this group willingly—to make a difference in the world. To help the people in need—the people who can't help themselves. Are you afraid?"

"Gentlemen!" someone shouted. "I am more convinced now than ever that we must take a stand. But the Tsar will tear Russia apart to find anyone who opposes him." The speaker was a tall man with a long mustache, bushy eyebrows, and a small cleft in his chin. He stood erect with a taut military deportment.

"Très bien," said Marguerite. "My cousin is in the French Army. Surely he knows what he is talking about."

The soldierly man continued. "I know the Russians to be vile creatures. We must stand up to the Tsar in the name of France and all that is good. After all, did they not remain motionless as the Prussians bombarded our beautiful Paris?!"

The crowd murmured in accord.

"Please, I need your full attention," Marguerite resumed command. "This failed attempt will put the Tsarists on high alert. We may have to work in solitude to overthrow the Tsar. We cannot depend on help from Russia as the revolutionaries are in hiding from the Okhrana."

"What can we do?" someone asked. Another echoed the same question. "What is your plan for us?"

"It is best that I talk to each of you in private—for secrecy's sake. But, please, trust me when I say that once we act, you will be heroes of the people. We will avenge our Russian brothers!"

Marguerite's cousin held court in the back of the room, surrounded by several men peppering him with questions.

Émile rose from his seat and announced to Vincent, "I am going to meet Marguerite's cousin. I want to find out more about the Tsar and what he knows."

Vincent grunted, still singularly focused on his journal. Émile started toward Marguerite's cousin, then, hesitating briefly, pushed his way past two men blocking his way.

"I am Émile Bernard," he declared, holding out his hand. The man peered down at him, noting that Émile's smooth hand was that of a nobleman, not the calloused palm of a provincial farmer. He was four to five inches taller than Émile and had an air of superiority about him. Taking Émile's hand, he introduced himself. "I am Ferdinand Esterhazy. Count Esterhazy, if you like." The Count continued to speak with the group around him and Émile listened intently. "I can assure you that Marguerite is correct. Listen to her. Russia is not a friend to France. I know firsthand that the French army is closely watching both Germany and Russia.

We cannot allow these two countries to become allies."

"Indeed, are you sure that they are trying to become closer allies?" someone asked.

"What does your intuition tell you? The Tsar needs Germany to look the other way while Russia subdues the Balkans. I cannot give you any more details. If I do, I may compromise secret military information. Gentlemen, I must go now." The group slowly dispersed as Esterhazy made his way across the room to Marguerite. He leaned in and whispered in her ear and kissed her on the cheek before leaving.

Émile returned to his place next to Vincent. "This has been a very interesting night. What do you think?"

"What? Oh yes, very interesting. I am almost ready to go. Just a few more details." Vincent completed his sketch and the two got up to leave.

Marguerite stopped the men before they reached the stairs. "Émile, Vincent. Could I have a private word with you?" They stepped over by the stone wall, away from the others who were heading toward the stairs. "The plans we are making are progressing quite well. The Commune will play a vital role in removing the Tsar from power. But I must confide in you that we need help. I think you two would be perfect to assist us in moving the plans along. Because you are artists, you could easily move about Europe without drawing suspicion."

"What would you have us do?" asked Émile.

"I am in the midst of several paintings," added Vincent. "I need to finish them."

"Your help would not be needed for a few months. But you must be prepared to leave on a moment's notice. Our plans are highly complex and not without risk."

"What would we do?" repeated Émile.

"I cannot say at this time. But I want to know I can count on both of you. I have so much at stake personally. When the time comes, I want to be able to call on you."

"How much risk will this entail?" Émile asked. "Putting a noose around my neck is not something I take lightly."

"I cannot promise that you will be free from peril but I can try to minimize your exposure. As we get closer to the time, I will explain more. For now, just think of the impact you could have on history."

"My art will be remembered..." Vincent thought aloud.

"Yes, Vincent, but freeing the Russian people from tyranny will only add to your fame. Think about what you could achieve." Rising from her seat with her eyes on the stairs, she spied Pierre. "We will talk again soon. I hope you will not disappoint me," she said as she ushered out her two guests.

Pierre descended into the basement and joined Marguerite. "I just passed your two artists as they were leaving," he said. "Can you count on their help?"

"I'm not sure. I may have overestimated their zealousness."

A look of concern crossed Pierre's face. "Marguerite, you really must succeed this time. I don't want your failure to reflect poorly on me." Marguerite countered, "You think I am not trying? The Commune will be firmly linked to the next attempt!"

"I will delay my report to the Chancellor. Any further mistakes could mean a death sentence for us all," warned Pierre.

"Thank you, Pierre. We just need more time."

"Time is what you have very little of."

Chapter 17
Paris – Winter 1887

Summer turned to fall and fall to winter, and the van Goghs' popularity among the yet-to-be-discovered artists grew with each passing season. Vincent exhibited his art at the Grand Bouillon—Restaurant du Chalet on Rue de Clichy. Theo would not yet display his work at the gallery. Like the Café du Tambourin, the restaurant showed the works of lesser known artists. The result was an eclectic group of art decorating the walls.

Vincent and Émile were sitting at a corner table critiquing the newest exhibits when Vincent spied an unfamiliar face at a crowded table nearby.

"Who is that in the corner opposite us?" Vincent asked Émile.

"Oh, that is Paul Gauguin. He draws quite a crowd, doesn't he?"

"Does he have work here?"

Émile looked around the room, "Over on the far wall. I think he has four, maybe five canvases."

Vincent got up and walked toward Gauguin's display. "These are very pleasing."

"He was included in the last Impressionist show."

Laughter from the corner filled the air. "I must meet him," said Vincent.

"Come. Let me introduce you."

Gauguin was tall, slim, and very tan. His narrow face and high forehead featured a prominent nose and a well-kept mustache. His chin carried a short, cropped Van Dyke beard.

His hair was short but unkempt.

"Paul!" shouted Émile, catching his attention.

"Émile Bernard. So nice to see you. Are you exhibiting anything here?"

"No, not right now. When did you return from the Islands?"

"I've only returned from Martinique a month ago. I must say, there is a lot going on in Paris that I missed."

"Paul, I want you to meet Vincent Van Gogh. Vincent has some work on display here as well."

"Vincent. Good to meet you. Where are your pictures?"

Vincent pointed to the opposite wall. "There. I have five pictures over there."

Gauguin looked in the direction of Vincent's display then back to the man. "Are you related to Theo Van Gogh at Goupil?"

"Theo is my brother."

"It is truly good to meet you! I haven't seen Theo in a long time. How is he?"

"He is well and his business is thriving. Say, why don't you come by our apartment this evening? Theo will be there."

"I would be delighted. Until tonight then," Gauguin nodded.

From that night on Gauguin spent many evenings with Theo and Vincent discussing color theory, the use of oils on Japanese silk, and other techniques. Vincent found himself enamored with Paul and looked forward to his weekly visits.

One night, Vincent decided to approach Paul with an idea.

"I have been thinking. Perhaps this would be a good time to start an artist colony. Would you be interested?" he asked, gazing at Gauguin. "It has been on my mind for some time. We could have a new society, a partnership. Paul, you and I could be the driving force behind it."

"I don't know, Vincent," Paul replied. "I'm happy with my work here and I've been able to display in the local galleries. Where would you go?"

"To the south of France where the weather would be more to our liking. You would still be able to exhibit wherever you wanted. But just think of the work we could accomplish if we were away from the bustle of Paris and freely collaborating with each other."

Vincent continued, his voice rising. "We could invite Émile to join the colony. The three of us could share a flat." Then, looking at his brother, he said, "Of course, Theo, I would want you to be a part of this as well but I know your health is not good. You should remain in Paris. But you could be our primary sponsor."

"I don't know, Vincent. Have you mentioned this to Émile?" asked Theo.

"Not yet. I think he would truly enjoy the healthy lifestyle, not to mention the beauty of southern France, as well as the chance to work alongside Paul."

"Establishing an artist colony would be a very ambitious undertaking," murmured Theo. "You might be caught up in administrative duties, leaving you less time to paint."

"There are those who can handle the business aspects of the partnership. We would be left to create," Vincent replied. Glancing sideways at Paul, Vincent tried to gauge his reaction. Paul sat upright, his stony demeanor revealing nothing of his thoughts.

The conversation soon drifted to other unrelated topics and they all returned to their drinking. Gauguin left in the wee hours of the morning fighting a nagging headache.

Chapter 18
Paris – Winter 1887

Vincent decided to let his artist colony proposal to Paul rest for the time being. Paul had not reacted to the idea in the manner Vincent had hoped, so he did not bring it up again. Instead, he avoided Paul and spent a good deal of his time at Le Tambourin rather than face his friend.

It was early afternoon and the sun glared through Le Tambourin's open windows. The proprietress, Signora Agostina Segatori, had taken down several of Vincent's paintings that he had given to her in exchange for food and drink, and stored them in a back room. They were not selling, and the proprietress was frustrated. Her misdeed triggered a round of fire from Vincent. He fussed at Signora for not returning the collection to him.

The air was heavy with unresolved anger. Vincent's outburst was interrupted by a sudden call.

"Vincent!" Émile greeted his friend. He regarded Vincent's taciturn mood warily. "Marguerite wants to meet with us this evening," he said quietly.

"Just the two of us? What for?"

"Yes, just us."

"Do you know what she has in mind?" Vincent, sidetracked from his argument with Agostina, let his fury subside while she retreated into her kitchen.

"No. She said she will discuss it with us tonight."

"When and where does she want to meet?"

"The café on Rue André Antoine, eight o-clock this evening."

Vincent arrived promptly at eight to find a café with one lone patron, Émile, relaxing at a timeworn table at the far end of the room. The air was hazy and dense. The windows were closed and heavily curtained.

Émile was drinking espresso and swiftly ordered another for his friend. Vincent removed his coat and hat and placed them on a wooden rack in the corner near their table. He was suitably dressed for the brisk night air, sporting a short coat, wool trousers, and a buttoned-up shirt. Émile was similarly clad in a casual natty coat and a coordinating scarf. Vincent eased himself into a chair next to Émile, placing his pipe and tobacco on his right and his sketchbook and pencil on his left.

"I am glad you made it, especially on such short notice," said Émile.

"I told you I would be here."

Marguerite appeared abruptly at the table, with Pierre in her wake.

"I didn't see you come in," said Émile, a bit startled. She was being oddly surreptitious, and it left him a bit unsettled.

"I took the liberty of coming in through the rear entrance. I did not want to be seen tonight. How are you Émile, Vincent?" She and Pierre took seats on either side of the artists.

"We are well," said Vincent. "Likewise, it is good to see you."

Marguerite was modestly dressed in a dark ankle-length dress. She wore a simple box hat with black netting that partially concealed her face. As she turned back the veil and looked directly at Vincent, he thought that her eyes appeared bluer than before, despite the dark circles below them.

Vincent lit his pipe, which was filled with pungent tobacco, and blew smoke across the table. Marguerite leaned back, her piercing blue eyes vacillating between Émile and Vincent. "It looks like we have the room to ourselves tonight. That is very fortuitous, considering what we have to discuss."

Vincent looked up from his pipe and started to say something but Marguerite raised her hand in a manner that said, please do not interrupt. "When we last spoke, I asked you to consider helping us with our cause. I did not ask this for myself but for the rest of the Commune and our Russian comrades who struggle under oppression." Her elegant fingers splayed on the table, she continued, "We now have a plan. We have most of the resources in place but we need your assistance. We… I… need you to deliver some vital supplies to St. Petersburg shortly after the New Year. You will be given sealed crates at La Gare du Nord. You will check these onto the train as baggage. Once you get to St. Petersburg, you will be met by one of our Russian comrades and taken to a safe house where you will be given further instructions. While you are there, you should take the time to paint some street scenes so that your cover will be protected. If all goes well, I expect you will return before April in time to see the flowers bloom."

Émile looked at Vincent but Vincent did not return his gaze. He was tightly gripping his pipe. Émile lowered his head, "I cannot go to Russia right now and certainly not for so long. I will be missed."

Silence.

"I want to help the cause, but going to Russia is… well, quite difficult. At least right now." Émile raised his head and was met with Marguerite's steely gaze.

Vincent chimed in. "I cannot leave Paris. Theo and I have too much work to do."

An uncomfortable silence lingered in the air. Finally, Marguerite leaned forward over the table and signaled Émile and Vincent to do the same. "I want to be clear. Both of you are involved in the plans of the Commune, whether you acknowledge it or not. Whatever we do, you do as well. If you refuse this assignment, you will have to help in other ways."

Sweat formed on Émile's brow and dripped into his eyes. His hands were trembling. "What do you have in mind?"

Marguerite leaned back and stared back and forth at the two artists. "The Commune needs financial support."

"I have no money!" exclaimed Émile.

"Nor do I," said Vincent.

"I am aware of your financial situations. There are other ways in which you can help the Commune raise money. You are both artists, are you not?"

"Yes, of course," said Vincent.

"And you know several other artists in Paris?"

"Yes," added Émile.

"Well, then," Marguerite's raised her hand, "there you have it. You two are smart. You may not be required to risk your life as your comrades do to further the cause, but you do have the means to help finance our efforts."

Vincent and Émile sat breathlessly, waiting for the cannonade to drop.

"Bring me two paintings of value that can be sold to help fund our activities. In this way you can be of help."

"I could paint you a picture. Émile, you could do the same," Vincent offered.

"You misunderstand," Marguerite said, "I don't want your worthless daubs of paint. You need to procure works of value. You claim to have connections with artists of some renown. Secure some of their works. Or better yet, I understand that your brother's gallery, Goupil, has several valuable works. Take two of them."

"I cannot steal from my brother!" protested Vincent.

"You would not be stealing from your brother, but from the gallery. Listen carefully, your loyalty is in question. If you do not do as I ask, you will pay a high price. And not just you, but your family, Émile, and your brother, Vincent. So, you have a decision to make: Prove your loyalty and remain a member of the Commune or disappoint and… well, the choice is yours."

Émile leaned in close to Vincent and said in a low voice, "You know this could be a way to get revenge on Goupil for the way they treated you."

"But it would be stealing from Theo!"

"No. No, it wouldn't. Theo oversees the entresol. We could take the paintings from the storeroom. Theo would never be connected to it and Goupil would finally pay for your mistreatment. Besides, think of the good it would do. The money would help the cause."

"I don't know," Vincent hesitated.

With his back to Marguerite, Émile whispered, "Vincent, Marguerite will have us killed. Have Theo and my parents killed if we don't do this."

"We could go to the police."

"What would we say? 'We want to report that we are part of a group that is trying to overthrow Russia and the leader has threatened to kill us?' No, this is a good solution. It solves our problem and keeps us out of trouble."

"Perhaps..." Vincent said slowly.

"Gentlemen," interjected Marguerite. "I will assume you agree. Notify Pierre when you have the paintings and he will collect them. Remember, we have long arms and you and your families are within our reach." Marguerite lowered her voice. "Besides, you joined the Commune to make the world a better place. This is a small thing to ask in comparison to what we are asking of others."

Marguerite rose and beckoned Pierre to do the same. She leaned over the table and said, "I really dislike delivering threats. It is beneath me. Do as I say, give Pierre two paintings of value that can be sold on the black market and you will have fulfilled your obligations. If you don't, well, the alternative is most abhorrent."

The alley door opened and Pierre and Marguerite stepped out to meet a waiting carriage. Snow was falling weightlessly, dusting the passageway with white flakes.

Pierre whispered to Marguerite, "You must have seen this coming?"

"Of course."

"Why do you think they will steal paintings for you?"

"Because I understand them."

"Without these two in Russia, how will you tie the assassination attempt to the French?"

She glared at him angrily. "We have other means for making the connection."

He continued pushing. "Have you considered simply forcing them to go?"

She maintained her composure but her gaze was steely, fixed upon his eyes. "I have. But I do not think it necessary. If it is, I am prepared to do whatever it takes. It could be beneficial to have these two alive back in Paris. It could make for a rather compelling connection." She softened just a bit. "Pierre, the Chancellor will be mollified. Ease your concerns."

"Be careful, Marguerite. This is your last chance."

Pierre escorted Marguerite to the carriage with his hand on her elbow. She gave him a murderous look as she took her seat. Pulling the curtain back, she said, "I am fully aware of my obligations. Do not forget your own. Home, driver!"

Chapter 19
Ville d'Avray – Present Day

Maggie stood just inside the open front door talking to a local gendarme. Flashing blue lights lit the surreal scene. Several policemen roamed through the jumbled rooms, some snapping photos, others applying a sticky black powder to tabletops and chair backs.

"So, you have no idea who would want to break into your house?" the young officer was asking. He was jotting down notes in a small pad, and could not have been more than twenty-five years old. Mark, standing next to Maggie, leaned in.

"No, not at all," he said.

"Are any valuables missing?"

"It's hard to say," Maggie replied, "We haven't had time to go through everything."

"Anything obvious missing?"

Mark spoke up. "Not that we can see, but like my wife said, we haven't had time to go through everything." He was exasperated from answering the same questions over and over from different officers, with Maggie translating the officers' French and halting English.

A commanding figure appeared at the door, framed in the evening sun that was about to disappear behind the horizon. He removed his hat and surveyed the devastation. The junior officer paused to see who had arrived, then snapped his attention to the door.

"*Commissaire!* We were not expecting you!" he exclaimed in French.

Commissaire Gastineau looked at Mark and nodded

toward the gendarme, "Please, if I may interrupt."

"*Certainement, Commissaire.*" The gendarme stepped aside.

"Monsieur McFadden, and Madame, I am sorry to meet you again under such circumstances."

"Yes, me too." Mark sighed.

"Yes, well, you must appreciate this is an unusual crime for our village. Is there a place where we can talk?"

"Yes," Mark nodded, "in the kitchen."

Mark sat next to his wife while Gastineau took a seat opposite the couple at the kitchen table. Maggie looked at Mark and squeezed his hand. Her eyes were swollen and red.

"Now tell me exactly what happened," said Gastineau. "Include as many details as possible, please."

"Well," she said, gathering her composure, "we just returned from Amsterdam. We took a taxi from Gare du Nord. When we got here, we found our house…" she gestured to the mess around them, "like this."

"What time did you arrive home?"

"Around 6:15 p.m."

"When did you call the police?"

"We looked around to assess the damage and then immediately called the police. So I guess it was around 6:30."

"Does anyone else have a key to your house?"

"No."

"Who knew you were going to Amsterdam?"

"There was Anton Lambert, a close friend of ours. He's head of oncology at Hôspital Hôtel-Dieu," Mark answered.

"And Victor Durand," added Maggie.

"Yes, a fellow named Victor Durand. He is an assistant director at the Museé d'Orsay," Mark added.

"Why would you tell this Victor Durand you were going to Amsterdam?" asked Gastineau.

Mark looked at Maggie then back at Gastineau. "Detective," Mark started.

"Commissaire," he corrected.

"I'm sorry. *Commissaire.*"

"Please continue. You were about to explain why you told M. Durand of your travel plans."

"Yes. Well, do you remember the gun we came to see you about?"

"Of course," replied Gastineau.

"We found two other items along with the gun," explained Mark.

"Really?" Gastineau's left eyebrow arched.

"A letter and a journal."

"Go on."

"The letter indicated that someone may have killed the owner of the journal. The journal appeared to be owned by an artist."

"And why do you believe this?"

"There were several sketches in it accompanied by notes. The kind of notes that an artist would make about his work, like paint choices, visual aspects, technique, and the like."

"I see." Gastineau jotted down some notes into his book. "And so you took this journal to M. Durand?"

"That's right. We wanted to know if he could identify the artist."

"And did he?"

"He suspected, as did we, that the journal belonged to

Vincent van Gogh." Mark glanced at Maggie. Just uttering it aloud, he knew it sounded implausible.

Gastineau put his pen down and stared impassively at Mark, then at Maggie. After a moment, he picked up his pen and asked, "Is that why you went to Amsterdam? For research?"

"Yes, we wanted to compare drawings in the journal to works in the Van Gogh Museum," she said

"And what did you learn?"

"Many of the pieces in the museum are also sketched in the journal. And, there are notes in the journal next to several of the sketches that describe the scene and where it was," Maggie offered.

"Did you show the journal to the authorities at the Van Gogh Museum?"

"No. We thought it best to keep it in a safe place. We put it in a bank repository."

The young gendarme reappeared. He bent down and whispered in Gastineau's ear.

"*Ça c'est bon*," said Gastineau. "The gendarmerie has completed their work and are ready to leave. I hope you do not mind, but I have a few more questions."

"Anything," replied Mark.

"How did you meet M. Durand?"

"Anton Lambert introduced us. Anton knows Victor somehow and offered to introduce us when we told him of our discovery."

"Ah. So M. Lambert also knows of your discovery."

"Yes."

"How many other people know?"

"I… I'm really not sure. I don't think we mentioned it to anyone else," Mark hesitated.

Maggie responded, "I haven't mentioned it to anyone."

The room went quiet as Gastineau reviewed his notes. Taking a deep breath, he said, "So, please correct me if I misstate anything. You discover a gun, a letter, and a journal hidden in this house."

"All three items were in a box buried in a stone column in the basement," Mark clarified. "I can show you."

Gastineau demurred and continued. "Thank you. The letter indicates that the journal's owner was possibly murdered. You come to the local police station to inquire about the gun's ownership. You then discuss your find with your friend, Anton Lambert, who introduces you to Victor Durand, a director at the Museé d'Orsay. He indicates to you that the journal could have belonged to Vincent van Gogh. You tell both Lambert and Durand you are going to Amsterdam to visit the Van Gogh Museum and upon your return, your house is ransacked with apparently nothing missing. Did I leave out anything?"

The couple sat quietly, then Mark said sheepishly, "There is one more thing."

"Please go on."

"After we visited Durand at the museum, someone stole my briefcase as we got off the train."

"Did you report the theft?"

"Yes, but the police were not optimistic about finding the thief or the briefcase."

"Did your briefcase have anything of value in it?"

"No, it was empty. But we did have the journal in it on

the way to the d'Orsay."

"And you removed it from the briefcase?"

"We were at the train station looking through it and realized we were about to miss our train so Maggie quickly put the journal into her carry bag—just to save time."

"I see. Is there anything else?"

"I can't think of anything."

"Who knew you were going to see M. Durand?"

"Only Durand and Anton. We met Durand's assistant at the Museum when we arrived."

"Do you remember the assistant's name?"

"I don't. Do you, Mags?"

"No, I don't either." She turned to Gastineau. "Do you think the thief was after the journal?"

"It's quite possible. Nothing seems to be missing. All of your jewelry, money, and items of value appear to have been. Yet the house is in shambles. Furniture knocked over, drawers emptied, bedding sliced open. Whoever broke in was looking for something specific. It is also clear that the intruder spent quite a bit of time here. A search this detailed takes time. The perpetrator knew you would not be home."

Mark was deep in thought. "That would mean there are very few suspects."

"Not as few as you might think. Word of mouth spreads quickly. Before any accusations are made, we must be quite certain of the facts."

Gastineau saw the distress in Maggie's face. "I am sorry for your misfortune, Madame."

"We came to France for peace and quiet and to soak in the culture. This is not what we expected."

"D'Avray is normally a very peaceful town. Major crimes are rare here. That is another reason I suspect this break-in is related to your discovery." Gastineau's brow furrowed. "It is amazing that these items you found lay undiscovered for such a long time."

"As I said, it was hidden in one of the stone support columns in the basement. It was not meant to be found."

"Yes. I will tell you that after you left the police station, I became curious. It is very odd to find an early twentieth-century gun hidden in a house in France. Sometimes we find weapons from World War II, but rarely do we find them from earlier times. I searched to see if I could learn more about the people who owned this house."

By now, Maggie was feeling much more composed. Gastineau's news seemed promising. "Were you able to find anything?" she inquired.

"I have a great interest in French history. I called several people I know who work in the archives around d'Avray and found that the owner was indeed a Monsieur Frederic Chemin."

"That confirms what we found in the town hall," observed Mark.

"Yes, but did you know that he is a direct ancestor of Josephine Fournier?"

Maggie said. "I know that name. I've seen her picture in the paper. Doesn't she lead a political party in France?"

"She does not lead but is the power behind a new conservative movement called *'Les Nationales Républicains.'*"

"That sounds a lot like 'republicans'," Mark said.

"You are not too far afield, Monsieur. *Les Républicains* believe that France is the strength and continuity behind

Europe. Their philosophy is 'France above all else.' Their support comes mostly from outlying areas but they are gaining strength with Parisians, especially after the terror attacks in the city."

"Was the Chemin family prominent in the 1880's?" Maggie asked.

Gastineau leaned back in his chair. "That is another interesting fact. Frederic Chemin was married to a Marguerite Devereaux. She also owned a house in Paris, but in her own name. In the late 1800's it was unusual for women to own property, especially expensive property."

Mark was nodding at Maggie. "The letter we found was addressed to a Marguerite. She may be the one who wanted the journal. But why, and—how was it worth killing for?"

Maggie explained. *"Commissaire,* the journal contains sketches of a young woman labelled Marguerite. It also has pictures of this house and our basement. If the journal was van Gogh's he must have been here."

"That is possible," said the policeman.

"The journal also referred to a group called the 'Commune.' I remember reading about a movement after the Franco-Prussian war called the Commune. Could these be related?" inquired Maggie.

"Madame McFadden, you know your French history."

"My mother lived in France—I know some through my mother and had a keen interest in French culture and history in school," said Maggie.

"And Language—your spoken French is very very good," he smiled. "If you will allow me, I will try to expand on your knowledge.

"After the Prussians invaded France, Bismarck laid siege to Paris. The people suffered greatly. When France finally surrendered, Bismarck seized the Alsace and Lorraine regions, and demanded that France pay f200M in retribution. Even more important to Bismarck was the unification of the Prussian empire and the independent southern states into what is now called Germany."

Mark remarked, "I know a bit of German history—I've read about how manipulative Bismarck was," said Mark.

"Yes, indeed. But for France, the worst was yet to come. The army was disarmed but the Parisian National Guard was permitted to maintain a standing force in order to maintain civil control in Paris. These circumstances gave rise to the Paris Commune in 1871."

"So that is the 'commune' in the letter?" Mark asked.

"It could be, but I don't think so," said Gastineau. "Recall that the Paris Commune existed in 1871 and was disbanded shortly thereafter. The journal you found was apparently written later."

"What happened to the Paris Commune?" Mark asked.

"The Paris Commune was a government like no other—all things decided by committee. The Commune came into conflict with the French Government that remained after Napoleon was defeated.

"The Commune tried to eradicate all evidence of the monarchy. Paris came under siege again, but this time from the French army. Frenchman against Frenchman. Cannon fire in the city. Buildings set ablaze by the Commune. Sadly, the army became judge and executioner. Parisian National Guards were shot on sight. The death toll was in the thousands."

"How horrible!" Maggie shook her head.

"The Paris Commune was eventually defeated, and the rightful government restored. But Paris would never be the same. In fact, the Paris Commune came to be the model for Karl Marx and Vladimir Lenin for their own communist revolution."

Surprised by this statement, Mark exclaimed, "Really?!"

"Yes. But as you know the French are resilient. After the retribution was paid to Germany, Paris rebounded. In fact, Paris hosted the Exposition Universelle in 1889. Our Tour Eiffel was the centerpiece of the Exposition."

"M. Gastineau, you should be a history professor," beamed Maggie.

"French history is my passion. Police work is my duty."

"But where does that leave us with the journal's 'Commune' and van Gogh's 'Marguerite?'" wondered Mark.

"That is an excellent question and, unfortunately, one that I have no answer for," Gastineau replied. "The Paris Commune was dismantled in 1871. I cannot speculate as to the journal's 'Commune.'"

Chapter 20
Paris – Winter 1887

St. Nicholas Day passed quietly and the New Year heralded in with exuberant celebration throughout Paris. Yet for all the revelry, this particular night seemed dark and foreboding. The stars and the moon were rendered invisible by low, threatening clouds, and the wind ripped through the avenues at such tremendous speed that Émile tottered and leaned to maintain his balance. He ducked into the deep shadows of a doorway, checking and rechecking his pocket watch, and pulling his scarf close around his neck. Damnation, he thought. With this wind, the temperature must be nearly freezing! Just then a lone figure, stooped and plodding, rounded the corner.

"Vincent, I was beginning to think you would not come!"

"I thought about not coming. But I'm here. The only reason I am here is to get some justice for the way Goupil treated me and the way it is treating Theo. We must leave the work in the entresol alone. We cannot hurt Theo."

"Theo will be fine. We will only take a couple of pictures from the back rooms. Did you bring the key?"

"We must hurry and return the key before Theo wakes."

The storeroom behind the main gallery was cluttered with canvases: some waiting to be inventoried, some to be returned to the artist or owner, and some waiting to be displayed. To the sides stood a number of unopened wooden crates.

Émile and Vincent looked quickly and silently through the stacks of paintings.

"This one is a prize. A small Rembrandt like this would please Marguerite."

"No, not a Rembrandt," responded Vincent.

"Here. This one is perfect," whispered Émile.

"Yes. A Caravaggio. Well known and yet not very well done," said Vincent. "We can also take this Monet. He paints so many, this one will not be missed. Neither of these has been inventoried yet. Hurry! Let's get out of here before we are spotted."

Émile pulled up a carriage he had hidden around the corner from the gallery. "I will give these to Pierre as soon as possible."

"Be careful with them. I don't want Theo to know I had anything to do with this."

"Vincent, I don't want to be caught either. I'll be careful." Émile snapped the reins and the carriage disappeared into the darkness.

Chapter 21
Ville d'Avray – Present Day

It was close to midnight before Gastineau left the house. Maggie and Mark were exhausted but too anxious to sleep. "I better call Maman and let her know what happened," she said, reaching for her phone.

"Don't you want to wait until the morning?"

"No, you know how she is—she'll be up. Hold on and I will put her on the speaker phone."

The phone was answered almost immediately. "Hello. Margaret, are you all right? Isn't it very late in Paris?" The voice was firm and denoted with a French accent.

"Yes, Maman. We are fine. I have you on the speaker phone so Mark can talk to you, too."

"How are you Maman Chapin?" asked Mark.

"Mark, my son, I am well. But why do you call so late?"

Maggie took a deep breath, "Maman, I wanted to let you know that our new house was broken into while we were in Amsterdam. Nothing seems to be missing, but the house is a mess."

"Margaret Lucille." Maggie knew that a lecture was in the offing when her mother used her two given names. "This is disturbing. Perhaps you and Mark should come back to the U.S. for a time."

"Maman, please, everything will be fine. We are not hurt and, like I said, nothing seems to be missing. Mark and I think it may have been some teenagers up to no good."

"Listen you two—sometimes nothing is as it seems."

"Why do you say that, Maman?"

"It may be a simple break-in. I don't want to belabor my point but I think it's best that you leave the matter to the police. At any rate, I am happy that you are both safe. Mark, keep my daughter out of harm's way, will you please?"

"Of course, Maman Chapin."

"I must go then. Please call me tomorrow and let me know how things progress with the police investigation. Bonne chance, la France." With that, the phone went dead.

Maggie pushed the red disconnect button. "She sounded unusually concerned, which isn't like her. I didn't even get a chance to tell her about the briefcase incident. It's probably best that I didn't, though."

"It is natural that she should worry about her little girl. She'll be fine. Your mother is the spunkiest woman I know… next to you of course."

They worked for another hour, putting clothes and other items in order, then slept for some restless hours. They awoke past sunrise, feeling groggy from stress and insufficient sleep, but once awake Mark brewed a pot of coffee and they returned to their work.

"It could have been worse," he observed. Maggie was on one knee picking up shards of glass that had been a precious Louis XVI table lamp.

"Really? How so?" she asked.

"For one thing, we could have been here when they broke in. Who knows what they might have done to us."

"Maybe. But if we were here, they might not have broken in at all, and none of this would have been destroyed."

"Look, Maggie, it's only stuff. It can be replaced."

"It saddens me to know that they've rummaged through

our personal belongings. I'm not accustomed to feeling this way—so vulnerable."

"I know. I understand. But this will all get better with time. We just have to take more precautions."

"Like what?"

"One thing we need is a security system."

Maggie looked at the black fingerprint ink residue on the table. "I hope all this dusting was worthwhile. This powder is hard to clean up."

"It's probably better to use a hand-held vacuum rather than trying to wipe it up. Why don't we take a break now and go get something to eat?"

"Ok. Let me wash up. I'm filthy and stinky from this work."

"I like your filth. And your scent, too," Mark said as he kissed her cheek. "Actually, you smell like lavender."

Maggie sighed. "You never change." Then she smiled.

They sat at a sidewalk café watching local people come and go. "The cappuccino is delicious," said Maggie, licking foamy milk from her upper lip. "You know what we forgot last night?"

"What?"

"We didn't tell Maman what Gastineau found out about the house."

"We didn't have the time. She hung up so quickly."

"Well, don't let me forget the next time we talk to her."

The couple sat staring out at the people passing along the sidewalk.

"You're awfully quiet. What are you thinking?" Maggie asked.

"I keep going back over what Gastineau said last

night. The only people we told about our trip to Amsterdam were Anton and Victor Durand. You didn't mention anything to Madame Rousseau, did you?"

"No, I didn't. But Mark, you've known Anton for twenty years. You don't really think he would break into our house, do you?"

"No... no. But I don't know Durand."

"But he is a friend of Anton's, and a museum official. I can't imagine Anton introducing us if he didn't think he was anything but legit."

"Yeah... could be... probably."

"The more I think about it, I think it was kids. Some teens out having fun tearing stuff up."

"If it were teens or vandals, wouldn't they have taken other stuff—things they could sell for drug money? I don't know... if it were kids, they sure did themselves proud. What a mess they created." Just then Mark's cell phone rang. "It's Anton," he said to Maggie.

"Hello, Anton. How are you?"

"Very well, my friend, and you?"

"We're okay," Mark replied slowly.

"You do not sound like you mean it. Is there a problem?"

"Well, our house was broken into and vandalized while we were in Amsterdam."

"Mon Dieu! That is terrible! Was anything taken?"

"That's the strange thing—the house was ransacked. All the drawers were emptied, the couches and beds slashed. But as far as we can tell, nothing is missing."

"How awful! What did the gendarmes say? I assume you called them."

"Yes, we did. They took fingerprints and looked over everything. But in the end, they were not very hopeful of coming up with anything."

"Maybe the fingerprints will lead somewhere."

"I'm not sure they found any prints other than ours. I'm doubtful that we'll learn who did it."

"How is Maggie taking this?"

"As you might expect, she's upset."

"I understand. Please tell her I inquired about her."

"Certainly. But that's not why you called…"

"I wanted to ask you to meet Sarah and me in Paris for dinner, but that may not be appropriate now."

"Oh, no—that's a good idea! Not tonight, we need to catch up on sleep. But any other night is fine. We probably need the distraction. And seeing old friends like you is always good!"

"Excellent. I have a small restaurant off the Champs-Élysées in mind. Saturday? Around eight?"

"That would be excellent. I'm sure Maggie will be up for it."

"Wonderful! *Très bien*. I will make reservations and email you the details."

"Looking forward to seeing you and your family."

"Oh, I almost forgot. How was your trip to Amsterdam? Was it fruitful?"

"Somewhat. It does look like the journal belonged to van Gogh, comparing the handwriting in the journal and the letters we saw in the museum. And many of the sketches in the journal were studies of paintings we saw there on display."

"That is so exciting! I can hardly wait to see it! It appears to be quite a find, your notebook."

"That's not all."

"There's more?"

"The policeman at our house last night helping with the investigation discovered that our house was once owned by an ancestor of Josephine Fournier, the politician."

"No! How intriguing! Her popularity is rising in France."

"So we've heard. It's a shame we can't talk to her about the house. She might know about its history."

"I may be able to help in that regard," Anton said.

"Don't tell me you know Josephine Fournier?"

"Not Josephine, but her mother, Madame Chauvenal. She is a major donor to the cancer institute. I have met her several times and have been to fundraising events at her Paris home. Perhaps I can arrange for you to meet with her."

"Anton, that could be very helpful!" Mark responded, after a breath.

"I cannot promise, but I will try."

"Well, thank you for anything you can do."

"It is my pleasure. Until Saturday, *au revoir.*"

"*Au revoir,*" Mark replied.

"Nicely pronounced," Maggie winked at him. "What was that all about?"

Mark relayed what Anton had told him about his connection to Josephine Fournier through Mme. Chauvenal. "He may even arrange for us to meet her."

"It would be fascinating to see if Mme. Chauvenal has any information on the house—or if she knows anything about the so-called 'Commune.'"

"We may learn something soon enough. For now, we have the challenge of cleaning up our place."

Anton sent details of their dinner reservations at an intimate Parisian eatery near the Tuileries.

"This is so quaint, so old world, and so French," Maggie said, taking in the long, unshuttered windows and sky-blue paneled building.

"Anton had high praise for it. It's one of his favorites. He's always favored the traditional Parisian cuisine and that's what we should expect here."

A tiny gray-haired woman with a tight chignon met them as they entered the bistro and took them to Anton and Sarah's table, where an open bottle of red Burgundy sat gathering its first breaths of air. The men shook hands. Then Anton gave Maggie a quick hug, and Mark pecked Sarah's cheek.

Once seated, Mark looked around and saw that nearly all the tables were filled.

"This place is popular," he observed.

"Very popular indeed with the locals," Sarah remarked.

Anton poured wine into the two empty glasses. "Here's to good friends," he exclaimed, raising his glass.

"To friends," the others answered in unison. The tinkling of glass resonated.

"Mark, I hope you don't mind, but I told Sarah about your break-in."

"Yes, I am so sorry," Sarah said, taking Maggie's hand. "I hope nothing of value was taken."

"Thank you! No, nothing of value, except our peace of mind. Just knowing that someone came uninvited into our house and rummaged through all our personal belongings made me feel very queasy. And several things were damaged beyond repair—furniture, pillows, our bedding."

"I'm so sorry to hear this. Please, let this evening be a new beginning for you two in France," Sarah proposed.

"I'll second that!" Maggie said with no uncertainty in her voice. "By the way, Sarah, how are the two little boys?"

"Ah," Sarah giggled, "not so little but certainly 'all boys'! Guillaume and Louis are now eight and ten years old. Very smart and very boisterous. They cause me many sleepless nights!"

"Isn't that what children are supposed to do?" asked Mark, grinning.

"Yes, and they do it well! Tell me, I don't want to pry, but are there any children in your future?" asked Sarah.

"We really don't know. Mark and I are getting a little long in the tooth and have discussed adoption."

"You and Mark would make great parents! Whatever happens, I'm sure it will be for the best."

Anton looked at Mark. "Pardon me for changing the subject but I wanted you to know that I called Mme. Chauvenal."

"Really? What did she say?"

"She was most gracious. She said she could see you on Wednesday at two o'clock. Will that work for you?"

"Perfect!"

"Here is her address and phone number. There is no need to call unless you cannot make the appointment. She'll be expecting you."

"We'll be sure to make it! Anton, we really appreciate this."

The two couples dined on *escargots à la bourguignonne* then gruyere cheese soufflés served with fresh white asparagus. The chocolate soufflés were judiciously ordered ahead of time so they appeared just as everyone finished their main course.

At that moment, Mark noticed Anton's eyes on the front door. Anton was watching an odd-looking fellow shuffling toward them. It looked as though his legs were about to collapse under the weight of his corpulent body.

"Ah, it's Victor. I hope you do not mind, my friends, but I invited Victor Durand to join us for dessert and a nightcap. He works long hours and does not have a wife to go home to, nor does he have much of a social life. I also thought you might want to discuss your trip to Amsterdam with him."

Mark looked over his shoulder to see the museum director conspicuously jostling his way through the tables and chairs.

"Victor, I am pleased to see you!" Anton shook Victor's meaty hand vigorously.

Durand dabbed at beads of sweat trickling down his forehead. He was dressed in a tired wool suit with broad lapels. The coat would not button around his mighty girth. His belt was hidden, barely able to do its job of keeping up his pants. His breath came in quick, short gasps.

"Thank you for inviting me. I am sorry to be late. But art is a demanding lover." Durand shook Mark's hand and awkwardly took each of the women's hands, using only the tips of his fingers. A chair was brought to the table and he sat with a grunt. Another chocolate soufflé appeared before him.

"*M. et Mme. McFadden,* I hope you are enjoying our lovely city," he said with a forced smile. His teeth were tinged yellow from cigarettes, and he smelled of massive amounts of musky cologne. A Givenchy Gentleman knock-off, Mark thought to himself.

"Victor," Anton said somberly, "Mark and Maggies' house in d'Avray was broken into this week while they were in Amsterdam."

"That is terrible! Have they caught the culprits?"

"No, unfortunately not," answered Mark. "I doubt we will ever know who did it."

"How was your trip to the Van Gogh Museum?" Durand asked. "Did you discover anything new? You did not take the journal with you to Amsterdam, did you?"

"No, we left it in d'Avray. We thought it would be safer here. We did see several paintings that were sketched in the journal though. We are now convinced the journal is authentic."

"If you would permit me, I would like to examine it again. This time in more detail."

"Perhaps later. We have some other priorities just now," Mark replied, hoping that this simple explanation would suffice. "For one, we need to get our house back in order."

"I will come to your house if it is more convenient for you," offered Durand.

Mark stole a sideways glance at Maggie, then said, "We don't keep the journal at our home. We decided it simply wasn't safe to do so."

Durand's eyes grew wide. "But where do you have it?"

"We've decided to keep it in a bank repository for the time being," answered Mark.

Victor looked down at his soufflé, which had collapsed along with, apparently, his spirit. "That is probably wise," he said softly.

Chapter 22
Paris – Winter 1887

Émile was nervous as he sat in the café on Rue André Antoine. Arriving early, he had already consumed two coffees and was staring at his third. The wind whipped noisily against frosted windows. He reflected on Vincent's increased moodiness over the past few days, and murmured to himself, "I hope he does not change his mind."

A cold breeze blew through the café, sending a shiver up Émile's spine as he closed his eyes. He sat bolt upright when the chair opposite him scraped backwards across the floor. The sound only deepened the chilly aura of the room.

"You hope who hasn't changed his mind?" Pierre asked as he took his seat. His thick mustache was shrouded in tiny icicles. He leaned back in the chair, awaiting a reply, then said impatiently, "Well, who are you worried about?"

"No one. I was thinking out loud."

"Do you have the items?"

"Yes," came the whispered reply.

Shortly, a steaming brew of fresh coffee was placed in front of Pierre. The hot liquid melted the small flecks of snow on his heavy mustache and he absent-mindedly dabbed his mouth with a napkin, then continued.

"Before you go any further, I feel it necessary to explain a couple of things to you so there are no misunderstandings."

Émile wriggled in discomfort under Pierre's steely gaze.

"Against my strong advice, Marguerite took you into her confidence. You were among the few who were made privy to the Commune's mission."

"But…"

Pierre raised a palm to silence Émile. "This mission Marguerite has planned will change the course of history. It is not the folly of fools."

"I understand."

"I don't think you do. This little tribute of yours is just a start. You are part of the Commune. If you disappoint Marguerite or me in any way, you will be dealt with in the most severe manner. Now, what have you brought me?"

Émile straightened in his chair and exhaled deeply. "Van Gogh and I have procured two suitable pieces. One is a Caravaggio and the other a Monet."

"Very good. I have to admit, I am surprised," he smirked. "Marguerite will be pleased. You have given yourself and van Gogh a reprieve. Where are the paintings?"

"I have them in a carriage behind the café. Please don't let anyone know what van Gogh and I have done."

Pierre stood and placed a hand on Émile's shoulder. "Do not worry. This is our secret. Now, take me to the paintings."

Later that afternoon Pierre, lost in his brooding thoughts, waited on the broad avenue for Marguerite. Suddenly a voice rang out, rousing him out of his reverie.

"You must have an enormous weight on your mind to stare for so long into the heavens," the voice said.

Pierre spun around. "Ah, there you are, Marguerite!"

"Oh, my dear friend." She placed her hand on Pierre's arm and started walking leisurely down the boulevard. "So," she said, "what news do you bring?"

"These artists surprised me. I expected them to act the

cowards they are, but you now have two new pieces for your art collection."

"Wonderful. What are they?"

"A Caravaggio and a Monet."

"My, that is wonderful. I expected something much less. But you are right, they are cowards. If they had any bravado, we would have a very different situation to deal with. Please deliver the items to my home." The couple halted. Marguerite looked up into Pierre's angular face, seeing his concern.

"You worry so, mon cheri. Don't. All is well." Marguerite retreated alone in the direction they had come from, leaving Pierre alone, gaping after her.

Chapter 23
Paris – Present Day

The McFaddens drove down the narrow avenue west of the Bois de Boulogne. Giant oak and chestnut trees lined both sides of the street, casting long shadows on the pavement. The trunks stood like sentinels guarding the mansions that lie behind the walls and across large expanses of carefully manicured lawns and gardens.

"These are amazing homes," Mark said in awe as he drove slowly in search of Mme. Chauvenal's address.

"These are not ordinary *maison,* my dear. These are mansions—*manoir*—estates."

"Yes indeed. These are not the humble *maison* of *le bourgeois.*" He smiled over at her.

"Bien fait! Hey, slow down, I think we're close."

Mark squinted out his window. "They could make the numbers easier to see."

"They probably don't want to be seen. These are people who value their privacy. There!" Maggie exclaimed. "That's it. Just like the picture from Google Maps."

"Nice wall. Impossible to scale, for sure. Where's the entrance? Or do we park on the street?"

"Looks like there's a gate up ahead."

The mansion was surrounded by an eight-foot high stone wall, interrupted by capped posts every twenty feet. Inset from the wall was an intricate wrought iron double gate. There, cameras turned to identify visitors. Mark looked out of the car's window to face a video screen, speaker, and red button. A man's deep voice broke the silence.

"Je peux vous aider? Can I help you?"

Maggie leaned over Mark and answered in French. "We are Mark and Maggie McFadden. We have an appointment with Mme. Chauvenal."

"Un moment, s'il vous plaît."

The gates began to rattle and then slowly moved inward. The voice returned, instructing them in French.

"Go straight," Maggie translated. "There should be a circle in front of the house. He said to park on the right and go up to the door."

Mark inched the car through the gates, crunching the tiny gravel that separated the driveway's stone blocks. The drive wound briefly through large oak trees, flanked on either side by flower beds and hedges.

"This is something, isn't it?!" Mark said.

"Old money, to be sure," noted Maggie. "I'd love to have gardens like these at our place."

"Don't get any ideas. We're doing well, but this is out of our league."

The large stone mansion loomed before them like a faceless creature, framed between two ancient oaks. In front of the imposing structure lay a circular drive wide enough for three cars. In the center of the drive, directly in front of the main door, a sculptured fountain spouted streams of water toward a robed female figure. She held a torch in her right hand, high above her head. Her face was tilted slightly upward; her head was adorned with a laurel wreath.

Mark stared at the figure. The sun reflected off the pristine white marble, creating an aura of diffused light.

"Marianne," said Maggie.

"Who?"

"Marianne. The statue. It's Marianne, the French goddess of liberty. The original is bronze and is in Paris, but this marble one is magnificent. Come on. We can't stand out here all day." Maggie tugged gently on Mark's arm.

The granite mansion was two stories with ornate overhangs and gargoyle rain spouts. Three steps led to massive ten-foot high oak double doors. As Mark and Maggie approached the entryway, one of the doors swung open and a middle-aged woman attired in a black, long sleeve dress and white apron stood before them. Her hair was streaked with gray and pulled up into a French twist. Her face was expressionless.

"Monsieur et Madame McFadden?" she asked in a voice that sounded as rough as the gravel they had just passed over.

"Oui," Maggie replied.

"Entrez-vous, s'il vous plaît. Follow me."

Mark stopped just past the threshold to take in the stunning panorama. The foyer was the full height of the two-storied house. The floor was cream-colored marble so shiny that it appeared to be translucent. Fresh cut flowers perched spectacularly on a round antique table directly under a crystal chandelier in the middle of the foyer. Full length portraits of women in long, flowing gowns adorned the walls. A grand staircase stretched in a gradual arch to the second floor.

"Quite lovely," Mark whispered with awe in his voice. Maggie nodded in agreement.

The maid led them past mahogany French doors that closed off the rooms on either side of the foyer, toward a light-filled room at the end of the main hall. Mark nudged

Maggie and pointed to a portrait on the wall. Josephine Fournier was looking down on them. Her cerulean blue eyes followed them as they traversed the entryway. Maggie felt a little uneasy.

The maid spoke. "Would you prefer to speak English?" she asked her guests.

"Please, if it is not inconvenient," Mark replied.

"Of course."

They entered a massive, mahogany-paneled office that boasted a partner's desk at one end of the room with an oversized credenza behind it. A round table sat inside an alcove overlooking a verdant garden. Portraits and paintings filled every possible space on the walls. A leather couch and two overstuffed leather chairs were arranged around a heavy wooden table in the middle of the room. The maid gestured to the leather chairs.

"Please be seated. Mme. Chauvenal is in the garden. She will be here in a moment. Would you like some tea or coffee? A pastry perhaps?"

"I would appreciate a cup of coffee," Mark answered politely.

"Madame?" asked the maid.

"Do you have green tea?" Maggie asked.

"Certainly. *Monsieur*, would you prefer American coffee, cappuccino or espresso?"

"Yes, American coffee, please."

She left the room, leaving the couple to gape at the elegant surroundings.

"This artwork is amazing!" gasped Maggie. "Look, I think this is a Caravaggio!"

Mark came alongside Maggie. "Look over here." He led

her to a full-length portrait of a woman in a red formal dress, standing next to a large brown and white dog. Her black hair hung loosely over her shoulders. Her translucent bright blue eyes bore right through Maggie.

"Mags, this is the woman in the journal." he whispered. Maggie read the small brass nameplate imbedded in the frame. "Marguerite Devereaux." They both stared up at the massive portrait. "It looks like we've hit the jackpot," said Mark, as he turned to admire the other furnishings and paintings.

"Look over here," Mark pulled his wife toward a round table with several photos of people taken during World War II and after. They both bent down to inspect one particular sepia image behind a gold-plated frame.

"That is my mother and me with Charles DeGaulle," announced a steely voice from behind them. Mark and Maggie turned to her. "It was taken right after the liberation of Paris. My mother was an operative for the underground. I was a young girl, but war makes you grow up quickly. I ran messages between the various underground factions in Paris and to the west."

Madame Chauvenal stood imposingly next to the leather sofa. She was dressed in a floral gardening apron that wrapped around her bodice. As tall as Maggie, she was thin with salt and pepper hair, more salt than pepper. The lines in her face, while barely visible, made her look dignified and experienced. But it was her eyes that captured both Mark and Maggie—blue as the summer sky, almost translucent.

Mark stepped forward to introduce himself and Maggie, but his words were cut short when two massive brown and white spotted hounds came out of nowhere.

"Please do not be afraid. These dogs are well-mannered," the woman directed.

"They took me by surprise! I'm Mark McFadden and this is my wife, Maggie." Mark offered his hand.

"What a lovely name for such a lovely woman," remarked Mme. Chauvenal as she greeted them. "Please, make yourselves comfortable. I see Claire has arrived with refreshments. Thank you, Claire."

The maid entered with a silver tea set and deftly poured the coffee and tea into delicate porcelain cups. She then placed a cappuccino in front of Mme. Chauvenal along with a platter of pastries and disappeared.

"Beautiful dogs," observed Maggie. "We are both dog lovers. May I pet them?"

"They are my babies. But I would not advise petting them. They are quite protective of me." She made a slight gesture with her hand, palm pushing downward. The hounds immediately lay down, heads up, ears forward and alert. "They are *Braque français*—French hunting dogs. This one is Hugo," she said pointing to the dog to her left. "He can be rather difficult at times. I named him after Victor Hugo. This one is Lucie. She is my prize. She is named after Lucie Aubrac, a clever and fierce underground fighter during the war."

"So well behaved," Mark observed.

"Mme. Chauvenal, you said your parents were with the resistance during the war?" said Maggie.

"Yes, that is correct."

"My mother is from Paris and her parents also fought with the resistance."

"What is your mother's name?"

"Her name is Rena Chapin. Her mother was Ines Lebeau. My mother changed her name after the war."

The old woman caught her breath, then looked up toward the ornate molding. "I do not remember the name Lebeau. There were so many patriots fighting the Germans, I could not know them all. But, I'm sure you did not come here to admire my dogs or talk about the war. When Anton called he said you had purchased a home in Ville-d'Avray that may somehow be connected to one of my ancestors."

"That's right. Maggie and I bought a lovely old house that, quite honestly, needs some restoring and tender care."

The old woman chuckled. "I'm afraid many of our old homes here in France need some attention. Not everyone has the means to maintain these lovely domiciles. By the way, how is it that you know Anton?"

"We went to university together—Stanford, in California."

"Ah, yes. An excellent school. Please tell me more about your house. And you may call me Anna."

"Certainly. Well, while we were working in the basement of our new home, we came across an old wooden box buried in one of the support columns. We have reason to believe the box dates back to 1890. Naturally, we were curious to learn more. When we searched the local records, we found that the property was owned by a Frederic Chemin and Marguerite Devereaux. We were later told that they were distant relatives of yours. We wondered if you could tell us anything about them and the house. In that box was a note addressed to 'Marguerite' and a journal."

Mme. Chauvenal sat quietly listening to Mark's story.

When he finished, she picked up her cup and thoughtfully sipped her cappuccino. Mark was looking at her expectantly, waiting for a reply. Finally, she said, "Marguerite Devereaux was my great-grandmother. Her portrait is there, behind the desk. I know little about Frederic and I'm unaware of any family-owned property in d'Avray. That is not to say they did not own the house. I simply don't know. But you mentioned a letter?"

Mark continued. "Yes, we found a letter addressed to 'Marguerite.' It referred to someone's untimely death. I believe the exact words were 'that poor wretch'."

Anna took another sip of her cappuccino, gazing directly at Mark. "Curious. I wonder what that means."

"We were hoping you could shed some light on what we found."

"I'm not sure. Please tell me about the journal."

"Well," Mark began, "it appears to be an artist's journal. It is full of sketches and notes about color and perspective. There are sketches of our house in the journal and of Marguerite."

Anna shifted slightly in her chair. "My, my. Do you know who kept the journal?" she said.

"We believe it may have been a van Gogh journal," said Maggie.

"Why, that is extraordinary! And you say that Marguerite's portrait is in the journal?"

"Yes."

Mme. Chauvenal rose and crossed the room to contemplate the portrait behind the desk.

"This is Marguerite Devereaux. She was quite a

woman. She survived the Prussian war and Paris siege. I'm not sure exactly what her role was, but I believe she worked with the French Republic to resist further German occupation. I am surprised that any of my ancestors would be mentioned in a van Gogh journal. Are you certain the journal was his?"

Maggie replied, "No, this is speculation on our part, but from what we have discovered so far, everything points to the journal being his. There are several sketches in the journal that are remarkably like some of his paintings. We have more research to do to determine its authenticity."

"I don't profess to know everything that my ancestors were involved with. But if you would like, I will see if I can find out more about my great-grandmother. I must tell you, you have piqued my curiosity."

"Any help you can give us would be greatly appreciated," Maggie said.

"Oh my, the time has gotten away from me. I am so sorry but I have another engagement. Laurent!" she called.

A tall, square-jawed man appeared in the doorway.

"I'm afraid I have to leave you now. Laurent will see you out. Please give him your address and telephone number. I will be sure to call you if I discover anything."

"Thank you, Madame," said Mark.

"Yes, you are quite welcome. Likewise, please do me the favor of letting me know if you learn anything, especially as it relates to my family."

"We most certainly will," answered Maggie. "Anna, may I ask you one more question?"

"Certainly, my dear."

"I've noticed you have a great many pictures and portraits of the women in your family; however, I don't see any men from your family."

"Oh, quite right, my dear! It's very simple. You see, the women in our family have always been the strong ones and so much more interesting than the men!" Then added with a cheery wave, *"Bonne chance, la France!"*

Chapter 24
Paris – Late Winter 1887

Émile sat in a corner of a café near his parents' house and his backyard studio. He was drinking a coffee, nibbling on a croissant and perusing a newspaper. Turning the page, he let out a gasp.

"Mon Dieu!" he exclaimed. The headline of the article read "Explosion Near Russian Palace. Second Assassination Attempt in Year. French Implicated." Reading quickly, he rose from the table, threw some coins down, and hurried through the front door.

Shortly, he was pounding on the van Gogh apartment door, calling for Vincent. But there was no answer.

Wandering about Montmartre, Émile decided to try Tanguy's shop but had no luck there. Eventually, he found Vincent warming himself over coffee at one of his familiar haunts.

"Vincent, have you seen the paper?"

"No. What is it that leaves you so excited and breathless? Sit. Have a coffee and a bite to eat." Vincent motioned for Émile to be seated.

"No, I cannot eat right now." Émile opened the paper in his hand and pointed to the headline. "Read this."

Vincent hastily read the article and looked up. "Marguerite's plan failed again."

"But you know what this means, don't you?"

"No..."

Émile sighed heavily. "There will be an inquiry and the Russians will be looking for whoever is responsible, perhaps even looking for us."

"But we had nothing to do with this!"

"Not directly, but we are still part of the Commune! If the Commune is suspected, then we will be suspects! I'm nervous, Vincent. No, I'm beyond nervous! I think we should take a trip, a vacation perhaps, and get away from all of this. I don't want to be around if there is an investigation."

"Theo's manager found out about the missing paintings and is frantic," Vincent said.

"Does he suspect Theo?"

"No, but Theo is nervous about what may happen. He could be dismissed."

The two men sat in silence, each alone with his thoughts. At last Vincent spoke. "Émile, I have my paint box and easel with me. I am going down to the river to paint. You may come along if you wish."

"No. I am going back home to think this through. Perhaps I will see you later."

Vincent rose, gathered his supplies and headed toward the door. Émile reread the article and rubbed his furrowed brow.

In another café, Marguerite was on her second coffee and reading the same headlines. She chuckled as she studied the article, then put it aside. She reached for her fur-lined coat, adjusted her hat, and gathered her black leather purse. She tossed the paper into a bin as she exited the café.

The frigid air was damp with the promise of snow. A brisk wind was gathering, compelling passersby to brace themselves against its unwelcome chill. Marguerite was not the least bit bothered by the weather. She strolled leisurely down the avenue as if it were a summer's day, peering into the shop windows. The reflection of a carriage caught her eye. A gentleman alit from the carriage and approached her. Without turning around, she said, "Bonjour, Pierre. It is a good morning, is it not?"

"I am in no humor for your small talk, Marguerite. I need information. There were few details in the paper. What have you?" he responded.

Turning from the window, she put her arm into Pierre's and continued her saunter down the avenue. "I have a telegram that tells me the Okhrana has found some terribly incriminating evidence linking the incident to some fanatical French group called 'The Commune'."

"Will the Russians believe it?"

"Why, yes, I'm certain they will. Why wouldn't they? My contact in the Okhrana believes the evidence is quite damning."

"More importantly, will it become public?"

"In time. Patience, mon ami. Eventually one government will blame the other for trying to assassinate its leader."

"I am not a patient man. And neither is the Chancellor. He is under great pressure. Alexander is making overtures to the French president. He is in desperate need of money."

"I am aware. It should only be a few days before the Okhrana charges France with the assassination attempt. In the meantime, I will follow my daily routine, so you will know where to find me." Marguerite let go of Pierre's arm and continued alone down the avenue. Staring after her in deep thought, Pierre finally returned to the carriage and rode off.

The inhospitable cold brought tears to Vincent's eyes as he trudged through the vacant Paris streets. Despite his heavy boots, thick pants, snug coat and hat, the bitter wind chilled him to the bone.

"I don't think I can hold a brush long enough to paint in this dreadful weather," he mumbled to himself. He stopped in the middle of the boulevard, and then abruptly turned in the direction of Rue Lepic.

By the time he reached his apartment, he was thoroughly frozen and feeling irritable at his lost chance to paint another Parisian scene. He set his easel and paint box down in the middle of the foyer, removed his hat and coat, and poured himself a Cognac. He could feel the dark amber liquid burn from his tongue all the way through to the deepest depths of his belly. Not only did the brandy warm him, but it eased some of the tension that had built up on his walk home. He then turned his mind to his art.

Looking from his blank canvas to the ornate oval mirror that adorned a patterned wall, Vincent decided on another self-portrait. He had not started the day with a self-portrait in mind, but as he looked in the mirror the color of his beard, the weathered texture of his coat and the tawny hue of his skin all came into focus. Perhaps a self-portrait would be best today after all. As with any other subject, he sought to master his own portrait through trial and error.

He worked rapidly and without a break. His likeness came into view as if popping out from the canvas. One moment there were only paint smudges and a vague outline of a head. The next moment a shape had taken form and Vincent was looking back at himself from the canvas. He used short, defined strokes to depict his well-trimmed beard and reddish hair, which stood straight back off his brow. He stippled his hair with a bit of olive white and added more of the same to his beard. The image was quickly and cohesively coming into view.

Vincent spent time painting intensity into his eyes. He wanted viewers to appreciate the serious nature of the artist. Only his ear was somewhat undefined—perhaps an afterthought, appearing like a bulb of cauliflower on the side of his head. The light skin tones around his neck were accented with darker shading, giving dimension to his pronounced Adam's apple. Unlike many other portraits and paintings he had done before, this time Vincent did not outline the face and head in a dark color. Instead, he blended his hair and perfectly erect figure into the background. This resulted in his face and eyes standing out as a focal point of the work.

Vincent, wholly absorbed in his art, did not hear Theo enter the apartment. Theo regarded his brother quietly, acutely aware of his single-minded approach to each and every undertaking. Theo silently slipped into the room and peered over Vincent's shoulder at the work-in-progress. "This is a bit darker than I would have imagined," Theo said softly.

"What? Oh… Theo. I did not hear you come in. You startled me! What did you say?"

"This is very good, but darker than I would have imagined."

"My spirit is not light, dear brother. How was your day at the gallery?"

Removing his coat and hat, Theo said, "My employer is still searching for the missing paintings."

"Have they looked everywhere? Do they suspect someone took them or have they simply been misplaced?"

"I don't really know. I am keeping my focus on the entresol. But it is distracting and worrisome."

Vincent looked from the mirror back to the canvas. "I am just about finished here. Would you please pour me a Cognac?"

Theo poured them both a snifter of the amber liquor, setting Vincent's down delicately on a side table. He then sank, exhausted, into an armchair and reached for his nightcap, savoring each sip as he slowly emptied his glass. By the time Vincent had finished the portrait, Theo had fallen asleep, his empty glass in his lap. The sun had set and darkness filled the room. Vincent was wounded that his best friend could not keep vigil with him.

The next morning, the sun shone brightly on the boulevard, providing a break from the unbearable winter that seemed to drag on forever. Marguerite read the article on the front page of the newspaper. A satisfied smile crossed her lips. The report was good, very good indeed. As Marguerite was silently feeling jubilant, Pierre appeared before her. "Ah, Pierre. Good morning to you. I take it that you have read this morning's paper?"

"I have. It is good news."

Ignoring his reply, Marguerite began to read aloud to Pierre: "The Russian State Police have linked the bombing outside the Anichkov Palace in St. Petersburg to a French terrorist group calling themselves 'The Commune' with apparent ties to the NV. The Anichkov Palace is the home of Tsar Alexander III. Fortunately, the Tsar and his family were at their primary residence, the Gatchina Palace, when the bomb went off. Russian diplomats have demanded action from the French government to immediately find and deliver the conspirators to Russian authorities."

"As I said, I read the article. Now what do we do?"

"We wait. The personal items and the guns will lead the investigation to different Commune members. The Russians will be leery of any alliance with France. The Chancellor will have several options now in dealing with the Tsar."

"I hope you are right."

"I am, my dear Pierre, I am."

The next day Émile and Vincent were walking along a winding dirt road on Montmartre. Fields of grasses made brittle by the previous night's frost lay on both sides.

"I am very nervous. Scared, actually. The news article might as well have published our names and proclaimed us conspirators," moaned Émile.

"A trivial matter. The more important issue is the stolen paintings. Theo is ill with worry and believes his job in jeopardy," said Vincent.

"This is not trivial! We could be charged with attempted assassination! The paper this morning said the Russian police were starting an investigation in Paris."

"Worry about Theo if you must worry. This Russian thing will pass," Vincent answered dismissively.

"Does Theo's manager suspect him?"

"No, I don't think so, but he may hold Theo responsible for the loss."

"That's unfortunate. But, Vincent, I feel compelled to leave Paris for a while. My parents have a small house in Brittany. I will go there until things cool down. I advise you, my friend, to do likewise. Leave Paris as quickly as possible. Go to some remote place where you are not known. Some place where you can disappear."

"No," he said. "My brother needs me and I will stay here."

"Very well," Émile said. He put his arms around Vincent and held him for a brief moment. "I shall miss you. Until we meet again." He turned and walked down the hillside.

Chapter 25
Ville d'Avray – Present Day

Mark pulled out of the driveway onto the narrow tree-lined street. The shadows of the trees on the roadway resembled oddly shaped pieces of a jigsaw puzzle.

"It looks like we have found our Marguerite," said Mark.

Maggie did not reply.

"Mags, are you here?" Mark persisted.

"Yes. Sorry... I was just thinking, it's odd that Mme. Chauvenal used the exact same phrase as Maman. *'Bonne chance, la France.'*"

"It's probably a wartime phrase that was popular when they were young. But back to my observation. It looks like we've learned who Marguerite is."

"Yep. The sketches in the journal don't do her justice though. The woman in Mme. Chauvenal's study was really stunning."

"Mags, do you think Mme. Chauvenal knows more than she let on? I mean, about our house and its connection to Marguerite?"

"Maybe. I don't know."

As they considered the events of the past hour, neither noticed a dark blue Renault Clio that pulled out behind them, following at a safe distance.

"Traffic is at a standstill. It's as bad or worse here than anywhere in the States," observed Mark.

"It's a good thing we aren't in a hurry."

Just then Mark's cell phone rang. He punched the Bluetooth connection and answered. "Hello. Mark McFadden."

"M. McFadden, this is Commissaire Gastineau. I hope I am calling at a convenient time."

"Yes, no problem, Commissaire. Maggie and I are sitting in traffic, trying to get home before dark."

"My apologies. Are you in Paris?"

"Just returning."

"Ah, that explains the traffic. Paris is like any other European capital in that respect. Many cars! All trying to move at the same time!"

"That seems to be the case."

"M. McFadden, I would like to meet with you and your wife, today, if that is possible."

"Maggie is right here. I have you on speaker phone."

"Very good."

Maggie replied "We can certainly meet but I'm not sure how long it will take us to get home. It may be late by the looks of this endless parade of cars."

"No matter. Where are you now?"

"We are near the Bois de Boulogne."

"Excellent. I will come to your house later this evening."

"Could you tell us what you want to discuss?" asked Mark.

"I think it better if we talk in person. Until then, *au revoir.*" The phone went dead.

"I wonder what this is all about," Mark said, wrinkling his brow.

"I dunno. He was pretty abrupt," Maggie frowned. "I guess we'll find out soon enough."

They inched their way through Paris, the dark blue Renault Clio weaving in and out of traffic behind them. Darkness had fallen by the time Mark turned into their driveway. The Renault Clio slowed, as though to park. Two sets of wary eyes watched the American couple disappear into their house. As the Clio lingered, a black Renault Mégane pulled around it and turned into the McFadden's driveway. The Clio sped away.

Gastineau stepped out of his Renault and strode toward the house.

Mark opened the front door just as Gastineau was about to knock. "Commissaire, what perfect timing. We just walked in the door. Come in. I was about to check our outside lights to see if they were on. Mags! Commissaire Gastineau is here."

"I'll be right there," the response echoed from upstairs.

"I'm going to put on some coffee. Would you like a cup?" Mark offered as he led Gastineau into the kitchen.

"Yes, that would be nice. Coffee is a habit that I cannot break. It is ingrained in the French blood."

Maggie entered the kitchen, pulling her hair out from under the neckline of a freshly donned cashmere sweater, and greeted their guest warmly. "Please, don't get up. Mark, I'll take a cup of coffee, too. *Monsieur* Gastineau, what brings you out so late?"

"Before I get to the reason for my visit, I would like to ask where you were today."

Mark and Maggie looked at each other. "Why do you ask?" Mark wanted to know.

"Let's call it professional curiosity."

"Well, we met with Mme. Chauvenal at her home."

"Impressive! In France for just a few months and already you are invited to meet with someone who is considered a national treasure!"

"We really don't know her. Anton, our college friend

who lives here set up the meeting."

"Ah," he flipped open his notebook. "That would be Anton Lambert."

"Yes."

"And Monsieur Lambert introduced you to Victor Durand of the Musée d'Orsay?"

"Yes, but—wait. What is this about?" asked Mark.

Gastineau shrugged. "Just routine questions. You see, I have found that M. Durand may not be what he seems."

"What do you mean?" Maggie's eyebrows lifted.

"When I inquired about M. Durand, I discovered that he is well known to the section of the Paris police that investigates art theft."

"He is the director of the museum," Mark interjected. "Don't the police seek him out for his expert opinion?"

Gastineau eyed Mark, his face expressionless. "Non, they know him as a suspect in many art thefts and forgeries."

"What?!" exclaimed Mark. "Victor Durand?! That can't be true."

"Cannot be true because he is a friend of M. Lambert or because he works at the d'Orsay?"

"Well… both."

"Monsieur, I am sure you are not so naïve as to believe art directors cannot be criminals. M. Durand is suspected of aiding—perhaps even orchestrating—several high-profile art forgeries and thefts over the past ten years. It seems his personal hunger for art has led him into much debt."

"Debt does not make him a thief…" Mark countered.

"No, it does not. But some of his associates are part of

an organized syndicate that deal in stolen art and forgeries worldwide."

"Oh my God." Maggie breathed.

"My sources tell me that M. Durand may be in debt to the wrong people."

"Then why don't you arrest him?" asked Maggie.

"What we know and what we can prove are two different things, Madame. If we could prove his involvement, we would arrest him."

"If he suspects that the journal we found is van Gogh's, it could be his financial salvation. He would want it, wouldn't he?" suggested Mark.

"Yes, Monsieur."

"Do you think he broke into our house or that he stole Mark's briefcase?" asked Maggie.

"Possibly. But he was out of town the same time you were in Amsterdam, so it is unlikely that he broke into your house himself."

"Where was he?" Maggie wondered.

"Amsterdam," replied Gastineau with a hint of a smile. "It appears he was watching you, perhaps to make sure you did not turn over the journal to the Van Gogh Museum."

"How did you find this out?" asked Mark.

"The division in charge of investigating art theft had someone follow M. Durant because of an on-going investigation. His sudden departure to Amsterdam aroused further suspicion. It turns out that he was following you two."

"Following us?" Maggie and Mark exclaimed in unison.
"Yes."

Maggie turned to Mark in disbelief. "I can't believe this."

Gastineau continued his line of questioning. "Now, please tell me, why did you visit Mme. Chauvenal?"

"Because you told us her ancestors owned this house in the late 1800's. We thought she could tell us something about Frederic or Marguerite Chemin that would give us hints as to why the journal, the gun, and the letter were hidden here."

"What did she tell you?" asked Gastineau.

"Only that Marguerite Devereaux was her great-grandmother. But other than that, nothing really. She didn't seem to know anything about the house," replied Mark.

"We are wondering if Mme. Chauvenal is withholding information. She seemed reluctant to tell us anything," Maggie added.

"Mme. Chauvenal is revered by many in France. She risked her life as a girl running messages for the underground. De Gaulle himself dubbed her a 'heroine of the republic.' She also has business interests throughout France and Europe. Her daughter is the power behind a national political party—a position I'm certain Mme. Chauvenal supports. I'm afraid it is not my place to speculate on what she knows or does not know."

With that, Gastineau rose from his seat, gathered his belongings, and bid the couple farewell. After Mark saw the policeman to the door, he returned to his place in the kitchen with Maggie. "This whole thing is unbelievable. It feels like we're in some kind of alternate reality."

"It does," agreed Maggie. "I want to talk to Maman and find out if she knows Mme. Chauvenal."

Maggie's mother picked up on the second ring. "Hello,

Margaret. I hope you and Mark are enjoying Paris. Have the gendarmes discovered who broke into your house?"

"We are well, Maman. A lot has happened here. The police have not found who broke in but some things have come up that we want to discuss with you."

"Go on."

"The journal we found, you remember?"

"But of course."

"Mark and I are convinced that it really is van Gogh's."

"My, that is marvelous. What an excellent discovery! And a valuable one at that!"

"Do you recall that we took the journal to an art director at the d'Orsay?"

"Yes, briefly."

"Well, it turns out that Commissaire Gastineau, the police officer in charge of our case, believes that Victor Durand, the art director, may be involved with an art theft ring."

"Mon Dieu! Margaret, you and Mark must be very careful."

"We are. We think that Durand is interested in the journal. We put it in a bank repository for now—to keep it safe."

"Margaret, I cannot help but worry. Criminals seldom let little things get in their way. And you may be dealing with professional criminals."

"Maman, please don't worry. We will be careful. Plus, we have Gastineau looking out for us."

"The police can only do so much, my dear. They cannot be with you at all hours of the day."

"I have some other news, Maman. This house was once owned by a Fredric Chemin, who, we discovered, was an ancestor to Josephine Fournier, the politician. As it happens,

Anton, Mark's friend from college, knows Madam Fournier's mother through the cancer institute. He arranged for us to meet her today. We spent the afternoon at her mansion near the Bois du Boulogne."

"My, you two are getting very involved in Parisian life."

"It seems so. But there's more. It turns out that Mme. Chauvenal, Fournier's mother, is a descendant of a woman mentioned in van Gogh's journal. Anna Chauvenal and her mother were in the French underground just as you were. Isn't that amazing, Maman?"

There was silence on the line.

"Maman? Maman, are you still there?"

"Yes, my dear. I am still here."

"Don't you find these connections remarkable?"

"Yes, indeed. Truly amazing."

"You don't sound very excited, Maman."

"I am thrilled."

"Mme. Chauvenal is somewhat of a celebrity in France. We saw a picture of her and her mother with Charles De Gaulle. Is it possible that you two could have met? It seems like you and she have a common history, am I right?"

Silence again.

"Maman?"

"Yes. We were a part of that movement."

"Is it possible you know Mme. Chauvenal from the war?"

"That was a long time ago. There were many of us in the resistance. It was impossible to know them all."

"I just thought..."

"Margaret, I want you and Mark to be careful."

"Oh, Maman, you worry too much. We are fine."

"Yes, well I must go now."

"But why the rush? Don't you want to chat some more?"

"I do, but I really must go. I must get ready for an appointment. *Bonne chance, la France.*" The phone went silent.

Maggie stared at the phone in her hand.

Chapter 26
Paris – Late Winter-Early Spring 1888

The following day, Vincent went to see Père Tanguy to pick up paint supplies and canvas. As was their understanding, he took along some of his completed work and asked old man Tanguy to display them on his walls. "Theo will settle the bill later," he told Tanguy. To Vincent's immense displeasure, which he voiced in no uncertain terms, Tanguy immediately hauled the canvases into the back room. He laid them against a stack of other artists' work left at the shop for him to sell. All at once Père's scowling wife appeared in his way, thick arms folded across her bosom, ready to fire away at her poor battered husband. He raised his hand to his wife and said, "Please, I've suffered enough today! First Vincent, now you!"

Vincent scurried down the street with his supplies cradled in his arms, his head bowed. He was both infuriated and vexed by Tanguy's sullenness. How can his work sell if Tanguy doesn't even bother to display it? "And that woman," he grumbled. "What on God's earth is she here for except to torment me?"

As Vincent came upon a small patisserie, his nose caught the mouth-watering scent of fresh baked goods. Vincent breathed in the bakery delights. "Ahhh… that's just what I need. Some decent food, a smoke, and a cup of coffee will improve my disposition." He entered the café and placed his supplies next to an unoccupied table. He approached the counter and eyed the display of breads.

"What will you have," the woman behind the counter asked. She looked like she enjoyed her work and ate every bit of the profits.

"A petite loaf and a coffee, si'l vous plaît. And some fresh butter, also." Vincent rummaged through his pockets and found some coins. He had just enough to pay for the coffee and bread. He returned to his table with his food. There, discarded on the table next to his, was a newspaper. He reached over and snatched it up and as he was spreading it out in front of him, he saw the bold header on the article in the lower right column of the front page:

France Denies Involvement in Assassination Attempt

Vincent devoured the article in the same manner as his bread and his coffee. So the Russians are looking for Commune members. It seems that Émile was right after all, he thought. The report went on to quote French President, Marie Carnot, who denounced the actions of the Commune and further stated that "all of France will assist in the search for the conspirators."

Vincent laid the paper down on the table. He picked up his supplies and walked out of the café. He walked toward the Louvre and finally came to a bench by the Seine. He did not feel the cold penetrate his heavy coat as he stared at the snow and ice-covered water. Finally, he rose and walked back to the apartment.

Theo was sitting in an armchair when Vincent arrived. He was completely spent after a long day at the gallery. Vincent regarded his brother.

"How was your day at work?" asked Vincent, setting

his supplies in a corner.

"Long. We sold six paintings from the work in the Entresol. The new artist exhibit seems to be doing very well."

"Would you like to go out for dinner?" asked Vincent.

"I am simply too tired tonight, my brother. I think I will go to bed early. But thank you anyway."

"Theo," asked Vincent in a small voice. "I hate to ask you, but do you think I could have some additional money this month? Not much, but I've come up with some extra expenses and I don't want to be short later on."

"Of course. How much do you need?"

"Could you spare a hundred francs?"

"That's a lot."

"I wouldn't ask if I didn't really need it. You know the price of pigments. Canvas costs have risen too."

"All right. Take the money from my bag."

"Theo, I really appreciate this and I appreciate you. Despite our differences, you are still my best friend."

Theo went to his room and shut the door, leaving Vincent alone with his thoughts.

When Theo arrived home the following evening, the apartment was dark. He turned on the lights and looked around. Vincent's art supplies, canvases, perspective frame, coat and hat were gone. He must be working late, he thought to himself. I hope he is not spending the money I just gave him on whores and absinthe. Then he noticed a folded paper on the table with his name on it. He opened it warily and read:

My dear Theo:

At long last I have decided to leave for le Midi and start the artist colony that we have discussed so many times. I know this seems like a sudden and irrational decision, but trust me when I tell you, I have given this much thought. I will write more when I am settled. I hope you will not be angry with me. I look forward with great pleasure to your visits.

With a hearty handshake,
Vincent

Theo gaped at the letter for several minutes. He could not understand what had gotten into Vincent and why he would leave without even a proper goodbye. He crumpled the paper and threw it into the trash can. He turned toward the sherry decanter and reached for a glass. It was time for a nightcap to steady the nerves.

Chapter 27
Ville d'Avray – Present Day

Mark awoke the next morning, rolled over and reached for his wife and found her missing. He propped himself up on one elbow and stared in foggy confusion at the empty spot beside him. Quickly, he hopped to his feet, put on his slippers, and wrapped himself in a terrycloth robe. His footfalls were met with creaks and groans from the old wooden stairs. Except for the birds singing from the open windows, not a sound came from the first floor.

"Mags," he called. Nothing. "Mags!" he called again, this time a little louder. He turned the corner into the kitchen. He found Maggie bent over the table, her head resting sideways on her arm, her hair draped over her face.

He bent down and brushed her hair from her neck and kissed her. "Mags, wake up."

"Huh? What? What time is it?" She looked at him with sleep-laden eyes.

"Eight-thirty. Want some breakfast?"

"Oh," she sighed. She wiped the spittle from her mouth with the back of her hand. "Coffee, please!"

"You stayed here all night? Why couldn't you sleep?"

"Kept thinking about what Gastineau said and how Maman reacted when I mentioned Mme. Chauvenal."

"I thought you said she didn't say anything."

"It's not what she said, it's what she didn't say. I got the feeling she wanted to tell me something but thought better of it."

"Mags, yesterday was pretty eventful and you were tired

last night. I'm sure if your mother wanted to tell you something, she would have. She's not the kind to hold back."

Maggie let out a long sigh. "You're right. I'm probably imagining things."

Mark's cell phone rang.

"Monsieur McFadden, this is Victor Durand, from the Musée d'Orsay. I hope I am calling you at a good time."

"Oh, er, M. Durand. Yes, of course, this is fine."

Maggie mouthed "Durand?" Mark nodded.

"Very good. I have continued to investigate the journal you discovered. I wish to see the journal again; would it be possible?"

"I'm not sure. As I told you, we now keep it in a safe deposit box."

"I believe it is important to verify its provenance. When would it be available for my inspection?"

"I'm not sure when it will be available, M. Durand."

"I can meet at any time. I could even come to your house."

"I'm not sure..." Mark said slowly.

"M. McFadden. I have a sense of urgency about this. The journal could be a treasure."

"M. Durand, I cannot make promises, but I will discuss our schedule with Maggie. I have your number. I will call you back once we've figured out what our plans are."

"Please, and thank you, sir."

"Goodbye, M. Durand." Mark pushed the red button.

"What was that all about," asked Maggie.

"Durand wants to see the journal again."

"Bet he does."

"Says he wants to check its provenance."

"Yeah. We should let Gastineau know about the call."

Mark dialed the police station and asked for Commissaire Gastineau.

Gastineau's voice came through the mobile phone's speaker. "M. and Mme. McFadden. To what do I owe the privilege of this call?"

"We're sorry to bother you but we just received a call from Victor Durand."

"I am not surprised. Did he want to meet with you again?"

"Yes. He wants to see the journal again."

"What did you tell him?"

"Nothing really. I told him we had not decided what to do—I held him off. We wanted to discuss this with you." Mark and Maggie huddled together over the phone, stealing glances from each other.

"Excellent. When does he want to meet?"

"As soon as possible."

"If you do not mind, can I call you back? I want to check with my colleagues at the Sûreté."

"Yes, of course."

"Good, I will call you later today."

A few hours later Mark's phone rang again.

"M. McFadden, this is Phillipe Gastineau again. My colleagues are very interested in having you meet with M. Durand. They believe you offer an exceptional opportunity of luring him in and finally breaking the ring he works for."

"M. Gastineau, is this safe? We're not trained in this sort of thing," said Maggie.

"I can assure you that you will be under surveillance at all times."

"But, if you are correct, Durand has already had our

house broken into and my briefcase stolen. My wife is right, we're not police."

"Monsieur and Madame McFadden, you two are in a position to help the Sûreté put an end to years of looting. I implore you, please help us. I will personally oversee your safety."

Mark exchanged a look of agreement with Maggie. "Okay, Commissaire. We're in."

"Someone will be watching you, you will wear wires, and we will be monitoring your conversation. My colleagues suggest you arrange to meet Durand later this week for lunch."

"We can do that," Mark said hesitantly.

"Good. Please call me after you have set up the lunch with Durand and I will meet you at the police headquarters before you see him. We will go over everything in detail. Until then, I advise you to not talk to anyone about this."

"Yes, of course," responded Mark.

"Very well. I sincerely appreciate your help." The phone went silent.

Maggie sighed deeply. "What have we gotten ourselves into?"

Chapter 28
Arles-sur-Oise – Late Winter-Early Spring 1888

A passenger train pulled into the Arles station. The harsh winter had taken its toll on the train platform, which was now suffering from decaying wood and rusting nails. Vincent felt like the old planks—worn from the winter cold and the many hours that he spent en route to his new home. He gathered his belongings and stepped off the train. It had snowed during the entire journey and Arles was covered in almost two feet of glorious white topped with a thin layer of crunchy packed ice.

Vincent waited next to the train for his art supplies to be unloaded. He tried to warm himself by pacing along the platform, breathing heavily into his cupped hands. "Perhaps I was too hasty in leaving Paris," he thought out loud.

"Pardon me?" The question came from another passenger who had just left the same train. He appeared to be a businessman returning home from Paris. He watched the odd-looking stranger warily.

"Nothing," replied Vincent. "I didn't think it would be so cold here."

"This is one of the worst winters we've had in many years," he said to Vincent. "The snow just seems to pile up daily. It has wreaked havoc on our crops. I'm not sure if our fruit trees will survive."

"I'm new in town," said Vincent. "Are there places to stay within a short walking distance?"

"There are several in this vicinity. What kind of lodging are you looking for?"

Arles-sur-Oise 1888

"Something not too expensive."

"Well, my good man, there are a couple of choices nearby. You might try the Hôtel Carrel. On Rue de la Cavalerie. A coachman will know it."

"Thank you, my friend." Vincent turned to a porter standing nearby. "Please take my things to a carriage." Vincent watched as the porter loaded his bags onto a waiting carriage and climbed aboard.

"Do you know Hôtel Carrel?" he asked the driver.

"Yes, of course, it is not far."

"Is it reasonably priced?"

"It is. Not many rooms though. Not many boarders, either."

"Take me there," said Vincent. His apprehension grew at the thought of having to face new surroundings. It would take time to adjust to these unfamiliar environs and he fervently hoped that it was worth the move away from Paris and his beloved brother.

The coach traveled along the Rhône past a large open park. During the day it was frequented by mothers with prams and once night fell, one often saw townspeople exercising their dogs or lovers strolling arm-in-arm. But today the park was deserted. The weather was simply not conducive to leisurely promenades. The cold wind coming off the water formed tiny icicles on Vincent's beard, encrusting his face with a hoary muzzle. The carriage turned left, away from the river and down a narrow street. It came to a halt in front of a limestone building marked by a single brown-stained door. The portal was flanked by a solid oak frame that had once been rich with vitality but was now weathered with age. The building consisted of just two levels. A wrought-iron balustrade was visible on the second floor. A sign suspended over the door read: "Restaurant and Hôtel Carrel."

"This is much better than I expected," Vincent mused, pleasantly surprised at the geniality of the inn. The driver unloaded his bags, canvases, and supplies and carried them inside, placing everything on the floor in front of an unpretentious mahogany desk. Vincent paid the driver and rang the bell on the desk. The clamor startled the innkeeper, who had been sneaking a short nap behind a closed door. He jumped to his feet, grabbing his apron as he received Vincent at the desk.

"Bon soir," said the short, chubby man. "You must be chilled to the marrow. Why, sir, you are trembling! Come and sit. Have something to eat and drink."

"I am looking for a room. Do you have one available for a single man?"

"We have a delightful room on the second floor, monsieur. How long do you want to stay?"

"I'm not sure. At least a week, maybe longer."

"We can arrange for a week. If you would like to stay longer, you must let me know in advance so I don't rent the room to someone else."

The innkeeper, Albert Carrel, and his wife, Catherine, helped Vincent move into his new quarters. The room was simple but warmly decorated, and Vincent thought the iron stove was large enough to heat an entire house. There was a single bed, a nightstand, table, bureau and a chair. There was ample room for Vincent to stack his canvases.

Vincent used the Hôtel Carrel as his base of operations for a few weeks. During the day, he ventured into the countryside to paint and visited shops in search of art that he thought might interest Theo. At night, he frequented the Café de la Gare where he became a regular fixture, taking his meals and drinking late into the evening. It was here where he came to know the proprietors, Joseph and Marie Ginoux.

When he was not painting or writing letters, he was reading, but the nights were long and Vincent took refuge in the local bordellos for the companionship that he missed. He found the women of Arles to be full-figured and Rubenesque in their beauty, which appealed to him greatly. Despite that, the nightlife in Arles was a far cry from that of Paris. Only the bordellos, a handful of cafés, and the Café de la Gare were open late into the evening.

Returning to the Hôtel Carrel early one evening, Vincent was met in the front lobby by Madame Carrel. "You have a letter, Vincent. It arrived this afternoon," she said as she handed him the envelope.

"Merci." Vincent sank into a nearby divan and opened the letter. It was from Émile.

Dear Vincent:

I was happy to receive your letter and to know that you arrived in Arles safe and secure. I have just returned from Brittany after a brief stay. There is much going on here! Russian police continue to search for anyone associated with the assassination attempt on the Tsar.

You are the smart one, leaving Paris. It appears that Marguerite has done likewise for she is nowhere to be found.

Thank you for the invitation to Arles but I must remain here with my family. These times are difficult. I must advise you to take all precautions. Be mindful of strangers!

Theo misses you. He does well with the Entrosol but his health is not good.

I will keep you apprised of events as they unfold—when I am able. Please destroy this letter once you have read it.

Your friend,
Émile

"Ah, Bernard, Bernard, you worry so much for someone so fortunate," Vincent murmured.

Chapter 29
Paris – Present Day

The hired car maneuvered through the Paris streets. Mark and Maggie sat in the backseat looking out at the light rain bouncing off the chic and colorful umbrellas of pedestrians. Only in Paris would one find such beautiful, art-inspired umbrellas, Mark thought to himself. Maggie turned her gaze from the bright streets to his shoulder. "I'm very nervous about this meeting," she said.

"Gastineau said he would be watching us. And we're wired so he can hear everything that is going on. Don't worry. Everything will be fine."

"I know, but I can't help being anxious. Let's go over it one more time."

Mark pursed his lips. "He said we should ask Durand if he could sell the journal—cash only. We have to get Durand to admit that he has sold art in this manner."

"Sounds simple enough," Maggie said slowly, but it was clear she wasn't convinced.

The two sat blankly staring at the Paris street scenes, caught up in their own thoughts. The silence was broken by the familiar ring tone Mark had reserved for Anton's calls.

Mark pulled the phone from his pocket. "Hello, Anton. Good to hear from you. What's up?"

Maggie looked quizzically at Mark, mouthing the words, "What does he want?"

Mark raised a finger. "I'll check with Maggie but I'm pretty sure Saturday works for us. We'll meet you at the main entrance of Les Invalides at two," he repeated, looking at Maggie. There was a moment of silence on Mark's end. Then he said, "Oh, so you know about that?"

Maggie's head whipped around like she had been struck by a heavy-weight fighter. She gaped expectantly at Mark.

"Yes, I'm sure he can be of help. Thanks. See you Saturday."

"What was that all about?" Maggie asked.

"Anton suggested that we spend Saturday playing tourist and then have dinner at his place."

"Yes, but what else did he say?"

"He said Victor was looking forward to our meeting and that he could help us establish the journal's authenticity."

"That's strange that Anton and Victor share so much."

"Yes, but they are friends. I suppose it's natural," Mark replied thoughtfully.

The car stopped in front of a building with a dark, red wood façade. The placard above the front door said, "Le Petit Roi." Mark and Maggie dashed through the rain and into the restaurant without a glance at the posted *carte du jour*. Once inside, they stomped their feet to remove the rainwater. Maggie gently smoothed her hair.

A round figure appeared at the archway separating the front of the restaurant from the rear of the building. Durand hesitated before shuffling over to the couple.

"Monsieur and Madame McFadden. It is so very nice to see you again. I am sorry about the weather, but I simply don't have control over it! Please follow me. I have a table in the back."

The back room was cozy, a few tables scattered about the room. A large ornate floor to ceiling bar took up one wall. Paintings by local artists filled the remaining walls. Durand took them to the back of the room, to the most remote table. The restaurant was otherwise empty.

"Please, sit and be comfortable. I arrived early to secure a place where we could talk in private." A smile came across his face, making his cheeks look like pink balloons, ready to burst. He pulled out a chair for Maggie.

"Thank you," she replied, sitting opposite the director.

A waiter appeared at their table and took their orders, then disappeared. Eager to get down to business, Durand turned his attention to the McFaddens. "Have you the journal? I would like to study it straight away."

"Before we go any further," Mark folded his hands with his elbows on the table and leaned forward. "We've been considering our options and we've decided that we want to sell the journal. Do you think you could find a buyer?"

Durand's eyes widened as he straightened in his chair. "Sell it? Why would you want to sell it? You do not know its value, if it has any value at all. It has not been properly examined."

"Monsieur Durand, I think we both know the journal is authentic—that it belonged to van Gogh," Mark said.

"I do not agree. I need much more time with it to verify its provenance."

Mark regarded Durand. "You strike me as a cautious man, but your persistence in obtaining the journal indicates to me that you believe it to be van Gogh's."

"I suspect that to be the case, but..."

Mark leaned in. "M. Durand, we have made up our minds. After our trip to Amsterdam, Maggie and I are certain that this is a lost van Gogh journal. We don't want to get involved with third party claims and the years of litigation that will most cer-

— 203 —

tainly follow. We want a fast cash sale and be done with it."

The conversation halted as the waiter brought their orders. When he left, Durand spoke up.

"Monsieur, you could take the journal to any number of auction houses and sell the journal."

"That would open us up to scrutiny—which we want to avoid. There would be questions as to how it came into our possession, then debates as to who its rightful owner is. Chances are that we would not have any rights. No rights—no money. So, my question for you, M. Durand, is can you find a buyer who will pay cash and keep our names out of any transaction?"

"You make this sound like you are looking for an accomplice rather than an art professional."

"Call it whatever you want. We just want a good price for it and we want it quickly," Mark answered evenly.

"I am a well-established, respected director of the Museum D'Orsay. I am not a middleman or as you say in America, a 'fence.' Nor do I find buyers for an antiquity whose provenance has not been determined by a professional."

Mark looked at Maggie, "Well, I think we're done here. We should go." The couple pushed their chairs back in unison.

"Wait," said Durand. "Wait," he repeated, lowering his voice. "You two surprise me." He motioned for them to sit. "Perhaps I can be of some assistance. So, you want to sell the journal. But what if it is not authentic?"

"I think we both know it is," said Mark.

"If I were to broker a sale, I must be certain the work is authentic. That means I will have to take possession of it and run at least some rudimentary tests."

"Hmm," said Mark rubbing his cheek. "No, I don't think

so. I'm satisfied that it is the real deal. Can you help us, or do I have to find someone else?"

"No! Okay, okay. How much do you want for the journal? And how do I know that you won't cut me out of the deal once I find a buyer?" Durand asked.

Mark looked at Maggie, then turned to Durand. "Two million Euro. I'm a man of my word. You will get your fair share—a small percentage of the purchase price. Much more than you could make at the museum in a year."

"Monsieur! You must be joking! Without so much as any proof of its authenticity, no one will pay that much!"

"This journal is worth much more than that. Are you in or are you out?"

Durand studied Mark's face. "You are very bold, my friend. What made you think you could ask me to sell the journal?"

"You did not go to your supervisor nor any other official, yet you are very persistent about getting your hands on the journal. I asked myself 'why?' I began to think there was something else in the mix. Perhaps it is professional reward or true interest in art. But I think not. You do not strike me as a man who is obsessed with his professional reputation. Why else would you be relegated to a basement office away from other museum officials? So I thought to the root of all evil: money. A find of this magnitude would either boost your reputation or make you wealthy. I suspected the latter would motivate you."

Durand finally spoke. "Perceptive of you." He leaned forward and whispered. "Money may be the root of all evil, but it does make life bearable, even enjoyable. Very well, I will find you a buyer. But, a word of caution. Do not cross me. We are in this together. You, me," Durand looked at Maggie "and your wife.

Do we understand each other?"

"Perfectly."

Victor leaned back in his chair, smiling, *"Très bien.* Now, let us have a drink to celebrate our collaboration."

"No, thank you. How long before I hear from you?"

"Soon, I expect. Very soon."

The couple rose and walked toward the door, leaving Victor Durand to celebrate alone.

Gastineau was waiting at their house in d'Avray. "You did well. I heard every word."

"I have to admit that I was scared shitless, er, I mean…"

"I know what you mean, Monsieur McFadden."

"What now?" asked Maggie.

"We wait. Once Durand gets in touch with you, we will form our plan."

"I still don't like it," said Maggie. "What if he just decides to come here and pay us a visit?"

"We will have someone watching your house. I do not think Durand is a violent man. He is a pawn in a larger game."

"Yeah," said Mark "well, what if he has a violent associate who decides to come for a visit?"

Gastineau walked to the door. "Please, trust us. We will be on guard. In the meantime, please continue with your usual routine."

Shutting the door, Mark looked at Maggie and shrugged. "In for a penny, in for a pound."

Chapter 30
Arles-sur-Oise – Spring-Summer 1888

The four-room house was just a few doors down from the Café de la Gare. Vincent fell in love with it immediately. It had a living area and a kitchen on the ground floor and two bedrooms on the second. The house had been vacant for many years, as evidenced by the peeling exterior paint. Despite its flaws, Vincent thought it the perfect place to set up his studio. He quickly rented it, telling Theo in a long letter that he could cut costs by using the house as both a residence and a studio. With money received from his brother, he hired a local man to do repairs that included repainting the exterior a cheery yellow and the shutters black. In the interior, he focused on the first floor. He intended to make the large living area into his studio and sleeping quarters. By springtime, Vincent had moved his art supplies and his canvases into his new house, bidding farewell to the Carrels and the hotel.

At last, summer brought the warmth that Vincent expected of southern France. He continued his feverish pace, painting multiple canvases each week as well as sketching and letter writing. But his appeals to Émile and Gauguin to join him in Arles went unanswered. Alone, Vincent filled his evenings smoking and drinking while watching the ebb and flow of patrons at the local cafés and bordellos.

In a Paris café, Marguerite was sipping coffee with her cousin, Count Esterhazy.

"I am concerned," Esterhazy said, pointing to a copy of

a newspaper lying on the table. The headline read: *Kaiser Dead. Wilhelm II Ascends To German Throne.*

"You promised to use your influence with the Germans to help me. Now this! Three Kaisers in one year! How can I trust you to keep your word?" Esterhazy demanded, nostrils flaring.

"Stop worrying, dear cousin. Have I ever let you down?" Marguerite soothed.

"I didn't mean to imply that you would let me down. It's just that there are things beyond your control. You are overly confident in your ability to manipulate people."

"Have patience!" She hissed. "I have the Germans where I want them. Ah, here is our comrade now." Esterhazy turned his head to see Pierre striding across the room toward them.

"Esterhazy, I haven't had the pleasure of your company for some time. Are you being useful or are we wasting our money on you as usual?" Pierre asked, scornfully.

"Well, you must know, I have a new position that puts me closer to the intelligence branch. Despite what you think, Pierre, my connections will prove to be quite useful in this operation."

Marguerite shot a disapproving glance at Pierre. "Pierre, why must you be so hurtful to Ferdinand? You should treat him with respect."

"I will—when he earns it. But now you and I must talk. Alone."

Gathering up his cap and briefcase, Esterhazy rose from his chair. He turned to Pierre and opened his mouth as if to speak but said nothing. *The bastard isn't worth it,* he thought. He nodded to his cousin and walked briskly away. Pierre lowered himself into the seat that Esterhazy had just vacated.

"Pierre, must you be so hard on him? He is working with us, not against us. Remember, we are on the same side! All you do is criticize him," she chastised.

"He will cause us trouble one day. You will see. If he were not your cousin..." Pierre's jaw tightened, and he went silent.

Marguerite let the matter drop and asked, "What news have you for me today?"

"This new Wilhelm is not someone the Chancellor expected to have to deal with. I understand Frederick's death was completely unexpected."

"So I have read. How does that affect us?"

"The new Kaiser is different than his brother. He may present us with some challenges. I think we must redouble our efforts to drive a wedge between France and Russia. The Chancellor was most impressed by your approach. He wants you to act again, but this time it must be more dramatic and with more direct links to the French."

The waiter appeared at their table, ready to take their order. Marguerite brushed him off. When he was out of earshot, she leaned into the table and whispered, "These things do not just occur overnight. There is much planning involved. Staging is critical."

"That, Madame, is entirely your problem. The Chancellor wants further action, quickly and with stronger ties to Paris. Those are his words. The French are making strong overtures to the Tsar. The Chancellor does not want anything, I repeat, anything, to bring the two countries together. Did you not read the speech he made to Parliament? He predicted the Balkans will be the next flash point. Germany is not ready for another war, not yet. We must have assurances that France will stay isolated. A two-front war would devastate Germany."

Marguerite let out a deep sigh. Why am I the lucky one, she thought.

"He believes in you. Even I must admit, you have always delivered on your promises. But it has cost our treasury dearly."

"Your point is not lost on me, Pierre."

"I must tell you, I think you have motives other than protecting Germany and the Chancellor. He deems you a patriot. I think you are something quite different. I see how you use your influence and money—German money no less—to advance yourself and your family in the French aristocracy. You are playing both ends against the middle and it will come back to haunt you."

"Are you and the Chancellor getting adequate value for your money?"

"He says yes. I have yet to decide."

"Well, my friend, his is the only opinion that counts. Tell the Chancellor I will not fail him. It may take some time and additional money, but he will get what he asks for."

"Someday, Marguerite, you will disappoint, and I will be there to gloat."

"Until that time, Pierre—adieu."

Chapter 31
Arles-sur-Oise – Summer-Autumn 1888

Isolation... anger... despair... angst... these were the myriad of emotions Vincent experienced as summer dragged on. He was on his own in Arles, isolated from the familiar environs of Paris and his artist friends. He felt the need to keep himself as busy as possible to ward off his growing anxiety. Fortunately, Theo had forgiven him for his hasty departure and was sending him money each month along with paint and supplies.

One evening, rather than sit alone in his studio, Vincent set off to take in the clamor of the café. Evenings at the Café de la Gare, especially during the summer months, were filled with a flurry of activity as men came and went amidst boisterous laughter. As Vincent entered, he was greeted by a familiar voice, that of his friend, Milliet, a French lieutenant, fully dressed in his colorful military garb. A waiter took Vincent's order as he seated himself at his friend's table.

"Vincent, I haven't seen you in a while. What have you been up to?" he asked.

"Hello, Milliet. I went down to the shore to sketch. It's quite lovely there. Serene and yet life-affirming."

"What did you sketch?"

"Fishing boats on the shore. Waves lapping the beach, men with their nets, women in sun bonnets."

"What do you do with all of these paintings, my friend?" asked the lieutenant.

"I keep several at my studio but I have sent many to my brother and a few to other artists."

"Ah, I see! Has your brother sold any?"

The waiter returned with a glass of green shimmering liquid and placed it in front of Vincent. Vincent peered into his absinthe for a few seconds before he spoke.

"Not yet. But Theo's displaying three of my landscapes at a very prestigious art show in Paris, Le Salon des Indépendants. I'm sure that this will be a turning point for me. It is, after all, a showing by nontraditional, innovative artists such as I."

"Well, then, a toast to your future success!" The lieutenant raised his glass and, with his customary exuberance, downed the rest of his drink. Vincent quietly took a small sip of his absinthe, sheepishly eyeing his friend. He had already read a review of his work by the noted art critic, Gustave Kahn. Kahn was not complimentary, stating that Vincent paid too little attention to the value and precision of his tones, among other artistic shortcomings.

Vincent was livid—and hurt. But as his passion for his art intensified, he became more troubled. Cognac, absinthe and cheap whores occupied his nights. He found it difficult to become aroused. He blamed his condition on age, not syphilis.

Furthermore, Vincent was unable to convince any artist to join him in the Yellow House. Both Émile Bernard and Paul Gauguin had refused, as had several others. Paul was not much of a correspondent, but he wrote to Vincent a couple of times with complaints of his health and his shared dismal financial situation. Ill and unable to work, Gauguin was staying in Brittany at a hotel near the sea, eating on credit and producing very little art. He implored

Vincent to intercede with his brother for money. This was just the opportunity that Vincent was waiting for—a chance to lure Gauguin to Arles.

He proposed to Theo that Gauguin be paid a stipend to come and stay with Vincent in the Yellow House. In return, Gauguin would send Theo two paintings a month. This was not exactly what Gauguin had in mind, but given his dire financial straits, he accepted the offer.

As he awaited Gauguin's arrival, Vincent increased the financial demands on his brother. Theo knew Vincent was living from hand to mouth and continued to help him as best he could. Vincent wrote often of his intent to cut back on his expenses by sketching more and using fewer canvases and oils, but other expenses took their place, like the furniture and curtains Vincent purchased to prepare Gauguin's room for his impending arrival.

August expired and September was coming to a close. Gauguin still had not arrived in Arles. In October, Vincent wrote again to his friend:

...I must tell you that even while working I think continually about the plan of setting up a studio in which you and I will be permanent residents, but which both of us want to turn into a shelter and refuge for friends, against times when they find that the struggle is getting too much for them.

...I have been thinking of you with very great emotion as I prepared your studio...

Vincent slipped further into a fragile state. The passing of time without companionship, and the ups and downs of promises made then broken, left him bitter and anxious. He lay down to sleep but sleep would not come easily. After several hours of tossing and turning, he drifted off. He woke suddenly, sweat covering his body. His bedclothes were wet to the touch and his hair matted against his skull. He jumped up and poured water from the ewer into his hands and splashed his face with the cool liquid. Beads of moisture formed on his craggy face. He was vaguely aware of where he was, but the fog of sleep was swirling in his head. He remembered falling into an abyss, the darkening sky closing in on him and obliterating all light. His arms and legs had flailed in an inky darkness as deep as the eye could see. It all seemed so real, and he shook from the image in his mind.

He lit a lantern. As he looked around the room, gathering his senses, his angst increased. He longed to be with Theo, to share a drink, a meal, a conversation—anything with the one person he truly loved.

"Mon Dieu, get a hold of yourself! For God's sake, get yourself together!" he whispered. Looking out the tiny window toward the park, Vincent realized that it was nearly morning. "I must get a grip. A firm grip," he sighed.

Turning back, facing his bed, he realized he was too weary and hungover to work. He sat on the bed, cradling his head in hands. Slowly he lay back, "Please, no more dreams!" he pleaded silently as the death grip of sleep took him once again.

Chapter 32
Paris – Present Day

The weather was perfect for an outdoor excursion on the day they had planned to meet Anton and his family in Paris. The deep blue skies were sprinkled with billowing white clouds. Mark and Maggie asked the taxi driver to drop them off near Les Invalides.

"I hate to be late," said Mark, tugging at Maggie's arm. He hurried her along, quickening his pace.

"Anton will wait. After all, this is Paris. Who's really ever on time in Paris?" she asked flippantly.

Just then Mark saw an arm thrust skyward. "There's Anton. And Sarah."

The couples hugged and pecked at each other's cheeks. "Did you have any difficulty finding a place to park?" asked Anton.

"Not at all," replied Mark. "We took a cab. I figured it would be easier since we didn't really know where we were going. Besides, I'm not particularly fond of driving in Paris."

Anton chuckled. "No one is. Let me gather up the boys and perhaps we can behave like tourists." Anton called to the two boys running in the open courtyard. They answered immediately, laughing and skipping their way to the adults.

"Guillaume, Louis, do you remember Monsieur and Madame McFadden?"

Maggie bent over and extended her hand. In French she said, "I'm sure you don't remember me but I knew you when you were little boys. Now you are young men! Do you have any girlfriends yet? I'll bet they chase after you in the playground, don't they?"

"Non!" they replied in unison. Guillaume added, "But Louis is looking for a girlfriend!"

Maggie laughed. "I'm sure he will find at least one—maybe two!"

"Come," coaxed Anton, "let us show you parts of our beautiful city."

The couples roamed Les Invalides, the French Army Museum and the site of Napoleon's tomb. Next, they strolled along the Seine, walked under the Eiffel Tower and took in some of the Paris gardens. Before long, Anton was looking at his watch, "It is now six. I know you Americans dine earlier than we do in France. I suggest we make our way to our flat. We'd like to show you our home and cook for you."

"Should we get a taxi?" asked Mark.

"It is not necessary. We are close. Our building is just up the avenue at Rue Decamp and Rue de Longchamp."

Anton's apartment was on the fifth floor of a corner building that overlooked the Place de Mexico. The front door opened to an expansive two-story foyer with alabaster marble floors and floral print wallpaper above a decorative chair rail moulding.

"Oh my," cooed Maggie. "This is lovely."

"Thank you," answered Sarah. "We sometimes have to entertain for Anton's work and we like to keep it inviting. Let me show you the rest of the apartment."

The living room ceilings, like the rest of the house, were fourteen feet high, set off by elaborate painted crown molding. Persian rugs adorned the parquet floors. The furnishings were a tasteful mixture of Louis XIV integrated with modern accent pieces. "We have been told that Louis Pasteur once lived in this building," said Anton. "Somehow, I doubt it."

Adjacent to the living room was the kitchen where two people were busy preparing dinner. "This is Jordain, our chef, and Florence, his wife. Florence makes the finest soufflés in Paris," beamed Sarah. "I spend much of my time in the kitchen," said Sarah, leading them into the spacious room. "Most Parisians don't linger here as you Americans like to do. I love the conviviality and warmth of your eat-in kitchens. French kitchens are typically designed for pure functionality; they are small and utilitarian with no place to relax and enjoy a small meal. We even have a full-sized American-style refrigerator and have added room for a morning table. I like to have breakfast here and sometimes I like to bake and have company in the kitchen."

Maggie fingered the marble countertops and admired the abundant work area. A splendid glass chandelier hung over the center island. Each cabinet looked as though it were an exquisite piece of furniture made just for that space.

"Come, let's make ourselves comfortable in the den while Jordain and Florence work their magic," said Anton. The den boasted four floor-to-ceiling windows with heavy satin drapes. Sheers had been pulled to diffuse the light from the setting sun, basking the room in a soft, rosy glow.

"Where did the boys go?" asked Maggie.

"Oh, they have their own rooms on the other side of the apartment. They'll join us in a little while."

"This is my special room," said Anton. "My 'man-cave' as you Americans like to call it. This is where I relax. I find it very soothing."

"I can certainly see why," said Mark. Anton handed a glass of white wine to each of his guests. "A Sauterne from the Bordeaux region," he announced. "A little bit sweet but with a lovely, slightly citrus nose. I hope you enjoy it."

Maggie breathed in the fruity aroma of the wine. "Ah." She took a sip. "Anton, this has a nice balance of sweetness and acidity. I think I detect a little peach in it. Lovely. I am loathe to admit it, but as much as I enjoy California wines, they don't quite equal the French labels."

Mark walked the perimeter of the room, admiring the dreamy landscapes and lifelike portraits. "These are magnificent," Maggie said as she came alongside Mark. She slipped her hand into his as they inched around the room. Suddenly, her grip tightened and they both stopped. She bent close to inspect a nearly monochromatic portrait of a man with a large black and silver mustache. He was dressed in a black suit with a white collared shirt and a white kerchief. His eyes were dark and threatening, framed at the top by high arching brows and below by deep circles. His hair was mostly silver and revealed a high forehead. In the lower right-hand corner, a signature could be discerned. It simply said: 'Vincent.'

"I see you've found my prize possession," said Anton, coming up behind them. "This is a portrait of one of my ancestors, Pierre Schlairet."

"Is that Vincent van Gogh's signature?" asked Mark, pointing incredulously.

"It is indeed. The family is not certain how van Gogh came to paint Pierre but it is thought to have been commissioned because Pierre was a prominent member of

Bismarck's cabinet."

"Otto von Bismarck?" asked Maggie.

"The same. He was most likely involved in diplomacy between Germany and France after the Franco-Prussian war. The family rumor was that Pierre was placed in France by Bismarck after the war and, after France repaid the reparations, he chose to remain in Paris."

Mark began to say, "I think we've seen…" but Maggie squeezed his hand and he halted in mid-sentence. He turned to face her and their eyes met. She was silently pleading with him to say no more.

"I'm sorry, what did you say, Mark?"

"I don't think I've seen a van Gogh in any private collection. This is amazing!"

"Thank you. I think Jordain is ready for us in the dining room. Sarah, do you want to call the boys?"

Chapter 33
Paris – Present Day

Mark and Maggie huddled in the back seat of the taxi. "Anton and Sarah have a beautiful home. I didn't expect a place so large and decorated in such style," said Maggie.

"Yeah, he sure has done well."

"I didn't think we should say anything to Anton about his van Gogh," whispered Maggie.

"I got that. I have to admit, I was a bit surprised to see a van Gogh in Anton's apartment. I didn't think van Gogh sold any paintings during his lifetime."

"Just one. But he certainly was not commissioned to paint any official portraits. He may have given some of his work away, though. I'm pretty sure that the figure in the painting is the man van Gogh sketched in the journal."

"I'd like to take a second look at the sketch," Mark thought aloud.

"Yeah," agreed Maggie. "Such an odd coincidence."

Monday afternoon they went to the local bank in d'Avray and, after retrieving their safety deposit box, were escorted into a private area. Mark opened the lid. "Did you bring the latex gloves?"

"Yep, got 'em right here."

They carefully leafed through the journal until they found the sketch of the mustachioed man.

"Okay, here's the picture of Anton's relative. Vincent called him 'Pierre.' It is definitely the same man."

Mark squinted over Maggie's shoulder to examine the

sketch in the dim light. "It sure is!"

"This is really very strange," Mark mused. "This Pierre, Anton, van Gogh, Marguerite, Madame Chauvenal... all somehow interrelated.

Mark met her gaze and replied, "Mags, I just do not believe in happenstance."

"I don't either. See what you can find about Anton's painting. I want to know what the public records show."

Mark pulled out his phone and searched the internet for van Gogh's oil paintings. "Man, this guy was prolific! I've got a site that lists his paintings by category, year, and subject. There are hundreds!"

"Look for portraits from around 1887 to 1890." She shifted to his side and watched as he went from one record to the next. "There. That's it!" she exclaimed. *Portrait of a Man with a Mustache.* 'Whereabouts unknown. Private collection. Winter 1886-1887. Oil on canvas.' Well, we know where it is. Mark, I have to ask, does Anton come from money?"

"I didn't think so. He went to Stanford on a fellowship. I always thought his parents were working class folks. At least, that's what he led me to believe."

"Well, he sure has money now. That van Gogh alone is worth a fortune."

"He had me fooled. Hell, I bought most of the beer in graduate school because he was always broke," Mark grumbled.

"Let me assure you that any hospital department head who has a van Gogh, a private chef, and a luxury apartment is not broke."

They returned home later that day and Mark sat watching the sun move lower in the sky. At any moment it would disappear behind the trees surrounding the old house. His stomach rumbled.

"My stomach is talking to me. Do you want to get a bite to eat?" he asked.

"Sounds good to me. I didn't realize how late it was. Let me change my shoes. I'll be ready in a minute," Maggie replied.

A sharp rap at the door drew Mark away from his laptop. "Who could that be?" he mumbled to himself. He opened the door to find Phillippe Gastineau standing with his hat in hand.

"Commissaire, what brings you out at this hour?"

"Monsieur McFadden, I am sorry to bother you, but may I come in?" he queried.

"Certainly," Mark said, stepping back to allow his guest into the room.

"Is your wife at home?"

"Yes, she will be down in a minute. We were just going out for dinner. What's going on?"

"I am sorry to interrupt. But if you don't mind, I will wait until your wife is present to say what I have to say."

"In that case, please have a seat.""

Maggie bounded down the steps, fastening an earring onto her left earlobe, oblivious to the rap at the door. "So where do you… oh! Commissaire! I didn't realize you were here!"

"Good evening. And I do apologize for the inconvenience, Madame."

"It's quite all right." Maggie looked quizzically at Mark.

"The Commissaire wants to talk to us," explained Mark. "We were just waiting for you."

The officer took his notebook from his suit coat. "Have you spoken with Victor Durand since our last conversation?"

"No," answered Mark. "Why do you ask?"

"It seems M. Durand has not shown up at the d'Orsay since he met with you."

"Really? Is that unusual?" asked Maggie.

"Yes. No one seems to know his whereabouts. He has not called into his office and there is no answer on his cell phone or at his house."

"When we left him, I had the impression he was going to look for a buyer for the journal. Maybe he is out trying to scare up some money," Mark shrugged.

"That could be, but..."

"Do you think something happened to him?" Maggie asked with mounting alarm.

"Are you positive he did not say where he was going after you left him?

"Positive," said Mark.

"Did he appear nervous or afraid?"

"No. He seemed calm."

Gastineau let out a deep sigh. "Have you noticed anything out of the ordinary this past week?"

"I'm not sure what you mean by that."

"Any vehicles or people that might be following you?"

"No, M. Gastineau. But you're making me nervous," said Maggie. "What's going on?"

Gastineau leaned forward. "I have something else to

tell you," he said. "I do not wish to alarm you but I feel a warning is necessary. My colleagues at the Sûreté just told me they suspect M. Durand may have been involved in the deaths of four petty art thieves over the past six years."

"What?" Mark sputtered. "Do you really mean Durand is a murderer?"

Gastineau raised his hand to halt Mark's outburst. "I just learned this myself. The Sûreté only suspect his involvement. They do not know for sure."

"Are you telling me that you may have put Maggie at risk?" he asked shrilly.

"I assure you that you are not in any danger."

Mark cut him off. "Really? You don't know that—"

Mark's rant was interrupted by his cell ringing.

Gastineau pointed to the phone, "You may want to get that."

Mark hesitated a moment. "Hello, this is Mark McFadden," he answered, trying to disguise the anger in his voice.

"Monsieur McFadden, this is Laurent calling on behalf of Madame Chauvenal. I hope I did not call at an inconvenient time."

"No… no. Please go on."

"Madame asked me to invite you and Madame McFadden to dine with her on Thursday evening at the estate. If you are available, of course."

Mark's shoulders relaxed slightly and his demeanor steadied. "Laurent, we would be delighted. What time should we arrive? Oh, and what is the dress code, if I may ask?"

"Seven o'clock for cocktails. Dinner will be served at eight. It is casual. A cravat is not necessary."

"Please tell Madame Chauvenal we would be delighted. We are looking forward to seeing her again."

"Excellent. I will let Madame know you will come. Thank you."

Mark looked at his wife. "Madame Chauvenal has invited us to dinner on Thursday night."

"I must say," remarked Gastineau, "you are mingling with the highest that French society has to offer." Abruptly, Gastineau announced, "I must be on my way."

"M. Gastineau," chided Mark, "I don't think we were finished discussing the danger you've put us in."

"I assure you that you are in no danger if you follow my directions and keep me informed of everything you are doing and the people that you see. Please telephone me right away if you are contacted by Durand." Gastineau walked quickly to the door. *"Adieu."*

The door closed gently behind him. Maggie turned to Mark. "That was a very strange reaction, don't you think?"

"What do you mean?"

"Here we are, in a heated conversation about Durand being a murderer and you get a call inviting us to Mme. Chauvenal's and suddenly he has to leave?"

Mark shrugged. "Maybe he just saw his opportunity to get out while he could—before I tore him a new asshole, that is."

"I don't know," Maggie said thoughtfully. "There was something odd in his behavior."

"I wouldn't make anything of it, Maggie."

Maggie went to the window and looked out. Gastineau was looking back at the house. Then he climbed into his Renault and left. "I don't know," she said to herself.

Chapter 34
Arles-sur-Oise – Autumn 1888

Vincent had been working steadily on a painting for Joseph Ginoux, the hotel proprietor, for three long nights. Finally, he put the last brush stroke on the white figure of Ginoux standing at attention by the billiard table of his café. He motioned for the proprietor to come see the fruits of his labor.

"I have decided to call this *The Night Café*," he told Ginoux. The owner's shoulders slumped and his arms fell to his sides. "This does not look like my place. It is lifeless and the crowds are missing!"

"This is not simply what I see, but it's what I feel when I look upon this room," Vincent explained. "I've tried to show the café as a place where one can lose himself completely. Can you not see the powers of darkness in this piece?" He was not up to justifying his work. It spoke for itself.

Ginoux's less-than-thrilled reaction thrust Vincent into a foul mood. Wordlessly, he snatched up the canvas and headed back to his room. As he placed his canvas on the floor against the wall, he noticed an envelope with familiar handwriting. "Ah, Theo," he mused, "I'd rather you were here instead of your letters." He opened the envelope and began to read, his disappointment subsiding as he took in each sentence. A smile crossed his face. Gauguin had finally agreed to come to Arles and would arrive in a fortnight! "This is the change I longed for! Thank you, God! Thank you, Theo!"

Giant marshmallow puffs of smoke billowed from the steam engine as it approached the Arles station. Gauguin's impending arrival made Vincent giddy with excitement and the carnival-like atmosphere of the station was almost too much for him to bear. The aroma of fresh bread and chocolate filled his nostrils. He paced back and forth across the massive stone ramp that led passengers from the the trains.

He had prepared for Paul's arrival for several days, putting the Yellow House in perfect order. He had purchased two beds with complementary nightstands, wash basins, and curtains for a cozier touch. He filled the rooms with his paintings, which had recently been much more colorful, reflecting his positive outlook for a productive endeavor with his colleague and friend.

The steam from the locomotive in the near distance seemed to hang in space, the train never making any forward progress. The anticipation felt as agonizing as the loneliness he had been experiencing in Arles. Slowly, the light from the engine made its way through the smoke into his line of sight, the whistle growing louder with every passing second. At last the train made its final approach to the platform and came to a stop just beyond the station so that the last passenger car and freight car were aligned with the platform. All along the station people were craning through the windows to catch a glimpse of lovers and friends making their way down the aisle toward the exit. The jovial conductor helped people off the train, careful that each woman was offered his hand as she descended. Nearby, the rail workers unloaded crates from the freight car.

People quickly filled the exits to welcome their travelers

with handshakes and embraces. Their lively chatter further heightened Vincent's excitement. Then he spied his friend, standing tall and lean in the doorway, coat open, his wavy hair slightly stirring in the light breeze, about to make his own dramatic entrance. Gauguin was striking in so many ways and Vincent felt his heart flutter with exhilaration at the sight of him. Oddly, Paul was peering back into the train as though searching for someone. Just then, Vincent made out the silhouette of a woman. Gauguin stepped off the train, his arm extended toward her. Gracefully, she stepped down onto the platform. They could have been lovers, the way they looked at each other. She giggled as Gauguin murmured in her ear.

Feeling a bit guarded, Vincent watched until a young man drew near to the woman and embraced her. The two strode away, arm in arm. Gauguin's smiling eyes followed her as she left the train station.

Gauguin immediately spied Vincent approaching. He steeled himself and forced a smile. Patience. Remember you need the money. Consider this the price of accepting the stipend. God, I hope this place has women and bars. I'm going to require some pleasurable diversions, he thought.

"Paul! I've been looking forward to your arrival. I'm delighted to see you. You look well. Are you fully recovered from your illness? I expected to find a much frailer fellow! Instead I'm greeting a robust Casanova! Your handshake is as hearty as ever!"

"Hello, my friend. Yes, I am in reasonably good shape. Likewise, it is wonderful to see you, too. How have you been? Your letters have told me quite a bit about your artistic endeavors. You've been a very busy fellow!"

"I'm well enough, but now that you're here, I'm certain I'll be even better. Come, our house is not far. I've done what I could to make it comfortable for you. I hope you will find it to your liking."

"One moment, please, Vincent. I must retrieve my trunk from the train." Turning to the freight car, Paul said, "Ah, there it is."

"Allow me to get it for you, Paul. It looks like you already have quite a load."

"Many thanks, Vincent."

The two men walked down the platform and into the small station. Gauguin one pace ahead of Vincent, who was struggling with the cumbersome trunk. It was growing heavier with each footstep.

"Where are the coaches?" asked Gauguin, looking around the open surroundings.

"I thought we would walk, which is usually my preferred mode of transportation, but this is very heavy! Wait, there's a coach," Vincent said pointing to a one-horse taxi. Gauguin motioned to the driver and the carriage pulled in front of them. Gauguin placed his bags, including his paint box and supplies, into the front passenger seat and climbed into the carriage while Vincent, unaided, wrestled with the oversized trunk. At last he was able to hoist the trunk into the back of the carriage. Perspiring, he squeezed himself next to the load, facing Gauguin. "Two Lamartine, driver!" wheezed Vincent. "It is the yellow house on the corner."

"I received the paintings you sent," Gauguin said, hunkering down into his seat. They were quite lovely. Émile also got the paintings you sent him."

"Excellent. I hoped you would like them. I have spent a lot of time working on my technique, experimenting with color and varieties of paint."

Peering out the window, Paul asked, "This seems like a large park. Are we near the center of town?"

"Well, the town of Arles is actually on both sides of the river. Our studio and house are on the other side of the park."

"I imagine this is lovely in springtime," Paul mused. The carriage came to an abrupt stop in front of the yellow house. The driver jumped down from his seat to assist the travelers.

"Is this it?" Paul asked, making little attempt to conceal his disappointment.

"Yes, but it is much nicer inside. I've spent a lot of time and a small fortune fixing it up. It was a true eyesore when I rented it."

"Hmmm, yes, I can tell." Gauguin walked to the front door and examined the rusted doorknob, hesitating before entering. He surveyed his new surroundings. Directly ahead, at the end of the hallway, were stairs. On the right was a doorway that opened to the art studio. Half of the room was barren while the other half was filled with canvases, some empty and some completed. Supplies and an easel were perched against one wall. The clutter on one side provided a stark contrast to the emptiness on the other.

With a heavy sigh, Gauguin turned toward the open door just in time to see Vincent heaving the oversized trunk through the entrance.

Arles-sur-Oise 1888

"I see you have cleared a space for me in the studio," he noted.

Huffing, Vincent replied, "Indeed, the studio is for both of us. The bedrooms are up the stairs."

Ignoring Vincent's battle with the trunk, Paul started for the staircase. Vincent called after him. "This trunk is too heavy for me to carry up these steps. Can you help me?"

Gauguin turned to face Vincent, eyeing the trunk lying in the middle of the hallway. He waited a moment, then marched toward his belongings. Wordlessly, he reached down and took hold of one handle and lifted. Vincent took the other end and slowly the men hoisted the trunk up the stairs.

"Your bedroom is on the right, facing the street. Mine is on the left," directed Vincent.

The room was freshly painted in linen-white and a bed was positioned against one wall. A chair stood next to the bed and a small bureau with a ewer was on the other side of the bed. Across from the foot of the bed a window, framed by light curtains, overlooked the park, which was now gracefully covered with leaves of red, orange, and amber-yellow. Two canvases hung in the room. One depicted the room itself and the other a single, bright yellow sunflower.

"It is small, but nice," Paul remarked as he scanned his quarters.

"I wanted to make it as bright and cheerful as possible. This will be a wonderful time! I have been so looking forward to our collaboration. Let's set up the studio now so tomorrow we can start in earnest."

"I am a bit weary after the trip and would prefer that we wait until tomorrow to set up the studio. Let's see, where is the washroom?"

"We have to use the one next door or at the local café. I could get you a chamber pot, if you'd like."

"Ugh. No washroom? No, I don't want a pot in these close quarters. Perhaps we should take a break and see what the local café has to offer."

They left the house and headed to the Café de la Gare. As they entered the restaurant, a short bespectacled man hurried across the room to greet them and gushed, "So, you must be the new artist from Paris that van Gogh has told us about! I am Joseph Ginoux, the owner of this fine establishment. Welcome!"

Gauguin was slightly taken aback by Ginoux's enthusiastic greeting. He looked at the proprietor and then at Vincent. Momentarily, he extended his hand to Ginoux and said, "I am Paul Gauguin. A pleasure to make your acquaintance, kind sir."

"This early in the day we have lots of empty seats and we offer a full menu. Sit wherever you like. Coffee? What is your pleasure, gentlemen?" Ginoux was keen to accommodate his new and distinguished guest.

"I would like a coffee and a baguette," answered Paul.

"Coffee for me, Ginoux," added Vincent. The two men found an empty table off to the side of the room, away from the few remaining drunks.

"I did not expect to be so well regarded before my arrival. What have you told your friends about me, van Gogh?" Paul asked.

"I merely mentioned that you would be coming and staying with me." Vincent tried to downplay his eagerness.

"Well, I certainly hope you informed the gentler sex of

my arrival," smiled Paul. "Speaking of the gentler sex, who's that on the other side of the billiard table?"

"That is Ginoux's wife, Marie. She is very standoffish and aloof. No sense of humor."

"We shall see. She would be a good first subject." Gauguin grinned from ear to ear at his friend.

Pierre was seated next to Marguerite on a park bench in central Paris, taking in the crisp fall air. A light breeze was blowing, scattering the orange and crimson leaves all about. Children laughed as they played bilboquet or "catch the ball in a cup," using homemade canvas balls and strings of yarn.

"Are all of your plans in place?" Pierre asked his companion.

Marguerite kept her gaze on the children as she answered. "Yes, we are ready. We just received the royal itinerary. It was the missing piece. The men are now preparing the package."

"I'll feel better when this is done and the Chancellor is more at ease with the new Kaiser. He is finding Wilhelm quite difficult. He's making lots of demands on the Chancellor, taking his attention away from more critical things. He cannot see the forest for the trees."

"The new Kaiser is just trying to be his own man. The Chancellor has dealt with much worse."

"I'm not so sure." Pierre looked askance at Marguerite.

"Well, my dear Pierre, how the Chancellor handles Wilhelm is not in my control. I will complete my mission, and then he will have his opportunity to deepen the division between France and Russia. But, to finish up our business here, there are a few more requests I must make."

"What now, Marguerite?" he asked with a trace of exasperation in his voice.

"First of all, I expect that a few of these Commune members may become erratic once they hear of our actions. We need them to stay calm and in place to help facilitate the connection between them and our actions." Marguerite's face was serious, her voice low.

"How do you propose to do that?" Pierre wanted to know.

"We will have one last meeting of the group. Once the news is reported in Paris, I need you to set up this meeting. I will quell their fears."

"And your other requests?" Pierre asked.

"My cousin, Ferdinand, could use some help, especially financially. And he wants to feel like he's a true contributor. Push your colleagues in the German embassy to take him more seriously."

"He's a buffoon. I don't want anything to do with him," Pierre sniffed, his nose up in the air. "You're asking me to stake my reputation on that idiot."

"He may be a buffoon, but he is my relative. And your controllers promised to help him."

"Scheisse! Merde!" Pierre spat. "Well! Anything else?"

"Why, yes, one more thing. My payment. I expect full payment once our actions have been successful. And by that, I must be clear, Pierre, I mean full payment is due once the attempt on the Tsar's life is made and a connection to France is established."

"The Chancellor will decide when payment is made," Pierre shrugged. "It's not up to you or me."

"Then I shall see the Chancellor. I'm sure my presence in Berlin will be appreciated," Marguerite smirked.

Arles-sur-Oise 1888

"You are not to even try to see him!" Pierre half-stood in fury.

"Then I expect full payment as we discussed. You have my account numbers. Do not make me regret working with you or the Chancellor." Marguerite was now irritated.

"Do not threaten me, woman!" Pierre warned.

"Why, Pierre, I never threaten. Threats are the idle words of a coward. Now, I must go. I am sure we will speak later." Marguerite rose from her seat.

Pierre was glaring at her, his face red with anger. As usual, she had the final word.

"Au revoir, mon cheri," she said as she strode casually away from the bench.

The next morning Paul quickly unpacked his clothes and painting supplies. He looked at the paints and canvases that Vincent was using and decided that he did not want to use what he perceived as inferior products.

"I don't see why we can't use the same paint and canvas material, Paul. It would be cheaper since we could purchase them in bulk."

"I have my favorite paint. If you want to use the same paint as I do, then you can change. As for your canvas, I prefer a rougher surface so the paint will adhere better."

"My canvases are fine. They are also less expensive."

"Art, dear Vincent, should not be constrained by mere capital. I will ask Theo to send me paints of my own choosing. Now, will you accompany me to find a bolt of jute that I can use for covering?"

That evening, Vincent introduced Paul to the locals at the Café de la Gare. Gauguin's stature and good looks made him very popular with both sexes and he, the acknowledged gregarious savage, was particularly attracted to forbidden fruit.

Marie Ginoux, dressed in a simple but revealing dress, was serving food and drinks. She lingered over each of the men, teasing them with a slight show of her décolletage.

As she approached their table, Paul raised his glass. "Madame Ginoux, you have a remarkable face. I should like to paint your portrait so posterity can enjoy what I have the pleasure of seeing now." His smile revealed perfect, even teeth, if a bit stained by tobacco. His prominent nose, which, on any other man would have been an unpleasant distraction, suggested an unrestrained, virile manner.

Blushing, she purred, "Monsieur Paul, you are a rogue!"

"Not a rogue, but a savage! Have you ever had a savage, Madame?"

"Oh, I shall not be teased!" She feigned a coy demeanor, barely concealing her delight.

Paul reached up and touched her arm. Marie looked down into his deep blue eyes. He said, "I really must paint you, Madame. Please allow me the pleasure and come by my humble studio later this week. If you want, I shall even be on my best behavior! But if you don't want me to, I shan't!" He gave her a sly wink.

"Perhaps, Monsieur, perhaps," she demurred. As Marie walked away from the table, Vincent looked at Paul and then at Marie. "She has never spoken to me except to take my order or demand payment."

"You have to be charming and patient," Paul said as he watched Marie. "I will paint her and she will enjoy sitting and anticipating what's to come later."

"You can't be serious…"

"Oh, but I am!" And he gave Vincent another sly wink.

A few days passed. Gauguin was alone in the studio. Vincent had gone into a remote area of Arles in search of fields and bridges for his next subject. Unlike Vincent, Gauguin preferred to remain in the studio painting "a tête" or from his head. He stole a look at Vincent's work that was lying about.

"Van Gogh wastes so much paint. There must be four or five layers on some of these canvases," he muttered to himself. He came upon *Starry Night Over the Rhone.* "More second thoughts. Looks like people standing on water." He came to *The Night Café,* which Vincent had painted for Joseph Ginoux but had not yet given to the proprietor. "This does not do the café justice. He simply doesn't capture the liveliness of the restaurant. We view this place in completely disparate ways." As he glanced around the studio, he saw that Vincent had left his journal behind. He picked it up and opened it. "My, my," he murmured, "some of these sketches are quite good. Excellent, in fact."

He thumbed through the book. "Van Gogh even annotates his drawings. He does have some intriguing observations. Oh, what is this?" He had come across a sketch of a beautiful young woman. In fact, there were several sketches of her in the book. There were also renderings of several men in different poses. One appeared as though the subjects had been drawn in an underground room or perhaps a basement. There were names by several of the figures. Pierre, Marguerite, Ferdinand, Louis. He finally came across a pencil sketch of Émile Bernard. Beside the drawing was a scribbled note, "Émile Bernard at the Commune Meeting." Curious, he thought.

He continued to look through the journal. The last third of it was empty, waiting for Vincent to fill the pages. Paul picked up a pencil and tapped it on the page, considered making a notation, but thought better of it. "If I encroach on his private space, he might just kill me and throw me under one of his bridges or in a field of sunflowers." He chuckled at his own wit. Instead, he sat down at his desk, found some paper, and hastily penned a short note to Émile whom he had not corresponded with for a while.

My dear Émile,

I am getting settled in Arles quite nicely. Vincent has been on his best behavior. His painting, however, confuses me. It's a dichotomy, really. Some canvases are bleak and humorless, others colorful and cheery. He embraces the accidents of thickly applied paint. I, however, detest an over-worked surface.

How is your lovely sister? I do miss Madeleine and our pleasant evenings together. Does your father remain angry with me?

On another note, I happened upon van Gogh's journal. I didn't mean to pry, really, but I couldn't tear myself away from his sketches. They were quite good, actually. Not like his paintings. Interestingly, he had several sketches of you and your "Commune" group. I wasn't aware of this camaraderie of friends... Why did you not invite me to join this group? Marguerite looks very appealing indeed! It's no surprise that he chose to sketch her several times!

Do come for a visit before the weather turns foul. I'm sure Vincent would welcome you with open arms. I would enjoy your company as well!

Yours, Paul

Arles-sur-Oise 1888

Gauguin's musings were interrupted by a knock on the front door. He opened the door to find Madame Ginoux dressed in an indigo dress with her hair pulled up into a small chignon. Loose curls framed her face, enhancing her sultry expression.

"Are you ready for me, Monsieur?" she asked. "Is now a good time for a sitting?"

"Madame, what a pleasant surprise!" Gauguin offered her his hand. "Yes, of course. Please, come this way." As he was ushering Madame Ginoux into the studio, Vincent returned from his long walk. He watched in disbelief as Paul seated Marie in a chair and took up a seat facing her, sketchpad in hand. Vincent excitedly grabbed his canvas and tripod and prepared to paint alongside his colleague.

"I did not imagine that Madame would arrive so shortly after your brief encounter! I hope that you do not mind if I paint with you, Paul."

"Please excuse my friend, dear Madame. He seldom has anyone pose for him, especially one so lovely as you." Gauguin gave Vincent a scornful look.

The two men worked side by side. Paul sketched his subject with charcoal while Vincent painted furiously with oils. Madame Ginoux was a willing subject, maintaining her erect posture without any complaints. Occasionally, one of the artists would ask her to look this way or that, tilt her head just so, or adjust her hair, all of which she promptly obeyed. At last Gauguin announced that he was finished for the day. "I will try to make my final work worthy of your time and beauty, Madame."

"Monsieur Paul, it has been my utmost pleasure." She

held out her hand and the debonair Gauguin brushed his lips across her pale skin.

Vincent was rushing to add the last bit of color to his canvas as Paul escorted Marie to the front door. "Au revoir, Madame. I eagerly await our next meeting," Gauguin told her. The door closed and he returned to the studio. Vincent was adding more paint to his canvas. "Vincent, really, must you be so inconsiderate? You did not even bid Marie adieu or accompany her to the door!"

Vincent continued his brushstrokes. Rising from the canvas he waved his brush in the air and exclaimed, "Why did that woman leave? I needed only a few more minutes."

"Did you not hear what I said?"

Still looking at the canvas, Vincent mumbled, "So inconsiderate. So like a woman."

Gauguin looked at his housemate and shook his head.

"Did you say something?" asked Vincent. "Paul?" When Vincent glanced in Gauguin's direction all he saw was the tail of Paul's coat floating through the doorway.

Chapter 35
Paris – Present Day

The BMW made its way down the tree-lined street near the Bois du Boulogne. Rays of filtered sunlight shimmered through the trees, casting a wondrous aura over the boulevard. Mark stopped his car at the stone piers and waited for the wrought iron gates to grant passage.

Maggie gazed out the passenger window and sighed as she took in the dreamlike landscape. "It's even lovelier the second time."

"Indeed, it is," Mark acknowledged, maneuvering the car around the brilliant white marble fountain to the front of the mansion. Claire was waiting for them at the entrance, erect as the proverbial pillar of salt, hands clasped at her bosom, her granite face not betraying a single thought.

As they approached the front step, Maggie greeted Claire cheerfully. "It's nice to see you again."

The maid opened the door and ushered the couple down the hallway to the same room as their first visit. "Madame will be with you shortly," she said curtly. After her offers of coffee and tea were declined, she stepped away.

Mark leaned over to Maggie and whispered, "She's not much of a conversationalist, is she?" Maggie grinned. The pair roamed around the perimeter of the room, examining the portraits and other paintings.

"There are millions of dollars of art hanging on these walls," observed Maggie. "That Caravaggio you are admiring alone is worth millions."

Just then there was the tiniest bit of rustling and Mme.

Chauvenal appeared, accompanied by her two hounds. Figuring her covetous remark had been overheard, Maggie was embarrassed and promptly apologized. "I'm sorry but I am just in awe of your collection, Mme. Chauvenal."

Madame stepped around the settee. When she stopped, the dogs halted, ears up. Deep, low growls emanated from the stalwart creatures as they eyed the two strangers.

"Hugo! Lucie! Is that any way to greet our guests?" With the slightest gesture of her hand, the dogs relaxed on their haunches and looked up at their owner, waiting for her next command.

"Quite all right, my dear. And you must remember to call me 'Anna.' Please forgive my childrens' ill behavior. As I mentioned before, they are very protective of me." She beckoned her guests to sit as she took her place on the leather sofa. "Thank you for coming. I couldn't stop thinking about what you found hidden in your house. The thought of learning more about my ancestors excites me. Imagine my surprise and intrigue, knowing you may have discovered some of my family secrets. Oh, Claire, please bring Maggie and Mark a drink. What will you have, my dears?"

Claire appeared before them when Maggie said, "Claire was kind enough to offer us some beverages when we arrived, but we declined. We are fine. Nothing, please."

"But I insist. We have some very fine red wine—from the Bordeaux region."

"Well, if you insist. It's difficult to turn down a beautiful Bordeaux," said Maggie.

"I'll have the same, please," added Mark.

"*Certainement.* And for you Madame?" Claire asked the older woman.

"*Chartreuse, merci, Claire.*"

"And I shall have glass of wine too, Claire." A throaty, feminine voice rang out from behind Mark and Maggie.

"Josephine!" exclaimed Madame Chauvenal. "I am delighted that you could join us!"

A tall, delicate woman glided into the room, clad in a blue silk Versace blouse and an eye-catching graphic knee-length Prada skirt, and Christian Louboutin shoes. She set a matching handbag on the table. Her jet-black hair hung loose, barely touching her broad shoulders. A nickel-sized blue topaz ring dominated a slender finger of her right hand. A delicate silver necklace with an oblong pendant graced her long neck. Her dangling earrings were equally exquisite.

"Maman, you look wonderful as usual, but a little thinner," she said in French, bending down to peck Madame Chauvenal's collagen-filled cheek. "I hope you are eating well." She turned to the guests and said, "I am Josephine Fournier, Anna's daughter."

"Madame Fournier, it is a pleasure to meet you," Maggie extended her hand. Mark did likewise.

"Please, call me Josie. All my friends do. I hope you don't mind if I intrude upon dinner. Maman has told me of your discovery and I so wanted to meet you and see the journal for myself."

"It would be our pleasure," said Maggie.

Josephine looked at Mark. "I understand that you discovered a life-saving method of treating cancer? That is a magnificent accomplishment."

"Thank you but I was merely part of a research team."

"Ah, yes. Modesty. An admirable quality! In my profession, we have no such humility."

Claire arrived with a tray of drinks, serving Madame Chauvenal first. She took the glass from Claire and said, "Did you bring the journal and the letter?"

"No, I'm sorry. We keep it in a bank for now. But we did bring pictures of several of the pages," answered Mark.

"Excellent! But before we delve into the past, perhaps we should have dinner. Josephine, we are having your favorite tonight, *duck á l'orange.*"

Josephine beamed. "Mark, Maggie, I hope you like duck. I can attest that Eduard, Maman's chef, prepares the best *duck á l'orange* in all of Paris. It practically melts in your mouth."

"Oooh, I love duck," Maggie said enthusiastically. As she was speaking, they all rose to follow Madame into the dining room.

The formal dining room was elegant. The ceilings were fourteen feet high and accented by ornate crown molding. The mahogany inlaid table could easily seat twenty people and was centered under two five-tiered Baccarat crystal chandeliers. The chairs were Louis XIV. A pair of matching walnut sideboards with hand-forged iron locks graced opposing walls. Florentine papered walls were filled with the works of popular French artists.

Gilded soft-paste porcelain dishes of varying sizes were strategically placed at one end of the immense table to accommodate four people. Maggie noted that the dishes were French-inspired. A dark blue lapis design was overlaid with veins of gold and looked superb against the delicate lace tablecloth. The flatware was Vermeil 18k gold. By her estimation, just the place settings had to be worth many thousands of dollars.

"Please, make yourselves comfortable," Madame invited. "Josephine, dear, kindly sit by me." She pointed to the chair to her right as she took the seat at the head of the table.

The sommelier appeared from a side door, his round eyeglasses held in place by a prominent knot on the bridge of his sharp nose. He was carrying a bottle of Olivier Leflaive Chardonnay Saint-Aubin. Gently, he announced, "I think you will enjoy this glorious wine. It has a few very distinct notes of almonds and exotic fruit, perhaps even a floral note as well. The finish is smooth and long. I hope you will find it to your liking." He poured a small amount into Mme. Chauvenal's glass and watched as she swirled the liquid in her mouth and waited for her approval.

"Excellent choice," she murmured. The sommelier continued pouring.

Mark and Maggie sipped politely, as did Josephine. The first course was served.

Mme. Chauvenal gazed across the table at Maggie. "Josephine, Maggie's grandmother was in the French resistance," she said, barely picking at her food.

"Really? Maman must have told you that she and her parents fought with the resistance. That is quite a coincidence. You must have relatives here in France?"

"I'm not sure. My grandfather was killed during the war and my grandmother moved to the U.S. shortly after the war. My mother was a young girl when they moved to the

States. She really has told me very little about the family."

"That is so sad," said Josephine. "Have you spent much time in France?"

"Only as an adult. I'm not sure why, but my mother never returned to France after she moved. But she always talked about missing France and especially Paris."

"I hope you can convince her to come soon. France is delightful, but like so many other countries, she is facing many troubling issues."

Mme. Chauvenal broke in. "Josephine is quite right, but we came here to dine with our new friends and learn more about their discovery."

When everyone had finished their meal, they retired to the den. Four leather chairs were evenly spaced around a small round table. The ever-present hounds followed the elderly woman to the table and lay on the floor directly behind her chair.

Mark sat down with Maggie on one side and Madame on the other. "As I said earlier, we have the journal and the letter in a safety deposit box, but we took some pictures and had them printed so it would be easier to see some of the detail." He withdrew the photos from the inner pocket of his jacket and passed them to Maggie.

Maggie arranged the photos on the table. "This is the journal cover. You can see that it is covered with paint splotches. These are several of the sketches in the journal. You can see that there are several notes written in the margins."

Josephine stood behind the two women and peered over their shoulders. "This is truly amazing. To think van Gogh carried this journal with him and drew these."

"This is where the reference to the group called the 'Commune' starts." Maggie pointed to one photo. All three women bent forward for a closer look. "This is the first sketch of Marguerite and this is another."

"Maman, that's our Marguerite!" exclaimed Josephine.

"Yes, so it is."

Maggie turned a few more photos.

"There she is again," said Josephine.

"This is a sketch of a man called 'Pierre'," said Maggie. "And next to this other picture, if you look at it closely, you can make out the words, 'Marguerite's cousin'."

"Maman, do you recognize this cousin?"

The older woman leaned in close to inspect the picture. "I'm sorry, I don't."

The three women continued to examine the photos with Maggie pointing out various notes. Finally, Mme. Chauvenal looked up. "This really is a treasure. You said you have the letter addressed to Marguerite?" Maggie handed the photo of the letter to her. "The original is not in very good shape I'm afraid."

Looking at the single photo, Madame Chauvenal's eyebrows arched.

Mark immediately noticed Madame's quizzical expression and asked, "Do you recognize anything, Anna?"

She hesitated for a second and then spoke. "Pardonnez-moi. I was trying to connect this note, the Commune and this mysterious cousin of ours."

Josephine took the photo from her mother.

"Hmm. 'FE.' Who might that be? Maman, do any of our ancestors have a last name that begins with an *E*?"

"Not that I am aware of. I must say, this journal, this

letter... they raise several questions. I thought I knew our family history but apparently there is a great deal that I do not know." She looked at Mark. "Would you mind if I kept these, just for a little while, so I can research our family more thoroughly?"

"Of course," replied Mark.

"You have been most helpful. I do appreciate you sharing your findings with us."

Mme. Chauvenal rose, and as she did, so did the hounds. "I am afraid it is getting late and elderly women must get their rest. Laurent, could you please show Monsieur and Madame McFadden to the door?" Then to Mark and Maggie she said, "Again, thank you for coming. I hope we will see each other again soon."

"It has been our pleasure," said Mark.

"Yes, thank you for a wonderful evening," added Maggie.

As they walked out the door, Maggie heard Mme. Chauvenal call, *"Bonne chance, la France!"*

Chapter 36
Arles-sur-Oise, Paris – Autumn 1888

Vincent sat alone over breakfast at a patisserie. He glanced at a local newspaper lying on the table next to him.

The headlines read: *Royal Train Derails: Tsar Injured.*

He picked up the paper and read the article. "I imagine that Émile will shit himself!" he thought.

In Paris, Émile was also taking in the same shocking headlines. The paper described the carnage resulting from the train accident. Seven people had been killed and the Tsar injured. Alexander was portrayed as a hero of Russia, risking his own life to save his wife and children. There was no cause reported for the accident nor were any perpetrators identified.

"Mon Dieu," Émile whispered. "If this is tied to the Commune, we are all dead!" Small beads of perspiration broke out across his brow and his hands began to shake. He rushed back to his studio. Throwing off his coat, he sat at his makeshift desk and searched for pen and paper.

"I must get a note to Vincent." With trembling hands, he started writing.

Dear Vincent:

I received the painting you sent. Thank you. I hope you are getting along with Gauguin. He can be charming one minute and difficult the next, whatever he chooses to be.

Did you see the news from Russia? Our comrades may have acted again.

Paul wrote to me not long ago and it seems he has found your journal. He has seen the sketches you made at our Commune meetings. This could be disastrous!

Please, for our sakes, destroy your journal and any other links to the Commune that you may have. Time is of the essence.

Be safe.
Your friend,
Émile

He sealed the letter and hurried to the post. If he got the letter there before noon, it might just make it to Vincent by the end of tomorrow. He hoped that he wasn't too late.

The Café de la Gare was crowded. Vincent sat at the end of the table near the wall. Gauguin sat at the other end, near the billiard table in the center of the room. The men playing pool stopped to chat with Paul. Madame Ginoux approached the table.

"Good evening, Monsieur Paul. How are you tonight?"

"Fine, ma cherie. You are looking well. It is very busy tonight, yes? Is it possible for you to sit with me?"

"Oh, Monsieur Paul, I don't think so. My husband needs my help. We are short on staff as usual, I'm afraid."

"Perhaps later you could help me," he said with his characteristic wink.

Marie blushed and turned away, stealing a furtive peek at Gauguin from over her shoulder.

Vincent spoke. "Her husband is a very jealous man. You should take care, Paul."

"He is no match for me. Besides, it is up to him to keep her happy. If he cannot satisfy her, then he doesn't deserve her."

Changing the subject, Vincent said, "I heard from Émile today."

"What did our friend Bernard have to say? Did he mention his sister?"

"His sister?" asked Vincent.

"Yes, Madeline. We had a close relationship in Pont-Aven this past summer."

"Goodness, Paul. You seduced his sister? She's but a mere child!"

"She was very willing. I would have married her but her father stood in our way."

"But, Paul, you are already married!"

"My wife has told me to never come back. Just as well. There are too many women to be confined to just one. Besides, I like the chase better than the capture." Gauguin let out a chuckle.

"How did Émile react to your seduction of his sister?"

"I don't think he was happy, but he'll get over it. It's not important," replied Gauguin. His eyes were fixed on Marie Ginoux as she moved from table to table.

Vincent shook his head and took a drink. Paul surely had the sexual appetite of a wild beast. He couldn't decide whether he should admire or despise the man.

"Paul," Vincent said. No answer. "Paul! I'm speaking to you!"

Gauguin snapped out of his reverie. "Sorry. What did you say?"

"Émile, in his letter, he said you went through my journal."

Without taking his eyes off Marie, Paul replied. "Journal? I don't remember. Maybe... I don't know."

Vincent became indignant. "The journal is mine. It's private and not meant for your prying eyes!"

Gauguin turned his attention to Vincent and said, "All right. It's nothing to worry about. I'm not interested in your sketches and ramblings anyway."

The two artists spent the rest of the evening in irritable silence while they downed one drink after another. It was well after midnight when they returned home exhausted and spent. They stumbled their way up the stairs to their respective rooms, to sleep off the evening's overindulgences.

For Vincent, a peaceful sleep was not to be. His night sweats were returning. Vincent stirred, his body damp and clammy. He was not fully awake and the darkness of his bedroom engulfed him. In the distance he could hear a strange banging sound but could not determine its source. He reached out into the darkness, trying to grasp something, anything that might help him pull out of the inkiness that surrounded him. He pushed his body up and put his feet onto the floor, his hands clutching the side of the bed.

"Oh, God. Not again! I must be going mad! Go away you demons, begone!" The banging ceased and he heard voices.

"Demon, are you speaking to me or am I still dreaming?" The voices became louder and Vincent finally realized that there were people in the hall outside his bedroom. His paranoia increased and he felt light-headed. He slowly gained a foothold, rising from the bed and making his way to the door. The voices were muted.

"Are there really people out there? Am I still asleep? Is this a dream?"

The voices stopped. Slowly he cracked the door and peered into the hallway. A figure was standing just outside the door. The person turned and looked in his direction.

Arles-sur-Oise 1888

Quickly, he closed the door. He couldn't see her face but he recognized the dress as the one she was wearing earlier this evening. "Mme. Ginoux. Was that really her?" he said to himself. He climbed back into his bed, dreading the nightmares that were sure to come.

The morning brought with it a sadness that Vincent could not fight. The dreams and night sweats and the image of Madame Ginoux leaving Gauguin's bedroom plagued Vincent as he readied himself for the day. He was emotionally off-balance, tired, and feeling wholly uninspired. How was he going to accomplish anything today in this frame of mind? He stumbled into the studio where Gauguin was waiting.

"Well, finally up I see," Paul smirked from his side of the studio. "Where are you going today?"

"The old bridge."

"Vincent, you always go out, away from people and activity. I am going to Les Alyscamps. I want to observe the people, particularly the whores. They make great studies. Come with me and you can paint or sketch them too, or catch the autumn leaves. They should make a fine subject for your next project."

"All right. If you insist," he replied.

The two men left the Yellow House and walked in silence across the park, then headed south along Rue Voltaire. They passed the old Roman amphitheater, stopping only when Gauguin saw something or someone he wished to sketch. They came upon an old homestead where women were harvesting late crops, potatoes and parsnips. Gauguin sketched for a while, planning to finish the rest later, from memory.

When Paul was done, the pair made their way down the Avenue des Alyscamp toward the ancient Roman cemetery and church just outside the walls of the city. The avenue was awash in color and lined with tall, spiraling trees that formed an honor guard for those strolling along the pedestrian way. The cemetery had been Arles' main burial ground for over 1,400 years. Aristocratic families from all over Europe had shipped the bodies of their loved ones for entombment there. But the construction of a railway and a canal had removed all vestiges of its former glory and it had become a favorite spot for couples to enjoy a quiet rendezvous. Often, single women, elegantly clad in their finest dresses, would stroll along, baring an ankle or perhaps revealing their soft, plump bosoms. If a gentleman were so inclined, these ladies could be had—for a price.

Gauguin slowed his pace as they neared the old section of the Avenue. "How long are you intending to stay?" Vincent asked Paul.

"For quite some time, I think. I am feeling inspired by the Arlésiennes."

"Very good then, go ahead. I will remain here. Come fetch me when you are ready to leave."

Gauguin nodded and continued his leisurely stroll. Vincent would see him occasionally tip his hat or chat with a couple as he made his way down the avenue. How does he do it, he wondered to himself. An accomplished seaman, talented artist, handsome and charming—he has it all. Vincent suddenly realized that he was envious of his friend.

Resolving to bring his resentment under control, Vincent sat down on a large rock, journal on his lap, studying the expanse ahead of him. Slowly, the scene presented itself. His calm returned. He took in a deep breath and picked up his pencil. As his right hand guided itself over the page, images began to form. Trees took shape, stones of the hardscrabble street came into view, and human forms emerged on the pathway. Vincent made notes about colors and textures, perspective and depth. As the sun faded, his sketch took on an urgency—as if the scene would disappear if he did not finish quickly. Tomorrow, Paul and I must return, and I will bring my canvas and paint, he thought. This will be a great study in yellow.

"Well, I see you made the most of your time here." Paul was standing just a few feet behind Vincent, peering over his bony shoulder at the journal.

"What? Oh, it's you, Paul. You startled me. I think I was in a trance!" Vincent said. "What do you think, shall we return tomorrow and paint together? I've made lots of notes about color."

Paul hesitated. "Perhaps." In truth, he was not looking forward to another day together, for he knew it would lead to more heated discussions about artistic style and their divergent approaches. They packed up their supplies and trudged back to the Yellow House to have dinner at home for a change.

It was cold, damp and malodorous in the cellar of the remote Paris house where the group of gathered men waited for their host to arrive. Despite the commotion created by their excited talk, they could discern footfalls on the wooden stairs. Heads turned to see the hem of an emerald dress descending into the basement.

"Gentlemen, please be seated," Marguerite commanded.

The room quieted as the men slowly took seats. Fog rose from their collective breath.

Marguerite began. "I am sure you have all read the paper and have seen the reports coming out of Russia. We have finally made the impact that we wanted."

"What do you mean?" someone bellowed.

"I mean, the Tsar is now fearful for his life. He will be pressed by his own countrymen to act more humanely. The train wreck provided just the impetus that the Russian peasants needed. Now we can expect them to rise up and overthrow their oppressors."

The room filled with chatter. "What about the claim reported yesterday in the paper that the NV is working with the Commune?"

"Allow me to explain. We are using the NV to help hide our involvement. I promised you that we would take the utmost care to keep you out of harm's way. This is part of the design; to steer the Tsar's attention to the NV."

Another voice called from the crowd. "There were accounts of casualties—French casualties—in the train wreck."

"It saddens me to say those accounts are true. We lost two of our comrades in the derailment. But you must know that they did not die in vain—while they were unfortunate losses, they did much to further our objectives. We are taking care of their families and will see to their children's safety." Marguerite looked around the room as she spoke. "Gentlemen, it is important for you to carry on your daily lives as if nothing has happened. If you panic, or behave unusually, or depart from your routines, you could endanger yourselves and our cause. We all depend on one another for our continued well-being. Now please, return to your homes and families with the knowledge that you have altered the course of history. You have made the world a better place."

Marguerite turned to Pierre, but he spoke first.

"Very good, Marguerite. Let's hope the Chancellor can make the best of this situation."

From behind, Marguerite felt a gentle touch on her elbow. She turned to find Émile Bernard standing before her. He was noticeably nervous, shifting from one foot to the other. His pale complexion was ashier than normal.

"May I speak to you in private, Marguerite?"

"I am a bit busy now. Can we do this later, Émile?"

"It's very important that I speak to you now," he insisted.

"Very well." Marguerite steered the young man to a far corner of the old foundation. Émile's eyes darted about, carefully observing the men as they left the room. Pierre was staring at him from across the basement, his face screwed up in annoyance.

"What is it that you want, Émile?"

"I have come across some very disturbing information," he said softly.

"Yes, please get on with it." Marguerite said, barely concealing her irritation.

"Van Gogh kept a sketch pad and notes. He drew pictures of the Commune, including us and several others."

"He did what?" she blurted.

Pierre's head jerked around and he took a half step toward the couple.

"He listed names by the sketches and specifically mentioned

the Commune." Émile was fidgeting with his coat sleeve.

Marguerite stared at Émile in disbelief. Her cold blue eyes penetrated him to the core. He felt as if he was being carried away on an iceberg into the frigid waters of the Arctic Ocean.

"This, I am afraid, is very bad. For van Gogh and for you. We cannot talk now but I will be in touch. Remain in Paris where I can reach you. Do you understand?" She did not wait for a reply but turned and walked toward Pierre. A smile crossed her face as she approached him.

"What did Bernard want with you?" Pierre asked.

"Nothing. He has an adolescent crush, that's all," she replied nonchalantly.

Chapter 37
Ville d'Avray – Present Day

The next day, the rain gave way and the sun pushed its way through bruised clouds. By early evening, the sky was clearing.

"This has just been a really, really miserable day," Maggie moaned.

"Yep, pretty dismal," said Mark as he stared at the glowing computer screen.

"You've been trying to find something on Pierre and this 'Commune' all day. Why don't you take a break and let's go into town for a bite to eat?" Maggie suggested.

Mark yawned and stretched his arms above his head, fingers intertwined. "What do you have in mind?"

"Oh, nothing fancy. Just something to get us out of the house. How about Café Le Pen?"

"Casual... Sounds good! That way, I don't have to change clothes. I can go like this."

"I need a minute to brush my hair and put on some makeup," said Maggie. She bounded up the stairs.

"Honey, you look great! Let's just go!"

"I'll only be a minute," she answered.

Mark shuffled some papers around and tidied up the desk while Maggie readied herself. Moments later they were in their car, headed for the café.

They were practically the only patrons in the restaurant. They took a seat by the window that looked out onto d'Avray's main thoroughfare and ordered. The food arrived quickly.

"How's your vichyssoise?" asked Mark.

"Creamy and refreshing. How about your sandwich?"

"Tasty, but then it's hard to mess up a ham and cheese sandwich. I think I'll order a T.N.T. Want a drink?"

"No. Just sparkling water for me."

"What? No wine or Tanqueray? How about dessert?"

"Not tonight."

"Are you feeling okay?"

"I'm fine. I'm going to the ladies' room—be right back."

Mark ordered his Tanqueray and tonic and stared absentmindedly out the window. The sun had disappeared behind the low-profile buildings and the streetlights began to flicker on along the empty street.

The waiter set Mark's drink and the bottle of Badoit on the table. "Is there anything else, Monsieur?"

"I don't think so. Just the check, please."

The waiter left to tally the bill. Mark sipped his gin and tonic. The café was beginning to fill up with customers. Mark never quite understood why Europeans ate so late. He looked at his watch.

"Damn, Maggie, did you fall in?" he wondered.

He summoned a waiter. "Which way to the toilets?" he asked.

The waiter pointed down the hall.

Mark thanked him and decided to wait just a bit longer. Finally, his glass held nothing but melted ice and a twisted lime slice. Mark looked at his watch again. Then he gazed over at the doorway leading to the bathrooms. Still no Maggie in sight.

"I'd better make sure she's okay," he thought.

The hallway to the bathrooms was dark, illuminated by a small ceiling light. Beyond that was a red light above a door marked *Sortie*. Mark hesitated, then knocked on the door marked *Femmes*.

"*Un moment,*" a woman said. But it was not Maggie's voice. The door opened and a short, elderly woman emerged. She squinted at Mark and pursed her lips. "*Pardon, Monsieur!*" she huffed as she shoved past him.

Mark caught the door just as it was about to slam shut and peered inside. There was only one commode and one sink. The room was empty.

Mark felt his heart in his throat. He walked quickly back into the restaurant and took another look around. There was no sign of Maggie. The waiter was clearing his table. Mark rushed over and put his hand on the waiter's arm.

"Did you see my wife?" he asked in English.

"*Pardon?*"

"My wife! Did you see my wife? She went to the toilet and never came back." Mark gestured toward the restroom.

"No, *Monsieur.* Are you ready to pay?"

Mark handed him a credit card, looking rapidly around the dining room and out the windows. He pulled out his cell phone and dialed. "Come on, Mags, pick up!" Then he heard a click and the familiar "This is Maggie McFadden. Please leave me a message at the beep."

Mark spoke with hushed urgency into his phone. "Mags, where are you? Call me! I'm worried!"

The waiter handed Mark the portable charge card reader. Without looking at the reader, Mark signed and took his card. He went back to the hallway that led to the restrooms.

The *Sortie* light caught his eye. Just outside the back door, were half a dozen cars, a couple of delivery trucks, and a portable storage container. No one in sight.

"Mags! Maggie!" he yelled. There was no response. He yelled again. He went back to the dining room. The waiter was standing at the bar, placing an order.

"Please, did you see my wife? We came in together. I can't find her anywhere!"

"I am sorry, Monsieur," the waiter said with a shrug. "I have not seen your wife."

"Could you ask your colleagues if they saw her?"

The waiter slipped into the kitchen. When he returned, a portly man in his late fifties was with him. "Monsieur, I am Frédéric Le Mans, the proprietor. What seems to be the problem?"

"My wife and I were here for dinner. She went to the ladies' room and I haven't seen her since."

"Perhaps she is still there…"

"No! No! I checked. She is not there! Did any of your staff see her leave?"

"I'm afraid not. Jacques asked the others and no one remembers your wife, Monsieur. I'm sorry."

Mark turned around and ran out the front door. His eyes swept the sidewalks. He ran to the parked car. There was no sign of Maggie.

"Okay," he mumbled to himself. "Calm down. There has to be something I'm missing here." He took a deep breath and exhaled slowly. He looked over the parking lot one more time, then took another deep breath.

He reached into his pocket for his phone and dialed.

"Gastineau ici."

"Commissaire Gastineau, this is Mark McFadden. My wife is missing!"

"What do you mean your wife is missing?"

"We went out to eat. She went to the bathroom and she has disappeared."

"Monsieur McFadden, what do you mean 'disappeared'?"

"Just that. She never came back from the bathroom."

"Where are you right now?"

"I'm at our car in the parking lot at Avenue Thierry, just down from Café Le Pen. That's where we had dinner."

"Wait where you are. I will there in a few minutes."

Mark could not stand still. He paced up and down the street and wove his way through the car park. Moments later he saw a flashing blue light approach. Gastineau's Megane pulled into the lot and he got out.

"Thank God you're here," Mark said.

"Monsieur, please be calm. Now tell me again. What happened? Please do not leave out any details."

Mark went through the events of the evening.

"When you went out the back door, did you see anyone or anything?"

"No."

"We must go back to the restaurant, monsieur."

Gastineau pulled out his phone as they hurried to Le Pen. He spoke in excited French and abruptly ended the call. "The police are on their way here."

"Do you think this has anything to do with Durand?"

"I do not know. Is it possible that your wife went off on her own without telling you?"

"No. That is not possible. She would not do that."

Flashing blue lights and the sounds of sirens came from down the street. Several police cars blocked the quiet street. Gastineau barked orders at the uniformed police and they immediately dispersed, some entering the restaurant while others went to the back of the building.

Gastineau continued his line of questioning. "Monsieur, I know you are upset. Please, tell me again what happened. This time show me where you were seated and walk through all of your movements."

"We were sitting here and just finished eating. I ordered a drink and Maggie went to the bathroom. When she didn't come back, I went to look for her. She wasn't in the ladies' room and the waiters hadn't seen her. I went out the back door and she wasn't there. I came back in and went to my car. I called you."

A policeman came and stood next to Gastineau and leaned in to whisper in the Commissaire's ear.

"What is it?" Mark asked. "Did they find something?"

Gastineau waved the police officer away and looked at Mark's bloodshot eyes. "No. The officers have found nothing."

"Damn it!" Mark looked around, blinking back tears. He felt as powerless as he was exasperated.

"Monsieur, I believe the best thing we can do is to return to your house."

"Are you ending the investigation now?"

"No. Not at all. But we must be realists. There may be a perfectly plausible reason why your wife has disappeared. On the other hand, the worst-case scenario is that she has been abducted. If that is the case, you will likely get a phone call and you should be home to receive it. The police will continue to search here and in the surrounding area, but let's hurry home in case she comes back there."

"Of course, you're right."

"Monsieur McFadden, you will ride with me. I will have someone bring your car later. Please give me the keys."

Once they arrived at the house, Gastineau opened the front door. Blue flashing lights illuminated the front room through the open door. "Stay here. I will check inside and motion to you when it is safe to come inside," he ordered.

He looked quickly through each room. Mark stood just outside, pacing back and forth. When Gastineau signaled, Mark went straight in and ran from room to room.

"Has anything been disturbed since you left?"

"No. Not that I can tell. Everything looks the same. What can I do? I feel so helpless…"

"This is very hard. We must wait and find out if your wife will return or you are contacted by a kidnapper. In the meanwhile, my men will continue to look for Madame McFadden."

Gastineau and Mark were sitting at the dining room table when Mark's cell phone rang. He reached into his pocket and Gastineau touched his arm. "Put it on speaker."

"Hello, Mark McFadden."

"Monsieur McFadden, do you recognize my voice?"

"Ah… Durand?"

Gastineau signaled for Mark to put the phone between them.

"Good. Are you alone or have you called the police?"

"What?"

Gastineau mouthed "alone."

"Are you alone?"

"Yes, I'm alone, why?"

"Good. Your wife is safe. At least for now."

"You have my wife?! You son-of-a-bitch!"

"Careful, Monsieur McFadden. You want her back, yes?"

"Yes! Yes, of course. Let me talk to her!"

Her wavering voice said, "Mark! Mark!! Are you there?"

"Mags! Are you okay?"

With that, he heard the phone being taken from her, and Durand was back on the line. "Now, listen carefully. This may sound like a well-worn cliché, but if you want your wife back safely, you will follow these directions to the letter." Durand was calm and spoke slowly. "At precisely ten o'clock tomorrow morning, you will go to the bank and collect the journal. You will then drive west to a town called Pontgouin. Wait at the corner of Rue du Pont de l'Aumône and Rue Saint-Jean. There you will receive further instructions. You will come alone. Once I have the journal, you will have your wife."

"So this is about that damn journal!" Mark exclaimed.

"That journal is my salvation, Monsieur McFadden. By the way, I have studied how long the trip will take from your house to Pontgouin. You should be at the designated corner by noon. If I see any police or if you are late, I will be forced to dispose of your wife. Do you understand?"

"Yes. I want to talk to her again."

"You have my instructions."

"Yes, let—"

The line went dead. Gastineau looked at Mark. "Now we have work to do."

Exactly at ten o'clock the next morning, the BMW pulled out of the driveway and headed toward the bank in d'Avray. Mark picked up the journal from the deposit box then ran back out and steered the car onto Rue de Marnes. The hundred-kilometer drive took just over an hour and a half, just as Durand predicted. Mark was weary and anxious, and angry. The bags under his bloodshot eyes were dark.

He pulled up to the curb where Rue Saint-Jean met Rue du Pont de l'Aumône. The corner was in a small industrial area. Dusty, older French model cars were parked along the low-profile curb. He shut off the car and looked around.

Minutes passed. A half an hour turned into an hour. Mark pounded on the steering wheel. "Come on!" he said. He laid his head back against the headrest and closed his eyes. Suddenly, the phone rang and Mark jerked straight up in his seat. "McFadden."

"Monsieur McFadden, you follow directions well. I am glad you are alone. That makes this exchange much easier. You have the journal?"

"I have the journal. Let me talk to Maggie."

"In due time. I am going to give you further directions. Are you ready?"

Mark took a pen from his inside pocket and found a piece of paper in the glove box. "Go ahead."

The BMW headed out of town on Route 920, following the snaking curves of the rugged country road. Mark came to a single lane bridge and turned right. He looked right and left for the landmarks that Durand had given him.

A small country road with the directional marker *La Roundiere* appeared on his left. The road was surrounded by fields with a scattering of trees. Beyond one large grove he saw a rutted farm road marked by two rotted wooden posts. He slowly angled the car between the posts. The car bounced over potholes, scraping the chassis and jostling Mark in his seat. Ahead he could make out an even smaller road, a farm path that jutted off to the right. The car bucked and twisted into weeds. "Oh God, please get me there. Please let my Maggie be safe," he murmured.

Under a large oak, Mark saw the car. It was in the shadows. No one was in sight. Mark inched the Beemer behind the old Renault. He looked around and opened the door. Slowly he stepped from his car.

There was a soft whisper of a gentle breeze.

"Durand!" he yelled.

"Durand! I've got the journal! Maggie! Mags!"

Mark approached the driver's side of the Renault. A rotund figure sat behind the steering wheel.

"Durand! Where's Maggie?" he called. He jerked open the driver's side door where Durand sat motionless.

"You miserable son-of-a-bitch, where's Maggie?" he yelled as he grabbed Durand's shirt, but the man was as limp as a rag doll. His slack body fell out of the car, landing wth the head twisted at a grotesque angle, his rumpled shirt soaked with blood the color of a Burmese ruby.

Mark stumbled, fell backward, and retched. When he wiped his mouth with his sleeve, he noticed that his hands were stained red. Alarmed and repulsed by this sight, he rubbed his hands on his pants over and over, desperately wanting to cleanse himself of the gory mess. Upon closer examination, he saw that Durand's head had been almost completely severed from his body.

Moments later, two black Land Rovers pulled next t the BMW. Gastineau jumped from the front passenger seat and ran to the Renault. His eyes fixed on Durand, he barked instructions. He then saw Mark, who was staring at Durand's body.

"Monsieur McFadden," he said, gently putting his arm around Mark's shoulder. "You need to step away."

"Where's Mags? Where's Mags? You don't think..." Mark did not finish.

"Please, Monsieur McFadden. Come with me."

"No. No! I have to find Maggie," he wailed, tears streaking his cheeks.

"Please," Gastineau pulled Mark's arm and guided him to the back of the Land Rover.

In the distance, blue lights flashed and sirens wailed. Mark sat staring straight ahead with Gastineau beside him in the Land Rover. A policeman bent down and whispered into Gastineau's ear. Gastineau nodded and turned to Mark.

"We have searched Durand's car and the surrounding area. Your wife is not here."

"And what about Durand?"

"He was garroted. He has not been dead very long. Whoever did this probably has your wife."

"You think she's alive then?"

"Yes, and you must think that as well. Come. We will take you back to d'Avray. We have preparations to make. And we must wait for the next call."

Chapter 38
s-sur-Oise, Paris – Autumn 1888

from the Yellow House could be heard in park across the street and throughout the neighborhood. Gauguin was raging against Vincent. "Why must you always be so pedantic? There is more than one way to approach painting."

"You claim, Paul, that all great artists draw from the head. I have come to realize that is not enough. The soul is where real art, real feelings, come from. I am certain that I am approaching my work in the right manner. I cannot be concerned with what people say about me. I have said this before: I want to paint what I feel and feel what I paint!"

"Yes but consider what the French master Delacroix once said. One must get one's studies from nature but that the ultimate picture ought to be made from memory. Do you dispute this?" Paul argued.

"No, but I am not entirely convinced. I have had these very discussions with my brother. As I have told him, I believe true painters are guided by that conscience—which is called sentiment, their soul—their brains aren't subject to the pencil, but the pencil to their brains.

"The soul needs to see the beauty and the despair around it. The head merely imagines it. Where is the truth in that? But Paul, in this way we are alike: we seek our subjects in the heart of the common people, the laborers, the whores, the peasants. While we differ in the techniques that we use, I refuse to believe that we are opposed to each other. I don't deny that you have surpassed me in many ways

Arles-sur-Oise 1888

but I think your criticism of me is unfair."

"You will never understand what I believe," said Paul. He rose from the chair in front of his canvas. "Look at your paintings. Paint on top of paint until you have to scrape it off and start again. I don't work that way. Degas does not work that way. Monet does not work that way!"

"My way is equally effective," Vincent insisted. "The clots of paint don't matter at all. If I leave them on for even a year and then scrape them off with a razor, I will obtain a much more solid color than if I had applied the paint thinly. And contrary to what you think, this scraping method has been practiced by the old masters as well as by the French painters of today. Even Theo agrees that my studies in the studio have become better rather than worse in color."

"You must try and vary your work. Use some imagination! Instead of concerning yourself with realistic detail or honing your skills of perspective, simplify your figures! Broaden your strokes! Ah, but there is no use in arguing with you. I am going out for some air. I am not sure that we can continue together. Our temperaments are simply incompatible." The door slammed as Gauguin left the house.

Vincent sat in his chair looking at the door to the studio. He lowered his head and cradled it in his hands. Sadness and frustration blurred his vision. "This was supposed to be a utopia of artists working in unison, appreciating one another. Why can't I ever make things work?"

He sat there for a long time, stewing. Raising his head, he looked at the blank canvas in front of him and his palette resting on the floor. He saw the empty chair where Gauguin had sat just a moment ago. He picked up his palette, tilted the tripod toward the empty chair and began to paint. His fury ebbed, and his face softened as he drew the lines of the chair. Focus and clarity returned once more.

Gauguin entered the two-story house across the park from the Yellow House. The building had once been a fine homestead but now was showing its age. Still, it was elegantly furnished, if not a bit dated, and he enjoyed frequent trips there.

"Good day, Monsieur Gauguin. It is a bit early for you, is it not?" the woman said as she opened the door. She wore a bustled skirt that rose just above her ankles, adorned by a skimpy bodice that exposed much of her soft, pillow-like breasts. Her cheeks were rouged in a deep rose, her eyes heavily rimmed with kohl.

"I need some relief and pleasant diversion, Madame. Is Rachel here?"

"Mai non, Monsieur. But she will be here later this evening. I'm sure another femme would entertain you though."

"First, do you have any brandy? I must steady my nerves."

"For you? Anything. Let me pour you some, my friend."

The woman went to the gilded sideboard and poured a small amount of unmarked liquid into a snifter. She handed it to Gauguin. He held the glass to his nose, inhaling the sweet aroma of the liquor, swirled it, and then took a sip, savoring the dark, smooth substance as it slid easily down his throat.

Just then a small, dark haired woman walked into the room. She was not as fashionable nor as flamboyantly dressed as the Proprietress. She had small firm breasts and a tiny waist. Her dress hung loosely over her shoulders, revealing youthful, soft alabaster skin. Paul appraised her as he swallowed the last of his brandy. Placing the glass on a nearby table, he took the young woman's hand and pulled her through the doorway. "I hope you have stamina, girl," he said as they climbed the back stairs.

Ferdinand Esterhazy sat at a small round table in the back of the café. He was pulling out his pocket watch several times to check the time, glancing at the door as he did so. "Where is she? She tells me to hurry and meet her at precisely on the hour and now it is half-past. Inconsiderate woman. Just…"

He looked up to see Marguerite brushing in past a departing patron. A waiter met her and as they exchanged words, he pointed toward the table in the back.

"Ferdinand, my apologies for my late arrival. I hope you will forgive me." Marguerite removed her gloves as she lowered herself into the seat opposite her cousin.

"Of course. I was surprised by your note, Marguerite."

"Well, I do appreciate you coming to meet with me on such short notice."

"I'm happy to oblige. But what is so urgent?"

Marguerite motioned toward the waiter. "Coffee, please, Henri. With a lump of sugar." She eyed her cousin. "Something has come up and I could use your help. You remember the Commune meeting you attended some time ago?"

"Yes, of course. What a bunch of lackeys. What about it?"

She chose her words carefully. "One of these 'lackeys' brought me some disturbing but thought-provoking news. It seems that within the group are two artists, Émile Bernard and Vincent van Gogh, and unbeknownst to me, van Gogh made sketches of the meetings."

"Really? That could be inconvenient for you."

Marguerite's brows furrowed. "Yes, well, we could also turn this to our advantage."

"How so?" asked the Count.

"Apparently, the pictures van Gogh drew included me and Pierre. He also added notes to his drawings."

"Won't these pictures put you at risk?"

"Possibly. But they may serve as leverage against the Germans. You see, if this journal has Pierre's likeness in it, then there is proof that the Germans are involved with the Commune. He is not aware of the journal and I am not going to mention it."

"I see. And you can use this information to increase your payment as well," Esterhazy remarked.

"Ferdinand, you have to think differently. Not everything is about money," she responded.

"That's easy for you to say. You have plenty of money! I don't. You know my wife left me and now I have only a meager army salary to live on."

"Quit your whining. I have seen to it that you are on the German payroll. Make the most of it."

Esterhazy started to say something but held his tongue when he saw the look in Marguerite's eyes.

She continued. "This journal could be a blessing in disguise. It might prove to be a real safety net for us. No harm can befall us as long as we have proof that Pierre and the Chancellor are behind the Commune. But, Ferdinand, no one must know we have it. Do you understand me?"

"What do you want me to do?" he asked.

"I understand that van Gogh has left Paris and gone south. I don't know exactly where but Pierre will probably be able to tell us. Certainly, Émile Bernard knows. At any rate, I want you to find van Gogh and get that journal and all the drawings he made of the Commune. But he must not know it was stolen. He must think that it was lost or misplaced. If he thinks it is stolen, he could raise an inquiry and involve the local police. He is a volatile man and I think perhaps a bit unstable. I've written down as much information as I have. Here." She opened her purse and handed Esterhazy a folded sheet of paper.

"This is not much to go on…"

"I'm afraid it will have to do. You can follow Bernard. Eventually he may lead you to van Gogh. Remember, stay out of sight. We do not want you to be seen. Bernard told me of the journal, but he may try to warn Vincent. I don't want Vincent to destroy it. So gather your things and leave quietly. Do not draw attention to yourself. Keep a low profile."

"Very well." Esterhazy rose, bid his cousin farewell, and headed for the door. Marguerite sat back in her chair, smiling to herself as he left the café.

Vincent and Paul continued to live in the Yellow House, making peace with each other on a day-to-day basis.

"Paul, there are some fascinating museums in Montpellier. Perhaps we could visit them together?"

"That's an excellent idea. Seeing more pictures might allow us to improve our work. And analyzing the work of others might be better than critiquing each other, which always seems to put us in a foul mood."

"There is a train tomorrow morning that we could catch. It would get us to Montpellier in the morning and we can make a day of it. There is a return train in the early evening."

The train to Montpellier was an old locomotive with few amenities. The seats were nothing more than mere benches that had seen better days; nevertheless, they were filled with people. Vincent and Paul made their way to a car at the rear of the train and sat as far away from the drafty doors as they could manage. The bench seats were frightfully hard and Vincent could feel every imperfection all the way down his spine. He sat erect against the straight back, grimacing with each bump in the track. Paul was next to him, absorbed in the local newspaper.

Vincent looked over Paul's shoulder and was startled to see the paper's headline: *French Conspire to Assassinate the Tsar.*

"May I see the front page?" asked Vincent, barely concealing his astonishment.

Gauguin muttered, "I'm reading it." But Vincent persisted, now agitated.

"Oh, never mind. Here," Paul said grudgingly, thrusting the page into Vincent's lap. "Perhaps this will keep you busy until we get to Montpellier."

The article elaborated on the Russian claim that a French Organization calling itself "The Commune" planned and executed the bombing of the Tsar's train in concert with the Russian socialist group, NV.

"This gives poor Émile just one more thing to fret about," sighed Vincent.

Paul looked up from his reading. "What did you say?"

"Oh, I was just talking to myself," Vincent replied.

"Yes, well, if you want to talk to yourself, please do so quietly and do not interrupt my reading," Paul said curtly. The pair continued their journey to Montpellier in silence.

The newspaper headlines seemed to scream out at Émile: "You are going to be discovered, declared guilty, and go to prison!" Panic overcame him as he read about the link between the ultra-nationalistic French "Commune" and the assassination attempt on the Tsar's life. The French government denied any involvement but agreed to cooperate with the Russian police in their search for any Frenchmen behind the plot. If only he had someone to talk to—someone to reassure him! Knowing that van Gogh had drawings of him at a Commune meeting only served to increase his anxiety.

"That bastard could get me thrown in prison. I must find out what Vincent drew in his sketchbook and destroy it. I have to go see him!" Mindful of Marguerite's warning to not bring any attention to himself by acting out of the ordinary, Émile decided to wait until early December to get away—an eternity.

Émile left his studio and walked toward Gare du Nord. As he walked down the street, he did not notice the tall figure watching from behind a lamppost. If he had looked, he would have recognized Ferdinand Esterhazy.

Vincent and Paul spent the day admiring and analyzing the paintings in the Montpellier Museum of Art. The dark hues of the old Dutch masters still held great appeal to Vincent. Paul appreciated their detail and the fine brushstrokes but was drawn to the more colorful, imaginative paintings of later artists. The two discussed and argued throughout the day about technique, color, and subject matter.

"You admire Daudet, Daubigny, Ziem, and Rousseau. I cannot bear those people. I love Ingres, Raphael, and Degas. But you detest them. We will never agree. Let's just admire our respective painters and move on," Paul said.

"We should discuss these things. If we fellow artists cannot talk about technique and color, then who can? And how will we advance our skills if we cannot talk? How will we establish our Studio of the South and persuade like-minded artists to join us?" Vincent asked.

"But Vincent, you don't discuss. You lecture. If I disagree, you say I am wrong. You are a romantic. I am a primitive."

"You are guilty of the same behavior," responded Vincent, lowering his head for a moment. "I don't mean to be argumentative. I have strong opinions and it is difficult for me to see another's viewpoint."

"You speak before thinking," Paul said coolly. "Can you be more considerate?"

"I will try. But my nature is to put myself in the moment and say what I feel. You know how passionate I am about everything! I don't mean to offend."

Paul let out a heavy sigh. He was hesitant to say it, but he wasn't sure that this studio was going anywhere if they were on opposite sides of every issue. This would be a topic for later. "Let's keep walking. We have much more to see before our train leaves for Arles."

They made the return trip mostly in silence. Once back at the Yellow House, Gauguin left without a word. Vincent checked the post, picked up three letters and went into the studio. He was tired from the trip to Montpellier and the bickering with Gauguin, not to mention his friend's constant threats to return to Paris. He had not eaten and was feeling weak. He sat in his chair with the tripod in front of him. An unfinished landscape reminded him of the work he had to complete.

He raised the letters to his chest, shuffling through them one by one. One was for Gauguin, one for him from Bernard, and one bore a return postmark of 54 Rue Lepic, Paris.

"Ah, Theo! I am glad to hear from you. Your timing couldn't be better." The letter began like many others from him. He inquired into Vincent's health, discussed the progress of his artwork, the sales at Goupil and Gauguin's success. Then came the bombshell.

...I was surprised earlier this week when Jo showed up at my door. She was in Paris visiting her brother. She looked well. She apologized for being so abrupt with me months ago. We are getting along fine now and have been seeing each other in the evenings. I must tell you that I am excited and nervous at the same time. Nothing would please me more than to start a new life with Jo. But that will be up to her. If she should desire to wed, I think an April nuptial would be lovely, don't you?

Vincent felt as if he had been struck by a bolt of lightning. He let the letter slip from his hands. "What more can happen?" he gasped. He rose abruptly and kicked his paint box, sending paint tubes and brushes everywhere. He paced up and down the small studio, ranting to himself. Finally, he stopped in the hallway, gathered his composure, then climbed the stairs to his bedroom.

Later that evening, Gauguin stumbled into the house, smelling of cognac and wine, which had numbed his limbs and his senses. He noticed Vincent's paint box opened and on its side with paint tubes lying helter-skelter around the room. The tripod was on the floor and several canvases were scattered about. He noticed the letters off to one side, one open and crumpled. "It must have been bad news." He reached down to pick up Theo's letter and began to read.

"Good for you, Theo!" he said audibly. "Getting married."

Thump. The noise came from upstairs. Paul waited, listening for another sound. When none came, he tossed the letter back on the floor and went to his room.

Thump. There it was again. Another thud, coming from Vincent's room. Gauguin quickly locked his door and took the added precaution of moving a chair to block it. I hope he stays in his own room, he thought.

Vincent lay in his bed unable to see any light. The oppressive darkness engulfed his whole being. Suddenly, he detected high-pitched laughter. It was faint but growing louder. Theo was laughing at him. His own brother! The laughter subsided; now there was only darkness. Tumbling into an unseen abyss, he could feel his arms and legs flailing around him. He tried to scream but his voice caught in his throat. Above him were two red glowing orbs, each with dark centers, growing larger and larger. All at once he had a frightening revelation: the demon was real! He tried again to cry for help, but he could not muster a single sound.

Vincent was fixed in space, unable to sit or stand. Then, between the orbs, a monstrous maw appeared, closing in on him. Twisting and turning, he fought with all his might against the faceless creature. Suddenly he fell, his stomach lurching as he hit the floor with a bang, tangled in his bed clothes that thankfully cushioned his fall. He opened his eyes. The darkness was still there, yet there were tiny pinpoints of light emanating from the window. Then the devil's eyes were gone. His head throbbing from the crash, he slowly untangled himself and crossed over to his chair. He could not bring himself to lie back down on the bed. His heart was beating in time with his fear and, eventually, he regained his senses. He went over to the ewer and splashed his face. Grabbing the towel from the side stand, he wiped his brow, his head, his beard and neck. He sank back into the chair staring into the darkness until the sun peeked through the window. "Morning, is it morning?" he muttered, "Theo, I am lost. Companionship and loyalty are all I ask. Alone is all I will ever be."

Chapter 39
Arles-sur-Oise – December 1888

The early morning train pulled into the Arles station on time. It was nearing Christmas and the winter cold was particularly biting this year. The usual crowd of sleepy commuters embarked and disembarked the single set of stairs leading to the passenger cars. Émile, wrapped tightly in an overcoat, scarf, and hat, walked quickly down the steps and then stopped to consult his map that he had brought with him. Locating the Place Lamartine, he went south along the Avenue Paulin Talabot. He soon found himself standing at the corner of his destination. He took in the expanse of the park across from the Yellow House, which he knew immediately from the drawings Vincent had sent him. The house was dark; he continued past, finally reaching the Café de la Gare. He entered, cautious not to run into Vincent or Paul.

"Monsieur, please sit anywhere you like," said Ginoux. The restaurant was nearly empty at this hour. A few men looked as if they had spent the night sleeping off their stupor at their respective tables. Émile went to the far side of the room and sat with his back to the wall, facing the door.

"Breakfast? Coffee?" asked Ginoux.

"Croissant and coffee, please."

"Very well."

Émile waited, his legs jerking up and down as if controlled by some imaginary string orchestrated by an unseen puppeteer. Dark circles underlined his eyes. He looked like he had not slept in days. As he warmed, he removed his coat.

"Are you visiting someone in Arles?" Ginoux asked as he placed the food in front of Émile.

"Uh, no, what makes you ask that?" said Émile.

"I haven't seen you before and I know almost everyone around here," replied Ginoux.

"I came from Marseille for the day, just to see Arles. I've not been here before."

"Did you arrive on this morning's train?" quizzed Ginoux.

"Yes. I was in Paris on business and decided to stop here on the way home," Émile stammered.

"So, what business are you in that brings you here?" Ginoux wanted to know.

Émile looked at the table and took a sip of coffee, gathering time to think of an appropriate response. "I sell art supplies."

"Oh, you know, we have quite a number of artists here in Arles. Why just down the block in that ugly yellow house next to the market are two artists from Paris. They might be interested in what you sell."

Despite the cold air, perspiration glistened from Émile's hairline and his upper lip. "Thank you for the suggestion."

"Ginoux!" A man called out from across the room.

"Excuse me, sir, I must attend to another customer. Have a good visit."

Émile quickly finished his breakfast, placed some coins on the table, and left the café. He walked to the park across from the Yellow House. The trees had already bared themselves of their leaves and the early frost had claimed many of the ornamental bushes along the path. He found a wooden bench and perched where he could easily observe the Yellow House. I hope van Gogh gets up early, he thought. It's too damn cold to wait out here for any length of time.

Vincent arose, his nightclothes drenched in sweat from an arduous fight with yet another demon. He was exhausted from the battle and the nightmare had brought him a sense of dread that left him restless and achy. Sleep evaded him for the rest of the night.

He rinsed his face, cleaned his teeth, and dressed. He made his way down the stairs and into the studio. He lit an oil lamp and looked around at the clutter that he had left a few days ago.

I should not give Paul any other reason to leave, he thought to himself.

He took a deep breath and proceeded to retrieve the tubes of paint and canvases that were scattered about. As he rearranged the canvases along the walls, he noticed an envelope that had slid behind them. He opened it to discover that it was from Émile Bernard.

"Poor old Émile, you worry for naught." Just then a creak came from behind Vincent. He turned abruptly toward its source. There stood Gauguin, his coat draped loosely over his slack shoulders.

"A letter from Bernard?" he asked.

"Yes," Vincent said quietly. Before he could say anything else, Gauguin announced that he was leaving for breakfast and disappeared, leaving Vincent alone in the empty studio. The strain of their relationship weighed heavily on Vincent's morning.

Émile remained steadfast on the bench, never taking his eyes off the Yellow House. The sun was beginning to emerge, casting faint spidery shadows through the leafless trees. He decided to move to a better vantage point when he spied Gauguin emerging from the house, tugging at his coat and heading toward La Gare. Where is Vincent, Émile said under his breath. Shortly, the door opened again and a disheveled man with a red beard and long-stemmed pipe exited, also in the direction of La Gare.

"Vincent… finally!" Émile dashed across the park. He came up behind Vincent and grabbed his bone-thin arm. Vincent whirled around, prepared to defend himself.

"It's me, Vincent! It's Émile!"

Relaxing, Vincent cried, "Émile, what are you doing here? Why didn't you tell me you were coming?"

"Vincent, we must talk. In private!"

"I was on my way to Café de la Gare to have breakfast with Paul. I'm sure he would be delighted to see you. We can make room for you in the studio if you want to stay."

"Please, Vincent, we have to talk. I've come all the way from Paris to see you. Do you know somewhere we can go and talk undisturbed?"

"What can be so important as to make you travel all the way from Paris?"

"Please, can we go someplace?"

"There is a patisserie not far from here." The two walked across the park. "How is Paris? How are your parents? Have you kept in touch with Theo?" Vincent queried.

"My parents are fine. I have not seen Theo in at least a year but we correspond occasionally."

"You should see him! His business is thriving! I am so proud of his success, something which has passed me by, I'm afraid," said Vincent.

"Perhaps when I return to Paris I shall see him."

"How long are you staying?"

"I have a return train this evening."

"Émile, why not stay for a while? You would really like it here. This cold weather is unseasonable, it is usually much more pleasant. Gauguin says he feels like a new man because of Arles."

"I have to be in Paris tomorrow."

"Here we are," Vincent announced. "They have excellent pastries, the best in Arles."

They took a seat at a rear table where Émile thought they would have some privacy. "I am so excited to see you again, my friend!" Vincent exclaimed, slapping Émile on the shoulder.

Émile replied, "You may not be so happy once you know why I'm here."

"Nothing could dampen my joy!" said Vincent.

"Vincent, please. We have serious business to discuss."

Van Gogh sat back in his chair. The smile disappeared from his face and his shoulders dropped. "What could be so dire?"

The waiter came and took their order. Émile was silent for a moment, mentally composing his words. "You have read in the papers about the attempted assassination of the Tsar?"

"Why, yes, of course. It's in all the papers. And your letters. I just read one today. Émile, I am not destroying my journal."

"Today? I sent that letter to you at least a week ago!"

"It was lost—misplaced. I just found it this morning," Vincent explained.

Émile groaned. "The atmosphere in Paris is most depressing. The Russian secret police are walking the streets, along with the Sùreté. It is only a matter of time before they start making arrests. There is a lot of pressure to find the French conspirators."

"Come, come, Émile. It cannot be that bad!"

"But it is! And I am frightened. I… we could be arrested and thrown into a Russian prison! You need to face reality!" The two men halted their conversation as the waiter placed demitasse cups in front of them.

"Gauguin wrote to me and said you had drawings of us at the Commune meetings," Émile whispered.

"Of course I do. You saw me sketch!"

"Vincent, you must destroy them! Marguerite emphasized how confidential the meetings were!"

"I will do no such thing. My journal is my life blood. It has drawings and notes that I use routinely to develop my craft," Vincent argued.

"At least destroy the pages that pertain to the Commune," Émile pleaded.

"No, I will not. They are an important part of my work. Is this why you came to Arles? To have me destroy my creations?"

"These drawings can't mean much to you. You have so many. Can't you see the danger they put us in?" moaned Émile.

"I see that you are scared of your own shadow. Marguerite assured us that she would protect us."

"She cannot protect us from the Okhrana! We will be found and jailed, or worse!" Émile was adamant.

"Have the police questioned you?" Vincent countered.

"Not yet. But…"

"Then you worry for nothing."

With a raised voice, Émile said, "Vincent, you are a fool!

This is serious." He softened his tone as heads turned in their direction. "Please, give me the pages… just the ones with the commune sketches and Marguerite's likenesses. I only need those pages, not the entire journal."

"No. I will keep my journal with me and away from prying eyes but I will not let you or anyone else destroy my work." Vincent stood up.

"Vincent…" Émile said in a pleading voice.

"We will talk again but not of this." Vincent started toward the door without looking back. Émile remained seated, suddenly feeling clammy. He withdrew a handkerchief and mopped his brow.

Vincent bolted out quickly, leaving the door to slam shut behind him. Angry with his friend, he elbowed his way down the street, oblivious to all, including the tall, watchful figure leaning against a lamppost across from the café.

"That must not have gone well," the man muttered to himself. He did not move but waited until he saw Émile emerge from the café, looking beaten and weary. "So he must have been unsuccessful. Looks like van Gogh got the better of the boy." Esterhazy lit a cigarette and turned in the opposite direction.

As Christmas day neared, Vincent's sense of loneliness and abandonment deepened. Painting became secondary to drinking. Absinthe had become his primary drink of choice since wine and cognac no longer offered the solace he desired.

A couple of days before Christmas, Paul and Vincent were sitting at their respective easels in the studio when Paul announced casually, but cautiously, "I am going to Paris for the holiday."

Arles-sur-Oise 1888

Vincent did not respond.

Paul continued. "You have been in such a dark place. I don't want you to drag me down with you."

Finally, Vincent answered. "You know that is not the reason."

"It is," Paul insisted.

"No. You don't care to be here with me or work together. You think me strange."

"I am going out for a walk." Gauguin donned his coat and hat and silently walked out of the house, careful to avoid coming near Vincent. He could not bear another argument with this madman.

Vincent sat and stared at the wall. Silence engulfed the room. He closed his eyes and leaned back in his chair. Voices came into his head.

"You are to blame. You! Only you!"

"I am not to blame," he said in a loud voice. "I try, oh, how I try! What am I to do?" The last words came out in a whimper. Tears came to his eyes, clouding his vision as the voices pounded in his head. The pounding grew distant and suddenly he realized that the noise was coming from the front door. Roulin peered in. "Van Gogh?" he yelled. "Van Gogh, are you here?" The mailman spied Vincent in his chair. "Are you all right? You are staring at the wall."

Vincent turned his head and looked at Roulin, "I am fine. Do you have something for me?"

"Yes, a letter from your brother." He handed the envelope to Vincent. He took it and looked at it as if he had never seen a letter before.

"I have to finish my deliveries. Are you really sure you are all right, Vincent?"

"Go. I am fine," Vincent snapped.

Roulin was taken aback by the sharpness of his reply. He knew Vincent was sometimes a bit grumpy and folks often described him as "queer" but he had always been civil to the postman. He hastened to the door and left Vincent staring at the envelope.

He slid his finger under the flap and opened the letter. As he unfolded the single sheet, a hundred franc note fell to the floor. Theo's words seemed to jump from the page and pierce his heart like a searing dagger.

Dear Vincent:
I have wonderful news! Jo has agreed to marry me. I told her I loved her and she has told me she loves me too... I am so inexpressibly joyful... We plan to marry in the spring. We will search for a new apartment, one large enough for a family. You will be most welcome to come and visit...
A great handshake to you and Paul,
Theo

The voices in his head grew louder. "Idiot! Even your brother doesn't love you anymore. He has found a woman to take your place. Fool, fool, fool!"

"Theo loves me! Nothing can break the strength and deepness of our brotherly bond!" Vincent shouted to no one.

"He tolerates you. He now has Jo to warm him at night. He doesn't need you," the voices answered.

"No, I am important to him! I matter!"

Slowly, Vincent began to reconcile himself to his inner voice. He knew it spoke the truth. He rose from his chair, threw on his coat and headed out the door. The arguments continued as van Gogh made his way down Lamartine. People stood aside to let the curious little man pass by.

The afternoon crowd was just gathering at Café de la Gare as Vincent walked through the door. He found a small table and collapsed into the chair, hoping to become invisible in the shadows of the faintly-lit room. Observing the state that Vincent was in, Ginoux approached his table with some trepidation.

"What will it be, Vincent?"

"Absinthe, with a lump of sugar." He sat with his coat on. He reached his left hand into his pocket and took out his pipe. With his right hand, he removed a pouch of tobacco, his journal, and Theo's crumpled letter. He eyed them thoughtfully. Ginoux appeared with his drink.

Vincent's life became more meaningless with every sip of absinthe. "Where can I find happiness? I thought it would be different here. Gauguin intends to leave and Theo has abandoned me. Bernard wants to destroy my work. I have no money."

Tears welled up in his eyes, overflowing into the green absinthe. His body jerked from his quiet sobbing. The fire from his pipe tobacco had extinguished. He paid no mind and ordered more drink.

Afternoon slipped into evening, and before long, the absinthe haze encircled Vincent in a faint aura of doom. The dizzying effects of the alcohol left him feeling as though he were floating above the crowd. He started to become faint. Guess I've had enough, he thought. He picked himself up and stumbled out of the restaurant.

Vincent weaved his way down Lamartine, eliciting stares from all those around him. He grumbled, his arms flailing at unseen foes, his clothes tattered and shabby. His breath stank of hard liquor. Some found him amusing, some were fearful of this odd drunk. Vincent was unaware of the attention he was drawing for he was totally immersed in a conversation with the voices in his head.

"I don't need Theo to be successful," he slurred as he staggered up to his front door.

Gauguin was sitting in the kitchen, nursing a nagging headache with a damp cloth, when the front door opened to reveal Vincent's disheveled figure.

"Paul. Oh, Paul. It's you! You're still here!" he cried.

"Yes, I'm here. Come in, quickly now! You are quite a sight!" He rose from the kitchen table and went to Vincent.

"Paul, I need you. Please don't leave me." He grabbed Paul's hands and fell on his knees.

Gauguin's face turned crimson. He hurriedly pulled Vincent away from the door and slammed it shut.

"What the hell's wrong with you? You are an embarrassing spectacle! Vincent, I swear you are unbearable!"

"Paul, Theo has abandoned me. He has a woman now. Bernard is angry with me, Russians want me dead. I need you."

"What are you talking about? You are too smashed to know what you are doing. Go to bed and sleep it off!" he bellowed as he loosened himself from Vincent's grip and headed for the stairs.

Despite Vincent's drunkenness, he was able to catch Gauguin at the top of the stairs, wrapping his arms around Gauguin's neck. The two men staggered under Vincent's weight and Gauguin became pinned against the wall. For a brief moment, Vincent stood eye to eye with his friend. Suddenly, Gauguin felt Vincent's lips on his mouth. The kiss so startled Gauguin that he shoved Vincent violently onto the opposite wall.

"What the fuck was that?" he roared, mopping his face with his sleeve.

Vincent, with his back to the wall, gawped at Paul with heavy, half-closed eyelids. "I need you. You must stay with me," he begged, as he slid to the floor like a rag doll.

"You're drunk," spat Gauguin. The disgust he felt sent him running down the stairs as far away from Vincent as possible. Seconds later, Vincent heard rummaging coming from the studio below, and then the door slammed. He went into his room, fell onto the bed and went into a deep slumber.

Vincent slept through the next day until late afternoon. When he awoke he was confused, foggy, nauseous, and his mouth felt as though it had been stuffed with cotton. He tried to recall the events of last evening. Did he really beg Gauguin to stay? Did he really kiss him?

"What time is it? What happened last night?" he asked, rubbing his temples.

The voices returned, loud and clear. "You have gravely offended your friend, Gauguin. Once again you have acted the fool."

"What have I done?" he murmured.

The voices continued. "You have ruined everything. The demon will most certainly come for you again!"

He rose from his bed and went to the wash basin. With hands gripping both sides of the basin, he steadied himself and looked into the mirror. Swollen red eyes looked back at him.

Suddenly, a torrent of emotions overwhelmed him. Sorrow was replaced by anger, anger replaced by guilt, guilt by repentance.

"I must pay for my sins!" he cried.

He spied his razor next to the basin. The voices in his head urged him, "Do it! Do it!" Vincent put both hands to his ears to quiet them. "Repent," commanded the voices. "You must make your act of contrition!"

He grabbed the razor and with one long swift move, slashed his left ear lobe in two. Crimson blood gushed out, pouring down his neck onto his shirt. Still angry and not yet feeling the pain that was about to engulf him, Vincent flung the razor across the room. He gazed at his left hand, which was holding the severed lobe, then at the mirror. Startled by the bloodied visage staring back at him, he suddenly felt a horrible queasiness overtake him but he managed to steady himself. He grabbed a towel and wrapped it tightly around his head. "Paul must know I am repentant."

Vincent started down the steps, marking his passage with droplets of blood that had not yet begun to congeal. He entered the studio in search of a small box. He found one on the floor by his easel, emptied it of its contents, and placed his severed ear inside. Blood soaked the interior of the box until it was almost as red as the ear lobe itself.

He found his coat on the floor and put it around his shoulders as he stepped out into the cold air. Evening had fallen, the sky moonless and starless. Was that an omen? For a moment, the ground swayed beneath him and he caught his breath. When the queasiness passed, he hurried to the Café de la Gare. Ginoux saw him immediately with the bloody towel around his head and quickly came to his side.

"Vincent, what happened? Are you all right?"

"Gauguin. Ginoux, where is he?" Vincent demanded.

"He's not here." Ginoux was alarmed not only by the urgency of Vincent's voice but also by his wounded and disoriented state.

Frustrated with the innkeeper's answer, head throbbing and fighting panic, Vincent dashed out the door into the lonely streets.

He knew where he had to go. Across the park was the bordello where Rachel lived and worked. A few minutes later, Vincent arrived at the door and was greeted by the proprietress.

"Good heavens! What happened to you?"

Ignoring her question, Vincent answered, "I must see Gauguin. He's here, isn't he?"

"He is presently engaged."

"I insist… I must see him." Vincent started up the stairs.

The madam heaved a sigh and nodded to a large, powerfully-built man lurking in the shadows. The Neanderthal grabbed Vincent and effortlessly pulled him down the steps. She repeated herself. "Monsieur Gauguin is presently engaged."

Convinced that he was getting nowhere with the proprietress and certain that he could not overpower the Neanderthal, Vincent removed the box from his coat and handed it to her. "Please give Paul a message for me," he said softly.

"What shall I tell him," she said, accepting the box.

Vincent leaned into the woman and whispered in her ear. "Remember me." He turned away and disappeared into the evening.

Rachel was on her hands and knees, Gauguin thrusting into her from behind. His movements took on an urgency with each thrust. Rachel steadied herself with a hand on the wall to keep Gauguin from pushing her head into the headboard. The thrusts slowed but with each lunge, he tried to drive deeper and deeper into the small redheaded girl. The final lunge came with a small, throaty sigh from Gauguin. He rolled over onto the bed, leaving Rachel on all fours as she gazed over her naked shoulder at her latest customer.

"Well, Monsieur Paul, you must have saved that up. I thought you were trying to send me to the moon."

"Yes, well, it's no secret that I am part savage," he smirked. Rising from the bed, he dressed himself, then prepared to leave. When he opened the door, the madam was waiting for him at the bottom of the stairs, box in hand.

"Your friend left this for you, Monsieur Gauguin."

"What is it?" he asked tentatively.

"I don't know. I didn't open it and he didn't say. He also asked me to give you a message."

Paul took the box. "What message? What friend?" he asked quizzically.

He opened the box and saw the bloody lump of flesh. His jaw dropped, and the color faded from his face.

"'Remember me' is all he said."

Chapter 40
Ville d'Avray, Paris – Present Day

Mark paced back and forth in the kitchen, cell phone pressed to his ear. "Yes. Yes, Maman Chapin, the police are doing all they can. Gastineau has it all under control." He paused. "Yes. Of course, I will, as soon as I know anything. Goodbye." Gendarmes were bustling throughout the house setting up electronics. Gastineau quietly approached Mark and gently touched his arm.

"Monsieur McFadden, please have a seat and I will explain what we are doing."

"Yes, of course."

"We are preparing for a phone call. We are sure you will be contacted soon. This equipment," the policeman said as he tapped a large black box with several switches, lights, and meters, "will intercept any call to your cell phone. We will then trace the call and triangulate its origin based on the mobile towers that are pinged. Unlike what is shown in the movies, we can pinpoint a general location very quickly but we have to be in the vicinity to pin the exact location.

"This box here will analyze the voice of the caller. It will tell us if he is under stress and, if his voiceprint is in our database, it will identify him."

"I hope all of this fancy equipment does its job," Mark said dourly.

"These men are very good at their work, Monsieur."

Mark started to get up from the table when his cell phone rang. Trembling, he picked it up. Gendarmes quickly donned earpieces and turned switches on the electronics.

Gastineau nodded to him. "Take it in the living room where it is quieter."

Mark moved as instructed. "McFadden."

A burst of static penetrated the speaker; then a strange, robotic voice that reminded Mark of the mechanical larynx of a throat cancer victim said, "Monsieur McFadden, you can tell the police to stop their futile efforts to trace this call. What is important is that you listen and follow my instructions carefully or your wife will join our friend Durand."

"Don't hurt Maggie! Please, is she all right? Let me talk to her!"

"Your wife is alive and well for now. How she fares in the future is up to you."

The ominous voice continued. "You will go to Gare de Lyon by taxi. Once inside the station, you will see a large arrival and departure board directly across from the rail tracks. Beneath this board is a flower cart. The vendor is a lovely lady. She knows nothing of this matter. You will stand next to the cart and wait. Further instructions will be given to you there. You must be there by four o'clock today. Do you understand?"

"Yes! I want to talk to my wife!"

"Monsieur, you are not in a position to make demands! I have more instructions for you. Are you listening?"

"Yes, I'm listening," he snarled.

The mysterious caller let out a menacing cackle. "Are the police making progress in tracing this call?"

The technician looked up from the electronic gear and shook his head. Gastineau let out a sigh and whispered,

"Keep trying." To Mark, he said, "Keep him talking."

Mark felt the anger building within him. "What else do you want me to do?" he growled.

"You will wear a tan blazer, dark pants, black shoes and socks. Oh, and you must wear a white hat—a symbol of virtue, yes?" He chuckled. "Do you have all of these items?"

Mark repeated the instructions with his eyes on Gastineau. "Yes, I have them all."

"Excellent. Oh, and the hat cannot be what you Americans call a 'baseball cap.' It must be a proper chapeau."

"Okay. I got it."

"You will put the van Gogh journal in the pocket of your blazer. Do you understand?"

"Yes."

"Very well. Now, for the most important part. And please make sure your guests listen carefully. The police are not to follow you or accompany you in any manner. Tracking devices are strictly forbidden. If you fail to adhere to these instructions, you will never see your wife again."

"Please, don't hurt Maggie. I'll do as you say."

"That is wise. Be at Gare de Lyon at four o'clock." The line went dead.

Gastineau looked expectantly at the technician. "Were you able to pinpoint the location?" he asked.

"No, sir. The call was routed through several relay stations and satellites. He was clever."

"Merde!"

Wearily, Gastineau looked at Mark and said, "It looks like you have an appointment to keep, Monsieur McFadden."

The taxi arrived at Mark's house at half past two. As Gastineau ushered Mark to the door, he said, "You will make it to Gare de Lyon in plenty of time. Remain calm. We are doing everything possible to get your wife back safely."

"What if your men are spotted?"

"My men are already in place. They are not wearing uniforms. There is no need for alarm, Monsieur. Please, go and retrieve your wife."

Traffic through Paris' 15th, 7th, and 6th arrondissements was painfully time-consuming. Mark stared out the back window watching buildings pass with agonizing sluggishness. The taxi crossed the Seine on Pont Charles de Gaulle, continuing until it reached the train station.

"How ironic," Mark murmured, looking at the street sign reading, "'Rue Van Gogh.'" He paid the driver and stepped onto the plaza in front of the clock tower on the north side of the train station. Patrons crowded the broad walkway and hustled in and out of the terminal's massive doors.

Mark hesitated. He could not discern any irregularities. If the police are here, they are well disguised, he thought. He walked quickly into the train station and halted a few feet from the entrance to get his bearings. Banners hung from the high-arching ceiling advertising toiletries, clothes, and the latest digital gadgets. Near the center, where trains lined up to greet their passengers, were large inlaid letters: 'Hall One.'

There, directly in front and above him, was a large electronic arrival and departure board. Underneath the board, on the side toward the trains, was a small hand cart overflowing with colorful bouquets. An older woman in an apron and matching bonnet was fluffing up floral displays. Mark positioned himself next to the cart, trying to appear casual.

"Monsieur?" she offered.

Mark turned to face the woman as she gazed up at him in anticipation.

"Non," he replied, waving his hands and shaking his head. He nervously scanned the terminal—shifting streams of people moving chaotically in every direction. The image blurred before him, his heart thumping so powerfully that he thought his chest would explode. He worried that the old lady could hear it.

Across the terminal he watched a mass of humanity disappearing into the floor, gliding down the ramps toward the track platforms. He repeatedly and reflexively glanced at his watch, with time seeming to slow. The atmosphere inside the terminal was heavy, adding weight to Mark's already overburdened shoulders as time ground to a halt.

"Come on," he seethed. "It's 4:20. Come on."

A dull ache in his back sharpened with each passing minute. He leaned against a stone wall under the board, trying to push the irritating pain away. The old woman was staring at him. He tried to smile but it was no use.

"Oh, for Chrissake! It's 4:30! Where the hell are you?" He was clammy with sweat, his shirt now sticking to him and making him feel even more smothered.

Suddenly a man with a briefcase was beside Mark.

Mark turned toward the stranger, who continued past him and stopped in front of the flower vendor. The man left with a large bouquet of Sorbonne lilies mixed with baby's breath, yellow roses, and white alstroemeria.

As Mark let out an audible sigh, he was startled by a tug on his arm. Standing at his side was a bespectacled boy, a young teenager. Blotches of fine facial hair failed to conceal severe acne covering his cheeks, forehead, and chin.

"Are you Monsieur McFadden?" the boy asked in a cracking voice.

"Yes? Yes! I am!"

The boy handed Mark an envelope. "Take TGV 6623 to Marseille. The train leaves at 4:57 from Track Nine in Hall Three. You must hurry." The boy turned to leave but Mark grabbed his shirtsleeve before he could get away.

"Who sent you? Who gave this to you?" Mark cried.

"You must hurry, Monsieur," the boy urged, "or you will miss your train. Go down that way," he said, pointing to a ramp leading under the station. "Go to Hall Three, Track Nine. Hurry now."

Mark looked at his watch. 4:52. He released the boy and ran toward the ramp. He pushed his way through the crowds, taking the escalator two steps at a time. He barely noticed irritated passengers cursing after him.

Once inside Hall Three, he looked for Track Nine. There was Track Fifteen, Thirteen, Eleven… then Nine! A voice over the loudspeaker was announcing the final call for Marseille.

The dash to Track Nine was quick. He bounded up the steps into the last car as the conductor took one final look up and down the platform. The train started with a jolt, testing his balance as a conductor appeared at his side.

"Monsieur?"

"Pardon," Mark mangled in French, his breathing labored, "I don't speak French, could you help me?"

"But of course."

Mark took the envelope that the boy had given him and handed it to the conductor. The conductor opened it and withdrew a single voucher.

"You are in first-class, Monsieur. Your seat is in the front car. You will have to go all the way forward, just past the first-class dining car." He turned the voucher toward Mark and pointed to numbers near the edge. "Your row and seat are here."

"Thank you. *Merci,*" nodded Mark.

The conductor moved past him and began assisting other passengers. Mark started toward the front of the car and onward through the doors into the next car. He rocked along with the train until he reached the first-class section, where he was blocked by another conductor who asked to see Mark's ticket. Satisfied that all was in order, he gestured Mark to move on ahead.

The dining car was brimming with men and women enjoying an assortment of libations, a scene that struck Mark as surreal. He squeezed along the narrow aisle, occasionally bumping a boisterous arm or a protruding foot of a reveler. His breaths were shallow, and the noisy car rattled him like the din of a lunatic asylum.

With a sigh of relief he finally reached the first car, and searched for his seat. It was on the aisle, and the window seat beside it was empty. Across the aisle, an elderly couple was sharing a wrinkled newspaper. Behind him were two businessmen huddled over a laptop. Directly in front a young couple doted over a sleeping baby.

Mark collapsed into the seat, drew a deep breath and exhaled loudly, grateful to be off his feet. The elderly lady turned and smiled at him, then continued reading. A conductor stopped beside him to punch his ticket. As he settled in the ache in his back began to ease, the rhythmic rocking of the train having a hypnotic effect on his tired mind. His eyes slowly closed and his head drooped to one side. Outside, the verdant pastures of southern France flew past as Mark twitched and shuddered in restless on-and-off sleep.

Chapter 41
Paris, Arles-sur-Oise – December 1888

On Christmas Eve, Theo and Jo sat together on the dark green divan in his apartment, planning their upcoming visit to Jo's parents in Holland to announce the engagement. Jo had spent most of the day preparing their evening meal. The aroma wafting from the kitchen made Theo's mouth water as he raised another glass of port to toast his bride-to-be. Moments later, a message arrived for Theo. The letter was post-marked 'Arles'."

"Good heavens!" exclaimed Theo.

"What is it, my love?" asked Jo.

"It's from Gauguin. He says I should come to Arles immediately. Something has happened to Vincent."

"What?" Jo asked.

"He doesn't say. Only that I should come straightaway."

"Then you should go. When is the next train?"

"But, Jo, I just arrived. This is our first Christmas together," Theo protested.

"We shall have many more, my love. Your brother needs you. Go and be with him."

The evening train from Amsterdam to Arles departed on schedule. It was an arduous fifteen-hour journey. Theo sat alone, staring pensively out the window. Just a short while ago, he was filled with joy at the prospect of spending the holidays with Jo. In an instant his bright spirits had dissipated, his joy now elusive as a butterfly. Theo pushed away feelings of resentment that had begun to creep into his consciousness.

The train pulled into the Arles station at mid-morning on Christmas Day. The air was crisp, the sky an azure blue with scattered white, puffy clouds. Theo stood on the platform scouring the area for a sign of Gauguin. A raised arm appeared above the crowd, waving in his direction. Gauguin made his way over to Theo, extending his hand in greeting.

"I am sorry to have sent you such a troubling cable. It is good that you are here. How was your journey?"

"Long. Tiring. I was with Jo celebrating our engagement when I received your message. Now, tell me, what is going on with Vincent? Is he all right?"

"He injured himself a couple of days ago. He is in the hospital and should be fine. At least, physically."

"Theo," Paul said, "I have tried to put on a brave face these past few months, but it has not been easy. Vincent is almost impossible to live with. He is abusive and angry. He is jealous that you are selling my paintings and not his."

"Yes, yes. But what happened?"

"About a week ago we went to the Museum in Montpellier. It was a good trip but Vincent was in one of his moods after we got back. He argued and shouted at passersby and at me. I wrote to you that I would stay, hopeful that this mood would pass. I believe I was a bit hasty in that regard."

"Paul, what happened?" Theo said sternly.

"I'm coming to it. Well, the other day, he was drinking and in ill humor. I could not bear to be around him and left the house. Later that evening, while I was out, I received a box from him. When I opened it, there was a piece of Vincent's ear inside."

"What?! Oh Lord! He cut off his ear?" Theo stopped dead

in his tracks.

"Not his entire ear, but a good size piece," Paul replied.

"What was he thinking? He must have been out of his mind!" Theo looked down at his feet.

Gauguin felt awkward. He looked around as if searching for the right words. "I discovered him on his bed," he continued, "covered in blood. I got him to the hospital as soon as I could. He is in good care," he told Theo reassuringly.

"Was he hurt badly? Were there any other cuts on his body?" asked Theo.

"No. They cleaned and bandaged the wound, and he seems to be recovering."

"Let's go straight to the hospital."

"Let me get a carriage for us," Paul suggested.

The wards at Hôtel-Dieu were nearly empty on Christmas. Even the sick wanted to be home on this one day. The two men entered the front door and Paul led the way to the ward where Vincent lay. The ailing artist's head was wrapped with a white bandage that extended under his jaw. There was a tincture of red on the right side where his ear was located. A man dressed in a white smock was bent over Vincent, inspecting the bandage.

"Oh, my God," whispered Theo, "he looks ghastly!"

The attendant raised his head and looked at Theo. Paul introduced them. "Doctor, this is Theo van Gogh, Vincent's brother."

The doctor offered his hand to Theo. "I am Doctor Félix Rey, attending physician. Vincent has suffered trauma to his ear. It appears that he cut off his ear lobe with a sharp object, probably a razor."

"Will he be okay?"

"Physically, he will be fine. There was a lot of blood loss, but the damage was limited to the ear. However, what caused him to inflict this harm to himself remains to be determined."

"He has had fits before but he's never hurt himself," said Theo.

Dr. Rey took Theo by the arm and led him away from the bed. The doctor was very young and sported a Van Dyke beard that lent sophistication to his otherwise youthful countenance.

Leaning into Theo, he said softly, "Your brother has suffered a break with reality. I am not sure what caused it but I have prescribed some medication that might help. He will remain here a few days and then we will determine what our next steps should be."

"Thank you, Doctor. I appreciate what you are doing for him. He has a volatile nature but he has never hurt himself before."

"You can stay with him for now, Monsieur van Gogh. I have rounds to make but I will be back to check on him later."

The doctor turned and left the ward while Theo moved slowly back to Vincent's bedside. Looking down on Vincent, he whispered, "What would make you do this? Oh, Vincent!" After a short silence, Theo continued, "At least you are cleaned up. I don't remember the last time I saw you clean-shaven."

Theo sat on the side of the bed. Vincent lay with his eyes closed and brows furrowed, his pupils darting back and forth under his heavy eyelids. Theo raised his legs onto the bed and rested his head on the pillow next to Vincent.

"Remember how we used to play as children? You were always trying to tell Wil and me what to do. We never listened. And then you went away to school. You were forced to grow up quickly. I was too young to understand what it meant to be an adult. Until father told me I had to work to help out."

He paused, looked at Vincent and the bandages wrapped around his head, then looked at the ceiling. "I remember when you started to paint. Mother thought it a waste of time. You are getting better, you know. A bit more work and you will be extraordinary. You are on the precipice of greatness, my brother. I know it."

The one-sided conversation continued as Theo reminisced about their misspent youth. He made light of Vincent's many transgressions that frequently earned him a smack on the derriere or to be sent to bed without supper. Finally, Theo put his feet on the floor and stood. Gauguin had left. When Theo reached the front door, he found Paul waiting for him in the hallway.

"How long are you staying?" Paul asked Theo.

"I will catch the next train back to Paris."

"So soon? Very well. I will come with you. I just need to pick up a few things at the house. I can have my canvases shipped by train separately."

Theo looked pained as he walked through the house where Vincent had spent such an agonizing time. Blood spatters remained on the floor and a larger mess covered Vincent's bed. As Theo surveyed the quarters that Vincent and Gauguin had shared, Gauguin packed for his trip to Paris. Before long, the two men left the house and walked in the cold night air to the train station. The small platform was nearly deserted as they waited for the train.

"He will be fine, Theo," Paul finally said.

"I hope so. He is troubled."

"Oh, I am certainly aware of that," replied Paul with a trace of sarcasm in his voice. "It has not been easy to remain here alone with him, especially in this armpit of a town. If it weren't for you, I would have left long ago."

Theo looked at Paul but remained silent. The train arrived before he could think of something to say to him. He did not look forward to this long journey back to Paris and felt a bit of angst over leaving his brother behind.

That night, while Theo dozed on the train, Vincent thrashed about in his hospital bed. Violent nightmares alternated with periods of dark calm. Then demons would appear from out of the depths of his sub-conscious and entangle themselves with childhood delusions. They seemed all too real. When he opened his eyes, an indistinct form hovering above him came slowly into focus.

"Monsieur van Gogh, can you hear me? Are you in pain? Monsieur van Gogh, please try to stay awake. The voice was calm, peaceful, and reassuring.

"My name is Dr. Rey. I have been looking after you since you arrived at Hôtel Dieu. Monsieur, do you know where you are?"

Vincent's eyes flickered as he took in his surroundings. He did not recognize this place. A sudden flash of fear overtook him and he pushed downward on the bed to raise himself up, only to have this strange figure gently push him back.

"Where am I?" he asked.

"In the hospital. You cut yourself. Do you remember?"

"I remember lying in my bed waiting for the demon to take me."

"No demon took you. You are safe now. I am Dr. Rey."

"Doctor... doctor?"

"You are in the hospital," he repeated. "Do you remember cutting yourself?"

Slowly Vincent put his hand to his ear and his face. "What happened to my beard?"

"We had to shave your beard to clean up the blood. Your beard was so matted we were afraid of infection at the site of the wound."

"I want to go home. Bring me my clothes."

"I'm sorry, Monsieur van Gogh, you must stay here for a few days. Please try to relax. You have a very nasty wound."

Vincent was too tired, too hungry, and too groggy to resist. He lay back and drifted in and out of sleep. The hallucinations returned. A leathery, horned figure sneered down at him. Laughing, it proclaimed that Theo had abandoned him. The laugh turned into a loud, cackling roar. He pushed and kicked at the freakish beast. He could feel its tentacles encircling him like a boa constrictor on a helpless mongoose. Try as he might, he could not free himself from the demon-monster. He felt the restraints clamp him to a sacrificial altar. Then the voices came, calm, soothing, heartening—

"Monsieur Vincent, you must not resist. You are safe here. It was merely a dream. We have restrained you for your protection."

The next few days were a mixture of agitation followed

by short bouts of tranquility. He learned that Theo had visited him in his depraved condition. But where was he now?

"Dr. Rey why did Theo not stay?" became a frequent question to which the doctor had no answer.

The letter from Arles arrived shortly after Theo was back in Paris. Vincent, it appeared, was mentally unbalanced and prone to physical attacks—hurting not only himself but others. It was reported that he berated other patients and chased the nurses. Letters from Dr. Rey confirmed the diagnosis of "mental alienation," a term widely used to describe insanity. To complicate matters, the Arles police had been tasked with determining Vincent's ability to handle being released.

Theo brooded over Vincent's precarious situation. With his impending marriage and the likelihood of moving to a larger apartment more suitable for a family, Theo fretted over the expense of a highly-rated asylum. He wrote to a local cleric at the hospital, the Reverend Salles, for a second opinion. He secretly hoped that the minister would tell him that Vincent was ready to be released. Instead, Salles only reaffirmed Vincent's delicate state of mind. Disappointed but resolved, Theo set a course to fight any distractions except that of his marriage to Jo. Thus, Vincent became merely a shadow at dusk; long and ghostly, but only noticeable if one turned his back to the sun. Theo decided to face the sun and went to Amsterdam to help Jo with the wedding plans.

Vincent ruminated constantly over Theo's hasty departure. He battered the doctor and the reverend with questions daily. "Any news from Theo?" he would ask. Their inability to provide any updates served to deepen his despair and the darkness in his soul lingered like an unwelcome visitor. Then one day, the rays of the late afternoon sun streamed through the windows and bathed Vincent in a shimmering light, and he felt a divine-like intervention. It was as if a fever was breaking.

An odd calm came over him and he whispered: "I must be my own man. I must get back to work. I cannot let events control me. I must be strong."

The next day, Dr. Rey noticed a marked improvement in Vincent's demeanor. The Reverend Salles agreed that Vincent seemed less agitated and in brighter spirits. Consequently, he was moved from isolation to a shared ward, where he kept to himself but performed well. By early January, they recommended that Vincent be accompanied to Arles for a day trip, and that, too, was successful—he remained calm, quiet, and thoughtful, and when he spoke, he did so reasonably and rationally. The following week, Dr. Rey agreed that Vincent was ready for full release.

Dr. Rey brought Vincent his shirt and trousers, which had been cleaned and pressed. Vincent dressed and when he donned his coat, he noticed one side was bulging. He placed his hand in the large pocket and discovered his journal. He fingered its worn leathery binder; it felt as familiar as an old friend, and he smiled.

"Be careful, Monsieur van Gogh," warned the doctor. "Do not exert yourself. And please be mindful of the discharge instructions that we have provided. Most important of all, avoid conflict or anything that might cause you undue distress. We are releasing you in the custody of Monsieur Roulin, the postman, who has kindly agreed to accompany you home."

Vincent's return to the Yellow House was greeted by an eviction notice from his landlord, along with the skeptical glances from a few neighbors. "Stay strong," he murmured to himself as he read the notice. It said he had until Easter to remove his belongings. Perfect, he thought. Just perfect.

The studio was in shambles. Painting supplies were strewn about the room, canvases pitched every which way on the floor. He could not recall throwing a tantrum before he went to the hospital.

"Clearly, I have forgotten how bad things were," he half-whispered. "I must call someone to clean up. I hope none of my work is damaged. Now, where are my paints?" He began to search through the rubble.

Over the next few days, he managed to restore order to the studio, with completed canvases on one wall and unfinished work on another. The cleaning woman was successful in getting up most of the blood and paint splatters, and she finished her work and departed quietly.

The next morning he awoke, refreshed from a long and much desired good night's sleep. He was ready to start the day with renewed vigor, but he was not yet prepared to face the public or go into the countryside to find subjects. Instead, he found his subjects in his little Yellow House. He searched among his canvases and came across a portrait of Augustine Roulin, the postman's wife, whom he had painted before his attack.

"This has such promise. *La Berceuse*. Augustine Rocking a Cradle. I will make copies of this, improving each with color and hue." He set to work, copying the portrait of Augustine sitting in a rocking chair and holding a rope attached to an unseen bassinet. He copied sunflowers and painted a scene of his bedroom, but then was distracted by the sound of pebbles hitting his windows.

"What now?" he yelled to no one in particular. "A bunch of schoolboys pelting my windows!" He hastened to the door and flung it open as though casting off an unwanted overcoat. As soon as the boys saw Vincent, they scattered in different directions. "Scoundrels, all of you! Go away and don't come back!"

Vincent was stomping about when Roulin appeared, mail in hand, his mail sack dangling from his hefty shoulder. "Van Gogh, what are you doing? It looks like you are chasing the children."

"Indeed, I am! The little shits keep watching me through the window as if I were an oddity on display for their viewing pleasure."

"Chasing them will only encourage them."

"Well, what should I do, just let them stare and throw stones at my windows? They interrupt my work! Besides that, they might break something and then who shall pay for that?"

"Come, let's go inside," said Roulin, calmly. "I have some news to discuss." The pair went inside and Roulin took a seat in the studio.

"Would you like some coffee?" asked Vincent.

"Yes, that would be lovely. It is cold and I've been walking since early this morning."

"Wait here while I make some."

Roulin looked around the studio. He set down his large sack, removed his hat and coat and sat in the chair formerly used by Gauguin. He scanned the canvases lining the walls.

There were three pictures of his wife in a rocking chair, three paintings of sunflowers, and one painting of a bedroom. Against the wall, separate from the other paintings, was a portrait of Vincent with no beard. Within that portrait was a painting of Gauguin in the background. He studied the self-portrait—it looked serious, almost menacing.

Vincent returned with a tray of coffee, lemon peel, sugar, and cream.

"Ah, this will help to warm me!" proclaimed Roulin.

Vincent set the tray on a rickety three-legged table Gauguin had purchased shortly after his arrival in Arles. "Please help yourself." He took a cup for himself, added sugar and lemon, then perched in the chair in front of the easel. "You said you had news?"

"Yes. I have taken a promotion and will be leaving for Marseille at the end of the month."

"Leaving? You are leaving?" Vincent made no attempt to conceal his disappointment.

"Yes. My wife and son and I will be moving shortly. Hopefully by month's end."

Vincent was quiet.

"It pays more money and with a small child, I can use it."

"I will be very sorry to see you leave. You have been a good friend to me, Roulin."

"Why, thank you, Vincent."

"Before you go, have your wife come over and select a painting." He pointed to the wall of paintings of Augustine. "I will make a present of one to her."

"I am sure she would like that very much. I'll tell her to come by. Now, how have you been, besides chasing little hooligans?" Roulin chuckled. "Your place looks much better, by the way. You've been hard at work."

"Those hooligans are no laughing matter. They drive me mad. Even their parents taunt me."

"Come now, Vincent, is it really that bad?" Roulin said with a smile.

"It is! I cannot go outside for a smoke or to enjoy some fresh air without being accosted. They encircle me like a ring of fire. I have even been followed."

"Who would follow you? I can believe that some would tease you, but follow you?" questioned Roulin.

"Tease, you say? It is not teasing. It's maliciousness. They call me names like 'the one-eared mongrel.' And yes, I have been followed. Just yesterday I noticed someone trailing behind me as I walked to La Gare and to the river."

"Who was it? Did you know them?"

"I'm not sure. A tall man, rather large, with a mustache. He was bundled tight in his coat and wore a hat low on his face so I could not make out his features. But he has followed me before, I'm sure of it."

"But you don't know him?"

"I don't know. I don't think so. He doesn't look familiar."

"Well, I wouldn't worry about it. It's probably just your imagination playing tricks on you."

"If that is the case, I wish it would stop," Vincent flinched.

"How are you sleeping?"

"Fine, when I do sleep. I don't sleep for long periods."

"Well, I must go and finish my route," said Roulin as he picked up his mail pouch. "We will speak again soon and I will mention the painting to Augustine."

Vincent escorted Roulin to the door. The cold air wafted its way through the portal, chilling him to the bone. He looked dejected; his heart heavy as he anticipated the permanent departure of a trusted friend. He blinked back tears as he bade farewell to his trusted friend.

Vincent spent the next couple of weeks in isolation, leaving the Yellow House only for the bare necessities. He penned a note to his brother, telling him how heartbroken he was that Theo had been forced to journey to Arles on his account. Vincent assured him that he was fine and that he should not worry about him. Then he inquired about Gauguin. Had he terrified him? Why hadn't he given Vincent any sign of life? He asked Theo to tell Gauguin that he was thinking of him and to please write.

The next day, Felix Rey, along with two other doctors, paid a house call to the Yellow House. Vincent was delighted to see them and eager to show Dr. Rey his art. Dr. Rey was quickly caught up in Vincent's unrestrained enthusiasm and agreed to sit for him soon. After a couple of hours, he left the house, convinced that Vincent was his old self once again.

Later that same exuberant day Vincent received Theo's engagement announcement:

Engaged
Theodorus van Gogh
and
Johanna Bonger
January 1889
Paris
Amsterdam
Reception Wednesday, 9 January
Weteringschans 121

"Well, this is not unexpected," he thought. "I wish Theo well, but I will not be there. Amsterdam is much too far." Days passed and Vincent remained in isolation, alternately working frantically and sitting disconsolately in his studio.

Chapter 42
Paris, Arles-sur-Oise – Late Winter-Early Spring 1889

Theo found a new apartment where he and Jo could raise a family together. Although it was further away from the artists' colony on Montmartre, it was nearer his office. In that respect it would give him more time to be with his young wife. He immediately started refurbishing the third-floor apartment at 8 Cité Pigalle, adding a new furnace and a gas stove in the kitchen. He had running water installed in the kitchen and bathroom. He wanted Jo's opinion and sent her swatches of wallpaper to look over almost daily.

Between his job at Goupil, apartment renovations, wedding planning, and his obsessive writing to Jo, Theo had little time to think about Vincent. He was overseeing the preparation for a Monet exhibition in the Goupil entresol when he received a letter from Reverend Salles.

Dear Sir,
Your brother, whom we had believed more or less cured and who had taken up his usual work once more, has again lately shown signs of mental distress. For three days he has imagined that he is being poisoned and is seeing nothing but poisoners and poisoned people everywhere. The cleaning woman, who looks after him with a certain devotion, noticing his more than abnormal state, considered it her duty to report it—and the neighbors brought it to the attention of the central commissioner. This man put your brother under surveillance, and this afternoon had him driven to the hospital, where he has been placed in an isolation cell. I have just seen him and his state made a very painful impression on me. He has

withdrawn into absolute muteness, hides himself under his bedcovers and sometimes cries without uttering a word. Today, according to the cleaning woman, he has refused all food; all day yesterday and this morning he has spoken little and at times his behavior has frightened this poor woman, who told me that while he was in this state she could not continue to look after him.

"Dear God! I have been so blind. What will I do now?" Theo could hardly contain his shame as he read the news about Vincent's arrest. He strode to his office in the rear of the Gallery and wrote a short note to the Rev. Salles.

Dear Reverend Salles,
Thank you for your letter regarding my brother, Vincent. I am sorry but it is impossible for me to come to Arles at this time as I am deeply involved in an important work project. I must therefore rely on your sound judgment. Do you think it absolutely necessary for Vincent to have constant supervision? Does he really need to be kept in a hospital cell or an asylum? If the answer is yes, are there local hospitals or asylums that would be less expensive than the ones near Paris? I fear the cost of Hôtel Dieu is more than I can financially bear, for the long term, but my brother's well-being is very important to me.
I look forward to your reply regarding my brother's health.
With appreciation,
Theo van Gogh

Vincent was kept in isolation in Hôtel Dieu with only a bed, a chair, a closet, and a small fireplace. Visitors were not allowed unless they were sanctioned by the hospital. Reverend Salles had seen to it that a fire had been lit to warm his room. The examining doctor felt that he needed a sedative to help him sleep, so one was administered shortly after his arrival. The effect was almost immediate. Vincent had been completely exhausted by his heated struggle with his captors.

Violent dreams of monsters and demons descended upon him once again. He found himself wandering through a field of sunflowers, but with a dirty mist hovering like a blanket of scum. There were rugged mountains in the distance. Suddenly a demon appeared before him. But was it a demon? Or a human that had mutated into something else? It sniggered at him, then raised long, ugly claws. Vincent shrank away in disgust and fear, then began running. As he fled the monster, he tripped and landed face down in mire. The demon was upon him immediately, raking its cold talons across his back, his legs, his arms. Its fiendish laughter filled his ears.

"I am always with you, Vincent. I will never leave you. You will never be alone again!" The demon cackled, then flew away. Vincent righted himself. This must surely be hell, he thought. He looked up toward the heavens and saw a small circle of light.

The light grew brighter and larger. It now filled most of his vision. "Please, God, if it is you, receive this poor wretched servant into your arms," he pleaded silently.

"Monsieur van Gogh! Monsieur van Gogh, can you hear me?" The doctor was holding a flame near Vincent's head, passing it back and forth from his left eye to his right. The attending nurse noted, "Doctor, I think he is moving. His eyes are flickering. He's trying to say something."

"Monsieur van Gogh!" he repeated.

Vincent sat up with a jerk, suddenly aware of the doctor and the candlelight. He gaped, slack-jawed and bleary-eyed, for he did not recognize anyone, nor could he remember where he was. Then he saw a familiar figure, the Reverend Salles, approach the bed.

"Monsieur Vincent, do you recognize me? I am Reverend Salles. You know me, don't you?"

Vincent's eyes narrowed as he squinted to focus. "Why, yes. I know you, Reverend." He eyed his surroundings, taking in the austere room. "Where am I?"

"You are in the hospital again. Do you remember being brought here by the gendarmes?"

"No... yes? I'm not sure. Maybe. When may I go home?" he said, rubbing his eyes.

The doctor spoke. "Monsieur van Gogh, you are ill and in need of medical attention. You will remain here until you are better."

"How long will that be? I want to return to my house and my studio. I have work to do."

"I am not sure how long you will be here. For now, you must rest and regain some strength." As the doctor ushered the nurse and Salles out of the room he instructed them, "We should let him rest. Nurse, please check on him later and make sure he is not agitated."

Vincent threw off his covers and attempted to get out of bed, shouting after them, "I need to go home! You can't keep me here!" But his legs gave out and he stumbled to the floor. He cradled himself and wept.

Outside his room, the physician spoke again with the preacher. "Dr. Rey was correct with his diagnosis. Vincent is mentally alienated. I will prescribe potassium bromide to help him through the next few days. That should quell his outbursts. In the meantime, it is my understanding that you are in touch with his brother, is that correct?"

"Yes, Doctor."

"Good. Please tell his brother that Monsieur van Gogh should be placed in a long-term care asylum. I'm afraid his condition may not improve."

"I will advise his brother accordingly, but I am not sure he can support the cost of a long-term confinement."

"Then Vincent may become a ward of the state." The doctor walked away, leaving Salles standing in the hallway. He could hear Vincent moaning and sobbing behind the door. Salles' worry felt crushing, but all he could do was walk away and hope that the second dose of medication would soon take effect.

Theo received regular letters from Salles, each explaining that Vincent was showing no improvement and requesting a decision on his brother's care, which Theo was loathe to do. He was in Goupil's mezzanine when another missive arrived.

Monsieur,
It is with great pleasure I tell you that your brother shows signs of improvement. The doctors have removed him from isolation and have allowed him to make day trips into the city. For myself, I fear this improvement to be short lived and would encourage you to consider an institution. I sincerely hope I am wrong.

Best wishes,
Salles

"Finally, some good news," Theo cried. "Now I can concentrate fully on the wedding, knowing that Vincent is better. I simply cannot worry about him right now. Perhaps the day trips will keep him in good spirits."

In Arles, Vincent returned to his residence on a day visit. He had hoped to resume his painting, but the medication made him lethargic and sleepy, and he lacked both motivation and inspiration—the fear of every artist.

He stared at a blank canvas before him for some time. When the sun began to fade, he rose, trance-like, and slipped on his coat to return to the Hôtel Dieu.

A group of neighbors had assembled outside the Yellow House. When Vincent appeared at the front door, someone snarled, "Go back to Paris, crazy man!" Then another, "Why are you out of the hospital, one-eared mongrel? Leave!"

Vincent said nothing as he made his way through the onlookers. An arm grabbed Vincent's shoulder and gave an emphatic shove. Still in a weakened state, Vincent fell to one knee. He bent his head and paused.

"He's weeping! The madman is crying!"

"Watch out, the mongrel might bite!"

Vincent rose slowly, steadied himself, and continued toward the hospital, his head bowed in silence. He had no desire for confrontations of any sort. He was grateful for the impending darkness that would enshroud him. Then he would be at the hospital, away from all this unwanted commotion.

Weeks passed and Vincent had stopped showing signs of agitation and hallucination. The police captain, doctor, and the minister met outside the ward to discuss another release.

"Are you sure he's safe?" the gendarme asked.

"I cannot be absolutely sure of anything, Captain. I cannot be sure that you are safe. But I have no medical reason to hold him any longer."

The captain smirked at the doctor. "I don't want disturbances. If he returns to the hospital, you will put him in isolation and you will keep him there!"

"That's fine. But for now, I have no authority to keep him here. Do you?"

"No," replied the captain.

The doctor turned to the pastor. "Then, Rev. Salles, would you please escort Monsieur van Gogh home? I would very much appreciate it if someone such as you actually got him safely to his house."

"Certainly, Doctor. I will be glad to see him home." Salles and the nurse went into the ward, leaving the doctor and the captain alone to continue a tense conversation.

"Are you doing the right thing?" the captain wanted to know.

Exhaling deeply, the doctor said, "I don't know. I hope so."

A few days later, a letter from Salles arrived at Theo's door. Theo's stomach churned as he took in the dreadful news.

Monsieur,
Your poor brother has been taken into the hospital again. As you will undoubtedly have heard from him, he had returned to his house a few days ago.

However, his behavior, and the way he talked, made me fear that the improvement which had taken place was only superficial. This fear, which we all had, proved only too well-founded. A petition signed by some 30 neighbours, informed M. the Mayor of the inconvenience caused by allowing this man his complete liberty and cited facts to support this assertion. The superintendent of police, to whom the document was submitted, has immediately had your brother taken back to the hospital with the express order not to let him leave. He came to my house to inform me of the situation, and to ask me to write to you.

It is clear that a decision has to be made. Is it your intention to come and take your brother with you, or to put him into an institution of your own choice? Or do you prefer to leave it in the hands of the police? On this point we should have a categorical reply.

Will you please without hesitation make your intentions known, and address them either to myself or to the Mayor or to the superintendent of police. We will only act after having received your reply and we will act according to your wishes.

I had rather hoped to have some better news, and that stopped me from writing to you sooner to acknowledge receipt of your letter and the 50 f. that it contained.

My deepest sympathies, and I assure you of my best wishes.
Salles

Theo groaned. "What do I do now? I have to go to Amsterdam soon. Vincent, is this your way of sabotaging my wedding?" He felt terribly guilty having such selfish thoughts, but felt intuitively a connection between Vincent's relapses and his own marriage.

The isolation in the cell was absolute. Even the demons did not come to taunt Vincent. The silence roared. Vincent tried to scream but nothing came out. He raised his hands to his face but could not see or feel his fingers. This must truly be hell, to not even know ridicule, he thought. He tried to imagine his paintings, *La Berceuse,* and others. No images appeared. He felt suspended in a vacuum, unable to breathe, with ethereal memories flickering but not able to fully form.

Then he felt a nudge. Could it be real? There it was again! And a voice twisting through from beyond the darkness. The nudge came again, and he shook.

The nurse stood over Vincent, trying to shake him awake. He was huddled in a fetal position under the covers, and she could hear him moaning and sputtering as if attempting to speak. But words were unintelligible.

"Monsieur van Gogh! Wake up! You have a letter from Paris, Monsieur van Gogh."

The blanket flew off and Vincent bolted up, eyes wide open, his head swaying back and forth. His eyes focused down on the nurse, and she took a step back from the cot, frightened by the bedraggled red-headed man gaping at her with menacing eyes.

"Here! Your letter!" She tossed it at the foot of the bed and ran out of the small room. Vincent heard the door latching in place.

He perched on the bed, turning the letter over in his hands as he tried to anticipate its contents. It had been several weeks since Theo had written. Consequently, he longed for news but at the same time, he dreaded any talk of his brother's nuptials. Finally, he tore open the envelope and greedily devoured its message.

My dear brother,
I hear that you are not better yet, which causes me a good deal of grief. I so wish you could tell me how you are feeling, for there is nothing more distressing than this uncertainty, and if you could tell me how things are with you, I might be able to do something sooner to give you solace. You have done so much for me that it is a great sorrow for me to know that, precisely at this time when in all probability I am going to have days of happiness with my dear Jo, you are passing through days of misery. She had the fond idea that, by reason of her wanting to live my life as much as possible, you might have been a brother to her, as you have always been to me. We hope from the bottom of our hearts that you will be able to recover your health completely, and that you will be able to resume your work within a short time.

While arranging my new apartment it is such a pleasure for me to look at your pictures. They make the rooms so gay, and there is such an intensity of truth, of the true countryside in them, in each one of them. It is really as you used to say now and then of certain pictures of other artists—that they give the impression of having been reaped directly from the fields.

If it were not so far away, I should certainly have come to see you, but I don't have the time for that, and I ask myself if my visit would be of any use to you.

Signac intends to go to the South within a short time. He will go see you. I am now having an exhibition of Claude Monet at the gallery; it is very successful. It will not be long before the public will be asking for pictures of the new school, for they certainly stir up the public mind. If you can, you would be most kind if you would give me, or let someone give me, news about you, for apart from the letters from Messrs. Rey and Salles, I know nothing about you.

I wish you better health, and remain your brother who loves you.
Theo

"Signac!" Vincent screamed. "You send Signac in your place!" He let out a long sigh. "Just as well. I have no place in his life now. He has his new wife. I wish the demons would return. At least I would have someone to talk to. To complain to. To fight with."

The long arm of Paris winter had reached its end and at last withdrew. As March rolled in, men and women emerged from their cottages and apartments to greet the arrival of songbirds and flower buds. Crocuses poked up from beneath budding trees—one of the very first signs that spring had arrived—and Paris itself transformed from a deathly world of pure ghostly white into a fairyland of early emerald greens. It was on a spring day like this that Theo stood, beaming at the sight of the crowded gallery, proud to wind up the last week of the Monet exhibit.

"Theo, the show looks to be very successful."

Theo turned toward the familiar voice. "Émile! I'm delighted to see you! It is a huge success indeed! The gallery has done very well and Monet is making quite an impact on the critics with his Impressionist techniques."

"Is Monet here?"

"He was earlier. He is reveling in the public's adulation. And becoming wealthy! We are actually getting bids for his work. He'd better get busy and paint more! This is our final week!"

"Have you heard from your brother?"

Theo lowered his head and became pensive. "Yes, he is not so well. He is back in the hospital, in isolation."

"Isolation? Why? What has he done?"

"It seems that his neighbors petitioned the local authorities to have him locked up. They are fearful of him. Imagine, being afraid of poor Vincent."

"Well, you know he can be difficult. And peculiar at times."

"Yes, but he does not deserve to be locked up. He is not even allowed to paint!"

"Have you been to see him? How does he appear?"

"I'm afraid I have been preoccupied with this exhibition, my new apartment, and my upcoming nuptials."

"Do you think Vincent will go to the wedding? Will the doctors permit him to attend?"

"Oh, that's not a good idea. He could disrupt everything. I feel badly that he won't be there but also a bit relieved. Does that make me a wicked brother, Émile?"

"Of course not. You have taken care of him for most of his life. You deserve complete and utter bliss on your special day. And I think Vincent, deep down in his heart of hearts, would want that for you too."

"I have asked Signac to drop in on Vincent. He was headed south anyway. It is not too out of his way to pay a visit to my brother."

"When is he leaving?"

"I believe he leaves in a week or two."

"Perhaps I will give him something to take to Vincent."

"That would be very thoughtful, Émile. Oh, I must take my leave; it looks like we have another Monet ready to sell! Until we meet again, my friend!"

Émile stood outside the apartment door and rapped three times. He could discern some noise from inside.

"One moment, please. I'm coming!" the voice bellowed.

Paul Signac opened the door. He was not much older than Émile, with a young face and well-defined features. He was dressed in a long apron with splotches of paint in varying colors covering most of the front. His hair was disheveled and a bright orange streak of paint had congealed on his right cheek.

"Émile, please come in. I was just working on my latest river landscape, attempting to perfect my pointillism technique. I'm afraid working with small dots of color is very hard on the eyes. You've given me just the break I needed! How are you?"

"I am well. And you?"

"Things are going very well for me at the moment. Except for these damn French politics!"

Émile laughed. "You will never be satisfied with French politics, even if you became King of France! You're an anarchist, Paul!"

"Well, that is probably true. So what brings you to my humble abode?"

"Theo van Gogh told me you would be heading south soon and would be looking in on Vincent."

"Yes. He asked me to check on his brother. I understand he is not well."

"Yes, unfortunately. I hoped you could give Vincent a couple of items from me."

"Of course! What do you have for him?"

"I have this small sketch and a letter. I wanted to let

him know that I am thinking of him." Émile hesitated, then continued.

"You know, Paul, Vincent has an eye for color and detail. He has spent a great deal of time improving his use of local color. He keeps detailed notes regarding his paintings and chronicles his thoughts on color theory. I would really love to see his notes. By the way, when are you returning to Paris?"

"I should be back in early summer. The south coast is simply too hot in the summer months for me to remain there any longer."

"I know what you mean. Well, would you mind asking Vincent if I could borrow his journal for a time? I will return it. Perhaps you could bring it back with you?"

"Certainly, I will ask him for the journal and bring it to you."

"Many thanks, my friend. A safe journey to you," Émile said as he set a small pencil sketch of Pont Neuf and a letter on the table.

Dr. Rey came through the door into the lobby at Hôtel Dieu. Paul Signac was sitting in a hard-backed chair gazing out the window into an open courtyard. He was looking forward to a relaxing stay in Marseille and a bit of sailing.

"Monsieur Signac?"

Paul stood up to greet the doctor. "Yes, I am Paul Signac."

"I am Dr. Rey. I am the physician in charge of Monsieur van Gogh. Please follow me and I will take you to Vincent's room."

The doctor continued to speak as he led Signac to his office. "Monsieur van Gogh has been experiencing symptoms of what we call 'mental alienation.' Lately, he has had fewer attacks, which gives us hope that the medication and rest has benefited him."

"When will he be able to go home?"

"That is difficult to determine. He is here because his neighbors are fearful of him. You see, sometimes he becomes violent. His behavior can be very terrifying to others."

"What sort of behavior are you referring to?"

"He paces, head down, and sometimes he chases people. He imagines things. On occasion, he speaks to himself in a loud voice. He is often volatile and quick to anger."

"That's the Vincent I know. He has forever been unpredictable."

"Perhaps, but it is not normal behavior. For now, he must remain here until his brother decides what to do or the authorities decide for him."

The two men passed through a double door that led to the hospital wards and down several corridors until they came to a ward labelled "Isolation."

"He is in isolation?" asked Signac.

"Yes, but only as ordered by the authorities. Personally, I don't believe he needs to be isolated. Here we are."

When the men entered the windowless room Vincent was lying on the bed, his hands behind his head, staring up at the ceiling. Paul thought the room looked more like a cell than a hospital room. There were no personal effects of any sort. He couldn't imagine living like this without a painting on the wall or a vase of flowers. Not even so much as a photograph! Only a small fireplace providing a minimal amount of warmth.

"Paul! So nice of you to come to visit with me! I'm

afraid my surroundings are a bit austere. Please make yourself comfortable, if you can." Although Paul was no substitute for his brother, Theo, Vincent was still delighted to see an old friend.

"Vincent, you look well. How do you feel?" Signac remarked as he shook Vincent's hand.

"I am much better, thank you. And you, how is the world treating you? Are you still experimenting with pointillism?"

"I am well. And yes, I am still working with tiny dots of paint. Seurat and I have enjoyed working together in this style. In time it will become less controversial, I am sure."

"Excuse me, gentlemen," interrupted Rey, "I have other duties to attend to. Just let the nurse in the hall know when you are ready to leave, M. Signac."

"Certainly, Dr. Rey."

"Theo wrote to inform me of your visit. What news do you have of my brother?" Vincent asked.

"He is prospering. And very excited about his upcoming marriage. He is like a small boy, unwrapping a new toy!"

"I wish him well. And the Goupil business, too."

"His latest exhibit was a one-man show for Claude Monet. To say it was a success is an understatement."

"Monet is quite talented. I'm sure his paintings are highly sought and will fetch an exorbitant price." Vincent paused. "Have you seen Gauguin?"

"No, I haven't. I heard he returned to Paris after your accident. I've heard he was very disturbed by the incident."

"Really? Is that so? Tell me now, what did you hear?"

"I heard that you made life difficult and treated him with no respect. He said he tried to help you with your painting but you refused his instruction."

"What lies! Anything else?"

"Not really. He said he took you to the hospital after your accident and that he stayed with you until Theo arrived."

"More lies. He's merely trying to make himself look good. I bared my soul to that man and he turned his back on me."

"Vincent, I'm not trying to antagonize you. Please..."

"Yes, I know. I'm sorry for the outburst. It's not your fault that Gauguin is such a self-absorbed scoundrel."

"Oh, I almost forgot to mention it. Bernard stopped to see me right before I left Paris. He wanted me to give you this." He handed Vincent the sketch of Pont Neuf.

"Oh, this is very thoughtful. A lovely sketch. I see he has greatly improved his charcoal work."

"...and this." Signac handed Vincent the envelope. "And that reminds me. Émile wants to borrow your journal. He says he can learn from your notes and sketches."

"He wants my journal? He asked you to get it for him?"

"Yes, he said he would return it the next time he sees you."

"I've told him before that I will keep my journal. He doesn't want to study it. He wants to destroy it."

"Why would he do that?" Paul asked doubtfully.

"He's afraid of what's in it."

Signac looked quizzically at Vincent. In a soft voice he asked, "Why would he be afraid of your journal?"

"It's not important. Émile is a frightened boy."

"Well, I guess it is time for me to be on my way," said Paul, sensing that he had touched a nerve.

"Many thanks for stopping by, Paul. I enjoyed your visit."

After Signac left, Vincent opened Émile's letter and began to read:

Dear Vincent,
I hope you are well and safe. I am sure you have read about the continuing investigation into the assassination attempt on the Tsar's family. Things are not good here. I am in much distress but trying to disguise it. I am considering going into the military to avoid the police and the Russians. I advise you to find some place safe. I believe all of our lives to be in danger.
I implore you once again to give your journal to Signac. He will deliver it to me and I will remove only the pages that link us to the Commune. Please destroy this letter after you have read its contents.
I remain your friend.
Émile

"Is Bernard that foolish? If the Russians wanted us dead, we would have been dead long ago!" He crumpled the letter and threw it onto the hot embers in the fireplace. The paper sent sparks up through the blackened chimney, and quickly curled to ash.

After much discussion, Salles and Theo agreed on a long-term care facility for Vincent. It was a well-known asylum not far from Arles in the town of Saint-Rémy. Salles made the arrangements for Vincent's transfer. When it was time to leave, a carriage was waiting for them.

In no time at all, they arrived at the front gate of Saint-Paul-de-Mausole Asylum. Rev. Salles stepped out, followed by Vincent, who carried a small suitcase.

"Driver, kindly return in an hour," said the reverend.

"Certainly." He snapped the reins and the carriage pulled away with a clatter.

"Doctor Peyron is expecting you in about twenty minutes. Before we go in, do you want to sit?"

"Please. This may be my last taste of real freedom." Vincent looked melancholic as he sat on the bench.

"Don't say that, Vincent. You have improved every day. I would expect you to be here for only a short while."

"I'm not so sure. It seems like everyone wants me here and the way events have unfolded have not been to my advantage. Look at what happened last week—the heat went off, the river flooded, and the water, mildew, and mold claimed many of my paintings at the Yellow House."

"But most of them were salvaged. And the Ginoux's will look after your paintings and furniture. Their storeroom is kept warm and dry."

"I wish I could have brought my paintings with me," he said forlornly.

"Well, the ones you selected, along with your equipment, will be here in a week. You can survive for a week without them."

"I have done that already. I guess that means that this—" Vincent waived his arms around the grounds of the institution, "is so much better than Arles."

"You will do fine here."

"Am I permitted to have visitors?"

"Not right away. Dr. Peyron will need to spend some time evaluating you."

"You mean determining if I am insane or not." Vincent

lowered his head and closed his eyes.

"Evaluating you and then determining who or how many visitors you can reasonably handle."

"Am I allowed out?"

"That is up to Dr. Peyron. But he is a very reasonable man. He only has the best intentions and will do right by you."

"Well, let's not put this off any longer." Vincent rose from the bench and headed for the building.

The men walked side by side through the stone archway that stood like a twin sentinels in front of the immense courtyard. On either side of the gateway the asylum extended for what seemed to Vincent to be an eternity. Like an impenetrable fortress, he thought. So solemn and institutional. The branches on the sturdy oaks were sprouting a new set of leaves to mark the advent of spring. The only sign of gaiety was in the light refrains of birds that could be heard throughout the vast grounds, and in the spring light upon the poppies and tulips lining the flowerbeds.

Vincent's breath caught as he spotted the billowing sunflower fields off in the distance. He glanced at his companion and whispered, "Perhaps I will be safe here."

Chapter 43
Train to Marseille – Present Day

Mark was jolted awake when the train signaled its passing through a small French hamlet with an extended horn-blast. He straightened, yawned, and rubbed his face in his hands.

"Where the hell are we?" He looked at his watch. 5:45 p.m. "Damn, I must have slept at least a half an hour."

Mark pulled the envelope from his coat pocket and reread the ticket voucher. A stop in Lyon and then on to Marseille. Arrival time is 8:46. "Then what?" he wondered.

A clatter arose as the rear door to the car burst open. A woman in a uniform similar to the conductor's emerged with a food and beverage cart. "Monsieur, something to drink, or perhaps a snack?" her blue-capped head tilted just a bit to one side.

"Yes, please. Could I have a Coke Light? What do you have to eat?"

"We have cheese and tomato sandwiches, crisps and crackers."

"Crackers, please," he replied, thinking they might settle his queasy stomach.

She placed a can of Coke Light and a glass on the tray in front of him, then offered crackers from a snack assortment in her basket. He chose one, and as he began to open it she slid an envelope next to the cup, then moved on quickly to the next row of passengers.

Mark stared at the envelope, then opened it and removed the typewritten message:

At exactly 18:30 go to the car behind the dining car and

proceed to the restroom at the rear. Knock twice. Wait, then knock twice more. Bring this message with you.

He looked at his watch. Five minutes past six. He peered up and down the car then folded the message and put it in his coat pocket.

At precisely 6:29 p.m., Mark stood and moved quickly toward the dining car. The raucous crowd had neither thinned nor quieted, and they barely noticed him as he maneuvered through them and out the door to the next car. He paused there and looked—no one seemed to take notice of him as he passed. The restroom was on the right-hand side of the car, a red "occupied" bar displayed on its door. He looked around to see if anyone was watching.

He breathed deeply and knocked twice. After a pause, he knocked twice more. He heard the latch move and watched the red sign flip to green. He cautiously pushed the door open, and saw a middle-aged man pressing himself against the wall and motioning for Mark to come in. Once Mark was inside, the stranger locked the door.

"Who are you? Where's my wife?" Mark demanded to know.

With a hairy-knuckled finger to his lips, the man cautioned, "Shhh. All in good time." He looked Mark up and down. "I'm glad you keep yourself fit."

"What?" Mark's brow furrowed.

"Take off your clothes," the man ordered.

"What? No, I don't think so!"

"This is not a game, Monsieur. If you want to see your wife again, you will do as I say."

"Where is she?" he demanded.

"Take off your clothes. We don't have much time."

Mark removed his hat and coat. "What's going on here?"

"Put your phone and watch in this bag," commanded the stranger.

"Okay, now what?" Mark asked.

"Just keep going. Quickly," he growled

When Mark had stripped down to his socks and underwear, the man handed him a large bag. "Put these on."

Bewildered, Mark donned the new clothing—a pair of ill-fitting beige pants, a light blue shirt, and a navy sport coat. Once he was dressed, the stranger handed him the journal and the letter from his original jacket. "I guess we didn't size you very well. Here, put these in your pocket."

The man took a gold watch, a Cross pen, and a cell phone from his own pocket and handed them to Mark. "Take these, too."

He then withdrew an envelope from his coat and handed it to Mark. "You are to go to the car behind this one and take this seat." He pointed to a TGV ticket. "Get off at the next stop, which is Lyon. Do not draw attention to yourself or your wife will suffer the consequences."

Mark faced him stunned but stoic. "What do I do then?"

"Go to the Café de Lyon inside the terminal and order a coffee. Do not return to the front of the train. Do not even look toward the front of the train. Do not look back at the train when you depart. Go straight inside the terminal café. Do not talk to anyone."

"What then?"

"You wait."

"Bastard!" Mark said under his breath.

"Yes, of course. Now, one more thing." The man took a

blond wig from the bag. "You will wear this and act naturally." He placed the wig on Mark's head and eyed him carefully. "Good. Now go. You have only a little time before you must leave the train."

The lavatory door opened and a blond-haired man exited. A few minutes later, another man in a white hat and dark pants made his way toward the dining car.

Mark went to the assigned seat but barely had time to sit before the train slowed for its stop in Lyon. Outside, the gentle rolling fields and cozy hamlets had given way to modern high rises, tenements, and rundown office buildings. Passengers rose to gather their luggage and prepared to exit the train.

"Lyon!" the loudspeaker announced as the train jerked to a stop. Mark looked out the window to find a large group of people milling around waiting to board. The aisle was not yet clear and he was impatient to get off. Finally, a polite gentleman gestured for Mark to go ahead of him. With an appreciative nod, he rose and joined the moving queue.

On the platform, he eagerly searched around for an entrance to the terminal. He thought of the man's warning about not looking back and shuddered to think what might happen to Maggie if he were to disobey the order. "Focus!" he said to himself.

Once inside the Gare de Lyon Part-Dieu, Mark stopped and looked around. The station had a similar construction as the DC Metro: marble floors, curved ceilings with square concrete sections, but the Metro could not rival the wealth of shops and cafés that the Gare de Lyon boasted.

"How am I going to find Café de Lyon in this mess?" he mumbled to himself.

Heads bobbed all around him, like marker buoys in a turbulent sea. They seemed to move in random but purposeful patterns. Mark walked toward a large open-air part of the station. Ahead, hanging from the ceiling, was an arrival and departure board. Just below it was a map of the station.

He bent over close to the map. *"Vous êtes ici...* I think that means 'you are here.' Okay, so now I have to find Café de Lyon." He put his finger on the map and traced up and down the main aisle. "There! It should be just around the corner."

He straightened and headed in the direction of the café, and soon spied a sign with a coffee cup logo. It read: "Café de Lyon." It was small, with well-worn wide-planked pine floors and a half-dozen wooden tables with straight-back chairs. A glass display counter of pastries and breads took up a large portion of the center of the room. Only one barista was on duty, and a young couple sat at the table closest to the exit. There were a few lone businessmen sitting around with newspapers. Mark ordered a cappuccino. He scanned the café for anything unusual but found nothing.

Mark took his steaming cup and positioned himself at a table near the back so he could see the door. The other patrons took no notice of him. The barista was occupied with his phone. "Who is it going to be this time?" Mark wondered. With each sip of his coffee, his eyes darted across the café, his shoulders grew more rounded, and his breath more rapid. His eyes began to tear up as he felt a surge of remorse and fear. He reached for his handkerchief and stopped. "Shit. Not my clothes." He took a napkin and dabbed his eyes, squeezing away tears.

He dabbed his eyes again. His jaw tensed. The barista was

still texting but one of the men reading a newspaper had left. The young couple was gathering their trash and tossing it into the bin. Within seconds they disappeared from Mark's view.

One man remained in the café. He folded his paper and turned to address Mark. "Do you have the time?" he asked in French.

Mark eyed him warily and finally answered, "I'm sorry I don't speak French."

"Oh, pardon me. I was wondering what time you have."

Mark looked at the watch that he had been provided by the stranger on the train. "Seven thirty-five."

The man thanked Mark, took his newspaper and left. Mark was now alone in the café. A couple of minutes passed. His leg jogged up and down nervously with quick, rhythmic motion. A tall, attractive woman dressed in fashionable jeans and a brightly colored designer t-shirt came through the door pulling a small suitcase. She exchanged words with the barista, who began preparing a latte. As she turned her head, her eyes met Mark's. He thought he detected a hint of recognition from her, perhaps a barely perceptible smile. She picked up her latte, paid the clerk, and walked toward Mark. He straightened in his chair.

She laid an envelope on the table in front of him. "Monsieur McFadden, you are to take the TER 17816 to Dijon. There you will transfer to the Trenitalia Intercité 221 to Venice. You do not have much time to catch your train. It leaves from Track Four in fifteen minutes." She bent close to Mark's ear and whispered "Again, Monsieur, do not arouse suspicion. Your wife wants very much to see you again." She stood up. *"Au revoir!"* she said merrily.

Mark started to say something but stopped himself. He sucked in three deep breaths and with each one, exhaled slowly. Within seconds, the woman had blended into the streaming crowd outside.

Mark scanned the terminal once again for directions. He found an overhead sign to Tracks One through Five. He hurried toward them, trying to appear calm but with his stomach again churning.

The old TER 17816 appeared to be more than ready for retirement. As bad as the outside was, the inside was worse. The rubber mat lining the center aisle was worn in spots, right down to the bare metal. The armrests were brittle with age. Faded seat fabric looked like it had been clawed by cats, and the windows were smudged with grease from hair and fingers. Mark wondered if the interior had ever been cleaned.

He showed his ticket to a conductor and was directed to a second-class car with general seating. At the rear of the car, a group of teenagers with multi-colored hair and leather pants were laughing and pushing each other.

The train rumbled and teetered as it left the station, like a tilt-a-whirl carnival ride just firing up. Mark took a seat next to a window, well away from the rowdy teens. He kept his eyes focused on the landscape outside as it crawled slowly by. Except for the teens, the car's only sounds were the clacking of rails passing under the antique carriage.

The TER 17816 rolled to a stop in the Marseille-Saint-Charles train station on Track E. A warm night air had closed in on southern France and the lights of the city cast a bewitching glow over the steel thoroughbreds sitting side by side at the starting gate, eager for their next journey.

A man sporting a white chapeau stepped off the train and turned toward the main terminal. His head was bent forward, his face concealed by the brim of his hat. Once inside, the man hesitated, and then strode toward a large arrival and departure board.

Gastineau watched closely as the man made his way across the terminal. He lifted a walkie-talkie, "Do you have him?"

"*Oui.* He is headed to the arrivals board."

"Keep a safe distance. We must not alert him or anyone else to our presence."

From his perch, high in the ceiling girders, the detective had a broad view of the station. He turned to the man next to him. "Any sign of our target?"

"*Non.*"

The white hat paused under the board and looked around. He paced indecisively with his hands in his pockets. He stopped once again and looked around, then started toward a corner of the terminal.

"Where's he going?" Gastineau yelled into the microphone.

"I'm not sure…"

A second voice cut in. "I think he is going to the toilet."

"Who is posted in the toilet?" barked Gastineau.

"No one, sir. There is only one way in and one way out," came a response from the walkie-talkie.

"Did anyone approach our man? Do we see anything out of the ordinary?" Gastineau asked.

"Non," came the replies. Gastineau heaved a sigh. The white hat was now out of his sight.

"Can you see the door to the toilet?" Gastineau asked his men.

"Yes, clearly," said one.

"Are you sure there is no other way in or out of there?"

"Yes, sir."

"Perhaps he is meeting someone in there," someone said.

"Let's wait a couple of minutes more. Lucien, if he does not come out, you go in and find out what's going on."

"Yes, sir," came the reply, with static.

Minutes passed. A bearded street bum came out, followed by an older teenager. Shortly after them was a well-dressed businessman. Then a cleric arrived and left.

Gastineau toggled the radio, "This has taken too long. Lucien! Go! Now!"

A young man in a white polo shirt hurried into the toilet. Within seconds he emerged from the restroom with a bag in one hand and a white hat in the other. He gazed up in Gastineau's direction.

"He's gone! His clothes, wallet, watch and phone… they're all in this bag!" he announced to his superior.

"Merde!" Gastineau spat.

Mark stepped off the train in Dijon and went directly to the main area. The circular station was equipped with several arrival and departure screens. "Where is 221… oh, there… Track B."

He followed the signs to Track B. The Trenitalia Intercité was a well-appointed modern train with sleeping berths. His ticket was for a private sleeping car. He slid the door open to find two folding bunk beds and a small sink. Mark plopped wearily onto one of the beds that had been pulled down to serve as a couch. He gazed out the window. "This is a fucking disaster," he moaned. "They're just running me in circles."

Once again, the city features fell away revealing nothing but dark undulating hills. Mark stared trancelike at the darkness. Occasionally he shook his head and rubbed his eyes to stay awake and focused. "I hope Gastineau is on top of this. What the hell will he do when he discovers I am not on the train?"

There was a firm rap on the door and Mark jumped. He got up and opened it. Standing with a clipboard and a bar code scanner, a conductor said, "Ticket, Monsieur?"

Mark sighed and handed the ticket to the conductor. The door closed and he returned to his seat, returning his gaze out the window. The compartment door soon opened again, and Mark turned to look. His eyes grew large as he stood up, staring at the door with his mouth agape.

Chapter 44
Saint-Rémy, Paris, Arles-sur-Oise – Spring-Summer 1889

Vincent sat in the asylum garden, sketchbook on his lap and pen in hand. He stared at the old cypress trees lining the pathway. A massive, diseased limb had been severed from the largest of them, rendering its form bizarrely unequal. "A hobbled giant," he mused as he continued his sketch. He thought the tree was not unlike him—wretched, grotesque, disturbed. I wonder if it has suffered as I have, he thought.

"Monsieur van Gogh!" A voice rang out down the path. Vincent spied an orderly hurrying his way. "Monsieur Vincent, Dr. Peyron would like to see you. Please come this way."

Dr. Peyron was a tall, slender man with a balding pate. He compensated for his lack of hair by sporting a thick handlebar mustache. Round metal-framed eyeglasses perched on a considerable nose, magnifying his beady eyes. One might have mistaken him for an accountant or a bookkeeper, such was his appearance. His office overlooked the courtyard with floor to ceiling windows. Natural light from the massive casements cast a hallowed glow upon the dark mahogany bookcases lining two of the walls. Upon entry into the room, one could hardly miss the richness of the mahogany's color and texture.

Dr. Peyron sat, hands folded, behind a large desk in the middle of the room with his back to the windows. Two leather-bound chairs were positioned across the desk, which was littered with books and papers.

"Monsieur Vincent, thank you for coming. I have reviewed your file and the letters from Dr. Rey in Arles. As you know, his initial diagnosis of your disease was 'mental alienation' but my own observations of your behavior indicate that your problems might be neurological in nature. I believe that you suffer from a form of epilepsy. I think it best to continue to observe you and perform more tests in order to confirm my diagnosis."

"I understand, doctor."

"Epilepsy is an illness that is often inherited. Is there any history in your family of epilepsy?"

"My uncle suffered seizures. There may have been others, I don't know."

"Yes, I am not surprised. Since this illness is most likely inherited, you must know that there is nothing you could have done to avoid the seizures."

Vincent was silent for a long moment. "That is a relief. I worry that I have done something to bring on the attacks. Is there a medication for my illness? Can it be cured?"

"We have some medicine that can help with the seizures, but I am not aware of a cure. You know, some of the most creative men in history suffered from the same malady as you. Michelangelo, Da Vinci, Sir Isaac Newton… It has even been suggested that Napoleon Bonaparte experienced epileptic seizures."

Vincent's thoughts deepened for a moment, then he looked at the doctor. "In that case, is it possible for me to resume painting and have freedom of movement?"

Dr. Peyron nodded decisively. "You may certainly resume painting. In fact, we have a small room on the ground floor that you are free to use as a studio if you so desire. Naturally there will be an extra charge for that space. I can discuss it with your brother, if you like."

Vincent brightened. "Oh, yes! That would be wonderful! I do think Theo will be amenable to renting a studio for me if the cost is not exorbitant. And am I free to roam? I have always enjoyed long walks as I am a keen observer of nature, and I must confess that I am tiring of this monastic existence. Also, I should like one day to return to Arles."

"I understand, Vincent, but we must take one step at a time—together. Before I can allow you to roam outside these grounds, I would like to observe you a bit longer. You may walk in the gardens, but please remain on the compound. For now."

"Yes, I will, certainly—thank you, doctor!" Vincent rose and walked quickly to the door. Despite such high spirits that he felt a quick urge to leap out into the hallway, he held a calm and dignified bearing. While a part of him had enjoyed the solitude of the asylum, he longed more and more to explore the Mediterranean-like countryside of the Provence region. It was very different from Arles. He was beginning to feel whole again.

Esterhazy was feeling antsy, drumming his fingers on the café table, and fidgeting in his seat when a figure appeared from the window glare cast by the midday sun.

Marguerite matter-of-factly took her seat. "Thank you, Ferdinand, for agreeing to meet. I hope I did not inconvenience you. Did you order coffee?"

"Hello Marguerite," he nodded. "Yes, I did order. And I thought you might like something more than just coffee. Here comes our meal now."

A waiter appeared with two demitasse cups, lemon twists, sugar, a basket of bread, and an assortment of meats and cheeses. Feeling famished, Esterhazy wanted to dive into the food but restrained himself until Marguerite served herself.

She opened the conversation as he loaded his plate. "Some unexpected and unwelcomed events have transpired recently. I'm sure you keep up with current events."

"Yes, I do." He paused over a slice of cured ham. "But please elaborate." Esterhazy's stomach signaled an urgency as he stacked the bread with ham, salami and cheese, and took a first eager bite.

"Certainly. The Russian secret police are still searching France for the people responsible for the attempt on the Tsar. But they have found nothing. I thought by now they would have in custody someone from the Commune. There are so many clues lying about. The Russians are incompetent."

"Marguerite, I am confused. You are a true French patriot, yet you set blame for the Tsar's assassination attempt on France. Why?"

She sighed. "It is complicated. Once France is implicated, we can turn the tables and reveal Germany as the true origin of the assassination attempt. It was Germany who used gullible Frenchmen as its pawns. That, dear cousin, will seal a long-term alliance between Russia and France while buttressing Germany. An isolated Germany will no longer be a threat to France. All of Europe will be behind us."

"Ingenious! But how will you 'turn the tables,' as you say?"

"By leaving a clearly documented money trail. The French will follow it and it will lead them to Germany."

"Brilliant."

"But the piece de resistance is the van Gogh journal. It is proof that the Germans were the architects of the plot. Pierre's likeness is in the journal, plain as day."

"As is yours, Marguerite."

"Yes, but once we have the journal in our hands, some pages may become lost… that is easily done." She set down her cup and dabbed the corners of her mouth with the napkin. "So. Now you understand its importance. The journal—have you secured it?"

"I have tried. But no, not as yet, I have not come across it. I have been through his entire house, followed him on foot, and even tried to pick his pockets, but to no avail. When he has it with him, which is almost always, he keeps it near at hand, or tucked away."

"You must keep trying. And take care that he not suspect you stole it."

Esterhazy sat upright like a bird ruffling his feathers. "You may not know, but Vincent has been committed to an asylum in Saint-Rémy. He is watched all the time. This will make it even more difficult."

Marguerite returned a scowl. "I leave it up to you as to how to secure it, but just get it! I'm leaving now." She stood abruptly. "Complete your mission," she hissed, then paused a moment and smiled. "As always, it is good to see you. Stay well." She turned away casually and sidled to the door.

Summer descended upon Paris early with unseasonable heat. The city stench seemed to return overnight, like a suffocating, dense fog that would not lift. The city parks and gardens filled up with people escaping the lethargy of the inner city.

Marguerite seemed unbothered by the oppressive heat as she strolled along the wide path leading to the Tuileries. A small orange parasol shielded her from the brutal sun.

"You are punctual today, Marguerite," sounded a deep voice from the side as she approached.

Marguerite turned to recognize Pierre's dark eyes peering over the daily newspaper. "Pierre," she said with smile, "you look so formal. You should wear something cooler in this heat. Is that suit wool?"

Ignoring her comment, Pierre rose to join her in strolling along the path. "I was wondering when I would hear from you," she said briskly. "You've been silent for some time."

After a few moments of awkward silence, he leaned toward her and said, "There have been some setbacks in Berlin."

She said nothing, but continued walking straight ahead.

"The Russians have dismissed the notion of a French plot against the Tsar," he disclosed.

She halted and looked away, her lips pursed, then turned back to him. "I did my best. Sometimes we wily French can defeat even the best laid plans."

Pierre drew a sharp breath. "This is serious, Madam."

"I am not making light of the situation," she demurred. "You must be patient. Sometimes these investigations can take new turns."

"The Chancellor has little of that. A further complication is the new Kaiser's meddling in Bismarck's plans for Germany."

"Does the Kaiser know how complicit the Chancellor is in this assassination attempt?" asked Marguerite.

His jaw tense, Pierre glowered at Marguerite. "You are never to mention that again!" he warned through clenched teeth.

Marguerite returned his angry glare, then continued with her walk. "Coming?"

Pierre caught up in a few long strides, then settled into her pace.

"Pierre," Marguerite said softly, "I realize the position the Chancellor is in. He wants a strong, united Germany, as we all do, but he has a Kaiser that does not trust him and a Franco-Russian alliance that may thwart any possibilities for a united motherland. His one hope, his one prayer, is to break the Franco-Russian alliance and replace it with a German-Russian pact. If this happens, Germany will dominate all of Europe and Bismarck will be chancellor for life."

Pierre nodded. "That would be best for all of us."

"Indeed," said Marguerite. "And I have come to understand that the new Kaiser has taken a liking to you. That you are working your way into his inner circle."

Alarmed by this news, Pierre grabbed Marguerite by the arm. "Where did you hear that?"

Marguerite looked down at his hand with such distaste that Pierre, suddenly ashamed, was compelled to remove it. "It is difficult to serve two masters, especially when one is a fool and the other is ruthless." She watched Pierre squirm in discomfort.

"I don't need a lecture from you, Marguerite. If I could prove you are using us, I would—"

"Would what, Pierre? Tell the Kaiser you plotted to assassinate the Tsar?"

"Marguerite, there is no proof I was involved in the assassination plot!"

"Let me assure you—there is proof, Pierre. You know I do not bluff." She smiled triumphantly, then her eyes narrowed. "You are caught in a difficult situation, Pierre. I am sure I can help you. I suggest you simply let me follow through with my plans."

Sweat beaded from Vincent as he labored at his easel. He took no notice of the droplets rolling down his face, arms and back, dampening his shirt and trousers. His hands were moving in short, strong strokes with a vitality he had not felt in some time. His focus on the canvas was absolute.

"Monsieur Vincent?" came a voice. He did not hear it.

The words repeated, louder. "Monsieur Vincent!"

He startled and a smudge of vermillion landed in the wrong spot. "Merde!" He turned toward the voice.

"Oh, Dr. Peyron! I did not hear you come in."

"I can see that, Vincent. You seem to be consumed with your work." The doctor gazed around the studio with a small grin at the multitude of paintings and sketches scattered about.

"Is there something I can do for you?" asked Vincent.

"Actually, I came to let you know that I have given much thought to your request to visit Arles. While I am still a bit uncertain I should do this, I have decided to grant your request."

Vincent raised his brush like a flag. "Well thank you, doctor! I am sure I will be fine! Seeing old friends will benefit me greatly. And I will be able to check on my furniture. Perhaps I could even bring a piece or two back with me?"

"Perhaps. Louis will accompany you, and you must follow his instructions to the letter. He has been told to watch carefully for any signs of relapse. If he detects any such signs, he is to bring you back without delay."

"I understand. Louis and I get along well. There will not be any problems."

"And this will be a day trip only. Out on the morning train, back on the evening train." The doctor was trying to look firm, but was feeling more bemusement, taking delight in seeing Vincent at his work and looking stronger.

"Thank you, Dr. Peyron. I appreciate your confidence in me."

The mid-morning train arrived at the Arles station and Vincent filed out onto the platform followed by his attendant. It was all so familiar to him and it gladdened his heart to be back in a place that had once welcomed him with open arms. But these feelings were shaded by apprehension as he recalled the neighbors' petition to have him removed. He pushed that thought out of his head.

"Louis, I would first like to go to Café de la Gare and check on my furniture. If there is time and she is willing, I will sketch Madame Ginoux in my journal."

"That is fine. Please lead the way, Monsieur Vincent."

On their way to Café de la Gare the men passed 2 Place Lamartine, where Vincent felt a pang. "That was my house and studio," he told Louis. He could see the high-water mark from the recent flood. Paint was beginning to peel and the building had clearly not been maintained after Vincent left. It looked abandoned.

"It is very nice," Louis lied. He felt the need to be polite to his charge, but he was not a good liar. Vincent didn't seem to care.

"Yes, it is—or, it was—a nice comfortable spot. I see the lock has been replaced on the door. Well, let's continue. We haven't far to go."

The two men entered the Café de La Gare, which reeked of stale beer, musty wine, and grilled meat that couldn't be readily identified. A haze hung over the room, fed by hand-rolled cigarettes, cigars, and a few pipes. Vincent stopped a server. "Would you kindly let Madame Ginoux know that Vincent van Gogh is here?"

"Monsieur, regrettably, Madame Ginoux is not here. She is in Marseille."

"Then is Monsieur Ginoux available?"

"No sir. He is with the Madame. If you like, please sit and I will serve you and your friend."

"Thank you, no." Vincent turned to Louis, "It appears that Monsieur and Madame Ginoux are away. I probably should have informed them that I was coming but there wasn't enough time. Let's go see Reverend Salles."

A carriage took them to a small house on the other side of town. Vincent knocked on the door. The charwoman answered.

"Yes, may I help you?"

"Would you please inform the Reverend that Vincent van Gogh is here to see him?"

"Monsieur, I am so sorry but the Reverend is out of town this week. He won't be back until next Monday."

"Oh, I see," said Vincent in a low voice. Disappointment now colored his face.

"I am sure the Reverend would have liked to have seen you, Monsieur. Would you care to leave a letter for him?"

"No, thank you. Please just tell him Vincent van Gogh was in town to pay his respects."

"I will, Monsieur. Au revoir."

"Louis," Vincent said, "let's go to the hospital. I should call on Dr. Rey."

The hospital entryway was filled with visitors. Vincent did not recall ever seeing it this busy. He approached the young man seated behind the lobby desk and asked for Dr. Rey.

"Oh, I am sorry Monsieur, Dr. Rey is in Paris for a conference. Would you like to speak with another doctor?"

"No, thank you. When will he return?"

"I don't think for three or four days."

Louis eyed Vincent. "I am sorry none of your friends were here. Is there anyone else you want to see?"

"No. Let's just walk for a while."

Louis saw the hurt in his eyes. He felt badly for Vincent, knowing how much he had anticipated the trip.

They walked along the boulevards, idly peering into shop windows and watching the town folk scuttle to and fro. They made their way to Vincent's favorite art store and purchased some brushes. Before long, they were back at La Gare.

"Let's go in and have something to eat and drink," Vincent suggested. "There may be some neighbors lingering around."

"Monsieur, please don't drink too much. Remember the doctor's orders," Louis cautioned.

"Yes, of course."

The two men sat across from each other at a large table. "Soup and a glass of absinthe," Vincent snapped at the server. Louis sensed a change in his demeanor since the morning.

"For myself, I would also like some soup and a glass of Bordeaux." He looked at Vincent. "Monsieur, do you see anyone that you know?"

Vincent surveyed the room. Across from the billiard table

in a dimly lit corner he noticed a gentleman with a thick mustache sitting alone. "Funny, that man looks familiar but I cannot place him. I'm certain I've seen him before, though."

"A neighbor, perhaps?"

"No, I don't think so."

"Anyone else you know?" asked Louis.

He took a second look. "No, none that I recognize."

Vincent seemed to have run out of conversation. Louis tried to engage him, but was met with silence. At last Louis announced that it was time to catch the train back to Saint-Rémy. Wary of his sudden change in demeanor, Louis thought to keep a close eye on Vincent for the rest of the trip.

The mustachioed man watched as the pair left the restaurant. He quickly called to the server and paid his bill. He had no time to waste.

Chapter 45
Paris – Present Day

"Mags!" Mark sprang from his seat. She flung her arms tightly around his neck and buried her face in his shoulder, and sobbed. "Oh God, I've been so worried," his voice broke as he too wept. He kissed and cradled her head as they cried, dampening his rumpled shirt collar. The door closed firmly behind her and a short, stocky thug nudged them deeper into the cabin with his pistol. "Sit," he ordered.

"What do you want?!" Mark shouted angrily. He had his hands on Maggie's shoulders and turned her away.

The man glared at Mark from under heavy eyebrows. Mark looked at the silencer on the end of the pistol. The gruff voice again commanded slowly, "Sit. Now!" as if talking to dogs. Mark guided Maggie to the bench seat.

A shadow passed over the cabin door.

"Anton!" Mark exclaimed, standing. The gunman shoved the pistol into Mark's chest, forcing him back down.

"Mark, *mon ami,* I am sorry that things had to go so wrong for you and dear Maggie."

Mark's face turned crimson and he started again to rise. "What the hell is going on here?"

Anton raised a hand. "Please sit back down and calm yourself. Samuel here is very protective of me. He has orders to shoot anyone who threatens me." Anton plunked down on the end of the bunk. "At least we have a beautiful evening for our ride."

"Anton, I asked you a simple question. What's going on?"

"Isn't it obvious?" Maggie cut in, staring at Anton. "Our

so-called friend wants the journal and is willing to do anything to get it."

"Your wife is very insightful." Anton held out his hand toward Mark and said, "Now, please give me the journal."

Mark begrudgingly handed it over. Anton leaned back on the bunk, legs crossed, his eyes on his captives. Slowly, he removed a pair of cotton gloves from his coat pocket and slid them over his hands.

Mark leaned back into his wife. "Mags, are you all right?" Mark teared up again as he looked into her face. He searched for any signs of bruises or marks but saw none. "I've been worried sick about you."

"I'm fine. He—" she nodded in Anton's direction, "has kept me tied up and gagged most of the time."

"I must tell you, my friend," the Frenchman said, leafing through the notebook, "this is a remarkable find. Very rare. Extremely valuable."

"You piece of shit! Why are you doing this?" Mark's face was a knot of fury. Samuel jabbed him again with the gun, reminding him who had the upper hand.

"Isn't it obvious? He needs the money," spat Maggie.

"I thought you were our friend."

Anton smiled. "I suppose not. At least, not anymore. It's really too bad." He continued to examine his prize. "Aha! There is something in here about my ancestor, Pierre. I should have known. You both looked like you had seen a specter when you saw the painting in my den." Turning more pages, he paused.

"Since you two are so very clever, I am confident you recognized the sketch of this woman—one of Mme. Chauvenal's ancestors. Her portrait hangs in the old crone's house. The sketches in this notebook do not do justice to her true beauty."

"Anton, why would you need money so badly that you would kidnap Maggie?"

Anton set the journal in his lap and gave Mark an exasperated look. "Do you think a researcher could live as I do? You are not so naïve as to believe I could afford my lifestyle on such a lowly salary. Besides, I am only following in the family business."

"What do you mean, 'the family business'?"

"My family have always been resourceful. Well, some more than others. During the war, when France was divided into the occupied zone and the so-called free zone, my grandfather worked in the office of cultural relations in Petain's government."

"What the hell is 'cultural relations'?"

Anton chuckled. "Almost anything he wanted it to be. Mostly it meant supplying pieces of art and other treasures to the German high command. My grandfather was very good at his work. He was so good, in fact, that he became quite wealthy selling and trading antiquities and jewelry."

Mark was calmer now, and solemn. "Stolen from the Jews, I assume."

"Mostly. But then again, my grandfather stole from virtually anyone who had something of value. When it came to acquiring wealth, he had no loyalties."

Mark's eyes bore into Anton. "I'm surprised he didn't go on trial for war crimes."

"Oh, he was very clever. He appeared to side with the

occupied French and passed on many privileges to important landowners and bureaucrats. He played both ends."

"He kept his fortune?"

"In Switzerland. As many Vichy leaders did. In the winter of 1942, Germany occupied the French Free Zone, thus ending the façade of French independence. My grandfather continued his accumulation, working secretly for the Gestapo."

"So, you are the offspring of Nazis. That explains a lot."

"Don't be ridiculous. My family were never Nazis. My grandfather knew Hitler would fall. That is why he hid his money in Switzerland."

"Right. Your grandfather taught you the business?"

"No. My grandfather died when I was very young. He taught my father the business. You see, Europe was a mess after the war. Black markets supplied everything from candy to art. My grandfather and father established the largest black market art organization in the world."

"Did your father teach you to be so ruthless?"

"Mark, Mark, Mark. Tsk, tsk, tsk. I am not ruthless. In fact, I am too kind and accommodating. If I were ruthless, Maggie would be dead and you would have been shoved out of the TGV door."

Mark looked at Maggie. He could see the venom in her eyes. She looked like a rattlesnake ready to strike.

Anton continued. "No, I am gentle. I made sure you two would reunite."

Maggie held silent while Mark spoke. "Some reunion. Why don't you let us go? You have what you want."

"Well, you see, it's not so easy. I'm sure you can appreciate my dilemma."

Maggie spoke up accusingly. "Did you kill Durand?"

Anton showed her a smug smile. "When I recruited Victor, I thought he would make the perfect associate. A respected associate director at the d'Orsay, connected to the established art community. He turned out to be an insecure little man who felt slighted and overlooked. Victor was a buffoon and a greedy one at that. He became a liability to my organization. He really did love art, but he accumulated much too much debt. To the wrong people, I might add. He saw this sketchbook as a way to reclaim his life. He is the one who kidnapped Maggie. I freed your wife and probably saved her life. You should thank me."

"Yeah, I might do that," Mark sneered.

"Victor deserved what he got. He betrayed me. He tried to rob you, twice in fact. Blundered both times."

"He's the one who broke into our house?" cried Maggie.

"He had his cousin break into your house. And steal your briefcase, Mark. You met him at the Museé d'Orsay. He was Victor's assistant."

"Where is he?" Mark asked.

"He and Victor are together," Anton replied nonchalantly., then turning, said "Now, I need to think."

Maggie stopped him. "But wait—how did you get the van Gogh in your apartment?"

"Oh, now that is truly an interesting story," Anton brightened with a smile. He slowly closed his eyes and reopened them, then looked directly at the McFaddens.

"History," he recounted, "is often filled with happenstance accentuated by intrigue. As I mentioned to you before, the man in the painting is one of my ancestors. He was born on the German side of Alsace around 1840. He served in the Prussian army and became an aide to Otto von Bismarck.

"Pierre Schoeffel was his name. He was a minor figure in Bismarck's plans to meld the various Prussian states into a united Germany and dominate the European landscape. After the Franco-Prussian war of 1870, France was a second-rate power. England still retained control of the seas and Russia was gaining influence and power. But by 1880, France was in the middle of a resurgence.

"What does this have to do with the painting?"

Anton's eyes narrowed. "You asked me a question. You must let me finish. I do not often get the opportunity to brag about my ancestors. Besides, you might learn something."

Maggie tugged at Mark's sleeve. "I'm sorry, please continue," he said reluctantly, not in the mood for a history lesson.

"As I was explaining, France was rebuilding its army and occupied a central place of European influence by 1880. Bismarck was concerned that France and Russia would join forces against Germany. My ancestor was sent to France to devise a scheme to alienate France and Russia. This is where history becomes coincidental. Just who do you think my ancestor fell in with?"

"How would I know?" Mark shrugged.

"You disappoint me. It is all in your precious journal."

"Explain," Mark said with a doubtful look.

Anton paused to glare back, then continued. "Pierre met a lovely young ambitious Parisian who also had ties to Alsace, although her allegiance was not properly vetted. Marguerite Devereaux, Madame Chauvenal's great-great grandmother. Together, the two conspired to alienate Russia and France. I do not know the details of their plots, but it is clear that Marguerite took German money and established her progeny as one of the most influential families in France. Until you discovered this journal, the connection could not be proven."

Maggie leaned in incredulously. "Does Mme. Chauvenal know all this?" she asked.

"But of course."

"That's hard to believe." Mark leaned into Maggie as he spoke. "She said she didn't know what her ancestor was up to."

"What was she supposed to say, 'my ancestors were plotting against France'?" Anton held a dismissive sneer.

"Well, what about the portrait?"

"Oh, yes. Van Gogh was in Paris during some of this plotting. He and some other naïve, left-leaning artists were recruited to help in Marguerite and Pierre's plans. I am sure they did not suspect they were being used, but they were. Along the way, van Gogh painted the portrait of my ancestor. As you can imagine, my ancestor could never let this portrait become public. So, after van Gogh killed himself, my ancestor took possession of the painting from van Gogh's brother. It has been in my family ever since."

"Seems that stealing art runs through your veins. Your family has been doing it for decades."

"I suppose so. Now, I must go. I have arrangements to make. Samuel, make sure our guests remain quietly where they are."

Chapter 46
Paris, Saint-Rémy – Spring 1889

"Johanna, Johanna Bonger-van Gogh, are you here?" Theo bellowed as he entered the apartment.

"Yes, Theo, I am here. Where else would I be? Did you miss me so much that you had to come home early?" She smiled at her new husband and the soon-to-be father of her child.

He reached for his wife and rubbed her enlarged abdomen. "Yes, I wanted to see you and little Vincent."

"It will do just to see me. Little Vincent is not yet ready to meet the world."

Theo removed his hat and announced, "I have received several letters today."

"From whom?"

"Dr. Peyron wrote to say that Vincent is recovering nicely. He is certainly not entirely well, but he may no longer have to be confined to Saint-Rémy."

"That's wonderful, Theo!"

"It is indeed! I also received a letter from Camille Pissarro. He suggests that Vincent could come under the care of his doctor in Auvers-sur-Oise. Pissarro says this doctor…" Theo pulled a letter from his trouser pocket and scanned it, "…this Doctor Gachet, is an excellent physician and also has an interest in art."

"Theo, Auvers is very close! If your brother was there we could look in on him more frequently!"

Theo hesitated. "We could."

"You must write Vincent and let him know about Auvers

and Dr. Gachet!"

"I will let him know, but I think I should meet Gachet before Vincent goes to Auvers. I want to make sure he is the right man to help my brother."

"That is wise."

"I also brought home this small art publication." Theo opened his leather valise and removed a magazine.

Jo took it. "*De Portefeuille*. I don't believe I've heard of this publication."

"It is well known in the Belgium art world."

She read the review. "This references the exhibit at the *Salon des Indépendants*."

"Remember I was only allowed to send two paintings. I selected *Starry Night* and *Irises*. I thought those represented Vincent's best work and illustrated his versatility. Unfortunately, *Starry Night* was not displayed very well. *Irises*, on the other hand, was at the end of a hall. It was perfect."

"Theo, this is wonderful! Listen to this! 'Who is there that conveys, in form and colour, the magnificent, dynamic energy the 19th century is again becoming aware of? I know of one man, a lone pioneer, struggling on his own in the depths of darkest night. His name, Vincent, will go down to posterity.'" Jo looked up at Theo. "You must send this to Vincent! He must see it! This will certainly lift his spirits!"

"Of course, I will. Let's hope this review results in some of his pictures selling. We could use the money."

"Theo, we are fine. Don't worry about such things."

"I am worried. Money is not coming in fast enough. When Monet left the entresol, Goupil lost a large part of its business. Some of the other artists' works are not selling

Saint-Rémy 1889

either. Gauguin, for example, has been painting religious figures and creating abstract sculptures. Our patrons don't want that. Besides, we have a family to think of now with little Vincent on the way. And my brother's treatment is not getting any cheaper."

"Please, my dear, don't fret. We will be fine."

Vincent stood erect at his easel in the bright air, painting the olive tree groves. The sun cast a hopeful radiance as it rose over the mountains in the distance. "Ah, there is such harmony in this visage. The morning sky seems almost supernatural in its glow. This work needs some yellow. Perhaps a touch of ochre."

"Ah, Monsieur Vincent, it is wonderful to see you out and enjoying this pleasant morning."

"Dr. Peyron! This is a surprise. I did not expect to see you so far from your office."

"Even doctors need to take advantage of such beautiful fall days. Your painting seems to have a life of its own!"

"As my brother said in one of his letters, I am stronger when I paint true things that are full of color."

"He is correct! But do you really see the earth in purples and browns?"

Vincent gave a small laugh. "This is how I feel it in my mind's eye. It captivates you, doesn't it?!"

"Monsieur Vincent, you have recovered quite well from your latest attacks."

"I can hardly remember them. Except for some dizziness, I feel perfectly normal."

Dr. Peyron agreed. "Yes, you seem healthy. For that reason

I have decided to allow you to travel to Arles. Again, Louis will accompany you."

"I'm very grateful, doctor. When may I leave?"

"You and Louis can take the early train on the day after tomorrow."

"Very well, I will finish up here and prepare for the journey. Thank you, doctor!"

"Please, Monsieur van Gogh, do not overexert yourself."

"I will not. Louis will see to that."

In two days' time, Vincent and Louis boarded the train to Arles. On arrival, they headed directly for the Café de la Gare, once again passing the faded Yellow House. This time, though, Vincent did not take notice of his old home—he seemed to have put some concerns away. At the Café de La Gare, the air was filled with the familiar stale smoke and odors of the previous night's activities.

Vincent was delighted to find that Marie Ginoux was working in the kitchen. She entered the dining area, wiping her hands on her apron and beamed at the sight of him. After introductions were made, the three of them gathered at a vacant table, chatting for a while about Marie's husband, the neighbors, and the hotel business. Vincent lost track of time, absorbed in the conversation.

"Monsieur Vincent, please forgive me for interrupting," Louis prompted, "but if you want to see Rev. Salles, we should go now or we will be out of time."

"Yes, of course." Vincent bade farewell to Marie and left the cafe, Louis by his side. It was a brief carriage ride to the reverend's house.

Arles-sur-Oise 1889

"Monsieur Vincent, it is good to see you looking hale and hearty," said Salles as he escorted the two men into the parlor. The room was formal but comfortable.

"Rev. Salles, you have always been so kind. I am delighted to see you. Louis and I stopped by to see you once before but you were at a conference in Paris."

"Oh, yes. I am very sorry to have missed you, Vincent."

Time slipped by as they chatted about Saint-Rémy and Vincent's art. Before long, Louis noticed that the sun was beginning to fade and reminded Vincent it was time to catch the return train. As they were leaving, Salles spoke. "I just remembered! Some time back a man came looking for you. I didn't get his name or why he wanted to reach you."

"Really? What did he look like?"

"He was a large man with a full mustache. He had a military bearing."

"Hmmm. I'm bewildered. I can't think of anyone who…" Vincent trailed off. "Well, no matter." He waved farewell and bid his friend adieu.

In the carriage ride to the station, Vincent turned to Louis. "This turned out just as I had hoped."

"I am pleased for you, Monsieur Vincent. Who do you think was looking for you?"

"I haven't any idea, Louis."

Chapter 47
Saint-Rémy, Paris, Auvers – Winter 1889-Spring 1890

Vincent felt a rush of elation as he read the letter from the Association of Les Vingt.

15 November 1889
Sir
The Association of Les Vingt, founded in 1883 with the goal of organizing an international exhibition in Brussels each year, comprising the works of its members and of twenty Belgian and foreign artists chosen from among those most sympathetic to the artistic principles it represents, requests that you do it the honour of participating in its seventh annual Salon by sending one or more of your works.
The exhibition will open in the second half of January, and will last one month...
...The association requests you, Sir, to kindly let us know as soon as possible if you accept its invitation, as the number of these is strictly limited, and to inform us before 15 December of the notes and comments you wish to see featured in the catalogue....

"Yes! At last! An exhibit at Les Vingt! I will write Theo and suggest the paintings to display. Let me see, I think *The Reaper* would be good. The yellows in it are wonderful. The sun floods everything with light of pure gold. I think it is the lightest work I've done. Also, a self-portrait. I only wish I had more portraits to choose from. Oh, and *The Red Vineyard at Arles.* That one is also a fine painting. I love the autumn reds and yellows and the way the sun is reflected on the water. I'll see what Theo thinks."

There were several sharp raps at the door. "Yes! Come in!" Vincent yelled.

The door opened and Louis stuck his head in the room. "Are you ready to go into town, Monsieur Vincent?"

"Yes, let me get my coat and sketchbook."

The two men started down the stone hallway, their footfalls echoing up and down the long corridor.

"I received a letter inviting me to display at a major Belgium art exposition right after the New Year!" Vincent announced to his companion. He was practically jumping with joy.

"That is good, Monsieur Vincent, is it not?" replied Louis.

"Oh yes, very good!" They walked briskly into the open courtyard. The day was bright with few clouds in the sky but still bitterly cold. Louis and Vincent strode into the town of Saint-Rémy and straight into a patisserie for coffee and a hot buttery brioche. They took a seat near the open fire, both men warming their hands near the flame.

"You know, Louis, it was almost one year ago that I had my attack in Arles."

"You should not think of it," replied Louis. "You are better now. You don't want to bring bad things upon yourself."

"I cannot help but remember the loneliness I felt. I sometimes have the same feelings even now."

"Have you told Dr. Peyron about your feelings?"

"He says they are natural, but I don't feel they are of my making or natural to me. I just want serenity. Sometimes I think St. Nicholas Day is a bad omen for me."

"You should concentrate on the good things. Think

about the invitation you just received and your brother's new baby coming."

Vincent lowered his voice. "Yes, his new family. I should be joyful for him."

The men sipped their coffee in silence. Vincent looked casually around the intimate café and spied a gentleman sitting in a far corner, clad in a dark wool coat and black fur-lined hat. His bushy eyebrows and thick mustache conveyed an ominous manner.

Louis followed Vincent's eyes and noticed the same man. "Say, isn't that the fellow we saw in Arles when we were last there?"

"I'm not sure. It could be. He looks very familiar somehow." Vincent frowned thoughtfully.

"Well, we should be going if you want to sketch and pick up some supplies," said Louis.

They bundled up against the biting wind and continued their way into the old Roman town, Vincent pausing every so often to sketch. He worked quickly with hands nearly numb from the harsh chill. They reached the art shop and stepped in to replenish his supplies. As they were leaving the store, Louis said, "Do you have everything you wanted, Monsieur? It is time for us to return to St. Paul's."

"I'm ready," Vincent replied. As they turned to head back home, Vincent looked into the window of a café and noticed the same mustachioed man poring over a newspaper and sipping coffee. Vincent slowed, all the while staring, trying to place him. Was it in Arles where Vincent saw him last? How odd.

On their return to St. Paul's, Vincent went to his studio to rest. His thoughts were interrupted by Louis' genial sum-

Saint-Rémy 1889

mons. "Monsieur Vincent! I have a letter for you."

"Thank you." Vincent accepted the letter, sat down, and opened it. It was a note from Jo.

My dearest brother:
I sincerely hope this letter finds you well. Theo and I are anticipating our first St. Nicholas Day as a family. I wish we could share it with you dear brother. You should see how big I have become. I feel little Vincent inside me, kicking to get out. It is remarkable to feel the life inside me.

Vincent swallowed hard at the mention of the baby. He did not need any reminders of Jo's pregnancy or of the imminence of the baby's birth. He sorely required a distraction in hopes of staving off the depression that loomed over him, so he turned to his steadfast ally, his canvas. Donning his paint-splattered apron, he reached for his palette and brush and set to work. Night was fast approaching.

Louis came to the studio later that evening to make sure the fire was lit and to check on Vincent. A waning moon was just a sliver in the night sky. He opened the studio door to find Vincent lying face up on the floor, a small rivulet of dried blood on his forehead and paint dribbling from the corner of his mouth. It appeared that he had been into his paint tubes once again.

In Paris, Jo sat in the parlor with Theo's sister, Wilhelmina. Wil had come to visit shortly after St. Nicholas Day to help Jo prepare for the baby's arrival.

As the two women sat together in the parlor sipping

their late afternoon tea—a habit that Jo treasured even as a child—Jo remarked, "Theo is so worried about Vincent, I'm afraid his health is suffering also."

Wil nodded in agreement. "Vincent has always been apt to have fits, but he always recovers. Mother used to think he was making it up, trying to draw attention to himself, but finally came to believe the fits were real."

"Oh, they're real," said Jo, "no one would want to be in an asylum! That's no place to live! His illness is serious."

"He must be getting worse. When did he have his last fit?"

"St. Nicholas Eve."

The door to the apartment opened and the women heard Theo's cheery voice: "I'm home! Where are my beautiful wife and my lovely sister?"

"Here, in the parlor! How was your day, my darling?" asked Jo.

Theo removed his coat and hat and bent over to give Jo a kiss on her cheek. "It was a good day. How are you, Wil?" he said to his sister.

"Very well! Jo and I were just talking about Vincent."

"I worry about him," Theo said thoughtfully. "These attacks come and go so quickly and without much warning. After this last attack, Dr. Peyron has forbidden him from painting because he was caught eating paint. I can't imagine what got into him! It's unfathomable."

"We were just discussing that very thing."

"Despite his bizarre behavior, art is a creative outlet for him," continued Theo. "I'm afraid he will never make a full recovery if he cannot paint," Theo perched next to Wil on the divan. "On another note, a good one I might add, I received a letter addressed to Vincent today. He has been asked to exhibit at *Salon des Indépendants* in March."

"That's excellent!" cried Jo.

"It is. His paintings will be in two major exhibits this year. The Vingt exhibit opened last week and this one will open in March."

"It seems that our brother is finally getting the accolades he deserves—from his peers and the critics!" gushed Wil.

"Yes, finally! The article by Isaacson and the articles by Aurier have certainly enhanced his reputation. Vincent is becoming a luminary in the art world. I must select the pictures for the Salon that reflect his best work."

Jo asked, "Do you think Vincent will be well enough to go to Brussels or Paris to see either exhibit?"

"I don't think so, but that will be Doctor Peyron's decision," replied Theo. "His mind is fragile right now and he could be unpredictable, even belligerent. He recovered quickly from his last episode. They isolated him for less than a week. He was even well enough to go to Arles and visit the Ginoux's. From his letters, he seems fine. He spares us the ill news, I'm afraid."

"You could keep him in Saint-Rémy, couldn't you?" Wil asked Theo.

"I'm not sure anymore. As he gains popularity, I don't want to be viewed as the one who keeps him locked away in an insane asylum."

"But it is for his own well-being! Surely anyone can see that!" Wil argued.

"Not everyone. When he recovers from his attacks, he is normal. One would never suspect what he has been through. Can I keep a 'normal' man locked away? People would think me cruel."

"But Theo, you know Vincent's attacks come without warning," said Jo.

"Yes, but there's no certainty that another attack will strike—or that Vincent will remain calm and composed. Without question, I must be careful to follow the doctor's recommendations. It would indeed be splendid to have him out of the asylum if that's what the doctor advocates."

"Could he come here?" asked Jo.

Theo looked at his wife for a few seconds. "Oh, Jo, I don't think that would be a good idea. Even when he is 'normal', he is not like you and me. He can be angry and violent and then sad and despondent. His mind does not work like ours. But enough about Vincent!" He looked at his sister and patted her slight hand. "Wil, I am so thankful that you could come and stay with Jo. I'm not sure what to do when the baby comes and she is in her confinement."

"Oh, speaking of the baby," cried Jo, "little Vincent is kicking! Come, put your hand here," she said, touching her swollen belly. Theo and Wil both put their hands on Jo. Within seconds there was a thump, then a small kick. "He is going to be quite the boy!" smiled Theo. "That felt like a fist followed by a foot."

"If he has any idea what's waiting for him outside in our senseless world, he'll come out fighting!" said Wil. And that he did—on the last day of January, 1890.

Gauguin stood motionless with his arms at his sides, frowning in deep thought, as he gazed at his artwork hanging on the Salon wall. There were two landscapes, a Pietà, an angel, and two portraits. The Vingt exhibit was one of the major showings throughout Europe. Bernard marched up and stood next to him.

"These are some of your best efforts, Paul. I really admire the techniques and subjects. This is Symbolism at its finest."

Paul said nothing but remained frozen in his spot. His once tanned, smooth face now looked lined with worry. Or was that weariness? Émile couldn't determine which. His eyes were bloodshot. Had he been crying? Or was he angry?

"What's the matter with you, Paul?" asked Bernard.

Gauguin's hands flew to his face and covered his eyes and cheeks. As he pulled his hands away, he moaned. "I am an enraged but broken man. My art, my life's work is demeaned by Aurier.

"And that damn van Gogh. First, he insults me by criticizing my subject matter and then he is praised in the journals. Did you see Aurier's articles?"

"Yes, I saw the one in 'L'Art Moderne' and one in 'Mercure de France.' But do not lament over his criticism, my friend. He impugned me for painting religious themes."

"So you did see them! Merde! Aurier likened van Gogh to a martyr! He completely ignored all of the work I did!"

"He did not acknowledge any of my work either," Émile reminded Paul.

"Yes, but here in Brussels, he ignores my work and praises that simpleton's drawings. Come, let me show you something." Gauguin led Bernard to an adjoining salon. He pointed to a painting on the wall called *The Red Vineyards*.

"There, see that? Anna Boch paid 400 francs for that!

I remember when van Gogh painted it. We were in Arles together. I advised him to be more definitive in his outline. You can see it in the figures of the workers. But, here, in the foreground, not so much. I painted the same subject but with Breton women and no one has noticed—it's clearly superior to this!"

"Paul, perhaps you are being a bit too critical…"

Gauguin turned and looked down into Bernard's young, unlined face. Émile could see the brutality in the older man's eyes.

"Really!" bristled Gauguin. "You like this?!"

"I do," Bernard nodded. He was determined to hold his ground on this tête-á-queue. "I think it is quite striking. It speaks to me of death, with the yellow sun setting in the background. But mind you, it's not an ugly, despairing kind of death—it's rather like the natural progression of life. It is radiant with color and thick, coarse brush strokes, and yet, it is a very sophisticated rendering."

"Well, perhaps you don't know shit either!" Paul snorted as he turned away from his fellow artist and stomped out of the room.

Émile was bewildered by Gauguin's behavior. "Why is Gauguin so competitive?! Sometimes I think he is the mad one. If he doesn't watch his temper, it will get him into trouble… just like Vincent," Émile muttered.

Theo and Jo strolled arm in arm along the Champs-Élysées. The wintry weather had begun to yield to the warmth of approaching spring. Trees whose limbs had been bared by the harsh cold were beginning to go early green with tiny buds.

"It is a shame that Vincent could not come to Paris for this showing," said Jo. "I think he would have enjoyed his brush with fame!"

"He is too ill. Just when he seems to improve, he suffers another attack."

"The poor dear. I just cannot imagine the agony he is going through."

"I think the cold weather brings on some of his fits. That and Arles. Such bad memories. He really should stay away from there, but he keeps going back as if drawn by some magnetic force."

Jo tugged at Theo's arm and pointed. In the distance the iron structure from the World's Fair towered above the Paris skyline. "How long do you think Eiffel's Tower will loom over Paris? I think it should come down. It's been months since the Fair closed."

Theo laughed. "My dear, that is an engineering marvel. It will last until our little Vincent has his own pint-sized little Vincent!"

"Goodness, I hope not! Please don't mention our baby. I feel depressed leaving him at home with a nanny at such a young age."

"Come now. He is fine. The doctor says he is healthy and growing as he should. Besides, we both could use some quiet time."

The couple continued along the broad avenue until they came to a massive wooden building. A banner across the building proclaimed in large letters *Ville de Paris Pavillion – Salon des Indépendants*.

"The crowds have thinned since the opening," said Theo.

"Yes, well, the President of the Republic isn't here now. He only comes at the beginning—and then only to be seen and heard," Jo answered.

The interior of the building was expansive with high vaulted ceilings and several adjoining salons. The Indépendants was the second most heralded exhibit of the year. Paintings adorned every wall, leaving little blank space between pieces. There were large and small canvases, watercolors, oils, and sketches. Small sculptures in various mediums of wood, glass, marble and granite rested on pedestals, while larger ones were scattered about the highly-polished floors.

Theo and Jo threaded their way past the art admirers into a third gallery. Along one wall were ten of Vincent's paintings hung at eye level. A small placard bearing the title, date and artist's name was next to each work. They paused in front of a painting of sunflowers.

"I wish Vincent could be here," Theo said, "he would be so proud."

"You can tell him all about it," Jo replied, smiling.

"His paintings are very well placed. The effect is excellent," observed Theo.

The couple stood for a while in front of each painting, taking time to admire the brush strokes and techniques and colors. Theo heard his name and turned to see Émile Bernard and Albert Aurier approaching him.

"Émile, Albert, a pleasure to see you!" Theo exclaimed as he reached out to shake their hands.

"Likewise, my friend," said Émile. "And Jo, you look splendid. How is the baby?"

"Little Vincent is well. He has the brightest eyes and most adorable little hands and feet," she giggled. "And oh, what a personality he has already developed!"

"I will have to come and see him," said Émile.

"Oh yes, please do. You are welcome any time!"

"Jo, this is Albert Aurier, the art critic who has remarked so favorably about Vincent's work."

"Indeed! I have read your articles on Vincent. You have been most kind. It is heartening to see that someone understands what Vincent has struggled to convey in his paintings."

"It can take some time for an artist to become truly appreciated. Vincent's moment will come, I can assure you. He is a brilliant artist. By the way, is he here today? Did he come with you?"

"I'm afraid not," Theo replied. "He is not well. He's had another attack that keeps him in St. Paul's."

"I am sorry to hear that," said Aurier. "His work is pure genius. He should be here to bask in glory, for he is the star of this exhibition! Perhaps his malady bestows upon him the temperament of a true Symbolist and allows him to see what is invisible to even the healthiest eyes."

"That is so kind of you," said Theo.

"I might add that he is also quite humble. He wrote to me to ask that I give Paul Gauguin his due. Vincent is a special soul."

Aurier looked at Theo. "I am not the only one who feels strongly about Vincent's work. Georges Lecomte wrote a very good piece in *L'Art et Critique* about his impasto. And Claude Monet told me he thinks his works are the best in the show."

"I am so grateful to hear that!"

Aurier shook Theo's hand. "Your brother will leave a lasting legacy. He is a master. I must go, but I hope to see you again and very soon."

"Monsieur Aurier, please come by our apartment to visit. I must show you a painting Vincent dedicated to our son. It is a blossoming almond tree. It speaks of hope and promise."

"I must see it then! Au revoir, Theo, Madame." Bernard and Aurier went on their way to the outlying salons.

Just then, Theo noticed an older man with a red shock of hair, a sad but gentle mustache and tiny nest of hair under his lower lip. All of him seemed to be the same color: red hair, a rosy complexion no doubt brought on by a recent cold, and pink ears. He was judiciously appraising Vincent's works.

"Dr. Gachet?" asked Theo.

"Why, yes, I am Paul Gachet. Are you Theo van Gogh?" he inquired.

"Yes. I'm delighted that you could come so we could meet in person!"

"I read the information you sent me about your brother. I also read the letters from Dr. Peyron. Your brother is fortunate to be in the care of such an able doctor."

"I agree. Dr. Peyron has been very generous."

"I must confess, from what I know, I don't think Vincent is mad. I suspect he has a physical ailment that can be cured with proper treatment. If not cured, at least properly managed."

"Really?" Theo looked astonished. "You honestly think he can be cured?"

"If my theory is correct, I believe he can be cured with the right nutrition and medical treatment," Gachet replied. "But I would have to treat him at Auvers. Do you think he would be amenable to moving back to the Paris area?"

"I believe he would, doctor. We will have to work out several things, including his discharge from St. Paul's, his relocation, a place to stay in Auvers and the like."

"I can help with living arrangements in Auvers. You just let me know when I can expect him."

"Thank you, thank you, Dr. Gachet!" Theo beamed as he pumped Gachet's fleshy hand.

"Don't thank me yet, my boy. We still have plenty of work ahead of us. In the meantime, please keep me informed of his progress and plans."

"I certainly will. Au revoir!"

"Good day, my friends." The doctor retreated, continuing to admire the art works on the walls.

The manservant stood at the threshold of the study to announce the arrival of a guest. "Madame, Count Esterhazy is here to see you."

Marguerite paused from her letter writing and peered up at him from the large mahogany desk. "Count? Ah, yes. The Count. Please escort him in."

Esterhazy marched through the door followed by the manservant. Marguerite had returned to her letter and did not look up. "Sit down, Ferdinand," she ordered. "I will be finished in a minute."

Esterhazy removed his coat, and held it out for the manservant in attendance.

"Would you like something to drink, Monsieur?" asked the butler.

"Yes, a small Cognac would be nice."

Marguerite spoke up, shooting a glance at the butler. "Never mind. The Count won't be staying long."

A look of irritation crossed Esterhazy's broad face. Noting this, the butler dutifully retreated and closed the door behind him.

Esterhazy sat in the large, over-stuffed leather chair facing the desk. He surveyed the ornate room—bookshelves filled with leather-bound volumes, framed photographs of Marguerite with well-known dignitaries, industrialists, and politicians. But no family photos, he noted silently. Esterhazy gazed at a Caravaggio on the far wall.

Marguerite sat her pen down and eyed him. "I appreciate you coming on such short notice, Ferdinand," she said. Despite the polite words, her voice sounded hollow.

He faced Marguerite, her steely blue eyes revealing no emotion. "I saw your luggage in the entryway. Are you going on a trip?" he asked.

"I am going to England. It will be good to see my daughter again. She is at Kings College. Such a bright young woman," Marguerite said with more than a trace of pride.

"You don't speak of her often. Is she well?"

Marguerite ignored the question. Her personal life was no business of his, even though they were related. "I assume you have been keeping up with events in Germany?"

"I have."

"Not to dwell on the obvious, but I want to be very specific and clear. According to the papers, Bismarck resigned.

Of course, that is only partially correct. Kaiser Wilhelm and the Chancellor have had a tumultuous relationship for the past year. Bismarck finally went too far in trying to quell the social unrest in Germany and the Kaiser told him he must step aside."

"I suspected as much," replied the Count.

Marguerite nodded. "Yes, I'm sure you did. Once the Chancellor resigned, the Kaiser learned about the secret non-aggression pact between Germany and Russia that the Chancellor referred to as 'The Reassurance Treaty.' The Tsar wanted to renew the treaty but the Kaiser knew nothing about it."

"I'm willing to bet that did not make the Kaiser happy," interjected Esterhazy.

"No. It certainly did not. He was caught completely off guard and was terribly embarrassed. Needless to say, the Kaiser refused to renew the treaty, thereby further alienating the Tsar."

"What does any of this have to do with me?" Esterhazy wanted to know.

"I'm coming to that. As you may have already speculated, the Kaiser wanted to know what other secret agreements the Chancellor had entered into. He started interrogating several of the Chancellor's close associates, including our friend Pierre. Pierre told the Kaiser that the Chancellor was behind the assassination attempts against the Tsar. He further informed the Kaiser that these plots were orchestrated to cause a permanent rift between the Tsar and France."

"Wilhelm should appreciate the subterfuge," he smirked.

Marguerite gave him a bruising stare. "Wilhelm was not

amused. He ordered Pierre to destroy all evidence of these plots by whatever means necessary. Anyone and anything associated with any assassination attempt formulated by Bismarck is to be extinguished. Erased in its entirety."

"That does not bode well for you, does it?" Esterhazy taunted softly.

"For us, Ferdinand. For us. Do not forget your involvement. You were at the meetings. You supplied French weapons. You are also culpable, my dearest cousin," Marguerite seethed, her nostrils flaring.

"What do you want of me, then?" Esterhazy challenged. She was an enigma to him, a puzzle that he could not solve no matter how he approached her. She could be charming one minute and ruthless the next.

"I want that artist's sketchbook! It has proof of direct German involvement. No one will dare touch either of us if we have that book."

"I've tried to get it, but that damn van Gogh fellow never lets it out of his sight. And to make matters worse, he is now in an impenetrable insane asylum."

"Get it, Ferdinand. But no one, I repeat, no one must know you have it."

"If I get it, what do I do with it? You will be in England!"

"Hide it in the country house as we discussed."

"How will I hear from you?"

"I plan to stay in a little village outside London called Harpenden. I will use the pseudonym Voilemont. Now, please leave. I have preparations to make."

"When will you return?"

"When I think it is safe. Go. Leave me to my work."

Chapter 48
Saint-Rémy, Paris – Spring 1890

Doctor Peyron leaned forward and peered over his cluttered desk at Vincent. "Monsieur Vincent, it is my considered opinion, that discharge and travel to Paris is unwise at this time."

Vincent was slouched in the leather armchair, glaring at the doctor. "I tell you I must leave this place! If I don't, I will wither away in this prison."

"Good gracious, Vincent, this is not a prison and you are not a prisoner!"

"I am confined and it makes it too difficult to practice my profession. I must have freedom of movement!" Vincent's eyes widened and his face became flushed with agitation.

"But you have been painting. You have a studio, art supplies—everything is at your disposal."

"I mostly sit in my room. I paint from memory and emotion. I copy pictures. I need real freedom to create," he moaned. "I need inspiration! I want to resume the peasant studies that I abandoned and I simply cannot do that here!" Vincent started to rise from the chair. He felt as though someone had wrapped his entire body in a restraint jacket. He could not breathe. He wanted air.

Peyron spoke in a low, soothing voice. "Please, Monsieur Vincent. I do not mean to excite you. Please, sit down."

"I'm sorry," Vincent said as he lowered himself into the chair. He looked down at his feet. "I believe it is impossible for me to endure here any longer. I will heal more quickly in the North. I will be closer to my brother," he said quietly.

Peyron leaned back in his chair. "Monsieur, you have had

several attacks over the last few months. Only just recently are you returning to your old self."

"The last two months have been wretched! But you know that my attacks are followed by longer periods of complete calm. I want to take advantage of this time to move forward. My brother has found a suitable doctor who will look after me."

"Your brother," said Peyron, "has written me about Dr. Gachet. He seems qualified to treat you. However, I would advise you to let some time pass in order to ensure your period of calm has arrived."

"I assure you, Dr. Peyron, it has arrived," Vincent spoke adamantly, becoming agitated.

Peyron raised his hand to quiet Vincent's rising voice. "Very well," the doctor said, "if I have your brother's consent, I will sign the release papers—"

"Excellent." Vincent began to rise.

"—but you and your brother will have to take full responsibility for your release and subsequent actions. Is that understood? Neither I nor this facility shall have any liability for you once you are released."

Vincent nodded. "As it should be."

Peyron called to the attendant standing outside the doorway. "Louis! Please see Monsieur Vincent back to his room." Then addressing Vincent, he said, "Please have your brother send me his signed permission to release you."

Jo was sitting in a chair rocking baby Vincent and humming a soft lullaby. "Do you think Vincent is strong enough to make the journey from Saint-Rémy?"

Theo, embracing a snifter of Cognac on his divan, gave Jo a thoughtful look. "I don't know. Doctor Peyron advises against it, but Vincent is vehement about leaving St. Paul and coming north. Once his mind is made up, he's very difficult to convince otherwise."

"When do you expect him to arrive? I will have to prepare the small guest room."

"I have written Dr. Peyron with my consent to release him. Vincent is packing and will send me a telegram when he reaches Tarascon. I plan to meet him at the train station."

"I am anxious to see him. This will be the first time I have seen Vincent as a sister. And he will get to meet his namesake!"

"It has been over a year since I saw him in Arles." Theo said softly, looking off into the distance with regret on his face. "I hope this time is better."

Chapter 49
On a Train Somewhere in France – Present Day

Mark leaned over onto Maggie's shoulder and whispered, "Mags, tell me what happened at the restaurant."

She leaned into him. "I came out of the bathroom and Victor was leaning against the wall. I thought he was dining there so I said hello. He gave me a funny look and said something like 'come with me.' I asked what he meant and he pulled a gun out of his coat! I was terrified! I just froze. He took me out the back door and shoved me into the back seat of a car. He took my cell phone, smashed it, and threw it in the dumpster behind the restaurant!"

"I looked everywhere for you."

"Yeah, well, Durand tied me up, put a blindfold on me and took me to some hotel—through an alley. I could smell the garbage. He kept asking me about the sketchbook and you."

"What did he want to know?"

"I think he was sizing you up, to see how you would react to my kidnapping."

Mark was incredulous. "What? How I would react?"

"Like, would you go off the deep end, do something unpredictable. Mark, he seemed scared and just barely in control—if that makes any sense."

"Yeah. In over his head."

"Well, next thing I hear is Anton's voice. The two assholes argued over the sketchbook and me. I thought Anton was going to rescue me. Instead, he just removed the blindfold and told me that he was sorry things worked out this way. He told Durand to go through with his plan—which scared the hell out of me! They locked me in the bathroom, and I was trying to listen, wondering what would happen next. I fell asleep in the bathtub! When I woke up they were there, and they threw me in the trunk of a car. I've never been so scared in my life, Mark. They said if I caused any trouble, they would kill you and me."

"Well, Anton did kill Durand."

"He's evil, Mark. He took me out of the trunk, blindfolded me again, put me in the back seat of another car, and drove me to another hotel. Just a while ago, he told me we were going to see you. He said he would not hesitate to kill both of us if we caused any trouble."

"I believe him. I called Gastineau when I couldn't find you at the restaurant." Mark told her about the surveillance, finding Durant, and his own ordeal.

"By the way, I don't think I like you as a blond."

"Oh." Forgetting it was there in all the excitement, he removed the wig and dropped it on the floor.

"Do you think Gastineau knows where we are?"

"I doubt it. He's not looking for a blond guy in these clothes."

"What do you think Anton will do with us?"

"This is an Anton that I don't know. He has everything he wants. I don't see how he—"

"Don't say it," Maggie stopped him.

"We have to find a way out of here."

The train slowed and a sharp rap at the door startled the huddled couple. Samuel shook his gun at Mark and Maggie to signal that they shouldn't try anything. He looked through the peephole and unbolted the door. Anton entered.

"This is our stop. I strongly advise you to behave and not cause a scene. Samuel gets a little jumpy and is quick to react—the results can be fatal. You will follow me. Samuel will bring up the rear."

The four marched down the narrow passage toward the front of the car. The train lurched, then halted suddenly. A conductor opened the door that connected the train cars. As he did so, he whispered something to Anton. Mark heard Anton reply, *"Merci. Très bien."* The conductor stood aside to let Anton pass. Samuel gave Mark a hard shove.

Once outside the train, Anton ordered everyone to follow him. "Be careful, there are no clear paths and you do not want to get lost here."

They plodded for about forty-five minutes through shrubs and brush before eventually coming to an overgrown footpath. Mark was grateful to walk on something that was halfway navigable. He could see the scratches on Maggie's bare legs. He knew she was miserable.

They followed the trail for another half hour as it zigzagged up an incline. The foothills of the Alps loomed in the distance.

A single lane road ran just below the crest of the hill. A work van sat on the shoulder of the road with the hood up. Anton approached the driver and said a few words. The side door opened. Anton motioned for them to get in. "Quickly!" he ordered.

The driver closed the hood and got in behind the wheel. Four large leather captain's chairs behind the solid partition separated the driver from the passengers in the rear. A folded table rested against one side of the van, underneath a well-stocked bar. Mark and Maggie sat in the two forward-facing seats while Anton and Samuel sat opposite them, their backs to the driver.

Anton pushed a button on the partition and ordered the driver to get going. The truck accelerated to the sound of crunching gravel. "We have a long journey, so please relax. Would you like a drink?" asked Anton.

"A drink? I don't think so. Where are you taking us?" Mark demanded.

"Suit yourselves. If you want anything, all you have to do is ask."

"How about letting us go?"

"That is entirely up to you. I do not want to harm either of you. We have been friends for so long. But rest assured, I will do what I have to do."

"You didn't answer the question. Where are you taking us?" asked Maggie.

"We are going to my chateau. It is lovely. It is too bad you cannot truly enjoy it. It is one of the great treasures left to me by my grandfather."

"What do you mean by that?" queried Mark.

"My grandfather occupied the chateau during the war. After the war, he kept it."

"Who are the real owners?"

"War has a way of altering many things. You know the phrase 'history is written by the victors'? Well, the chaos that ensued after the war gave my grandfather, a truly resourceful man, the opportunity to transfer the property to his ownership. And it has remained in the family ever since." Anton let out a guttural laugh. "I guess you call that creative bookkeeping."

"You're just a common thief. And a murderer."

"Oh, but I am so much more than a common thief." Anton sipped his aperitif. "I procure the unprocurable. I have delivered a terra cotta soldier from China to a Russian businessman, a Phoenician gold coin to an Italian olive oil baron, and even a document hand-written by Louis XIV to an English aristocrat. All for a hefty price, of course, and in the greatest secrecy. No common thief can do that!"

"So that makes you an uncommon thief then," Mark snarled back at him.

Anton did not take the bait. He chuckled smugly. "I can accept that."

The 300-kilometer drive took just under four hours. Mark and Maggie dozed fitfully. Then the van took a series of quick turns and came to a sudden stop.

"Now you will have a chance, however brief, to see and hopefully enjoy my chateau," Anton boasted. The driver opened the sliding door to reveal an imposing four-story stone mansion. Narrow-beamed spotlights angled up to accent the tall square turrets at each of the four corners of the house. The house itself seemed to disappear into a stand of sturdy trees, creating a strong and eerie presence. Small lighting fixtures placed along the borders of the circular driveway illuminated the path to the house.

Mark whispered to Maggie, "I don't see any other houses around. No neighbors, no signs of human life anywhere in the vicinity."

"Come," said Anton. "I am sure you are exhausted. You have time to sleep before breakfast." He led the way through the front door into a grand, marbled entryway. Elegant rooms jutted off both sides of the atrium. A wide oak staircase curved majestically up to the second floor. "Samuel will take you to your room. I have some business to attend to. I bid you a *bon nuit, mes amis.*" Anton disappeared into another room.

Samuel directed them with his gun up the grand staircase. The second-floor hallway extended the length of the manor. Paintings adorned the walls and a series of antique rugs covered the hardwood floors. Samuel stopped at one of the heavy oak doors off the hall. Mark turned the crystal doorknob and swung the door inward. The center piece of the large room was a four-poster bed draped with sheers on all sides. A marble fireplace was at one end of the room and two floor-to-ceiling windows overlooked well-manicured gardens. A small lavatory adjoined the room. Samuel waved them in with his gun hand and the door slammed shut. They heard the key click in the old lock.

Maggie walked around the perimeter of the room. "Well, at least we have a comfortable place to stay. Now what?"

"I don't really know. I'm having a tough time understanding all of this. Anton… I would never in a million years think Anton could do this."

"Me neither. I wonder if Sarah knows."

Mark jiggled the windows. "Locked. I don't know. It would be hard to hide this sort of thing. How have the authorities not caught on? It's incredible to me."

Maggie turned abruptly, "Did you call Maman and tell her what was going on?"

"Yes. I called her when I couldn't find you at the restaurant."

"Crap."

"Why? She deserved to know."

"She was already worried. Now she'll be through the roof. And if she can't get through to your cell, I don't know what she'll do."

"I gave her Gastineau's name and number. She's pretty resourceful. She'll get through to him if she feels she needs to."

Maggie plopped on the bed. "Well, what do we do now?"

"I think it's a good idea to get some rest. We'll need it."

"First, I'm going to take a shower. I smell like a spare tire."

Mark put his arm around Maggie. Tears ran down her cheek. "Everything will be okay, Mags."

"You are ever the optimist."

Chapter 50
Paris, Auvers-sur-Oise – Spring-Summer 1890

The whistle blared and steam filled the platform as the train squealed to a halt. Within minutes, Vincent stepped off onto the platform at La Gare de Lyon. The early morning air was cool and moist—a small thunderstorm had passed through the night before, leaving a trail of dampness in its wake. Vincent felt a surge of emotions as he looked around the platform: Anxiety… joy… weightlessness… exhilaration!

Just a few cars away, he spied Theo's arm raised in greeting. "Theo, thank you so very much for meeting me here!" Vincent cried as he hugged his brother. Theo could barely catch his breath under Vincent's deep, tight embrace.

"You look well, Vincent! You must have eaten like a horse. Have you gained weight?" asked Theo.

"I'm the same. It's just the passage of time and your failing memory! Quite frankly, though, Dr. Peyron threatened me with thirty lashes if I didn't clean my plate every night!"

Theo picked up Vincent's bag. "Come, we have a carriage waiting. All but one of your crates came yesterday."

"Did one get lost?" inquired Vincent.

"I'm sure it just took a bit of a detour. It will show up. Let's hurry, Jo is anxious to see you."

An early morning fog was lifting, imparting an eerie quality to the lifeless streets. No doubt the sun would soon appear and burn it off. But for now the brothers talked non-stop through cloud-skirted streets on their way to 8 Cité Pigalle.

The carriage pulled up to an apartment house in the middle of the block, which was lined on both sides by five-story buildings. He had grown accustomed to the quaint, petite structures of Arles and Saint-Rémy, and was unused to these canyons that crowded out every bit of natural light.

The men made their way into the foyer and up the stairs. When the door to the apartment opened, Jo ran to Vincent and put her arms around his thin shoulders.

"Vincent, I am so thrilled to see you!"

Vincent had not anticipated Jo's enthusiasm even though she had shown him a great deal of love and concern in her letters. All he could muster was a shy "It is a pleasure to see you, too."

Always the well-mannered hostess, Jo did not seem to notice Vincent's reticence. Taking his hand, she coaxed him onto a divan. "Come! Sit and rest. Would you like some breakfast? Coffee? Tea?" she asked.

"Oh, yes, please. The trip was very long and I did not get any rest. After my tea, I would like to sleep for a few hours and then see the city and museums. Perhaps visit Pére Tanguy," said Vincent. He looked around the apartment, taking in its furnishings and decor. At least one of his paintings adorned every wall. *The Potato Eaters* was the focal point of the dining room, while *Starry Night Over the Rhone* hung magnificently over the fireplace in the parlor. He peeked at the baby in the next room. *Almond Blossoms,* which he had created just for little Vincent, overlooked the crib. Vincent couldn't help but feel a swelling pride at the sight of his art in his brother's home, and the wondrous tiny being that was his namesake.

"Little Vincent looks peaceful," Vincent remarked. "I'm

anxious to meet the little fellow when he awakens."

"He has settled down a bit," replied Theo. "He has been ill with the colic, but now he is well."

"I noticed that you have a cough, Theo. How long have you had it?"

"For some time. Must be old age. Why don't you get some rest and we will tour the city later?" Theo showed Vincent his room and helped him get settled. Then he returned to the living room, quietly leaving Vincent to nap in the small bedroom.

Vincent intended to make the most of his short stay in Paris and filled his next few days with all the activities that Theo had planned for him. He took in the exhibits of Japanese art at the Champ de Mars and soaked up the colors of Monet and Pissarro. He was overwhelmed with wonder by the works of Puvis de Chavannes. Vincent had not witnessed work by a contemporary artist in more than a year and took joy in these marvelous sights.

When the day arrived for Vincent to leave for Auvers, Theo accompanied him to the train station.

"Thank you for putting me up," he said to his brother. "I had a wonderful time with you and Jo and little Vincent but I am also glad to leave. Paris is simply too busy for me right now. I find it too confusing and it makes me feel a bit lost. I look forward to the simplicity of the countryside once again."

"I understand, Vincent. I am delighted to have you living closer and to be able to see you more often! I have missed you, my brother. Have a good trip to Auvers. Please give my regards to Dr. Gachet."

"I will. When I am established, you and Jo must visit!"

"We will visit! I have so much to do though. I have the Raffaëlli show at the entresol and I am trying to convince Monet to return to Goupil. The owners are still angry with me for losing Monet's business and for the Caravaggio theft three years ago."

A sharp pang pierced Vincent's heart and he looked sheepishly down at the platform. "Why can't they forget the past? You have done so much for the gallery."

"They never forget, Vincent. It is their nature. You know how it is. They may live in the present, but they never forget."

The brothers embraced, and Vincent boarded the train for the hour ride to Auvers.

The village of Auvers-sur-Oise sat along a bend in the Oise River, surrounded by wheat fields and forests. The village had a storied history and throughout the years had maintained an intimate and antiquated charm. Its long, winding streets curved with the river. An old chateau could be seen in the distance overlooking the bucolic vista like a watchful governess.

Vincent left the train at the Chaponval station on the west side of town. He walked along the streets until he came to Dr. Gachet's home, a large two-story house on a hill surrounded by terraced gardens. Two stray cats eyed Vincent then ran off in search of better things. A rooster was crowing in the near distance. He knocked on the door. An older man, similar in size and stature to Vincent, answered. Tufts of red hair poked out above his large ears.

Auvers-sur-Oise 1890

"I am Vincent van Gogh. I am looking for Dr. Paul Gachet. He is expecting me."

"Ah, Vincent, my boy, I am Gachet. Do come in." He led Vincent into a well-appointed living room that held numerous antiques. Vincent immediately noticed the large stone fireplace occupying an entire wall. The plaster work enveloping it imparted a graveness that was reflected in Gachet's woeful face. Vincent wondered to himself what trauma had left such scars of sadness in this odd man's visage.

As he looked around the room, Vincent spied a lovely Pissarro, a winter scene with a red house, and two bouquets by Cézanne. The dining room boasted a large Chippendale table that could easily seat a dozen or more guests. A couple of Impressionist paintings lent some color to the otherwise cheerless room. At the end of the hallway, floor-to-ceiling French doors opened onto a flower garden that was enclosed by a six-foot brick and stucco wall covered with ivy.

"Please, sit and we can get to know one another," Gachet said as he offered Vincent a worn Queen Anne's chair, the fabric dull.

Gachet turned to Vincent. "I hope your trip was good."

"Yes, indeed. It is a short trip from Paris. I spent three days with my brother and his wife before coming here."

"And how is Theo?" asked Gachet.

"He looks well enough, but I fear he is under great stress at the Gallery."

"Yes, we all have our worrisome obligations, I'm afraid. Now please, tell me about you. How are you feeling? Are you experiencing any anxieties?" inquired Gachet.

"No, not at this time. In fact, I feel rejuvenated," responded Vincent. "I am extremely delighted to have freedom of movement again. I was so stifled and bored in the asylum that I was destined to be miserable. And to make matters worse, someone had to accompany me no matter where I went. I felt like a prisoner most of the time."

For the next few hours, Vincent and Gachet discussed Vincent's health, his attacks, and his work. Gachet struck Vincent as rather detached and distant, yet likable. His sad face would light up when he spoke of his days in Belgium and his association with the old painters. He proudly showed Vincent some of his own work.

Gachet looked at the clock on the mantel, "It is getting late in the day. I suggest you stay at the Inn, at least for the night. It is quite accommodating and very convenient. After you settle in, please come back and join me for dinner."

Vincent accepted the doctor's offer and left to find his way to the Hôtel Saint-Aubin. The hotel was a bit too expensive for his meager stipend, so after one night at Saint-Aubin, he moved to the Hôtel Ravoux, a smaller inn located in the middle of the village, owned by Gustave Ravoux, a Paris transplant, and his wife. The first floor was divided into a dining room and a poolroom. Winding stairs led to the second floor where Vincent settled in, anticipating that a second-story room might be quieter. The room's decor was scanty but had all he needed—one bed, a small built-in cupboard, a washstand, and a chair. A single window overlooked a small yard and barn behind the hotel.

Two days after Vincent settled in, his canvases and baggage arrived. "What do you have here, Monsieur van Gogh?" asked the proprietor.

Auvers-sur-Oise 1890

"These are some of my pictures and supplies."

"I don't think all of that will fit in your room! I have a back room on the first floor you can rent if you need the space," suggested Ravoux. He ushered Vincent to the back of the building, where an empty storeroom awaited him. "You may also have use of the barn to store some of your work."

"Thank you. This will do nicely," said Vincent.

Vincent was determined to develop a healthy routine so he would rise early and go out into the countryside to paint. Moreover, it was decidedly cooler in the mornings and Vincent discovered that he could accomplish more when the conditions were to his liking. He worked at a feverish pitch, completing some landscapes in less than a day. He varied his technique but mostly used short, quick, impatient strokes. The larger canvases quickly crowded his newfound space. It was then he decided to send some of them to Theo, desperately hoping that he would not stack them under his bed or put them in the termite-infested rooms at Tanguy's.

The bell above the door to the Goupil Gallery announced a visitor.

"Émile," Theo exclaimed, "how good to see you! Where have you been keeping yourself?"

"I have been preoccupied with my art and trying to establish myself. You know, trying to find that special niche where my work will be both recognized and well regarded."

"I do know what you mean. What brings you to the Gallery today?"

"I wanted to find out where Vincent is. I haven't heard from him for some time. Is he still in Saint-Rémy?"

"Oh my goodness, no. He has moved to Auvers-sur-Oise. I thought you knew," replied Theo.

Émile looked surprised. "When did he move there?"

"Just recently. Wait, I will give you his address. He is renting a room in the middle of town, just across from the town hall. I'm sure he would be delighted to hear from you."

"Perhaps I can visit him. Auvers isn't very far. Not like Saint-Rémy or Arles." Bernard looked around the entrosol. "Your Raffaëlli exhibit looks excellent. How is business?"

"Business is fine. Well, not really. The Gallery needs some high-end works." Theo's expression turned sour. "The owners want everything, including my life blood," he said in hushed tones.

"But surely it cannot be that bad!"

"Oh yes, it can. And it is," Theo groaned.

"I'm sorry, Theo."

They discussed their respective work, their latest endeavors, and the current affairs of the art world when a customer entered. Emile said to Theo, "I won't take up any more of your time. I must be going. *Au revoir,* my friend."

Émile stepped out onto the avenue, mulling over his next steps to retrieve the sketchbook.

"You look troubled, young man." The familiar voice came from behind Émile. He turned quickly to see who had spoken. The color drained from his face.

"Pierre," he gasped, "what are you doing here?"

"Looking for you."

"What do you want from me?"

"Come now. Walk with me." Pierre's voice was firm and commanding.

Once they were walking abreast Pierre inquired, "You have kept up on current events, I assume?"

"To what 'current events' are you referring?"

"I am going to be blunt with you, my friend. You have been a party to the assassination attempt on the Russian Tsar. That alone merits a death penalty."

"No one knows I am involved," Émile objected. He was doing his utmost to appear brave but his voice faltered and he swallowed hard.

Pierre grabbed Émile by the arm and drew him close. "I know," Pierre whispered into Émile's ear. "Marguerite knows. The rest of the Commune knows."

"But they won't divulge that information. It would mean the death penalty for them as well," Émile replied, shaking himself loose from Pierre's grasp.

"So you think. I am not so confident about that."

"Look, Pierre, I certainly won't tell anyone. What would I have to gain?"

Pierre steered the young artist down another avenue, leading toward the Champs-Élysées. "Some people just like to brag. Make themselves seem more important than they really are."

"I am not one of those people!" Émile protested.

"I hope not. For if you are, and I find out that you let slip any reference to the assassination attempts, you will not live to stand trial. Do you understand?"

Émile stopped and looked at Pierre. "I know how to keep quiet. You have my word."

Pierre stared at Émile, his penetrating eyes boring right through him. Émile could almost feel the heat from his cruel glare. Pierre finally asked, "Where is that other artist friend of yours? Van Gogh?"

"I... I don't know. He was in an asylum in Saint-Rémy. I don't know if he is still there or not." Émile nervously fingered the slip of paper Theo had given him with Vincent's address. Pierre considered what Bernard said. "Find out where he is. I want to talk to him. And you should hope he is as cooperative as you. Or else—"

"I'll find him! How can I reach you when I do?"

"Don't worry. I'll find you. Be quick about it. There are other people who are not as patient and understanding as I am," warned Pierre. He abruptly turned and disappeared as quickly as he had appeared.

Bernard nervously wiped the sweat from his brow. He could not stop the tremors that had taken hold of his body. "I have to get that sketchbook now. If Pierre discovers that I lied to him, he will kill us both."

Chapter 51
Auvers-sur-Oise – Early Summer 1890

Vincent was seated in front of a fresh canvas in his makeshift studio, thinking of his next project. A slight noise caused him to turn around. In the doorway stood a young man, eyeing one of Vincent's landscapes that was propped up against the wall.

"That is a magnificent painting," the young man said in an oddly breathy voice.

Vincent looked at him with an appraising eye. The peculiar visitor was tall and broad shouldered. His stubbled chin punctuated an otherwise fair complexion.

"I just finished it yesterday. I must take it to the barn to dry," said Vincent.

"Do you have other paintings in the barn?" he asked.

"Yes, a few."

The young fellow stepped hesitantly toward Vincent. "May I see them?"

Vincent thought for a moment, wondering what to make of this strange young man. "Yes, I suppose so. Follow me. What's your name?"

"I am Gaston Secretan. My father has a hunting lodge in Auvers. My brother and I spend the summer here."

"I am Vincent van Gogh. Are you interested in art?" he asked, pulling the studio door open.

"Very much so. But I don't get to draw often or go to museums. My father prefers that my brother and I play sports or hunt."

"That's a shame. Art is a worthy and creative profession."

The two reached the barn and Vincent led the young man through the side door.

"Oh my! Such beautiful pictures!" exclaimed Gaston, gazing open-mouthed at the paintings in the barn.

"Thank you." Vincent showed him several of his landscapes, explaining where each one had been created. After a few minutes, Vincent decided it was late and told his admirer that he was closing up. As he escorted Gaston from the barn, Gaston said, "May I come by tomorrow?"

"Certainly, if I am here, I will gladly show you more of my work." Vincent climbed the stairs to his room and bid a good night to Gaston. He closed the door behind him and lay on the bed, fully clothed. Sleep came quickly and dreamlessly.

A few days later, Vincent was resting on the wooden bench in front of the Ravoux. Daylight was fading as gaslight from the Inn trickled out from the windows behind him. He had discovered a beautiful late-blooming acacia tree behind the massive chateau that overlooked the river, and had spent the day painting a spray of its blossoming branches.

A harsh voice and a brush against Vincent's head interrupted his thoughts. "What an ugly ear! Mon Dieu, why don't you cover up that thing? It's disgusting." The speaker was an adolescent boy no more than sixteen years of age, sporting a fringed suede coat and leather chaps. An American cowboy hat topped his unruly hair. He was bent at the waist, inspecting the side of Vincent's head and squinting at the ill-formed, scarred ear.

"Go away! Leave me alone!" Vincent shouted.

Abruptly, Gaston appeared at the boy's side. "Monsieur, this is my brother, René," he explained. "Please forgive his brashness."

"Your brother is rude. He should be more considerate."

The younger Secretan straightened. "Can't you take a little teasing? I meant no harm."

"Well, whether or not you meant any harm is moot, young man. You did insult me."

René waved his arm dismissively. "Come, I'll make it up to you. I will buy you a drink," he said as he disappeared into the Ravoux.

Gaston said sheepishly, "My brother does not mean to be insulting. He doesn't take things very seriously, including the feelings of others."

Vincent begrudgingly accepted the offer and followed Gaston into the bar. After having spent some time with him, he discovered he rather liked the boy. Inside, the younger brother was already sitting at a small table where Vincent and Gaston joined him. René bellowed to the bartender: "Pernod all around!"

"But for me. I prefer absinthe," said Vincent.

"So you are the painter that Gaston told me about," René said to Vincent. "And a hard drinker, too."

"I am Vincent van Gogh. Yes, I am an artist."

"Are your paintings any good, Vincent van Gogh?" sneered René.

"René! Is that any way to address Monsieur van Gogh?" scolded Gaston.

"Sure. I want to know if he is any good. Maybe I will let him paint me."

"I am a fine artist. My pictures have been praised by

highly regarded art critics," Vincent responded curtly.

The Pernod arrived at the table. The strong anise aroma filled Vincent's nostrils. It had been a long time since he had drank absinthe and he was defenseless against its seductive fragrance.

"Let's drink to the celebrity among us! To 'Vincent-van-Gogh-the-fine-artist!'" With that pronouncement, René guzzled his drink in one great gulp. "Bar keeper, another round for the table!"

Vincent eyed the oddly dressed lad. "What is that costume you wear?"

"This is no costume! I bought this at the Paris Exposition last year. At the American display. You know Buffalo Bill Cody, don't you? He travels in his own show, 'Buffalo Bill's Wild West,' a circus with sharp shooters and all kinds of show."

"Oh," said Vincent. "I shall call you 'Puffalo Bill' then."

"You don't know how to say it," laughed René. "It starts with a 'B,' not a 'P.' It's not a pillow!" He ordered another round of Pernod then noticed Vincent had not yet finished his first drink. "You are not drinking! Can't you keep up? Are you going to let a boy out drink you?" he laughed with bravado.

Vincent downed one drink, and then another. More rounds came. The evening finally ended when Gaston announced that he was going home. "René, it's time for us to go."

"Well, Vincent-van-Gogh-the-fine-artist," slurred René, "I am sure we will see each other again!"

Vincent watched the boys leave and then staggered to his

room. He closed his eyes and felt the room spinning as he collapsed onto his bed. At last, a fitful sleep came.

The next morning Vincent awoke early, his head reeling from the previous night's libations. "I must remember that moderation is a virtue," he thought. He dressed, gathered his paint box, tripod and two canvases and trudged toward the western part of town. The sky was overcast and the air had a sweet pungency about it, signaling rain. Despite the weather, Vincent set his tripod overlooking a green wheat field that extended as far as the eye could see. He mixed his paint and attacked the canvas once again. In the distance he could see the rain coming down in torrents and knew the storm was headed his way. He hurried, grunting and twitching as he worked.

The rain held off and the morning passed without a drop. By early afternoon, Vincent's stomach was growling at him, complaining of neglect. He decided to leave his tripod and canvas there and walked back to the Ravoux for lunch.

The crowd had thinned out by the time he arrived. He ordered soup, bread, and coffee. When he was done, he left to return to his work. He had gone only a few meters when he noticed a familiar figure emerging from behind a garden wall.

"Émile!" exclaimed Vincent. "Is it really you?! I'm so delighted to see you after all this time! When did you arrive in Auvers?"

"I came in this morning. I need to talk to you. Alone."

"I am on my way to finish a painting of wheat fields. Why don't you come along? Have you heard from Paul? I haven't received a letter from him for a long time. How are you? Have you sold any paintings of late?"

"I am well, Vincent," replied Bernard. "Paul splits his time between Brittany and Paris. Look, Vincent, I must talk to you. It is important and I really want you to listen with an open mind."

"Go on."

"Pierre came to me. He threatened to kill me if I ever talked about the Commune or the plot to assassinate the Tsar."

"Why would you discuss it with anyone? Any mention of it might mean prison or worse."

"Yes," Émile went on. "I know that. But he also asked about you. He wants to talk to you. To give you the same warning."

"I don't want to talk to him! I have too many other things on my mind."

"Vincent, I lied about knowing where you were."

"Good," said Vincent.

"No, it is not good. The reason I lied was to keep your sketchbook secret from him. It has sketches of the Commune in it, including a drawing of Pierre."

"Yes, I know, I drew them."

"He must not know about those drawings. If he finds out about your sketchbook, he'll kill us both. Please, you must destroy those pages."

Vincent stopped and turned to look directly at Émile. In a firm, terse voice he said, "I have told you before: I will not deface my book! I will not let you or anyone else deface or destroy it! It contains a life-time of work."

"Vincent, this is a life or death situation! Don't you see, I'm scared!" exclaimed Bernard. He grabbed Vincent's arm.

Vincent shoved him away.

"Go! Go away and don't ask about my sketchbook again!" Vincent turned away. Émile remained, head down, feeling distraught. Across the street, behind the corner of a building, loomed a large mustachioed man. He whispered to himself, "Poor Émile, he is having a bad day."

Chapter 52
The French Countryside – Present Day

The penetrating pop-pop-pop sounds were like loud fireworks on Bastille Day. Mark and Maggie jumped out of bed and ran to the window to see where the noise had come from. In the moment the sun's rays were shimmering through the trees—a jarringly blissful sight soon interrupted by more loud bangs erupting nearby.

"Do you see anything?" asked Maggie, covering her ears.

"No, nothing! It sounds like it's coming from out in the hall. Get low!" He pulled Maggie to the floor and covered her with his body. Moments passed and then they heard running and shouting.

"Hurry, get some clothes on!" ordered Mark as he reached for his shirt and pants. Once dressed, they huddled together in a corner, listening to the chaos outside their door. A minute passed. Silence. Another minute passed.

"Hear anything?" Mark whispered.

"Nothing."

A key turned in the lock. A lone figure dressed from head to toe in black, wielding an AK-47, stood in the doorway. Behind him a body lay in a pool of blood.

The guard beckoned them down the hall with his rifle. In shock, the couple walked wordlessly down the bullet-riddled corridor, avoiding the lifeless body. At the grand staircase, they were met by a female guard who led them through the mansion to an oak-paneled study. At one end of the room was a large walnut partner's desk overlooking a garden and a small lake. On the other side of the room an ornate marble fireplace was surrounded by wing-backed chairs. Anton sat, slump-shouldered in one of the chairs with his eyes cast downward and his hands bound in front of him.

"Anton!" Mark called, his voice faltering.

"I see that you are finally awake, Monsieur et Madame McFadden. Welcome." The voice spoke from the chair opposite Anton. Mark led Maggie around the chair where they saw the two large spotted Braque français hounds. The dogs snapped their heads around to glare at the couple, teeth bared as they emitted a low sinister growl.

"Madame… Madame Chauvenal?" Mark stammered.

The matriarch motioned for Mark and Maggie to be seated. "I must say, you should be more careful of the company you keep. This one here," she nodded toward Anton, "is particularly nasty." She looked at Maggie. "My dear, I am sorry for the manner in which you were treated. But he has a way of acting that both infuriates and nauseates."

Maggie found her voice. "What's going on here?!"

"Our esteemed doctor did not tell you everything? I am surprised. He is such a braggart." Anton did not move but kept his eyes on the dogs hunched just in front of him.

"He told us his grandfather worked for the Vichy government during the war and stole art and antiques," replied Mark.

"He likes to tell that story. And indeed, it is partly true," she answered.

"Partly?" quizzed Maggie.

"Yes. His grandfather did work for the Vichy government as a cultural attaché. But he was an unimaginative public servant who could barely take care of himself. My mother took pity on Anton's family and helped them during those dreadful times. He owes everything to my family."

"That's a lie," Anton slurred.

"You see, even now he keeps up the façade."

Mark squinted his brow, his eyes wavering between Anton and the old woman. "What exactly do you mean, he 'owes everything' to your family?"

Madame Chauvenal stood and walked slowly around the office, hands clasped behind her back. She delicately touched the various paintings, figurines, and curios as she passed. "As I said, Anton's grandfather was a minor official in Pétain's government. His exact duties were to send looted treasures such as art, jewelry, and gold back to the Nazis in the North. He was not very good at this. His superior was under pressure to replace Anton's grandfather with someone competent. My mother stepped in and helped his grandfather by supplying him with artifacts the Nazis wanted. This way, Anton's family survived. Otherwise, Anton would not be here. His grandfather, his father, his mother, his aunts and uncles—they all would have been killed. You see, Anton is of Jewish ancestry."

"Liar!" Anton cried as he attempted to disentangle himself.

The room was filled with barking. The dogs were on top of Anton in an instant, ripping his shirt sleeve and tearing at his trousers. Blood spattered onto the antique silk Kashan rug beneath his feet. Helpless to defend himself, Anton let out an agonizing scream.

"Arrêtez! Lucie et Hugo, faire taire! Silence!"

The dogs sat, snarling at Anton. "Get him something to put on his wounds," barked the old woman. One of the guards left immediately to fetch some bandages. Anton sat, rocking back and forth, whining in pain.

Maggie was stunned as much by what Madame had just revealed as by the dogs' aggression. She looked at Mme. Chauvenal. "So, your mother stole from her own countrymen and supplied the Nazis?"

Chauvenal moved her intense gaze from Anton to Maggie. Her facial expression softened. "It was a small price to pay. You do not know how the times were. Hitler wanted all of France. All of Europe. The world. He would have done anything and everything to get what he wanted. My mother knew how to survive. We come from a long line of survivors."

"Fucking liar," Anton swore between moans.

"But you stole from your own countrymen?" said Maggie.

"Yes, but we saved so many lives. You see, at the same time we worked for the French underground. We rescued many Jews and Communists from the Nazi trains."

"Old crone! You are a witch and a fraud!" screamed Anton.

The old woman took a quick step forward and slapped Anton's face hard with the back of her hand. "That is enough! I have put up with you for too long." The dogs inched forward, snarling.

Blanching, Anton turned to Mark. "You want to know who the real villain is?" he said pleadingly, pointing to Mme. Chauvenal. "She is behind everything. It was her family that sent the Jews to the camps and stole their possessions. Sure, my grandfather and father helped—but only to save themselves. She and her family gave us no choice. If my grandfather did not do as he was told, he and my father would have been killed. Not by the Nazis but by her," he tilted his head toward her, eyeing the dogs warily. "How do you think her family became so wealthy? She certainly did not earn it. I work for her!"

"What?" said Mark. "Is that true? Are you two in business together?" He turned to Chauvenal, "Are you responsible for taking Maggie hostage?"

The old woman smiled. "No. I would never harm you or your wife. He is only looking to place blame on someone other than himself. Why, I came here to rescue you." She cradled her stomach as she uttered these words.

Mark became abruptly aware that Mme. Chauvenal appeared more fragile than he recalled. He chose to ignore her seeming infirmity and asked her skeptically, "How did you know we were here?"

"My dear boy, I learned from my Maman that you always keep an eye on those who can do you harm. I have known of this place for a long time."

"But how did you know we would be here or that Anton was involved?"

"She wants the book! There is something in it that she is afraid of." Anton glared at Mme. Chauvenal.

The old woman chuckled and walked behind the partner's desk, supporting her small frame by pressing her fingertips on the desk. "Even now, the poor boy tries to keep up the deception. I do not really blame him. He has been schooled since he was little to betray and belittle any person who could jeopardize his illegal endeavors. By the way, do you know how Anton got his name?"

"Pardon?" said Mark.

"Do you know how Anton got his name?" she repeated.

"I suppose his mother liked the sound of it. I have no idea."

"It is a little inside humor passed on by his father. You see, the business of dealing in stolen treasures was a lucrative business under the Nazis. Are you aware what the Nazi codename for the invasion of southern France was? Operation Anton."

Mme. Chauvenal stepped out from behind the desk. "Enough of this banter. We should get back to Paris." She picked up a large manila envelope from the desk and held it up, "I will hold on to this sketchbook for now." She pointed to Anton. "Take him," she said to the guards. "You two will come with me. It is a long journey back to Paris."

Chapter 53
Auvers-sur-Oise – Summer 1890

Gaston Secretan waited outside the Ravoux for Vincent to return from his foray into the Auvers countryside. When he saw the artist lugging his tripod and gear, he trotted over to greet him. "What have you painted today, Monsieur Vincent?" the boy asked, extending a hand to help him.

Vincent handed him the tripod. "A beautiful forest, just beyond the chateau."

"May I see?"

"Certainly. Help me put it in the barn to dry, will you?"

They walked to the barn, leaving the paint supplies in the studio along the way.

"It has so much feeling! I love the way the light dances on the trees!" the boy pointed.

"The shades of green give it dimension," said Vincent. "The browns add depth." It was a pleasure to talk with someone who appreciated his work, even if he did not completely understand the process. Gachet was like that too, although better versed in art than Gaston. Vincent lifted the canvas and hung it on a hook to dry.

The two enjoyed an amiable walk back to the Inn. "There you are," said René as Vincent and Gaston came through the back door. "I've been looking for you, Vincent-the-fine-artist. Come with me. I want to take you to my favorite bar. It's a small place not too far from here."

"This place is fine," replied Vincent. He had not forgotten the consequences of their last night out together and how he had felt upon waking this morning. On the other hand—it had been a good and productive day.

"The other place is better. And drinks are on me!"

Vincent thought a moment, then relented. "Very well, since you will buy."

The three men took a side street, crossed the railroad tracks, and turned down Rue Montmaur. They came to a small building with a sign in the window that said "Louis."

René entered, followed by Gaston and Vincent. René nodded to the barkeeper and snapped, "Pernod." He took his regular seat at a table in the back. A pool table separated them from the three other patrons in the otherwise quiet bar.

When the Pernod arrived, René said, "To Vincent," and gulped it greedily. "Another!" he roared at the bar man. Then he turned his attention to Vincent.

"Vincent, do you have a woman?" asked René.

"No, I am too busy to marry," he replied.

"I don't mean a wife. Do you have someone to screw?"

"Why?" asked Vincent.

"I want to show you what I bought." René reached into his pocket and removed several photos of women and men in various sexual positions. "What do you think of that?" asked René, feeling delight in the others' discomfort.

"René," sighed Gaston. "Really, do you always have to be so vulgar?"

"Vincent doesn't think it's vulgar, do you?"

"I don't need to look at this. If I wanted a woman, I would go to the local whore house," he retorted.

"That's just the thing. There are no whore houses in Auvers!" René laughed.

"Well, then I would just go to Paris," shrugged Vincent.

"That's a long way to go for a fuck," said René. "Besides, I have some friends that I'm sure you would like. Nothing like bringing the whores to you! We aim to please!"

"I'm not interested in your whores."

"What? Don't you like women?! Or do you prefer men, or boys, or… cowboys?" René was smirking gleefully now.

Vincent jumped up and pushed the table aside. "You are a little shit. I don't need to listen to your crap even if you buy all night!" He left the bar, slamming the door behind him with such force that all the patrons turned to look.

René was rolling with laughter but Gaston was not amused. "Why must you always act like that? Your behavior is shameful!"

René looked at his brother. "Oh, come on, didn't you think it was funny? He's such a queer fellow with his baggy pants and grotesque ear. I wonder if he's ever even had a woman before. What do you think?"

"I think that you ought to keep your mouth shut and leave the poor man alone. What did he do to deserve your spiteful humor?"

"Ha! That's just it—nothing!" The drinking continued until René passed out and Gaston had to carry him out of the bar.

Bastille Day was soon upon them and the people of Auvers celebrated with customary French pride. Vincent managed to avoid the crowds, especially René Secretan, by spending time alone in the countryside.

A few days after the excitement had passed, Vincent relaxed on a bench in town, enjoying the quiet solitude. He

Auvers-sur-Oise 1890

gazed upon the venerable town hall across from the Ravoux. Flags and decorations from Bastille Day still adorned its humble façade. *I should paint this once more before the town removes the flags*, he thought. He heard someone shouting his name.

"Vincent! Vincent van Gogh, the artist!" René Secretan was fast approaching him, followed by his brother Gaston, two other boys, and several young women. "Monsieur Vincent, we are on our way to Bar Louis. Why don't you join us?" said René.

"Ah, Puffalo Bill. I see you are dressed in your costume again." As he uttered these words, one of the girls placed her hand on the side of Vincent's head.

"Oh my, what happened? It must have been painful." Soon the others moved around to inspect Vincent's mutilated ear. He pushed them away.

"No, thank you. I am fine here," he said as he eyed the motley group of ruffians.

"Oh, come on, I am buying drinks for my friends. You should come with us," René urged.

Two of the young women grabbed Vincent's arms, one on each side, and coaxed him up from his bench. "Oh, please, Monsieur," cooed one. "We need a man to escort us, not these boys," whispered the other.

Surmising that he had no other choice—lest some unpleasantness ensue—Vincent rose from his seat and headed off with the group.

Bar Louis was quiet and they took their usual seats, with Vincent surrounded by the two young women and Gaston opposite him. "Pernod all around," ordered René. One of the women protested, "Oh, René, I want wine."

"Then you shall have it, ma petite. Garçon, bring the lady Champagne!" René shouted. "So Monsieur Vincent, what have you been painting?"

"Gardens, landscapes, a few portraits," he answered.

René turned to one of the girls, "You know, he sketched me fishing by the river. Perhaps one day I will be famous as one of van Gogh's subjects!" he spoke with exaggerated glee.

His companion draped her arm around his neck. "I'll bet it was a perfect sketch, for you are the perfect model," she purred.

"It was good," René said smugly, "but not as good as the real thing."

The drinks came and René raised his glass: "To Vincent!" The liquor was gone in one gulp. He ordered more. "I'll bet it's been a long time since you've had a woman," he smirked at Vincent.

As if on cue, the women put their hands on Vincent's legs and slowly moved them up to his crotch. They began rubbing him and kissing his cheeks.

"Two at once!" noted René. "Are you up for that? Well, is he, girls? Is he up for you both?" René leaned back as he roared in laughter.

One of the girls answered, "I think I feel movement! Yes, I feel throbbing!"

"I knew you could do it, old man!" René said merrily.

Vincent jumped up from his seat, shoving the girls away from him. "I will not put up with this humiliation!" He stomped out of the bar, incensed.

Auvers-sur-Oise 1890

Once again mortified by his brother's callousness, Gaston immediately rushed after Vincent, calling to him as he hurried to catch up. "I am so sorry! René does not consider the feelings of others. He is only looking for a good time."

Vincent kept walking. "He won't have it at my expense. I don't need his ill humor, his Pernod, or his whores."

"Please, do not think less of me because he is my brother. I bear you no ill will."

"I don't. Leave me now. You can come by tomorrow when I am calmer." Vincent returned to his room and brooded.

The next day, mourning doves cooed softly outside the window while meadowlarks conversed in a language only they could understand. The morning sunlight found its way into his room, bringing with it the faint aroma of freshly baked bread from the kitchen. Vincent quickly dressed and bounded down the stairs into his studio to gather up his paint gear, yesterday's events far from his mind.

He was intent upon working behind the old chateau on this beautiful summer morning. The sky was an azure blue, flawed by only a small scattering of clouds. Shortly he came to the hill that led to the chateau. He followed the southern side of the stone wall that separated the grounds from the town below. Behind the manse lay a wheat field to the west and a forest to the east. Vincent walked to the barn that stood between the field and the forest and looked out onto the open expanse—the chateau on his left, the barn and forest behind him. Perfect, he sighed happily. The sun was shimmering, amber wheat glistening beneath its rays.

He set up his tripod, then selected the large, frieze-style

canvas and prepared his greens, blues, whites, and yellows. He placed the stool in front of the canvas but, too energized to sit, chose to stand while he worked, propping one foot on it. He alternated his gaze from the field to the canvas. Then, when he had his vision set in his mind, he attacked with his usual vigor and determination. Short, thick strokes of color worked into form and his progress was punctuated with grunts, groans, and an occasional satisfied sigh.

The morning sun moved overhead, acting as a reminder, along with his hunger pains, that it was time to eat. Vincent chided himself for not having eaten at least a baguette before leaving. Still, this was a good time to take a break, he told himself. He cleaned his brushes and palette, then left the canvas, paint box, tripod and stool in front of the barn and headed back down the hill toward the Ravoux. He pulled out his pipe for a smoke as he made his way down the steep incline, touching his pocket twice to ensure he had not left his sketchbook behind.

Lunch at the Ravoux was simple: soup, a hunk of cheese, some crusty bread, and a glass of wine. After his meal, Vincent leaned back in the chair and puffed on his pipe. A few minutes later, he was on his way back to the chateau but had not made it very far when he heard a shout.

"Hey, artist! Van Gogh!"

Vincent turned to see René Secretan coming up behind him. He heaved a sigh. What now, he thought.

René strode up and turned sideways, pointing at him. "You offended me and my ladies the other night," he said with a sullen glare.

Vincent stared at the young man. "Is that the only costume you have?" he asked derisively. "You look like a little boy playing dress up, pretending to be a big man, which you are not. Where's your six-shooter, runt?"

A small group of men had been milling around and turned to watch the scene unfold. One of them let out a roar.

René was incensed. "It is not a costume. It is what I choose to wear and I like it."

"You tried to disgrace me in front of your friends," said Vincent. "Your parents should have taught you better."

"I was teasing you. And don't bring my parents into this. They don't care what my brother and I do."

"Perhaps they should," replied Vincent. "Why don't you go home to your mother and play with your toys." He turned, continued toward the chateau and said, "I have work to do."

The spectators let out another round of chuckles.

"What are you looking at?" René shrieked at them.

"I'll see you again, old man," René shouted after Vincent. Red-faced and seething in humiliation, he muttered angrily as he walked down an alley past a stack of discarded wooden crates.

"He thinks you a young fool." The words stung René's ears. He halted. A tall, broadly built man was standing in the shadows, puffing on a cigarette.

"What did you say?" The boy sneered at the mysterious figure.

"I said, he thinks you a fool. Someone not worth a trifle."

"And who the hell are you?" René asked, gritting his teeth.

The curious figure stepped from behind the crates. He sported a full mustache and a handsome fedora, but it was the silver-tipped, hand-carved walking stick in the man's left hand that drew René's attention. He stubbed out his cigarette as he regarded the brash youth.

"Nobody you know, young man. But certainly someone you want to know."

"And why would I want to know you?" spat René.

"Because I can help you put this artist in his place."

"How can you do that?"

The stranger started walking down the alley past the boy. "Come and I will explain."

Émile Bernard peeked around the corner of the town hall. He watched Vincent leave the Ravoux. He was about to leave his hiding spot when he spied the oddly dressed boy approach Vincent.

"What does that boy want with Vincent? And why is he dressed like an American cowboy? What a strange sight!" He watched their exchange and observed the boy retreating down an alley. Then he saw Vincent turn up a small lane toward the old chateau. Believing it to be safe, he stepped out from behind the town hall. He looked up and down. Suddenly a figure appeared in the alley from behind a stack of wooden crates. Émile froze. He watched as the man and the boy exchanged words. Émile could not see the man's face but was certain that he knew him. The pair walked further down the alley.

Bernard leapt back lest he be spotted, but then decided to follow them. The odd pair stopped and the man reached into his coat pocket and withdrew something wrapped in a cloth. Émile was too far away to hear what they were saying.

René watched as the older man retrieved an object from his coat. "What is that?"

"It is the thing that holds the power to make the artist respect you." He removed the cloth.

"A gun? I have a gun."

"But you have been afraid to use it, haven't you?"

"I'm no killer."

"This gun will allow you to act out your desire without repercussions. You can scare the life out of him."

"And just how is that?"

"The gun is loaded with blank ammunition. You can scare van Gogh without really hurting him. Next time, he won't know if you mean to harm him or just scare him. He will fear you. And with fear comes respect."

"It does sound like a great joke! Give it to me." René looked at the bright steel of the gun. The sunlight danced off the barrel and the receiver.

"But tell me this—just why are you so interested in helping me scare this artist?"

"Let's just say that he has offended me and my family. Now go. Van Gogh is painting up behind the chateau. I will be watching from a distance to see his reaction."

Émile stared at the pair standing in the alley. The man handed the item from his coat to the boy. "I wish I could hear what they are saying," he whispered. He watched as the two continued to talk. The cowboy stuffed the object into his waistband and bounded off. The man looked from side to side and then trailed after the boy at a distance.

Émile's heart leapt to his mouth. Now he was certain he recognized the stranger. Émile turned back to the main street and cautiously, made his way to Rue Alphonse Callè, the lane Vincent had taken to the chateau. Émile stopped before he entered the side street and checked to see if anyone was approaching. When he was satisfied the way was clear, he crept along the narrow street until he came to a cross street bordered by a stone wall.

"This was a bad idea," he whispered to himself. "Why did I think I could steal that damned sketchbook without Vincent knowing? Well, I've come this far, I have to get it."

Careful not to expose himself, he peeked left, then right, around the corner. There the cross street meandered east between buildings on one side and a high stone wall on the other. To the west, he saw a smaller stone wall with the chateau towering above it. "That must be where he is going."

Émile looked at the street name on a placard: Rue Léry. "I hope you are an empty street, Rue Léry," he said to no one.

Émile crept around the corner, using the wall as his cover. He headed along the wall toward the chateau until he came to an opening in the wall. A loophole for firing a musket, he thought. The hole was wider on the inside of the wall than the outside, affording better protection for someone guarding the estate. He put his head up to the opening and immediately saw Vincent disappear around the east side of the chateau. Émile intended to follow but just then spied a furtive figure stirring in the trees and low-lying brush beyond the castle. His face was obscured by shadows cast by the forest, but Émile could make out the familiar cowboy get-up.

"Now what is that silly boy doing?" Émile wondered. He crouched behind the wall, watching René dart from one tree to the next. The boy kept pace with Vincent as he made his way back to the barn where his easel was waiting for its master to return. Émile's breaths came in quick succession. He dabbed at the sweat that dotted his face and neck. "I have to get closer." He clambered over the wall and ran toward the chateau.

Crouched low, Émile scanned the tree line for the boy. There he was, sneaking from tree to tree and bush to bush, tracking Vincent. Émile slipped along the south side of the chateau to the northwest corner. Vincent was now in view again, his back to Émile, as he stood in front of his easel, apron in hand. Émile crouched down to close in on Vincent. A couple of abandoned hen houses and a dilapidated shed provided the cover he needed. He looked around for the boy but could not see him.

Then he saw movement in the trees once again and spotted the boy as he emerged from the trees and swaggered toward Vincent. Émile heard him shout, "Artist! Hey, artist!"

From his crouched position he watched as the cowboy strutted toward Vincent. Vincent sat on his stool and set his apron down on the ground next to his palette and turned to face the approaching annoyance. Émile could see the boy's fists clenching and unclenching by his side. Clearly, they were arguing. Again, Émile found himself too far away to make out what they were saying, but he could see that the cowboy was gesturing wildly and pacing in front of Vincent. The cowboy withdrew something from his waistband and pointed it downward at Vincent who stared up at the boy in disbelief.

The explosion startled Émile.

Vincent hurled backward off his stool.

The cowboy stood motionless. He shook the smoking pistol from his hand and let out a high-pitched squeal. Seconds later the boy was running back to the trees from where he had emerged. Émile sat, staring in shock.

Émile was just beginning to rise and gain his footing when a second figure appeared from the south stand of trees closer to the barn. The figure moved quickly to Vincent and, with his fedora in one hand and the walking stick in the other, bent over the recumbent body. He appeared to remove several items from Vincent's coat. The wary stranger looked around to ensure he was not being observed, then retrieved the gun and tucked it into his pocket. He bent over and dragged Vincent's lifeless body to the barn. Then he gathered up Vincent's belongings and trudged back into the woods.

Émile watched in horror as the man disappeared into the trees. He was hyperventilating so badly that he thought his lungs would burst from his chest if his heart didn't give way first. He rose unsteadily to his feet and ran to the barn where Vincent lie, taking care to watch the trees for any movement. Vincent lay on his back, his eyes closed. Deep red blood seeped slowly across his chest. Kneeling beside him, Émile took his hand. It was limp and lifeless. "Vincent... Vincent! Can you hear me? Please, Vincent, wake up!" There was no response.

Émile stood and stared down at his friend, a panicked sadness filling his chest, tears streaming down his cheeks. "Oh, Vincent!" Unsure of what he should do, Émile looked out the barn door and then ran toward the chateau. When he reached the corner of the building, he paused to look back at the barn.

"Marguerite, how could you do this! You sent your cousin to kill my friend!"

Chapter 54
Paris – Present Day

With measured footsteps, Mme. Chauvenal escorted Mark and Maggie out of the mansion and onto the wide gravel drive. Maggie scanned the surroundings and whispered, "This place is really isolated. I can't see a road or hear any traffic."

"Perfect place to lose a couple of nosy Americans," Mark quipped sarcastically. Several armed guards, all in black, surrounded a black Lincoln Town Car. Behind the limousine were a line of unmarked vans. Laurent stood erect, holding open the rear door to the Town Car. Mme. Chauvenal bent over and, with some difficulty, disappeared into the back seat. Laurent motioned for the McFaddens to get in the car.

Once Mark and Maggie were nestled in the plush leather seat opposite the old woman, Laurent dutifully took his place beside his employer. Mme. Chauvenal placed the manila envelope in her lap, gently tapping it with her fingers and gazing out the darkened window.

"This is a lovely setting. Anton will surely miss it. So unfortunate for him," she remarked.

Mark squeezed Maggie's hand, nervously moving his eyes from Madame to the pistol in Laurent's hand. Silence hung in the air like a dense fog. Finally, Maggie spoke. "What are you going to do with us?"

Mme. Chauvenal glowered at Maggie but remained silent.

"Well?" Maggie persisted.

"I mean you no harm, my dear. It is Anton that you should be concerned about. He is a thief, a kidnapper, and a murderer. His only thought is of his own financial gain. I have much more to consider."

"Like what?" Maggie asked.

The old woman sighed deeply. "I am your friend. You may not realize it just now, but I am. But Anton was right about the sketchbook. It does hold secrets that are best kept untold."

"Such as?" asked Mark.

"The book implicates my family in conspiracies, albeit old ones. However meaningless these may be, any rumors might hinder Josephine's political career."

"So, you are not greedy—merely power hungry," Mark stared hard at her.

"Monsieur, you clearly do not understand the position we are all in today. I am trying to save my beloved country."

"Really? How so?"

"Look around you. Bombings, shootings, and terrorist acts nearly every week. The European Union is too weak to act. Many countries in Europe not only welcome but harbor terrorists. France must look out for itself if we are to survive, if our culture is to endure."

"And Josephine is the answer?"

"Yes. Josephine understands what must be done and is not afraid to act. The recent terrorist attacks have raised the ire of the French and they want—no they need—someone like Josephine." Lowering her voice, she said, "But the press will make mountains out of any rumors. I cannot let that happen."

Mark studied Mme. Chauvenal's face. Her eyes were cast downward at the sketchbook, and her hands trembled slightly. "Why don't you simply destroy the book? Then there would be no threat to Josephine's reputation."

"I have considered that. But this book is part of my family history, our legacy. It would be wrong to destroy it."

Maggie squeezed Mark's hand and said softly, "Mme. Chauvenal, what could be so bad that it still haunts you over a hundred years later?"

The old woman lifted her eyes. "All families have secrets that cause them shame. We are no exception. In the late 1880's, Marguerite Devereaux fell in love and married Frederic Chemin. They had a daughter, but soon after she was born, Marguerite caught Frederic with another woman. Divorce was impossible in that time. So, they arranged to pursue their own lives apart from each other. Marguerite focused all her energy on the two things that were dearest to her: her daughter and her country.

"After the Prussian invasion of 1870, France was in disarray and needed allies. Germany was still a threat to France, so France turned to Russia for support." Anna turned her head toward the window as if viewing a newsreel from the past. She placed her hand upon her stomach and arched her back.

"Please. Go on," urged Maggie.

"Yes, of course. Forgive this old woman's aches and pains. You see, Bismarck was a cunning beast. He needed to create a chasm between France and Russia. But the Russian Tsar had no respect for the German Kaiser, so this rift would have been a challenge. Marguerite recognized the problem and wisely maneuvered herself into a position of trust within Bismarck's inner circle. She proposed to create the divide Bismarck wanted and shield him from all blame. Of course, she would be paid for her efforts. Paid very handsomely."

"Marguerite was a traitor, then?" questioned Mark.

"Oh, no. Quite the contrary. She was a hero. She took money from Bismarck but never intended to betray France."

"What exactly did she do?" asked Maggie.

"Her plan was brilliant. She recruited a few men and women who saw themselves as 'saviors' of France. She convinced them that the Tsar was brutalizing his people and that he must go. It was not far from the truth and these people were easily convinced of his cruelty. She organized a plot to assassinate the Tsar. This group of saviors would take the fall and since they were all French or had French connections, Russia would blame France and sever diplomatic ties."

"But you said she was a French hero. This makes her sound like a traitor," said Maggie.

"She never planned to actually kill the Tsar. There were many attempts, but none were successful and France was never really implicated. But Marguerite kept taking German money and delaying Bismarck from executing his own plans to divide France and Russia."

"How do you know so much?" queried Maggie.

"Marguerite kept a diary. It has been passed down from mother to daughter for generations."

"But that doesn't really explain why the sketchbook could damage you or your family," said Maggie.

"The journal connects Marguerite with the Germans after the Franco-Prussian war. Germany has never been a friend to France. Any association with a national enemy could put a label of traitor on my family."

"How were Marguerite and van Gogh connected exactly? Do you know?" asked Mark.

"One of the men she recruited for her cabal was an unknown artist. To her surprise, this artist kept a journal with notes and drawings—including identifiable portraits of the conspirators. No one could have guessed that the odd little man Marguerite seduced would keep a written and illustrated record. Or someday have the fame he now does."

"The journal and the letter seem to connect Marguerite to van Gogh's death as well," observed Mark.

"I suppose they could. Another reason to keep this," she raised the envelope, "secret."

"Then do you know who actually killed van Gogh?" Mark asked.

"I do not know. I do know that when she found out about the journal, she sent one of her husband's relatives to get it. Perhaps he overreacted."

Maggie hesitated, "Anna, do you know how the journal came to be hidden in our house?"

The old woman let out a sigh and cocked her head. "It is really very simple. Your house was used for the group meetings. Back then it was very secluded. When Marguerite sent this relative to get the book, she instructed him to put it in the basement. And, once it was secured and hidden away, they were no longer concerned with it, and never retrieved it."

"So, you don't know who actually shot van Gogh?" Maggie quizzed.

"No, and I do not believe we ever will know. Better to leave history alone and accept the romantic myth that he killed himself."

Dusk descended as the caravan entered an underground parking area in the rear of the mansion in Paris' Bois de Boulogne district. Madame Chauvenal led Mark and Maggie to an elevator.

"Laurent, please show our guests to the library. I shall be along in a while. Oh, Laurent, have Claire prepare them something to eat."

Laurent escorted Mark and Maggie through a labyrinth of hallways to the library. The couple entered the now familiar room. Laurent pointed to the divan, "Kindly, sit. Madam will not be long." Two men dressed in dark business suits stood next to each of the library doors. Laurent whispered to one of the men, then disappeared through the back door. Moments later, Claire appeared with sandwiches and tea.

"What do you think's going to happen?" Maggie whispered to Mark.

"I wish I knew. I'm having difficulty understanding this whole mess. Anton just..." he looked at the floor. "I just would never have believed he was capable of murder." He took a bite of his cucumber sandwich but could barely swallow.

"And that Mme. Chauvenal. How strange. She seems so refined, so matronly."

"Not now... not from where I sit," retorted Mark.

Without warning, Anton stumbled into the study with armed guards at either side. His face was flecked with blood, his left eye was swollen closed, and blood had clotted on his pants and sleeve from where the dogs had bitten him.

"*Asseyez!* Sit!" one of the guards snarled at Anton. Then looking at the McFaddens, he said in a calm, controlled voice, "Madame will be here momentarily."

The guard pushed Anton onto a chair. His head bobbed side to side and drool oozed from his mouth.

"Anton," whispered Mark. "Anton, can you hear me?"

"What's wrong with him?" asked Maggie with alarm.

"Drugged."

The two hounds entered the room with Mme. Chauvenal, their nails tapping the hardwood floors like the measured beat of a metronome. She perched in a soft leather chair and the dogs sat down beside her. She casually surveyed the room, first looking at Anton, then Mark, and finally resting her eyes on Maggie. Claire placed a steaming cup of tea in front of her then disappeared. She breathed in the fragrant aroma of the tea. "I hope you took the time to eat something. It has already been a long day."

"Yes, thank you," responded Maggie. "What's going to happen now?"

"Ah, a good question. I will have to deal with this filth," she nodded toward Anton. "He is truly disappointing. Disloyal. Greedy. And he meant to harm you two. I find that behavior reprehensible."

Mark looked at Anton, "What will you do with him?"

"That is not your concern anymore. Just know that he will be dealt with." With this she gestured to one of the guards and Anton was swiftly taken away.

Maggie's eyes followed Anton as he was ushered out the back door of the room. "What about us?"

"My dear, I do not mean you and your husband any

harm. You are but pawns caught up in this cat and mouse game being played."

Mark wrinkled his brow. "What does that mean?"

The old woman raised her hand and Laurent handed her the manila envelope. She coughed weakly. "I am still astonished at how fate intervenes and delivers the most remarkable gifts at the most opportune time. Just think, for you two to marry, buy that house in d'Avray, discover this journal, and then to seek out a meeting with me. Well, no one could have dreamed it possible."

Maggie stuttered. "I... I don't know what you mean."

"I know, child. It will soon become very clear, I'm certain. But in the meantime, you will be my guest here. Laurent will collect some of your things and bring them to you."

"So we're prisoners," Mark pressed her.

"Monsieur, there is no need for such drama. You are my guests. You have been through a harrowing experience and could certainly use some rest. Please take the time to explore this old chateau. But please do not attempt to leave. Laurent will see to it that you have everything you want."

"How long are we to be kept here?" asked Maggie.

"Not long, I hope."

"What does that mean, 'I hope'? Why can't you let us go now?" begged Maggie.

"You, my dear, are the reason you must stay."

"What? I don't follow." Maggie was perplexed by Mme. Chauvenal's statement.

"I know you do not understand." The old woman stopped, suddenly distracted by a rustling noise and the sweet scent of lilac.

"She means that you are the lure to draw me back. Back to face my demons." From the shadow of the main library entrance emerged a tall, thin figure with gray hair dressed in a simple blouse and skirt.

Rising from her seat, Maggie shouted, "Maman!"

Growls and barking erupted. Almost in unison, the guards raised their guns. Anna silenced the dogs with a wave of her hand. The guards took the cue and eased back against the walls.

"Maman, what are you doing here?"

"Rena, what a pleasant surprise," snarled Anna Chauvenal.

"Yes, I'm sure you are as surprised as you are pleased," replied Rena.

"Maman," Maggie cried. "What..."

"Please, Margaret. There is much you don't know. I had hoped to keep some things from you, but it is not to be."

Gesturing toward an empty chair, Mme. Chauvenal said, "Rena, come. Sit. We have a lot to discuss."

"I think I shall stand."

"That is your choice. But, please, come closer. Let me look at you. It has been a lifetime since we last saw each other."

Rena moved to the end of the divan and reached for Maggie's hand. Her eyes never left Anna Chauvenal.

"Rena, the years have been gracious to you. I admit, I did not expect you to arrive quite so soon."

"Maman, what's going on?"

"Shhh, *ma petite.*" Rena released Maggie's hand and stood facing Anna. "You should never have involved my family."

"Believe me, I never intended to. If your daughter had

not approached me about this sketchbook, I would never have known who she was. I was not sure where you were, if you were even still alive. And I surely did not know what you had told her, if anything." Anna rose and walked to the desk and picked up a small framed picture. "I can still remember you and me running through the Tuileries together as small children."

"Maman?"

"I have a much different recollection," Rena said, stiffly.

"Yes, I am sure you do. Those were difficult times."

"Difficult? *Merde.* Difficult? You and your family--"

Anna cut her off. "My family did whatever we deemed necessary to survive."

The two old women glared at each other. Rena clenched her fists, then unclenched them and decided to say nothing. Anna replaced the picture and sat back in her chair, the hounds at her feet.

"Maman, please, don't keep me in the dark!"

"Yes, Rena. Perhaps you should tell your daughter what is going on here."

Rena's eyes narrowed. Then just as quickly, her countenance turned calm. She sat down next to Maggie and let out a long sigh.

"Maman," whispered Maggie.

Another sigh. When she spoke, the words were slow, deliberate, and anguished. "It was another lifetime. Anna and I grew up near each other. She was the rich girl, I the poor one. But we made good companions. Our families spent some time together, but our circle of friends was vastly different. When the Nazis invaded France in 1940, everything changed. Hitler's army moved so quickly. We knew that if we stayed in Paris we would be under the Nazi's thumb, so we moved south. Anna and her family came with us. Their friends refused to leave Paris. It was a terrible journey. So many people on the roads. The Luftwaffe strafed everyone on the roads, killing innocent men, women and children. My father decided we should stay off the roads. We made it as far as Limoges. By then, Pétain had arranged a ceasefire with the Nazis. The north of France was occupied by Hitler's army, the south was a so-called 'free France.' But Pétain and his men were just Hitler's puppets. Our only hope was to hold out until the rest of the world woke up and came to our rescue."

"And that attitude is where we differed," Anna broke in.

Rena scoffed. "Differed? Yes, we differed all right. You were never taught that there are moral consequences to your choices."

"Stop. I will not hear of moral choices. Your father made a choice to allow you and your Maman to suffer. What choice did you or your mother really have?"

Rena's face flushed and her nostrils flared. She drew her breath in slowly, and calm returned to her demeanor. "May I continue?"

"Certainly, by all means," replied Anna.

"My parents joined a local resistance unit. My father quickly recruited Anna's parents. You must remember, this was the beginning of the war in France and there was no organized fight against the Nazis. Our priority was to protect those who were the most in jeopardy. It didn't take us long to realize that Pétain was ordered to round up all the Jews, Gypsies, Communists, Freemasons, and anyone else Hitler deemed undesirable and ship them to the North. We saw trains of boxcars packed with people. Women and children crushed and crying. Pétain's army, called the 'Milice', guarded the trains. It was a horrible, sordid thing to witness. Pétain took the opportunity to send his political enemies on the trains along with anyone he considered rebellious. That meant our families could be put on the trains if we were caught."

"Or if you were not clever enough to endear yourself to those in power," Anna added.

"Yes. Endear yourself to those in power," repeated Rena, dryly. "Anyway, we made it our mission to save as many of those unfortunate people as possible. The resistance established escape routes through the Pyrenees to Barcelona. Our parents," Rena nodded toward Anna, "would take families to a local safe house so they could be moved to safety. It was very dangerous and if any of the resistance or the refugees were caught, we knew the consequence would be death."

Rena paused and looked down at her feet. When she lifted her head, Maggie could see her fighting back tears.

"Oh, Maman," cried Maggie.

"It is all right. I haven't thought of these things for so long." She removed a small kerchief from her sleeve and dabbed her eyes. Maggie could see a fierceness in her mother she had never seen before.

Rena continued. "Since Anna and I were children, and girls at that, it was easy for us to carry messages between resistance cells and to and from the people we were trying to help. We came to look at it as a game. We would run through the streets as if we were playing hide and seek. The police mostly ignored us. If we did get stopped, we would say things like 'oh, please don't tell our parents we were playing in the street.' We were always released with just a stern warning."

Rena took a deep breath and gently shook her head. "One day, I accompanied my mother and father to the home of a wealthy Jewish family who lived just south of Vichy. I remember them clearly. They had a daughter my age and a son slightly older. My father brought a horse-drawn wagon to collect them and take them to a safe house, as were his orders. I remember my father was particularly nervous even though he had done this sort of thing several times before. My father had somehow learned that Pétain was sending his men the next day to take this family to the trains, so he was keenly aware that time was of the essence in getting them safely out of town. When we arrived at their house, they were not ready since they had not been expecting us. My father hurried them into the wagon with only a few of their possessions. My mother told me to remain quiet and not talk to the girl or the boy, and I obeyed.

The trip back to Limoges was long and arduous. We took the family to a farmhouse where they were to hide out in a storm cellar. My mother and I stayed in the wagon while my father took the family inside. When my father emerged from the farmhouse, he told us we had to return to their house in Vichy and collect some papers they had inadvertently left behind. He was unusually upset and very angry. I heard him curse at another man at the farmhouse. My father never cursed! He didn't utter a single word during the entire trip back to Vichy. I'm certain that he was mostly concerned for our safety. At any rate, when we arrived in Vichy there was another wagon in front of the house. It was filled with furniture and paintings, and other personal belongings. Standing next to the wagon were Anna and her mother. They were trying on coats and jewelry and laughing at each other. They were clearly taking pleasure in their new-found treasures."

Rena stared in fury at the old woman across from her.

"When my father saw them, he jumped from the wagon and ran into the house. I heard shouting and banging through the front door. My mother held me tightly as we waited for him in the wagon. She didn't say a word but I knew she was angry and scared. But I was young and didn't quite understand what was at stake. I wanted to see my friend but my Maman refused to let me go. I can still smell her old woolen dress pressed against my nose." Rena took a deep breath as if she were breathing in the scent of the dress even now.

"Enough," groused Mme. Chauvenal.

"Oh no. This is my story to tell and I will tell it! My father and Anna's father burst from the house, shouting, and pushing and shoving each other. Anna's mother came between them and said something to her husband that I couldn't hear. I remember all this as if it happened this morning. Anna must have heard what was said because she looked at me and smiled as if to say, 'everything is fine'. My father turned away from them and was moving toward our wagon when I heard the shot. He fell to the ground face first but managed to tell us to get away. 'Take the wagon and go!' he said. "Go. Now!' Those were his last words. My mother grabbed the reins and took off. When I looked back, Anna's mother was holding a gun. Smoke was curling from the end of the barrel. I never saw my father again. And I never saw Anna again until today."

Stunned by Rena's story, Maggie and Mark turned their gaze to Anna Chauvenal. She was resting all the way back in her chair, malevolence oozing from every pore. Her palms rested on her abdomen and she winced in pain. After an uneasy pause, she broke the silence in the room.

"My mother was always the strong one. She did what had to be done. Your father would have turned the resistance against us and ruined our business dealings with the Nazis. But this is all ancient history, Rena."

"Yes, Anna, it's history. It's our history, not theirs," she said pointing to Mark and Maggie.

"You know it is not that simple."

"It is that simple. I am here now. Isn't that what you wanted?"

"Of course it is. But now that you have explained things in such amazing detail, I do not see how I can let your daughter and son-in-law leave."

"I promise they will be silent on everything they know. I will stay here. Now let them leave."

"Maman, no, you can't do that," Maggie cried.

Rena looked upon Maggie as only a mother can. "This has been her plan all along. She wants to ensure that I cannot be a detriment to her or her daughter."

"No, Maman, she wants the sketchbook. She can have it and we all will leave. You agree, don't you Anna?"

Mme. Chauvenal threw her head back and laughed. "Oh,

my dear child, are you that naïve? The sketchbook is meaningless. Your Maman has always been the prize. She is the only one who could threaten Josephine's agenda."

"But I thought you wanted the sketchbook?"

"It is merely a trinket. A trinket that may be worth a small fortune, but still just a trinket when compared with our collection. That book alone could not harm me or Josephine. However, she could," nodding at Rena. "Now I am faced with a more complicated problem."

"You will not harm my family. You must know that I have made contingency plans. You didn't really think that I would come all this way unprepared, did you?"

"You look so smug," snapped Anna. "Of course I expected you to have a plan to get out of here. But it does not matter. There will be no one to come to your aid or to save your daughter."

In a low, confident voice Rena replied, "Don't you even want to know what I had in mind?"

"It is irrelevant."

"Anna, this is your chance to let all of us leave here. It really would be best for you and your daughter," urged Rena. "As much as I despise you, I have no desire to ruin your lives."

"You have no leverage over me. And I advise you to never speak of my daughter again. You will all disappear and that will be the end of this matter. Guards, take them away and dispose of them as we discussed!"

As the two guards moved toward the captives, Rena called out, "Josephine, have you heard enough?"

At that very moment, Josephine Fournier entered the

study through the back door. Her eyes were red, her cheeks flushed, and her heart thudded deep within her chest.

"Josephine, how long have you been listening?" Anna asked, her voice uncharacteristically wavering. She motioned for the guards to stand back.

"Maman, I heard everything. I cannot believe it. When Rena came to me with her story, I thought it was the raving of an old woman. I almost had her arrested. I always knew you were capable of terrible things, but this... How did you think this would really end?"

"Josephine, it is all under control. Our family is safe. Our secrets will remain hidden. Trust me."

Suddenly, the dogs were afoot and barking sharply. A deep baritone voice filled the room. "Madame Chauvenal, I am Commissaire Phillipe Gastineau of the Sûréte. Quiet your dogs or they will be shot!"

On his cue, several policemen, rifles raised, ran into the room and disarmed Anna's guards. Gastineau moved from behind Josephine and approached Anna, handcuffs at the ready. "Madame, I do not think these matters will be resolved as quickly or quietly as you planned. You have the right to an attorney, to make a statement, to answer questions, or remain silent..."

Chapter 55
Paris, Ville d'Avray – Present Day

Mark and Maggie stood in the driveway outside the Chauvenal mansion. Lights from the fountain illuminated the marble figure of Marianne. The driveway was filled with police cars. Several uniformed men stood in the courtyard, awaiting their next command from Gastineau. Maggie slumped against Mark and he put his arms around her shoulders.

"Are you all right?" he asked.

"Yes, I think so. I'm wondering what they're talking about in there," she replied.

"Probably asking your mother if she will testify against Mme. Chauvenal," Mark guessed.

"Then why ask us to leave?"

"I don't know. We'll find out when your mother comes out."

"I have always loved the figure of Marianne. She is so elegant, so majestic, so French," Rena remarked from behind them. Maggie ran to her mother and wrapped her arms tightly around her. "Careful, child. Don't break me. Remember, I'm old."

Maggie released her grip and looked at her. "Maman, you look so tired. When did you last sleep?"

"It's been a while. But let me look at you. I'm glad to see you are well. And you, Mark, are you okay? What an ordeal for the both of you!"

"I'm fine, Maman Chapin. When did you get here and how did you find us?"

Rena gestured toward Gastineau, who had appeared on the front step. "You have Monsieur Gastineau to thank. After Mark called me and told me Margaret had been taken, I called the police in d'Avray. When I finally spoke with the Commissaire, I learned that both of you were missing. I knew then that Anna was up to something. It was easy to track her, even from America. She does not keep a low profile, and through the years I've kept my eye on her whereabouts. I mistakenly believed that if I never returned to Paris, she would leave us all alone. After all, she and her daughter have had more important matters to attend to. But when you found that sketchbook and met with her, I knew something terrible was bound to happen."

Gastineau nodded solemnly. "I admit, I was very skeptical when your Maman told me her suspicion that Mme. Chauvenal was behind your kidnapping." He stepped toward Maggie. "But she is quite persistent... and persuasive. She called several times. But when she arrived at my office, I agreed to examine Mme. Chauvenal's background in more detail. And to my surprise, I discovered rumors of unsavory dealings. Which, unfortunately, could not be confirmed. Then Rena told me of the chateau near Limoges. My men discovered it had been owned by a wealthy Jewish family before the war. The family escaped France and a new deed was entered that transferred the property to a corporation controlled by Anton Lambert. I now knew that I had to take Mme. Chapin's claims seriously. I asked the local authorities to check on the property. They found the carnage left behind by Mme. Chauvenal and her men."

Rena continued. "I told Monsieur Gastineau that I

thought I could implicate Anna. After all, her main concern was her family and Josephine's ultimate success. The real leverage would be to convince her daughter of her mother's involvement in your kidnapping. That wasn't as hard as I thought it would be. When I explained my plan, she listened and agreed to cooperate."

"So tell me. What will happen to Mme. Chauvenal?" asked Maggie.

All three turned to Gastineau. He let out a deep breath. "This is very complicated. There is no perfect resolution."

"But what does that mean?" asked Mark.

"Mark, please," Rena admonished, looking at him. "Let the Commissaire continue."

"We have Anton Lambert in custody for the murder of Monsieur Durant and for your kidnapping."

"Yes, go on," Maggie urged.

"Any charges we file against Anna Chauvenal will never go to court."

Mark spoke, exasperated. "What? How can that be?"

Maggie chimed in, "With all the evidence you have against her?!"

Gastineau held up his hands in a defensive gesture. "She has been diagnosed with stage four pancreatic cancer. She has but a few weeks to live. She is entitled under French law to have a physician examine her and confirm the diagnosis. She has also surrendered her passport so she won't be able to go anywhere."

Rena broke in, "I begged Monsieur Gastineau to let her live out her life with her daughter. It is the humane thing to do."

"But, Maman!"

"Margaret, as you age, sometimes you become more… forgiving. Anna and Josephine have quite enough to deal with, they don't need legal issues as well."

"Maman, no one asked us what we thought. After all, we are the victims of their misdeeds."

"I know. I hope you will support me in this. You need to live your lives as well. Anna will not be around much longer and I truly believe Josephine is an innocent bystander in all of this corruption."

Gastineau's hands suddenly flew upward and he said, "That reminds me of something. Please excuse me. I'll be right back."

The three figures stood looking out on the sparkling fountain. The lights and the mist of the water created rainbows around Marianne.

"I can't believe you would let a killer and a traitor off the hook, Maman."

"I know," Madam Chapin said softly. "If I had revenge in mind, I would have acted differently. But now that you are safe, I just want life to move on. Besides, anything we do will hurt Josephine. She is a well-meaning woman who just happens to be the daughter of a sociopath. She is not like her mother. Sometimes, kindness and forgiveness are more potent weapons than anger and revenge."

Gastineau returned, carrying a manila envelope. He handed it to Mark. "I believe this is yours."

Mark took the envelope. "I guess I thought we wouldn't get this back."

"It is yours. You found it in your home."

"I thought the Chauvenals would keep it as their family heirloom," Mark said wryly.

Gastineau hesitated then said, "The sketchbook was not important to Mme. Chauvenal. Stopping Madame Chapin from telling her story and besmirching the family name was her only goal. Josephine demanded it be returned to you. Now you will have to determine what to do with it."

Days later, Mark and Maggie arrived at their home in d'Avray in a taxi. Rena met them at the front door. "Welcome home, you two. How was your trip?"

"Great," said Maggie. "The van Gogh museum was overwhelmed when we gave them the journal. They will determine its authenticity, of course, and assuming that all is in order, they will add it to their vast collection. We'll be recognized as the donors."

"I think you two did the right thing." Rena walked into the house and picked up the daily paper. "Did you see the headlines today?"

"No, we didn't have time," Maggie said. "Why?"

"Josephine Fournier announced that she is stepping away from politics. She wants to spend as much time as possible with her Maman before she passes. Anna is now bedridden and refuses to see anyone."

"It is for the best," Mark offered.

Rena held up the paper. "The papers are calling Josephine 'the French ideal'. Her selfless act of compassion will certainly be remembered. She is young. There is still plenty of time for her to realize her political ambitions if she chooses to re-enter politics."

"We can only hope she does." Maggie nodded.

Epilogue
Auvers-sur-Oise – Summer 1890

Vincent lay helpless on his bed for two days before finally succumbing to the bullet lodged in his abdomen. There were no trained surgeons in the area. A local doctor tried to extract the bullet with his fingers, probing and pushing until the pain from the cure was worse than the wound. Theo was notified of Vincent's predicament and rushed to his bedside. The two brothers spent Vincent's last days talking and sometimes weeping together. In and out of consciousness, Vincent refused to identify who shot him, then made the claim that he had shot himself.

Thus, Vincent's death was ruled a suicide—in the eyes of the Catholic Church, a grievous mortal sin. He was therefore denied burial in consecrated ground. The local church would not even allow Vincent's body to be transported by their hearse.

As a result, funeral services were held in the public room of the Ravoux Inn. Several of Vincent's paintings surrounded his casket. A few local residents paid their respects, as did Émile Bernard and Dr. Gachet. Paul Gauguin did not attend, and soon departed for Tahiti, where he painted paradise until he too died, several years later.

Vincent was interred at a hillside cemetery overlooking the fields of Auvers that he so loved to paint.

By the time of Vincent's death, Theo Van Gogh was in the throes of his own demise. Within a year of his brother's death, Theo became ill and delusional. He was admitted to a local sanitarium and died of complications from syphilis.

Joanna Bonger Van Gogh took up the mantel of praise for both Vincent and Theo. She tirelessly promoted Vincent's work and defended Theo's reputation. Her efforts were rewarded with the recognition of Vincent as one of the greatest artists of his age. Her son Vincent continued to promote his uncle's art, talent, and perseverance. His efforts ultimately brought about the establishment of the Van Gogh Museum in Amsterdam—uncle Vincent's true final resting place. As art is the man, so endures the very best of what became of Vincent, long after his pain ceased.

Sources

These are the major references used in the writing of *A Death in Auvers:*

Van Gogh, The Life
By Steven Naifeh and Gregory White Smith
Random House
ISBN 978-0-375-50748-9

Vincent Van Gogh, The Complete Paintings
Ingo F. Walther and Rainer Metzger
Taschen Bibliotheca Universalis
ISBN 978-3-8365-5715-3

The Van Gogh letters were sourced from:
www.webexhibits.org/vangogh

Letters are curated by Michael Douma. Most are written by Vincent van Gogh and Theo van Gogh, with translation into English by Johanna van Gogh-Bonger.

About the Author

Steven Schaefer lives in Maryland with his wife Ellen and enjoys motorcycling, golf, travel, and art. Steve and Ellen are regular visitors to her hometown of Gambier, Ohio and, whenever possible, spend their winters in Florida.

CPSIA information can be obtained
at www.ICGtesting.com
Printed in the USA
LVHW111445050722
722773LV00006B/438